The Seres Agenda

R. Scott Lemriel
(AKA - R. Scott Rochek)

PAGE PUBLISHING, INC.
New York, NY

First originally published by Page Publishing, Inc. 2013

ISBN 978-1-62838-082-8 (pbk)
ISBN 978-1-62838-083-5 (digital)

Printed in the United States of America

CONTENTS

PROLOGUE

UNEXPECTED TRANSFORMATION

For the first time, *The Seres Agenda* adventure uncovers what is soon coming to our planet Earth no one will anticipate. The following chapters do not reveal a prediction of the end of the world, a foreboding Armageddon, or a doomed fate for our planet. However, it is the pronouncement of the coming of an event that has never happened before, an event that will transform the Earth. This coincides with the predictions of today's living Mayan leaders regarding their Mayan Calendar that ended on December 21, 2012. They proclaim what is coming will occur during "the End Time" between 2007 and 2015. They foresee this will be "the end of evil as an experiment on Earth." I have included this claim because of what I found during my deeper independent explorations of the truth of this claim, and what I subsequently discovered is actually coming to planet Earth.

What has already begun that passed harmlessly through the end of the year 2012, and which will continue to expand for years into the future, initially involved the critical juncture of planetary and solar system alignments that otherwise would have been destructive to Earth. I have endeavored to share with people for several years now that something very significant has changed in Earth's destiny, and we will begin to see the benevolent effects of this in the near future. At the right moment, it will be apparent to everyone that our world is beginning to go through something extraordinary - something that never happened before in the history of creation. The destiny of our world has changed from a near future destructive direction to that of a worldwide event that will affect all life with an uplifting transformation.

Many other hidden comprehensive understandings continued to surface during many ongoing out-of-body journeys throughout my unfolding adult life. These explorations ventured into the primordial Sound, omnipresent force, original word or the first sound vibration that was sent out by the Creator to build all creation. This source behind all life, predominantly referred to as the Ancient One or Prime Creator by very advanced extraterrestrial human beings that have a vast understanding of its nature, originated the very first sound or word that created all that now exists. This omnipresent, omniscient, and omnipotent conscious energy field underlies, sustains, and supports all life everywhere in the multidimensional universe.

The extraordinary experiences into the unknown universe I encountered over the last forty plus years are all true. However, to paraphrase the statement made at the beginning of each episode of the old *Dragnet* police detective television dramas declares, "The episode you are about to see is true, but the names of the characters and the locations where the events took place have been changed to protect the innocent." Therefore, the continuing story throughout the pages of this book, based on many true-life experiences, you may understandably class as fictional to a degree. However, the wide panorama of information woven throughout the highly revealing story unveils the hidden truth suppressed in all of us long ago, and what is coming to Earth. What will take place worldwide will constructively uplift all life on the planet.

In the next few years, all mankind will know without a shadow of a doubt that highly evolved benevolent human, humanoid, and other extraterrestrial beings actually exist, as well as many other parallel physical dimensions, and higher realities.

Journey through the pages of *The Seres Agenda*, and you will discover an ever-widening hidden truth beginning to surface within your own knowing imagination. Then you too will come to inherently understand, as I have, that the rate of vibration on this planet is about to be greatly uplifted in quite dramatic, positive ways. This is necessary in order to prevent our world's otherwise coming destruction, along with all life.

You will then know for yourself that a new way is being prepared for you to gain the understanding, awareness, and insight to remain serenely balanced when this entirely unexpected worldwide transforming event takes place on Earth in the very near future. Fortunately, for us all, the decision to finally implement this constructive change is irreversible, or planet Earth would most certainly be doomed.

While you travel further into the astonishing revealing depth of *The Seres Agenda* with the human being named Mark Santfield, an adult in his mid-thirties, you will discover how his entirely unexpected profound adventures greatly transform and expand his understanding of the universe forever. He discovers that a classified second worldwide government, officially created after World War II, soon came under the influence and control of a non-human bi-peddle, diabolical totalitarian extraterrestrial race. Then he unexpectedly begins to awaken to the considerably important, key part that he is to carry out on planet Earth for its very survival.

As always, I wish each one of you, my fellow human beings living on Earth, only the very best during the uplifting transforming days that lie ahead for all of us.

Now, the amazing journey into Mr. Mark Santfield's unexpected discoveries about a wondrous truth covertly hidden from nearly everyone on Earth continues.

CHAPTER ONE

TAKEN
BEYOND EARTH

A sleek, silvery disc-shaped ship speeding through space, illumined around its entire circumference with a pale-blue light, swiftly passed by the planet Mars, and then it darted in a streak of light into the distant black void between countless stars.

Minutes later, the rapidly slowing streak of light coming from a vast background star-field gradually formed again back into the mysterious spaceship as it passed by the moon, headed in the direction of Earth.

It soon slowed to a stop, hovering above the cloud cover moving in high above the west coast of North America.

Inside, a lone alien pilot looked down and grinned with satisfaction at the blinking, faceted spherical blue crystal in the center of his semicircular crystalline control console.

Good! The one the Galactic Council selected is located. He will help... he must, he thought to himself with some relief.

Silently reflecting on the swift accomplishment, the visitor reached down at waist-high level and placed his right palm with spread fingers into the right illumined golden quartz crystal hand impression and it brightened, passing light through his translucent skin.

The rapidly descending spaceship passed down through the cloud layer, then darted below them through a small widening opening, sucking downward behind it whirling cloudy mists. It stopped a second later to hover fifty thousand feet above a verdant-forested crest along part of the High Sierra Mountains of northern California.

The extraterrestrial's hand passed over the top of a luminous green rectangular crystal and a just discernible human male, standing in a small clearing beside a two-man tent, appeared on a wide, vertical 3-D energy imaging screen that began to be projected a few feet above the control console. The alien's eyes sparkled with anticipation as his left hand touched a smaller red illumined, triangular-faceted crystal just above the left crystalline palm impression, and a circle of red light appeared around the image of the man. The image began to zoom closer, bringing the Earthman into clarity.

At ground level, the misty sprinkling of tiny warm raindrops hitting the man's upturned face was refreshing and the mid-summer air was rich with the scent of Ozone.

God, I needed this after all those months of madness in the city.

Mark Santfield felt relieved by the thought, as he peered deeper into his recollection of the past three months living under the smoggy skies of Los Angeles. That stint in the city was part of the research he was conducting for his new book about a suspected malevolent extraterrestrial presence operating behind a shadowy, hidden government on Earth. He had already interviewed several dozen people, men, women and a few children who all claimed they had been abducted by aliens and mistreated in some form or another, before they were returned to Earth with all memory of the experience repressed. That is, until deep hypnosis sessions clearly brought back the memories.

"Yeah, right!" he said aloud, smirking; but he did not feel an audible dialogue with himself on the subject was worth the effort as he continued in the silence of his own inner thoughts.

How the hell can all those people be abducted and have bizarre genetic experiments performed on them aboard some strange alien craft, then be whisked back home with total amnesia, no proof, and nobody else ever witnessing a damned thing?

11

He continued to muse over his reservation to believe any of them, while he was standing just outside his two-man tent below a cloudy, but still warm mid-summer day in the mountains. He was trim and just under six feet tall, in his mid-thirties with short, wavy brown hair, blue eyes, and a slight cleft chin. Although he never thought of himself as handsome compared to any famous men he knew about, his fiancée considered him to be good looking or as she put it, "a real catch." He grinned as he recalled her charming ways and vivid green eyes. Then he looked down at the tiny water drops beginning to softly thud into the dry, powdery dirt below his feet and his pleasureful smile widened. He glanced up at the sky and appreciatively gazed across the forested mountaintops and verdant valleys that surrounded him. He took in a deep breath of the clean mountain air, grinned like imp, and then started to joyfully sing with childlike abandon the old cheerful, classic lyrics to "The Song of The South."

"Zipadee-doo-dah, zipadee-a. My, oh my, what a wonderful day. Plenty of sunshine comin' my way. Zipadee-doo-dah, zipadee-a. Mr. Bluebird is on my shoulder. It's truth, it's actual, everything is satisfactual. Zipadee-doo-dah, Zipadee-a. My oh my, what a wonder... ful..."

But nothing else would come out of his gaping open mouth as a shiver of energy ran down his spine and goose bumps sprang up on his exposed arms through his short sleeve shirt. He slowly looked up to behold the clouds parting in a widening circle revealing a silvery disc-shaped extraterrestrial spaceship, surrounded by a luminous pale-blue aura, hovering below the center of the opening.

Oh...sh-sh-shit!

The stuttered thought remained in silence as an ensuing indescribable rush of adrenaline terror gripped him. His first impulse was to high tail it for the woods (he would have bolted), but a warm soothing glow began to emanate from his chest and he discovered, amazed, that all fear had left. A comforting, mellow male voice, clear as crystal, began speaking inside his head.

Be at peace. You are not in any danger. My name is Mon-tlan and I am communicating to you telepathically, mind-to-mind. I am also a human being, just the same as you; however, I am not from Earth. My home planet circles a sun beyond what you call the Pleiades star group. I am in the ship you see above and I have come to discuss with you a matter of extreme importance for all life on planet Earth. After you have personally experienced all that I have to reveal, you will understand the urgent nature that is behind my contacting you. Only then will I ask if you would be willing to assist a vast alliance of benevolent world systems to prevent the looming complete destruction of your planet. Will you allow me to bring you aboard my ship? I will respect your free will response to my request.

"Is this real?" Mark nervously blurted out.

Yes, Mark, it is, cheerfully replied Mon-tlan's firm voice in his head.

Mark was beginning to experience the oddest sensation of calm familiarity with the being behind the voice.

"Um, if I agree... will it hurt?" he cautiously asked aloud.

Soft, kind laughter filled his head and the benevolent voice answered, *I promise the teleportation beam is completely safe and painless. Once you are aboard, you will discover the experience was exhilarating. Mark, will you help us help your planet grow up and not be destroyed?*

Briefly spellbound by the astounding implications surrounding the monumental experience, Mark closed his eyes. Then he vigorously shook his head, rubbed his eyelids with the palms of his hands and took a deep calming breath. As he slowly opened his eyes, he cautiously looked up to discover the alien spaceship was still there, but it had moved closer and it was now hovering just a hundred feet above his head.

It was still radiating the same blue-white light aura around its entire silvery-gray metallic disc shape and he could make out more detail. Clearly defined on the bottom hull were three semi-spherical shaped pods spaced six feet apart in triangular position pointing downward. A circular spiral of overlapping thin metal sheets, similar to a camera's shutter, began to gradually become visible inside the triangular space between the pods. Mark looked back down at the ground to carefully consider the implications of what might happen next. Then he looked back up at the mysterious ship and shivered.

Well, I did want to do more research for my second book.

He pondered the thought further as he turned around to view the seeming security of his tent staked out on the ground. Then he looked back up at the ship and silently pondered another thought.

Now that's too damned ironic. I'm about to become one of those abducted people I interviewed, except, apparently I've been asked. Oh God, I hope I won't regret this. Well, here goes.

"What did you say your name was?" he cautiously asked out- loud.

My name is Mon-tlan, but if you wish, just call me Monti.

"Okay, Monti, but... um... will I be gone a long time?"

You will be exploring many truths for approximately three days or seventy-two Earth hours that have remained hidden from you and most other human beings on your planet. Yet, seven days will have elapsed by the time I return you to where you are now standing by your tent. I will explain how this is possible once you are aboard my ship. Are you ready?

Mark let his eyes caress the beautiful countryside surrounding his campsite one last time, before he focused back up at the ship.

"Well, alright, I would like to help if I can."

The thin, overlapping circle of camera shutter-like metal sheets on the bottom of the ship's hull began to spiral open and a transparent yellow golden cone of light projecting down from inside the ship washed over Mark's body, passing through every cell, creating a soothing sensation and an adventuresome Spirit began to well-up inside him.

He took one last look at the surrounding, lushly-forested tree line and froze in his tracks as his eyes fixated upon several moving sinister figures just behind the tree line, dressed in dark black clothing with camouflaging hoods pulled down over their heads. The taller of the three figures was gazing in Mark's direction with a pair of binoculars, and he motioned with a hand for the squatting man beside him to fire some type of yard long, silvery cylindrical shoulder-held device pointing in his direction. For an unknown reason, Mark felt a presence silently direct him to hit the ground, and he literally jumped forward, landing face down in the dirt just as a sizzling electrical sound split the air. A foot-thick beam of solid white light burned across the top of his body, and Mark involuntarily threw both hands over the top of his head as a shield. The full force of the beam hit his tent staked out on the ground a few feet away, violently blasting a heat wave backward that seared the tiny hairs on his hands, accompanied by a deafening, roaring sound similar to a jumbo jet taking off right next to him, and a violent shuddering like an earthquake under his body. The tent and the ground surrounding it shredded in an instant into millions of blistering bits of dissipating golden light particles. Mark glanced up to see the last moments of a disintegrating fireball of light and smoke evaporated into nothing, leaving behind a round black scorched circle of dirt where his tent had just been.

Mark turned his head toward the forest tree line to see the three men running in his direction over the several hundred yards between them, brandishing some kind of handheld weapons pointed directly at him. Refracted sunlight passing through clear crystalline appearing handgun barrels was creating an eerie full spectrum halo of light around their black glove-covered hands. Adrenaline terror rushed down his spine, and Mark jumped to his feet to run for his life in the opposite direction. He glanced over his shoulder in time to see all three men simultaneously extend their arms, aiming their crystalline guns, and he heard the sizzling explosive discharges of energy beam weapons split the air. He leaped in terror toward the ground; but to his astonishment, his body was instantly suspended just above the dirt, and tiny star-like sparkling points of golden light began dancing all over it before he simply vanished in a blinding whirl of golden energy.

The mysterious assailants stopped in their tracks with gaping mouths to see their three pulsing, inch-thick red energy beams harmlessly pass through the empty air above the vanishing transparent molecular energy of Mark's body to simultaneously hit a tree a hundred yards beyond him. In an instant, a vertical four-foot section of its trunk just above the ground was dematerialized inside a blinding, explosive white light and the remaining height of the giant fir tree dropped to the stump. Then its mighty two-hundred-foot-high bulk started to fall over until it crashed with a thunderous roar to the ground. The three mysterious assassins looked up in time to see Monti's sleek Scout spaceship flash a brighter light around the hull and it shot straight upward, vanishing from sight beyond the cloud cover. The taller enemy leader lifted a wrist communicator of some type to his lips and spoke a command in an alien language. A moment passed and dancing yellow flecks of upward whirling light appeared around their bodies before they too vanished from sight.

An instant later, Mark saw his hands reappear with the same tiny, star-like sparkling points of golden light dancing all over them, and the energy faded away. He looked up, still terrified, to discover he was standing behind a semicircular control console. Hundreds of various-sized illuminated, faceted crystal controls producing a dazzling display of every imaginable color spread out across the entire surface. The warm, friendly smile of an extraterrestrial human appearing male in his mid-thirties with slightly curly blond shoulder-length hair, and a matching short-cropped beard, was staring back at him. He was standing just three feet away behind the center of the console next to a sleek white chair. Mark's gaze immediately focused on the alien's striking, clear robin's-egg-blue eyes, and he was spellbound as he gazed into them. Then, without the slightest bit of doubt, he just simply knew the mysterious being standing before him was human, and quite benevolent. In fact, he was surprised he also understood this particular extraterrestrial was happy to greet an Earth person.

"Wow, that was incredible! I thought I was toast for sure down there. They were really trying to kill me," finally blurted out Mark relieved, not realizing he just said it aloud with gusto, and the sound of his own voice surprised him. "You mean... it's really true? I'm really aboard a spaceship?"

Monti chuckled, finding Mark's question a bit absurd and somewhat amusing, but he replied with a nod and a soothing baritone voice, this time using his own vocal chords.

"The beings who were after you below are not human, even though they may disguise themselves as such, and they most certainly would have killed you if they could. It seems I arrived in the nick of time, as I believe an old Earth expression states. Well, Mark, now what do you think about how you arrived aboard?"

"Actually, I feel really good - kind of warm and tingling all over," he exuberantly replied, a little breathless. "I've never been this clear-headed. I feel like Super Man." Then, Mark's jubilant smile dropped as he more somberly asked, "Why were they trying to kill me, and who are they anyway?"

Monti sighed and seriously replied, "They were sent to kill you by a rogue organization made up of mostly non-human beings. They are part of a totalitarian Alliance of worlds and I must tell you they have a deadly vested interest in Earth's future. This is why I contacted you at this time. You will understand more about this a little later. For now, welcome aboard."

Monti turned and placed both his palms with spread fingers into the luminous golden crystal control palm impressions and they brightened, radiating light through the translucent skin of his palms and fingers on both hands.

The ship shot out of Earth's upper atmosphere at incredible speed and slowed in seconds to stop in a hovering position in space a hundred miles above the planet.

While Monti was talking, Mark had been steadily gazing more closely at him, noticing the knee-length, light blue single-piece gown he was wearing, belted at his trim waist with a dark blue silken strip of material. It was tied off with a simple knot at his left side and the extra lengths were dangling down a foot over his hip. The top of the garment was designed with an open V-cut from the base of his neck to just above his solar plexus, and the symbol of a white gold-tipped pyramid above the center of a silvery galaxy was embroidered on the left chest area. Three blue stars in triangular position were set just above the apex of the pyramid. The visitor's feet were clad in simple, silken blue slip-on type shoes. He was completely human in appearance, firmly built, and stood perhaps six feet in height. He had smooth, wrinkle-free lightly tanned skin, and slightly sunken cheeks. Yet, Monti's cheerful eyes kept drawing back Mark's gaze because they appeared to be slightly larger eyes than most humans he had seen, and he could swear he could detect a subtle glowing energy emanating from them.

Then he remembered he had seen the phenomena before and he stated, wide-eyed, "Three days ago, a very unusual man calling himself Mr. Crystal mysteriously hinted I would soon meet someone very special, right after he introduced himself at the home of my finance's father. No doubt, he was referring to you. Yet, he could not have known they would attack me before then. Monti, I must know. Is he one of your people, as I suspect, and is our world already being run behind the scenes by the totalitarian extraterrestrial race you mentioned?"

Monti's vanishing smile became a somber expression, and he seriously replied, "Yes, Mark, Mr. Crystal is one of us. However, you cannot yet imagine how covertly and expertly the off-world totalitarian group has infiltrated your world. They were caught many times breaking a hundred-year-old treaty with the Galactic Inter-dimensional Alliance of Free Worlds. By treaty agreement, many races from the stars secretly established observation and scientific study bases in hidden locations. The treaty forbade any of them to make direct contact with any world leaders or the populace. However, a much larger and more dangerous cold war than took place between the United States and the former Soviet Union is underway between two different alliances of worlds, and Earth is caught in the middle of it. The non-human race I'm speaking of sees all mankind as cattle, and your planet as just another resource-filled world to be dominated and added to their totalitarian imperial kingdom."

"I don't understand," replied Mark, mystified.

Monti thoughtfully paused, and then touched several of the luminous faceted crystal controls on his console. The vertically rectangular projection view screen appeared above the console again, revealing the planet Saturn with its many rings and moons.

Monti pointed to it and stated, "Camouflaged within the rings circling this planet you call Saturn is one of our medium large mother ships or flagships. It's over a mile long."

He touched another crystal control and the screen changed to a close-up view of central rings, revealing a large cylindrical space ship stationed between the various-sized, icy-looking asteroid-type chunks that comprise the rings. A ship just like Monti's was flying straight toward the central section of the massive ship as it simply began to disappear by fading from sight. The view screen changed to a closer image as the vanishing ship completely disappeared just a few feet from the central section of the glistening, silvery hull of its parent vehicle. A moment later, it began to re-materialize inside a vast hanger bay that became visible through the parent ship's metal hull, which had become briefly transparent. While the Scout ship was landing beside eleven other similar ships, the hull returned to its normal solid, non-transparent state.

"As you can see," continued Monti, "we don't require open launch bays to exit or enter the parent ships. Our technology allows us to take our Scout ships into a halfway state or briefly into a parallel dimension by raising the molecular time rate of the ship's matter. Then, the ship can harmlessly pass right through the solid hull of the mother ship. Once inside, the Scout ship is returned to the same molecular time rate as that of the parent ship, and it can safely land inside the hanger bay." Monti steadily gazed at Mark, and then asked, "Will you come with me on the most revealing journey of your lifetime?"

Relieved, Mark sighed and replied, elated, "Everything you're telling me I've already dreamed about at night, and I had many visions about all this while I was writing my first book. The confirmation you bring to me is like giving fresh oxygen to a suffocating man. Yes, Monti, I'd be honored to go with you, learn all I can, and help in some way."

Monti nodded smiling and continued, "Then the people of your world may have a real chance to be taken off the quarantined status it is under per current treaty stipulations, and it could become a member of the Galactic Inter-dimensional Alliance of Free Worlds. When you return from this journey, you will be much changed for the better. You will then be capable of carrying out the diplomatic mission you are destined to fulfill for the survival of your people and your planet. We have technology the rogue totalitarian factions do not know exists, and we are about to implement it to protect your world. From the flagship, we can monitor all hidden activity on Earth.

"Yes, Mark, we know about the hidden government you wrote about in your first book, and they're quite real. This group poses a deadly threat to three-fourths of the planet's population. With your permission, I'll take you to the parent ship, and from there you can witness for yourself the very dire reality that a certain non-human alien group, and their allies are planning for your planet and its people. They already have a hypnotic control over the leaders of the secret second world government on your Earth.

"But, Mark, you must also know that we are not going to harm any of them to make this great change on Earth. To accomplish this we must be able to neutralize their subconsciously implanted terrorizing controls. Then, we can safely remove them from your world for a short time to rehabilitate them, and then return them. This must occur before we officially reveal our presence to all Earth inhabitants. That is, the truth about the existence of our entire Galactic Inter-dimensional Alliance of Free Worlds that is made up of many millions of inhabited world members, most of them human. We must act soon because the misuse of advanced subconscious waveform technology has already been implemented by the totalitarian race to control the subconscious free will of people all over your world. They want to make them a compliant slave race. At this moment, they are continuing covert illegal operations on your world to advance their dominating endeavors. Therefore, the determination has finally been made by all the Galactic Alliance members that they have both the ethical and benevolent right to stop their sinister plans from reaching maturity; for that would very likely result in the complete annihilation of your planet.

"For reasons that will become clear to you later, we cannot allow the destruction of your world to occur even accidentally. The repercussions of such an event would also create very harmful negative effects for hundreds of billions of those advanced beings in the Alliance that live in numerous parallel dimensions of the universe where many alternate Earth-type and other worlds exist. Great harm would also be caused to a vast number of other beings you know nothing about that inhabit some of the planets and moons within your own solar system."

Mark seriously pondered all Monti just shared with him, and then he curiously inquired, "What exactly did you mean when you said I would be permanently changed for the better?"

"Certain elements of your DNA and the majority of mankind on Earth have been purposefully shut down or turned off entirely," replied Monti. "You should have a hundred percent use of your brain, be naturally telepathic, and your bodies should last for a thousand years or more without disease of any kind. This is your birthright heritage. However, the human beings on your planet were long ago genetically deprived these abilities. I cannot go into the reasons for this more fully here, however you can explore the truth about all this aboard the flagship."

Several thousand miles away, two dark-gray triangular shaped spacecraft with tapered, rounded ends, three hemispheric pods under their hulls, and surrounded by pale-red anti-gravity auras were traveling parallel to each other when they shot upward out of Earth's atmosphere. They made parallel ninety-degree elbow-curved turns, and then sped up in the direction of Monti's hovering ship. The red energy fields surrounding the ships intensified, and the clear crystalline triangular pointed front end of each ship, positioned below a dark teardrop shaped cockpit window, simultaneously shot a fiery-red whirling basketball sized spherical energy weapon at tremendous speed toward Monti's ship.

Monti noticed a pink, spherical faceted crystal light up blinking, emitting a shrill warning sound. He instinctively lunged for the rectangular emerald green crystal next to it, and tightly grasped it in his right hand, lighting it up. The view screen revealed a now clearly visible transparent blue energy shield wavering between the ship and the two rapidly approaching red fireball weapons that were almost at impact. In the background distance, both triangular enemy ships sped up toward Monti's ship, just as both fireballs exploded off the force field, violently rocking the ship from side to side.

Mark fell to the floor but he jumped back up and yelled out, "Monti, what's wrong? What's happening?"

Monti was too busy to respond, as he jammed both palms of his hands back into the crystal-palm guidance controls.

The luminous blue energy shield surrounding the ship's hull brightened and the ship darted in a blur of light into a momentarily opened golden-violet energy conduit or tunnel that appeared directly in front of the hull. Two more red whirling fireball weapons shot right past the space where Monti's ship had been, just as the energy vortex doorway dwindled to a point of light and vanished with a swift sucking sound.

Monti turned to Mark from his seated position behind the console and stated relieved, "That was too close. Those two ships are from the treaty breaking rogue worlds. They call themselves Trilotew or the

Righteous Illumined Over-Lords of the Empire Worlds. Their agents on the ground must have had hidden ships waiting nearby monitoring my beaming you aboard before they tracked us here. Fortunately, I was able to activate the protective energy shield in time or they would have destroyed this ship. For now, we are safe from further pursuit. Their ships will not be able to follow us through the vortex because the Galactic Alliance controls and guards that particle opening. Mark, we have just passed through what we call a time-space warp or inter-dimensional vortex doorway. These natural openings exist throughout space between worlds and on the surface or in the atmosphere of many worlds like your planet.

"In fact, Earth is entirely unique in this manner, because it has a geometrically located grid system of inter-dimensional portal openings that surround the entire planet. These openings allow for travel into parallel dimensions, as well as swift travel to the far reaches of the galaxy. Different versions of your planet Earth exist in those parallel realities that you do not normally perceive, because they exist at a different molecular time or vibration rate. Another way of putting it is that we can travel into a higher dimension that vibrates at a faster molecular time rate, traverse a short distance, then come back down through another inter-dimensional opening to discover we have traveled across a vast expanse of interstellar space in the physical universe. This is possible because of the faster and slower molecular time rates between the two dimensions."

"I'm not sure I follow you, Monti, but I'm beginning to visualize a wider picture of creation than I've ever dreamed was possible before today," replied Mark, utterly fascinated. "Somehow, I now seem to be able to visualize what your saying on multi-dimensional levels. What did you do to me?"

Monti grinned, but did not answer as he touched another faced luminous crystal control, and the three dimensional energy view screen projected above the surface of the control console changed again. On it, Mark could see the spaceship he was aboard was passing through a kind of golden-violet hourglass shaped energy conduit that was gradually widening in the near distance. The planet Saturn with its huge surrounding ring system and moons were clearly visible in the near distance of the black void of space on the other side. Then the ship suddenly shot through to the other side and the view screen changed, revealing the energy conduit fading to invisibility in the distance behind the ship.

Monti continued, "As you could see for yourself, we just moved from a position high above the outer atmosphere of Earth through one of the inter-dimensional connective vortexes. This one opens into an area of outer space very close to the planet Saturn. We are now on course to rendezvous with the flagship. You can just make it out hovering in position between several of Saturn's foreground rings."

Mark leaned forward to see the image and the projected view screen changed again. He could now observe their fast approach to the giant mile-long parent ship, looming ever larger. Then he began to recall the recent experience he had with his fiancée just three days before his departure for a long anticipated solo camping trip in the High Sierra Mountains. They were both en route to visit her father at his secluded mansion located near the top-most heights of Beverly Hills, California. Amazed, Mark now discovered he had the ability to clearly visualize the experience all over again as if he was actually there, and a pleased grin unconsciously widened on his face.

CHAPTER TWO

WITH EYES WIDE OPEN

Oh God, I can just hear her," Mark hesitantly thought. *If I start down that road again, she'll hit the roof. Damn it, I have to say something.*

"It's the beginning of the end of all things as we know it," finally blurted out Mark Santfield to Janice Carter, his slightly younger shapely female companion in her early thirties, after he glanced down at the front-page headlines of *the Los Angeles Times* Sunday morning addition she had sitting on her lap.

He paused for a moment to passionately gaze at the women sitting next to him that was considered by many to be strikingly beautiful with emerald green eyes, long gently curled brunette hair and a straight regal nose that curved ever-so-slightly upward at the end.

He continued with gusto, "This may be the beginning of what I've been predicting now for years," he seriously continued. "The world is going through a transformation that will change the planet's entire surface. The proof is right in front of you. Just look at the stuff on that front page: tidal waves hit twelve coastlines of the world on the same day; violent earthquakes go off in seven locations at once; snow in the deserts; three remote extinct volcanoes suddenly blow their tops.

Good God, Janice, it's really about to happen."

She eyed him seriously, smirking back obvious impatience at his seemingly never-ending negative attitude about everything.

"Go on then, dummy. Keep it up," she coyly replied a moment later. "You'll just piss off everyone at the party; but I refuse to stand by your side this time and be embarrassed by your pontificating, negative predictions."

"Oh, don't worry, babe. After all, it is your Dad's party," he consolingly responded, motioning with a hand to relax. "I'm not really in the mood anyway. Oh, come on Janice, honey, cheer-up. I am doing this for you. I promise, I won't let you down."

He pulled the sleek blue, late model four-door Jaguar over to the curb in front of the ornate wrought iron gate crested with the symbol of golden-tipped, white-feathered eagle's wings. Dozens of other very expensive cars had already parked along both sides of the long private drive leading up to the entry gates. The gentle half moon curved driveway beyond it lead fifty feet up to a twenty thousand square-foot Roman style mansion estate, built nearby the two lane highway that ran along the mountain crest line high above Beverly Hills, California.

"Come on, let's have some fun," he impishly remarked.

Then he grinned wide at her, opened the door, jumped out, hurried around the front of the vehicle to the passenger door and opened it wide.

With a sweeping wave of his arm, he gallantly bowed low and cheerfully stated, "At your service, Princess."

She elegantly placed her hand in his and he helped her out of the vehicle. Then he surrounded her with his arms and passionately kissed her. When they parted a few moments later, she was blushing; but before he could say anything, she smartly straightened her blue silken dress and struck a very sexy modeling pose.

"Well, how do I look?" she coyly inquired, looking only to receive the anticipated response.

"Like a goddess!" he exuberantly replied, passionately surveying her radiant beauty and the firm curves of her body. "Now we'll see if your dream was worth the humbling you endured to get me on your father's guest list."

"Lead on," she regally commanded, as she gently placed her right hand on top of his open left palm.

Then she pushed the intercom buzzer set in left brick gate pillar with her left hand forefinger.

"Yes," replied a husky older male voice.

"Daddy, it's me," she replied and the gate began to swing open.

They stood back a few feet to let both gates swing back along each side of the driveway entrance. Then they began to nonchalantly walk hand-in-hand up the driveway toward the elegant mansion. Well-trimmed, healthy green grass and multi-colored rose flower beds in full bloom lined both sides of the driveway that continued around a circular water-filled courtyard. In the middle of it stood an elegant female angel statue with spread wings, spewing water from the palms of her hands into a wide, curved blue granite bowl at her feet. They walked around the fountain to the double front doors and rang the bell. A moment passed, then the large, ornate dark wood door on the right swung open inward. Standing stolid in the opening was a slightly balding, gray-haired burly man with a brown mustache in his late sixties, wearing an expensive dinner jacket.

"Well, daughter, it's about time you visited this house," he smugly stated.

"Father, is that all you can say after the emotional marathon we went through last night?" she defiantly replied, placing her hands on her hips.

"Now, daughter," he began, backing off, "Where's your usual sense of humor? So this is the young man you keep talking about. Are you treating my daughter well?" he inquired, seriously inspecting Mark from head to toe. "Damn well better be!" he hotly added. Before his daughter could soundly scold him, he quickly added forcing a pleasing grin, "Oh, don't mind me. I'm just exercising my fatherly rights."

Relieved, Janice grinned at him and stated, "Daddy, this is Mark Santfield, and Mark, this is Ted, my father."

Ted cordially extended his hand.

Mark grinned and cheerfully stated, "Well, Mr. Carter, I'm glad we get to finally meet," and he firmly shook Ted's hand.

"Just call me Ted. Everyone else does," he nonchalantly replied, as he stepped inside just behind the open front door.

Hand-in-hand, the couple casually walked through the majestic entryway and the door silently closed behind them.

Already inside were six couples, dressed in casual elegance, standing around the wide, stately oval entryway on a rich blue lapis lazuli bordered, tiled blue-gray granite floor. Several of them casually glanced at Mark and Janice, and then resumed their conversations.

A very large gold metal-framed crystal chandelier was hanging down eight feet from the white dome shaped ceiling like an upside down Christmas tree. It was glittering with reflected sparkling rainbow colors off a hundred teardrop-shaped crystals that gradually tapered down to one larger crystal at its bottom point, which was still ten feet above the granite floor. Directly below stood another smaller, winged female angel fountain, and water was also pouring from the open palms of both her hands into the circular blue granite pool below her feet. Twin polished oak staircases, at each side of the fountain, gradually curved around behind it to open onto a long, curved second level balcony walkway that lead in both directions to many other rooms. Mark and Janice walked a few feet behind Ted as he approached the angel fountain and stopped, then turned around to face them grinning.

"Well, you two can introduce yourselves to my guests. Most of them are already in the grand reception room through the open glass doors. In my study, I have something to attend to that will not take long. I'll join you shortly."

He walked a few feet over to the left staircase and headed up them toward the second level balcony.

Concerned, Mark looked at Janice and asked, "Now what? I don't know what to say to this class of people."

"Oh, don't worry, silly, I'll handle the introductions. I'm used to the formal chit-chat of this crowd." Raising her eyebrows, she impishly grinned. "Who knows, something interesting may turn up. Remember, that's why we're here."

Mark glanced at the quadruple-paneled French glass doors leading into the Grand Reception room, which were pulled back against each side of the wide entryway on recessed rails set below the stone floor. Just beyond them, he could see a massive deep-blue lapis lazuli bordered, tiled blue-gray granite floor inlaid with intricate mosaic hardwood patterns, and twelve Roman style gold-laced lapis lazuli stone columns encircling the entire room. Fifty couples merrily chatting away were standing around the circumference of the large room next to a dozen exotic, ornately carved wood-trimmed, glass-topped tables with matching intricately carved chairs, and several artfully placed luxurious couches.

Twenty feet higher up the wall surrounding the room were a dozen large horizontal oval concave, clear glass windows. Just above them stretched the long, gentle oval-shaped curve of the huge, white alabaster ceiling. A smaller oval section of the ceiling, built several inches down from the massive upper level, enclosed a bright recessed overhead light source that was brilliantly illuminating everything below in the expansive room. At the far end of the room was a large, ornate green granite fireplace fully alight with orange and blue-gold flames spiraling upward four feet from neatly stacked burning logs.

Who is he kidding? This place is more like the royal ballroom of a king's palace. I wonder if Ted could be involved.

Mark continued to silently ponder the very real danger that possibility represented, since his first book was trying to expose a shadowy hidden government to the world's people that knew nothing about it. He was also growing a little hot under the collar at the gaudy spectacle of privilege and power the place represented to him. It smacked of unfettered greed gained at the abusive expense of others; but he would not dare voice this to Janice. After all, he was not sure how her father had quite literally become the world's richest man with hundreds of billions under his control, or how he made so much money in the first place, and he was curious to find out more.

He was not exactly poor himself; but he knew he had made his money honestly after the sales of seventy-five million copies of his first hidden truth revealing research novel. The characters were fictional, but they were based entirely upon a sinister covert plan he actually uncovered by personal experience while doing research for the book. He dug deeper and discovered a small hidden group of powerful mega-billionaires devised this plan to financially control the world, and its various governments from a hidden classified government. More importantly, some evidence had recently turned up that convinced him this elitist group of power-mad men had come under the control of a totalitarian extraterrestrial race that planned to eliminate a sizable portion of the population on Earth.

His last book had thrown him into enough controversy over the last two years, and someone was monitoring his movements. Two days earlier, while he was leaving his house in Woodland Hills, California, he had spotted several men in a black late model sedan parked across the street. The man sitting opposite the driver was snapping dozens of pictures of him with a long telephoto lens. When they knew he had seen them, they sped away. He was becoming more frustrated about the whole affair, and this was delaying the release of his sequel book. It had been nearly ready for months, and the publisher was pressuring him to cough up the draft. Yet, he remained hesitant until he could find out more about the conspiracy he now knew was real beyond any doubt. He had not yet told Janice about everything he had uncovered that confirmed his suspicions, and he was not planning on telling her any more about those discoveries any time soon. He knew he was heading into certain dangerous territory, and he wanted to find a way to shield her and himself from harm.

Meanwhile, Janice was gazing at him concerned, and she touched his cheek to draw him out of his reverie.

"Will you relax? I promise, this night will be interesting. Come on, let's head inside and see what we can uncover."

Mark smiled at her self-assurance.

"Lead on, lady. This night, I'm all yours."

CHAPTER THREE

GUESTS FROM WAY OUT OF TOWN

Mark clasped her hand as she offered it to him, and hand-in-hand they strolled through the open entryway leading into the grand reception room. They had not taken two steps when they were simultaneously noticed by a middle-aged couple standing by one of the glass-topped tables near the left swung back louvered door. The regal man's goatee style beard and green eyes were striking but what caught Mark's attention was the reflected overhead light glistening off the top of his mostly bald head. Then he briefly gazed at the lovely shapely woman standing next to him with her with long black silken hair. She was wearing an expensive diamond and emerald necklace hanging down over the open front of her low cut blue and black silken dress. As they approached, they smiled at Janice and then at Mark.

"Well, Janice dear," bitingly began the woman with an obviously phony smile, and air of upper class distinction, "I see you finally decided to introduce your infamous controversial suitor to our little gathering."

"Oh, Cynthia Piermont, darling," disdainfully replied Janice with a quick phony grin in return, "I see you still haven't quite got the knack of pulling back your snippy little nose when it's poking its unwanted way into other people's business."

Cynthia's smile dropped to a fuming frown.

"Well, how dare you!"

She walked away in a huff, leaving behind her embarrassed consort looking all too apologetic for her behavior. He forced an appeasing grin at both Mark and Janice, and then extended a gracious, welcoming hand to Mark.

"It's a pleasure to finally meet you, Mr. Santfield. I'm Henry Throckmorton, Mr. Carter's general council."

Mark cordially nodded his head as they shook hands.

"Oh, please excuse Cynthia," continued Henry. "I don't know what's got into her, and believe me I had no idea she was going to make a snide remark or I wouldn't have agreed to be her consort for this event. For my part, Mark, you should know I've read your book several times, and I find it utterly fascinating. Although, I must also add that some of the people in this room were... well, how shall I put it, probably offended by some of the things you implied would likely personally concern them in some way. If you ask me, the snobs all deserve it. They all think they're above the basic law of the universe: that every action results in an equal but directly opposite reaction."

Still miffed by Cynthia's little jib, Janice interrupted, "Henry, you always were a level headed guy. I could always count on you to be straightforward with me, so how on Earth did you get hooked up with that shrew?"

Henry blanched and sighed before he glanced over his shoulder toward the fireplace in Cynthia's direction. She was already busily chatting away with several guests as if nothing had happened.

"Well, to answer your question, she is one of the wealthier members of this group, and she's directly involved with something your father is currently undertaking, something that could affect the whole world in some way. So far, that is about all I know. It was your father who asked me to accept her invitation to escort her here after I had politely bowed out, and he insisted that I treat her well. Now how could I refuse a request like that from your father?"

Then he winked at Janice; but she was not amused.

"Listen to me, Henry, we need to know what my father is about to do. I am worried about him. My senses tell me he may be involved in something politically very incorrect, and likely, completely illegal as far as our government or any government is concerned. If Mark is right about even half of what's in his book, then this little group is planning a very dismal future for the entire world. My father is just as tight-lipped about his business now as he was when I was a little girl, and I can't get anything out of him."

Henry looked at Mark, hesitantly rolled his eyes and sighed. Then he took Mark and Janice by the arms and headed them a few feet further toward the wall behind the table.

He looked around the room behind them to see if anyone was watching, then whispered, "I can't say too much here in this company. Hidden monitors line the entire room; except in this one corner where a blind spot exists and the receivers cannot pick up any soft conversations. You both must understand the power represented in this room actually runs the world today behind the scenes of elected governments. I could be in serious trouble just for saying that. Both of you are being told this now only because in recent days I have become concerned for my own safety. Let me explain. Yesterday, I came to the house to deliver a package that had obviously been delivered by mistake to my office, since some of your father's business interests are listed as operating from there. I believed your father was still in England because he was supposed to be there. Yet, when I walked into his study to deliver the package, I accidentally interrupted a meeting between him and two very unusual looking men, if you can call them that. Several very odd things immediately came to my attention, and I began to realize that neither your father nor his guests had arrived at the house by car or any other observable means I could discover. I could also swear, for a moment, when the two tall strange men saw me open the door and enter the room they were staring at me with malevolent intent through the red slits of cat-like eyes. I glanced at your father and when I looked back, his guest's eyes suddenly changed to normal appearing human eyes, and their taller statures diminished in height. I can tell you their continued gaze at me sent shivers down my spine. Janice, your father's face was a mix of fear and consternation when he saw me standing in the open doorway. He jumped up from his chair, walked up to me, took the parcel from my hand, grabbed my arm, and then promptly escorted me from the room, closing the study door behind us. Then he gazed into my eyes and forced a warm smile."

"'Henry, my good man,' he said to me, trying to appear very cordial, 'I should have told you I had to suddenly return from England. These two clients insisted on a personal meeting here, and they demand absolute anonymity regarding our interests. As you noticed, they are very touchy about such matters. Well, you could not have known, so no harm done. I'll straighten them out when I go back inside.'"

"Mystified by the whole experience, I asked, 'Ted, what the devil is going on? I'm your legal council on most business matters, but I've been left out of the loop on this one.'"

"Your father placed a consoling hand on my shoulder and replied, 'It was necessary but I'll have to explain more about that aspect of things later on. Trust me for now. Everything is fine. Head back to the office and I'll give you a call a little later.'"

"'Okay then, have a good meeting,' I reluctantly conceded, forcing my own smile, and I got the hell out of there at a brisk pace. The further away I traveled from your father's house and his two odd guests, the better I felt."

Deep in thought, Mark had his hand to his chin after hearing all Henry had to say.

Then he looked at Henry and solemnly stated, "Thank you for your trust in both of us. We will not betray your confidence. However, Henry, I must continue to uncover the truth about the two strange people that met with Ted. If I am right, they are not from anywhere around here. I mean from Earth, that is, and I do not believe their intentions for most of us on this planet are good ones. If it is all right with you, I would like to coordinate our very discreet investigations though Janice, until we can get to the bottom of this mystery and determine what, if anything, we can do about it because it could be very dangerous. Janice, I haven't told you about this, but both of you should know two days ago I caught several men taking pictures of me with a telephoto lens from a nearby car after I left my house. When they noticed I spotted them, they sped away. This was not the first time I noticed them tracking my movements either. I am sure of one thing; this all has something to do with the success of my first book.

Someone or something does not want the truth out there amongst the people."

"Why didn't you tell me, ya big lunk?" hotly demanded Janice.

"Look, Janice dear, I'm now concerned for your safety as well as my own, and I didn't want to alarm you until I could find out more. Besides, I suspect your father is involved in all of this somehow, and he may not even realize the danger he's in."

"What danger is he in?" she impatiently demanded.

Mark placed both hands on her shoulders to calm her, fondly stared into her eyes and answered, "If my hunch is correct, your father is being used by beings from another world. Somehow, they convinced him, and certain members of his worldwide group, that their business interests will be best served if they cooperated with their hidden alien agenda for the future of our planet. I further suspect this arrangement has been going on now for many, many years."

Henry glanced over his shoulder and looked back appearing nervously perplexed.

He quickly interrupted them with a big cheerful smile, grabbed both their arms and stated, "Well thank you, Janice, for introducing Mark and it's been a pleasure finally meeting you. I will look forward to reading your next book."

Just then, Cynthia and another couple walked by pretending to be engaged in conversation, but their attention was obviously focused with wide-open ears upon Mark, Janice and Henry.

"Go on, you two, and enjoy the party," cheerfully continued Henry, rolling his eyes in the direction of the three people who just walked by them.

He turned away and headed back into the room to engage in a conversation with another couple standing a dozen feet beyond them. Mark and Janice briefly gazed at each other, clasped hands, and then knowingly grinned as they started to walk across the large room, headed toward the fireplace at the far end.

THE MYSTERIOUS MR. CRYSTAL

The covert eyes from many of the couples standing around the huge room were casually glancing in the direction of Mark and Janice, while they nonchalantly walked across the center of the room toward the warm glow of the fire brightly burning inside the big green granite fireplace. Two well-kept women, about the age of Janice, briskly walked by her left side and turned in unison to smile elatedly back at her. Jubilant with surprise, Janice instantly recognizing them, and they threw their arms around each other.

"Janice!" delightedly stated the taller woman after they parted, and the shorter woman added, "You look beautiful."

"Mary and Joanne!" jubilantly responded Janice with equal delight. "My father didn't tell me you two were coming to the party."

"This must be Mark, your mysterious boyfriend," curiously stated Mary, a skillful diversion, and both she and Joanne gave him an appreciated full-length gaze.

"Hello, ladies," cordially responded Mark, and he returned a warm, friendly grin to them.

"Janice dear, we have got to catch up on things. We should find a place where we can talk together quietly. Delighted to finally meet you, Mark, but if you don't mind, can we borrow your fiancée for a few minutes?"

Janice snuggled his shoulder and cheerfully announced, "Mark, these two ladies from my college days are my dearest friends. I won't be long."

Mark grinned wide back at her and her two friends, then volunteered, "Go on, ladies, and have fun. I think I'll just hang here by the fire for a few minutes."

She kissed him on the cheek, and the three women walked away, already carrying on a very jovial conversation. As Mark turned toward the fireplace, he was greeted by a clean-shaven man about his height in his thirties, who had the most interesting robin's egg blue eyes, and shoulder-length golden blond hair. He was wearing an elegant dinner jacket similar to Ted, with an inch-long gold pin attached to the lapel. Its shape was like the fluid-form of some ancient Egyptian hieroglyphic symbol or similar ancient letter. Mark had never seen anything quite like it, or the stranger's slightly larger than average appearing eyes that seemed to be emitting some kind of subtle glow.

Suddenly Mark was aware the stranger's smile was benevolent, while his intriguing eyes continued to deeply gaze directly back into his own, and he was also amazed how completely unafraid and oddly uplifted he felt. Somehow he just knew the man standing a few feet from him, with his right elbow comfortably resting upon the fireplace mantle, was emanating genuine friendliness. With a cheerful grin, Mark extended his hand.

"My name is Mark Santfield. Perhaps you've heard of me."

The stranger's smile widened as he firmly shook Mark's hand and replied, "Yes, Mark, I know about you, and that you're doing important work, more important by far than you yet realize."

"Who are you, really?" asked Mark with curious suspicion.

"I'm referred to as Mr. Crystal by people from very far out of town, if you know what I mean."

Contemplating his innuendo, Mark momentarily continued to gaze into the stranger's compelling blue eyes, not quite knowing how to respond, and then he simply grinned.

"Yes, Mr. Crystal, I believe I do understand what you mean.

Please correct me if I'm wrong, but it's becoming clear to me now there are beings from locations way, way out of town, who don't have your good intentions toward all of us living on good old planet Earth."

Mr. Crystal nodded smiling, as Mark stepped up to the fireplace mantle to stand beside him for further conversation.

"Your insight into events taking place behind the surface appearance of things on Earth is accurate, but you don't yet know the full depth of what is hidden, and what is being planned. For reasons you already understand concerning quite a number of the people who are gathered here, and many others around the world, I cannot reveal more now other than to say you're on the right track. I believe the time has come for you to bring your fiancée and Henry, who you can trust, up to speed.

"Although your further explorations into the clandestine plans of these people, and their controlling off-world allies will become increasingly more dangerous, there are also those from way out of town who are part of a vast alliance of free worlds systems that wish you well. Even now, they are watching over all three of you, and they will continue to do so from now on. One of my associates will contact you soon, and if you are willing, he can show you the whole truth behind your suspicions, and the wonders of the universe at the same time. Until then, expect the unexpected, and trust your own feelings regarding what is benevolent or malevolent in intent toward you. Now, I must be going. My time here is very limited, before those with dominating designs on your world may detect my presence. It has been a pleasure meeting you, Mark. We will cross paths again. Farewell."

Mark reached to shake Mr. Crystal's hand, but the gold metal pin symbol on his suit lapel suddenly flashed a small pale-golden light, and he vanished in a silent oval vapor of shimmering pastel white light that swiftly faded away. Astounded, Mark waved a hand across the air where the stranger had been, and a nearby couple curiously looked in his direction, wondering what the hell was wrong with him. Noticing their gaze, Mark realized that somehow neither they nor anyone else in the entire room had seen Mr. Crystal vanish, or perhaps they had never seen him standing there in the first place. Improvising a cover, he began pretending to be interested in the construction of the mantle by curiously looking it over from end to end. He fondly ran his fingers along its smooth surface, turned smiling toward the observing couple, gave them an approving nod, and then walked away in search of Janice.

CHAPTER FIVE

ARRIVING ABOARD
THE MOTHER SHIP

Mark blinked several times, as he came out of his reverie of events that led to meeting Mr. Crystal. Then he gazed at Monti, who was still sitting behind the control console looking at the image on the projected energy view screen of their approach to the massive mile-long, cigar-shaped mother ship. Mark could see the Scout ship slowing its approach a few dozen feet away from the glistening silvery-white curved metal hull, midway along the parent ship's length. Horizontally positioned along the central length of the entire hull, as far as he could see in either direction, were a series of clear glass-like, four-foot wide oval view-portals.

Monti reached out and touched a four-inch tall blue, pyramid-shaped glowing crystal on the control console above the palm guidance controls, and the metal hull of the mother ship appeared to turn transparent.

From outside in space, Monti's Scout craft, surrounded by its own pale-blue antigravity luminous aura separate from that of the flagship, was gradually becoming transparent a little at a time. It slowly, harmlessly passed right through the parent ship's hull on approach to land inside the launch bay. In effect, the molecular time-rate of the

Scout ship was sped up, so that it now operated in a slightly higher parallel dimension than the mother ship. Thereby, it was capable of passing through the hull's slower atomic-energy time-rate fabric.

"Monti, did we just pass right through the solid metal hull of the mother ship?" enthusiastically asked Mark.

Monti grinned at the question and replied, "That's exactly right, Mark. The Scout ship is now operating at a higher molecular time rate within a slightly higher parallel dimension of the physical universe. Remember, I explained how we travel through natural warps or openings that exist on Earth, and at various locations within the physical universe. We travel a short distance within the other parallel dimension operating at a different molecular time rate, and then pass back down into the former reality to cover vast distances very quickly. Well, we can alter the molecular time rate of this Scout ship in the same way. Except, instead of going through a natural opening in creation, we raise or lower the ship's time rate to gain access to or exit the parent ship. Do you understand this now?"

Mark nodded he understood, and he looked back at the projected energy view screen to watch Monti's Scout ship as it gently began to land next to several dozen identical Scout ships. They were already landed inside the vast football field-sized hangar bay. Also landed in the distance by a triangular opening that appeared to lead into the massive ship's interior were several wider and vertically taller Scout-type ships. Glowing semi-spherical light sources in many parallel rows lining both sides of the ceiling were brightly illuminating the long oval shaped launch bay with natural appearing light. Below on the bay floor, many personnel were busy carrying out their duties on top of, around, and under the parked Scout ships. Not all were human, and this immediately caught Mark's attention.

"Tell me something, Monti. Some of the bi-pedal human-like beings working around that launch bay do not appear to be exactly human. Am I right?"

Monti kindly grinned and replied, "Right again, Mark. The personnel aboard this inter-dimensional Galaxy class vessel represent over a hundred planets in the Galactic Alliance. As you can see, those maintenance personnel are of human stock with variation as to skin color and texture, forehead size, height, shape and color of the eyes, shape and position of the ears, and several other interesting differences.

"The beings you see working on the nearest Scout ship with the smooth pale-blue skin, pointed ears, slight gill slits up under the back of their chins that you cannot see, who you may think look like tall Elves, are from a planet called Oceana. It actually exists in a slightly higher parallel dimension of the physical universe. In fact, they are one of the most ancient humanoid races in this galaxy. Their ancestor's mentors, called the Seres, were the original sponsoring benefactors of the entire Galactic Inter-dimensional Alliance of Free Worlds that began well over five hundred thousand Earth years ago.

"Yet, even with their obvious differences, Oceanan and Earth humans are capable of mating, and most of the humanoid species represented here originally came from the same ancestry long, long ago in Galactic history. Therefore, most of them are also capable of inter-marrying with Earth humans, and this explains why many of your ancient mythological historical records refer to mysterious ancient Gods who inter-married with Earth women. You should also know in a far more ancient Earth history that the people of Earth know nothing about, women from other worlds have also inter-married with Earthmen, but this was rare. What will amaze you even more is the fact no human being ever originally evolved on Earth. They came to your planet during the different, mostly scientific, colonizing events that took place over millions of years. This always takes place after the cyclic shifting of the planet's poles 180 degrees overnight occurs. The catastrophic event sinks much of the old mantle above sea level, and quickly replaces it with a new one from the sea floor. You can experience the full realization of these natural facts for yourself in the security of this Galactic Alliance flagship."

Wide-eyed, Mark was astounded by this enlightening historic information, and he was about to excitedly ask a question when he was distracted by what he saw on the view screen. He could see Monti's ship just touching down on the landing pad right next to the Scout ship with the crew from the planet Oceana working around, on top, and underneath it. The projected view screen simply vanished as Monti touched a control crystal. Then he touched another thin, rectangular green crystal, lighting it up, and a seam-like crack appeared in the hull directly behind Mark, who curiously gazed at it. Having not seen any indication that the ship's hull was anything but solid before, Mark watched fascinated as the widening seam formed into a vertical oval opening three feet wide and six feet high. Much brighter light from the landing bay streamed inside the ship, and a ramp with steps appeared right below the opening extending downward until it touched the smooth ivory white landing bay floor.

"Well, Monti, now what?" asked Mark, very intrigued.

"As promised, we will explore together many truths that have been hidden from you and the people on Earth. Then, with your permission, we will remove the hypnotic programming that has kept you from knowing who you really are, and where you came from. Mark, you have been the victim of a carefully orchestrated amnesia that was projected into your subconscious energy field. This was done right before your arrival on Earth, before you began to unconsciously operate a five year old male body."

"What?" blurted out Mark, mystified. "Someone actually suppressed all former memory of who I was, and everything I was sent to Earth to accomplish on purpose?"

"I know it's hard to accept, but don't worry about it for now. Trust me, everything will become clear to you soon. We should head inside the ship to meet several very important people who are anxious to meet you as well. Shall we go?"

Mark sadly shook his head, as the deeper realization of Monti's words began to sink in. He sighed deeply, and then looked up with a determined grin and replied, "Lead on, Monti. Now I'm really ready to help any way I can."

With a friendly smile, Monti nodded and placed a consoling, compassionate hand on Mark's shoulder. Then he headed out the opening and down the steps. Mark stopped at the opening, grinning enthusiasm, and briefly gazed through it at the incredibly expansive alien launch bay. Then he hurried down the steps.

Only the Earthman's clothing appeared to be oddly out of place compared to Monti, and the other human and humanoid personnel in the hangar bay, as they both walked a few feet away from the

Scout ship. They stopped next to a two-way moving conveyor type walkway that was flush to the surface of the hangar bay floor. Mark glanced to his right to see the walkway ran in both directions from the triangular opening at the far right end of the landing bay across the center of the floor to an identical triangular opening at the far left end. Monti motioned to Mark to step onto the conveyor and they stepped on it together. Standing stoically side by side, the conveyer rapidly moved them between several dozen neatly landed rows of Scout-class spacecraft, headed toward the triangular opening at the base of the far left smooth ivory-textured wall another hundred feet in the distance.

Moments later, they came to the end of the conveyor, and they casually stepped off it onto the launch bay floor directly in front of the fifteen foot high triangular opening. The smooth wall surrounding it gradually curved upward high overhead to become the long oval shaped hangar bay ceiling.

Monti politely waved his right arm toward the opening, and Mark enthusiastically walked inside. He glanced at the unusual luminous slanted walls as Monti stepped inside behind him, and they quickened their pace down the long triangular corridor.

CHAPTER SIX

THE
GRAND DECEPTION

After another hundred feet, the triangular corridor opened into a larger square chamber three hundred feet wide and sixty feet high. Mark stopped just inside the chamber to gaze at the four feet long and three feet wide clear horizontal oval observation windows that lined the curved walls on opposite sides of the room. Gazing through the windows to his left, Mark could clearly see many varying sizes of some type of ice-like crystals moving alongside the ship that made up Saturn's relatively thin ring system. They extended into the distance well below and above the mother ship that appeared to be moving in a synchronous orbit with the flow of rings around the planet. Through the oval windows to his right, he could see the vast layers of the enshrouding cloud cover moving across the massive gaseous world. Several of its small icy-looking moons were moving into view, just above the rings, high above the planet's left hemisphere and the largest orange-colored moon he knew was called Titan appeared to be slowly moving to the right high above the northeastern hemisphere. Monti stepped up behind Mark and stood by his right side. Then he gazed grinning at the astonished spellbound expression on Mark's face that clearly revealed the realization he was taking in a staggering sight most of his fellow human beings on Earth have never seen.

"Like any new discovery or experience, you get used to it after a while," kindly encouraged Monti.

Mark remained momentarily speechless before he slowly turned to look at Monti and solemnly replied, "My God, Monti, it's going to take a long time for me to get used to this."

He turned back still spellbound to gaze through the oval windows at the expansive icy rings of Saturn. Then he began to slowly look around the room to take in his surroundings.

Several oval glass-topped tables, with soft blue cushioned egg shaped chairs at each end were positioned directly below and in front of each oval window. The floor was carpeted with matching tightly woven blue material, and lights like those in the launch bay lined the curved ceiling in six parallel rows.

"So this room is some kind of observation area, right?" Mark curiously asked Monti.

Monti smiled and replied, "Yes, Mark, people come here to contemplate, talk together or just to peacefully gaze out through the windows at the majesty of creation that extends in infinite directions outside the ship. Several dozen of these observation areas exist throughout the length of this vessel. As I mentioned before, several important people are anxious to meet you. If you can turn your gaze away from the rings of Saturn for a while, I will take you to meet them. Please follow me."

Mark came out of his fixation on the overpowering majesty of the scene before him, slowly turned his head toward Monti and nodded his anxious consent. Monti turned and started to walk the remaining fifty-foot distance to the far side of the observation chamber toward another triangular entry hallway and Mark followed close behind him. The second triangular hallway was shorter than the first, and they had only walked fifteen feet before they passed through the opening on the other end to enter a geodesic dome-shaped chamber. It was a hundred feet across and fifty feet high. Twelve-foot tall, three sided hexagonal shaped, polished ivory textured control consoles surrounded the walls of the room that were lit up with hundreds of different sized and shaped faceted, touch sensitive crystalline controls. Many human and humanoid personnel with varying pastel colored skin, from smooth ivory and tanned Caucasian tones through the spectrum to smooth violet snake-like patterned textures, were sitting in chairs monitoring various energy projected view screens like the one on Monti's Scout class spaceship. However, these were much larger. High overhead, a transparent fifteen-foot wide convex domed canopy was centered in the ceiling. A foot-thick vertical transparent tube extended from the top center of the clear convex dome to a matching convex dome centered in the chamber floor. The inside of the tube, filled with powerful wavering pastel-blue static-like energy, was in constant radiant motion from end to end. Surrounding the outer circumference of the bottom observation dome were a dozen more of the oval shaped tables and chairs.

As Mark and Monti approached a table centered in the room, Mark glanced down to see a human man and woman, that appeared vibrantly healthy in their late-thirties, standing up to greet them. They were wearing simple, but elegantly designed single-piece slip-on type, silken blue uniforms belted at the waist with a dark-blue leather-like material, and matching slip-on silken shoes. The Galactic Alliance symbol of the white gold crowned pyramid, superimposed over a silvery galaxy with three blue stars positioned in a triangular formation above the pyramid's apex, were emblazoned slightly raised upon the right central chest area of their uniforms. Both of them were radiating warm friendliness toward Mark and Monti. The man's robin's egg-blue eyes and the woman's emerald-green eyes were also emanating the same subtle glow that Mark experienced the first time he met Monti.

"This is Commander Jon-tral and next to him is his Second in Command wife, First Officer Sun-deema. They come from my home world beyond what your people call the Pleiades star system," stated Monti, as Commander Jon-tral extended a hand toward Mark.

As Mark shook his hand, he had the same knowing experience that he was meeting two kind human beings, though considerably more advanced, who were from another planetary system far from the quarantined planet Earth. The radiantly beautiful woman extended her hand, and as Mark shook her long slender fingers, he clearly heard her sweet mellow voice right inside his head.

You are most welcome aboard the deep exploration and reconnaissance flagship of the Galactic Inter-dimensional Alliance of Free Worlds. It will be my privilege to be your guide during your short stay here and during the implantation removal process you will soon undergo. If there are any questions you may have regarding this or any other area of interest at any time, please do not hesitate to ask me and I will provide you with the answers.

Mark was unconsciously smiling at his gracious hosts, as he silently replied mind-to-mind just to see what would happen.

Thank you, gracious Lady, for your welcome words, and I thank you as well, Commander.

They both grinned and nodded they understood him. Thrilled by the prospect, Mark blurted out, "You mean both of you could hear me mind-to-mind?"

Monti answered for them quite pleased, "Mark, remember when I first telepathically contacted you?"

Mark nodded he did.

"Earth humans have the same telepathic capability; except, as I already mentioned, it has been purposefully suppressed, and this truth is one of the primary reasons you were brought aboard my ship to journey here. If you wish to help us save Earth from a terrible fate no one on your world would invite if aware of it, you must be set free from what was done to you before you arrived on Earth. First, you must remember your true self, your true eternal spherical energy form, or Atma - what you would call soul."

"It's odd, but now that you mention it, it seems at one time somewhere in the past I was completely familiar with all of you, and this inter-stellar space travel technology. Can you really help me remember everything that was taken from me?"

Commander Jon-tral grinned and replied, "Perhaps to start out, it would be best if First Officer Sun-deema took you on a tour of the ship. Then you can go with her to a type of crystalline chamber that can facilitate the full recovery of who you are and where you came from that remains suppressed in the depths of your subconscious mind. After that, the extreme importance of the mission you agreed to carry out with us will become self-evident."

Mark glanced around the room, curiously gazed at Commander Jon-tral and then asked, "So, if I'm correct, this area must be the control and command center of your mile-long ship."

"Yes, that's very observant of you," answered Jon-tral, pleased with Mark's insight. "An identical command center is located on the opposite end of the ship. Because of this dual command capability and the ship's cylindrical shape, as well as other structural characteristics, we can direct the ship to travel into any number of inter-dimensional openings to traverse great distances in space many, many times far beyond what you call the speed of light. You will comprehend more about how this is possible when you regain full recall of all that was suppressed within you."

"Mark, listen closely," more seriously continued Jon-tral. "As you already know, a great cyclic change is about to affect your solar system that normally reshapes Earth's entire mantle, and unfortunately most of the life on the surface is destroyed in the process. After the extinction event of your dinosaur era long ago, many different extraterrestrial colonization events took place on Earth. They involved both human and non-human explorers over many millions of years the people of Earth are completely unaware existed at any time.

"The hidden, misdirected elitist government members on your world have known for many years about this coming event; but they classified it far above "Top Secret" to keep humanity in the dark. They are planning to only save themselves by temporarily residing in secret underground bases, and in several off-world colonies within your solar system. Their totalitarian off-world allies promised to assist them to escape the catastrophe. However, the Trilotew totalitarians have ulterior motives for pretending to offer genuine assistance. In reality, they want to dominate your world and make slaves out of all humanity. When they finish using Earth's corrupted leaders, they will eliminate them and their families. If something unexpected destroyed Earth, the Trilotew would simply move on without remorse, as they have done in the past. Then they would attempt to conquer some other world that is not yet a part of the Galactic Inter-dimensional Alliance of Free Worlds.

"As Mon-tlan explained on your way here, galactic history reveals the ultimate effect of any hidden totalitarian alien influence on a world like your Earth. The result is always the same. Eventually, one or more hidden leaders will unexpectedly set off a prized, reverse-engineered extraterrestrial destructive device that will disintegrate the entire planet. Should that happen, and it is likely, Earth would become just another orbiting asteroid belt like the one between Mars and Jupiter. The Galactic Alliance will not let that happen under any circumstance for reasons that go far beyond just Earth's survival. Therefore, the implementation of *The Seres Agenda* will take place soon, regardless of whether or not the totalitarian faction wishes it. We will finally be able to prevent your planet from going through another destructive cyclic polar shift, and Earth humans can become space-faring members of the benevolent Galactic Alliance."

Elated, Mark grinned and replied, "But that's incredible. This means the repressive governments will be gone, and the people of Earth will actually get to play among the stars."

"I believe you're catching on," replied Jon-tral chuckling.

"Our immediate plan is to get you back home in time for you to effectively carry out your mission as the intermediary between the entire Galactic Inter-dimensional Alliance of Free Worlds and Earth's misdirected hidden government leaders, who are heading your planet toward annihilation. For now, with your permission, please go with First Officer Sun-deema and Special Mission Officer Mon-tlan. They will begin your reorientation process so you can gain back your true self."

Mark enthusiastically nodded his thanks to Jon-tral and Sun-deema. She smiled and headed toward the triangular exit on the opposite end of the room. Side by side, Mark and Monti headed toward the exit right behind her.

PARTING
THE SUBCONSCIOUS VEIL

As they casually walked along another triangular corridor, Sun-deema began to explain to Mark how he had been unexpectedly captured en route to Earth, and how he was subsequently deprived of the entire memory of who he was and where he came from through a diabolical process involving implanted, terror-based amnesia.

"The way to suppress a person's true identity," carefully began Sun-deema, "and the wealth of natural understanding they have as an awakened sentient being has been carried out on countless worlds throughout galactic history by those who seek to dominate all life. This is a sad commentary on a tumultuous past between the forces that respect and appreciate all life and those forces that seek only power, at any cost, to dominate all life."

Sun-deema smiled kindly, waiting for Mark's further inquiry.

"I know exactly what you mean," replied Mark with a disappointed shake of his head. "Back on Earth, the more power men acquire, the more corrupt they seem to become. However, I now begin to understand tyrants from other worlds have somehow orchestrated the destructive desire for power within certain families on Earth to believe they are elite over the rest of humankind. Based on everything I know

now, they could not have naturally evolved to be as evil as they have become on their own without such an influence. Correct me if I am wrong, but it also seems to me they are in very grave danger themselves. The ulterior motives of the totalitarian alliance will likely include the eventual elimination of this hidden ruling class of people on Earth, when they've been deemed to be no longer necessary."

Sun-deema nodded, grinning at Mark's insight and replied, "That's exactly what we discovered has taken place many, many times throughout galactic history on other worlds. This always happened after their citizens had been put through a covertly manipulated intrusion into their lives by a domineering race from outside their own world system."

Mark was now walking between Sun-deema on his right and Monti on his left, as they headed through the triangular exit and stepped onto a hundred-foot in diameter transparent circular, glass-like floor. He could gaze through the floor and around the circumference of the curved ceiling to discover the transparent circular floor equally bisected the top and bottom hemispheres of a huge spherically-shaped chamber. He estimated the amazing interior extended thirty feet above and thirty feet below the circular floor. Perfectly symmetrical, clear, eight-inch long by four-inch wide quartz crystals lined the entire surface of the spherical chamber. They were all pointing inward toward a smaller twenty-foot tall spherical structure centered in the floor, made of twelve identical pentagonal, glass-like transparent surfaces.

For some reason, the memory from a geometry class Mark had back in his college days came to mind. He recalled the pentagon sided shape was referred to as a dodecahedron. As they approached closer, he could see inside the hallow chamber through its transparent sides. Then he noticed a white cushioned chair was sitting on the floor in the middle of the chamber. Just outside the front of the chamber was a three-foot by two-foot oval-topped crystalline control console, supported by a green illumined four-foot tall octagonal crystalline pedestal. Several dozen various sized and shaped, multicolored faceted crystal controls that lined the console were similarly laid out like the control console in Monti's ship. As they approached the console, Mark could see to the left side of it a set of two-foot wide, clear quartz crystalline stairs that descended below the floor. They appeared to lead directly below the center of the dodecahedron chamber to provide access to the chair centered inside it. Sun-deema enthusiastically broke the silence.

"You can sit in the chair inside this chamber and wear a clear crystal helmet that extends around the forehead and temples. After activating the device, you will be able to recall any thought or emotion that has ever bothered you, such as the cause of the amnesia placed in your subconscious electromagnetic field or aura. You will directly experience what has been controlling you, buried in your mind at a frequency below your level of awareness, and you will begin to remember everything. Then I will guide you to permanently disintegrate the implanted controlling images.

"Mark, for a long period of time now we've been remarkably successful at freeing many other beings from such tyrannical subconscious control mechanisms. We have records of millions of human and humanoid beings dating back five hundred thousand years that have gone through this process in similar chambers throughout the Galactic Alliance. Each one of them were forced to forget everything they once knew about themselves, where they had come from, and all they accomplished during many lifetimes spanning many millions of years and much longer, before we helped set them free of the implanted illusions. As former victims, they all experienced an astounding awakening that was both extremely uplifting and enlightening. To some degree, the same has been true for any of us that were privileged at the time to observe the events."

Monti chimed in, "Mark, you're actually about to go through a most extraordinary process that will free you from all the subconscious programming that has kept you in the dark about your past. The official name for this device is the Frequency Harmonizing Mind-link Activator. To elaborate on what Sun-deema mentioned, it has proven to be very effective in removing what we call implants or three dimensional mental image pictures containing sight, sound, smells, motion, tactile sensations, and every possible emotion that will compel you to forget or behave in an abnormal manner for suppressive control purposes.

"In the past, entire planets have been enslaved in this manner by totalitarian invaders. The inhabitants and their leaders had been so subtly manipulated, they were not aware they were being taken over until it was too late. Now, your world is undergoing the same process. However, this time, we've been able to monitor everything they've been doing that's in direct violation of a treaty the totalitarian group signed with the entire Galactic Alliance, and we are preparing to permanently suspend all their activities on your planet. In fact, *The Seres Agenda* is also being implemented elsewhere in the galaxy right now to ensure this type of brainwashing will never take place on any world ever again. Well, Mark, are you ready to begin?"

Wide-eyed in awe, Mark breathed a sigh of relief and solemnly nodded his consent. Sun-deema smiled up at him, grasped his hand and led him down the stairs, while Monti walked over to the control console. A few moments later, Monti could see them reappear inside the chamber as they walked up the stairs out of an opening that remained hidden from view behind the white chair. She nodded for Mark to take a seat, and as he cautiously sat down in the chair, the sides and back fluidly changed shape to comfortably conform to his body size and characteristics. Mark grinned with satisfaction as he glanced around the room at the transparent sides of the chamber. Then his gaze came to focus on Monti, who he could clearly see through the transparent pentagon shaped panel directly across from him. He was still standing behind the middle of the oval control console in the outer spherical chamber smiling back, giving Mark an encouraging thumbs up sign. Mark nodded his thanks, as Sun-deema reached down behind the back of the chair and lifted up a four inch-wide and inch-thick gently curved, smoothly polished quartz crystal shaped headset. She placed it over his head and the three transparent, long curved oval-shaped finger-sized prongs fit over his forehead, across the top of the skull, and over his temples just above each ear.

"Wow, it's sending soothing sensations down my spine," stated Mark grinning, as he leaned back in the comfortable chair.

She stepped around to the front of the chair to face him and kindly stated, "I look forward to meeting you again after you remember who you are and all that's been suppressed within you."

Then she respectfully nodded and walked back down the stairs.

A moment later, she reappeared coming up the stairs by the control console. She walked over and stood beside Monti.

Monti touched a blue, faceted diamond-shaped crystal, lighting it up, and asked, "Mark, can you clearly hear me?"

He gazed through the clear pentagon panel directly in front of him and nodded that he had.

"Okay, Mark, we'll begin," continued Sun-deema. "Monti and I will be guiding you through the session so you will understand what was done, and how it affected you. Once a repressed memory surfaces, it also appears on the view screens, and your true nature or true self returns to your awareness. We will then guide you to disintegrate the former subconsciously implanted memories with a focused mental energy beam you will be able to consciously project."

She passed the palm of her right hand over a multi-faceted spherical green crystal, lighting it up, and all of the thousands of quartz crystals embedded in the walls surrounding the entire outer chamber started to glow with a faint golden light. At the same time, a low-frequency humming sound began to softly pulse through the room, and the pentagon-shaped panels surrounding Mark turned on, similar to transparent TV screens, emitting a thin, blue radiance. Then Mark heard Sun-deema's soothing voice again.

"Mark, concentrate on the thought that you want to know why you can't remember where you came from or who you were before you arrived on Earth."

Mark closed his eyes, but they immediately sprang open again. He was staring startled at the clear glass-like panels surrounding him, just as blurred images began to form and clear. Revealed before him on the screens was a human man of similar build to himself with slightly larger eyes, dressed in attire much like what Monti was wearing. The man was desperately struggling to get free from two tall, muscular, scaly green-skinned, bi-pedal reptilian aliens that had red, oval, cat-like eyes. They were tightly gripping his upper arms with long, claw-like fingers, forcing him through a spherical transparent red energy shield that surrounded a high-backed black obsidian chair centered in a dimly lit, crude octagon shaped laboratory. The surrounding field of energy then forced the man back into the chair, and straps made of the same red energy appeared binding his arms and legs to the chair's contours. The defiant man struggled with all his might to get free to no avail, as the two reptilian beings stood back a few feet. Then the taller one pointed a hand-held, long triangular, red crystalline device at the chair and the crystal lit up, compelling the man to involuntarily close his eyes. He continued to struggle, shaking his head to try to shake off what he was being forced to envision. Then he screamed in terror, and both reptilian captors gleamed in sadistic joy at the helpless predicament of their victim.

The images on the surrounding walls of the chamber suddenly changed in front of Mark and he could objectively see what the man on the screen was seeing, as if he and the man were now the same being. The first image Mark saw was when the man was happy and dressed in a single, form-fitting, silky-white Diplomat's attire. He was being respectfully honored and joyfully greeted by the welcoming, shaking hands of thousands of his fellow citizens that had lined up to greet him while he walked along a very advanced city street surrounded by many tall crystalline buildings that he remembered were on his home world.

The images changed again, revealing the man now being pushed off a cliff head-first by the same two reptilian captors. As the man tumbled down several hundred feet toward a volcanic inferno, Mark screamed in terror as he witnessed the man's body burst into flames, just before it hit the explosive lava that covered over his sinking body.

Once again, the scene changed and the man was now sitting on a smooth, oval-shaped, blue rock out in nature, surrounded by tall, tear drop-shaped bushy trees that were lushly covered with broad, silvery-green spoon-like leaves, and long strands of interspersed violet, star-shaped flowers emitting soft phosphorescent light. His happy eight and ten-year-old children, a boy and a girl, were sitting upon his lap giggling inside his arms wrapped around each, while he playfully, gently bounced them upon his knees. His happy, elegantly beautiful, green-eyed wife with long golden blond hair, wearing a soft white dress shimmering like a moonstone, walked up behind them and wrapped her arms around his neck.

The scene on the surrounding panels changed once more and the man was now standing spread-eagle, tied with thick ropes to several crude wooden posts in a prehistoric alien jungle setting. The same two reptilian captors approached him, brandishing long, curved, double-edged swords, and crude jagged-edged saws. They were laughing at the man's dire dilemma, as their long forked tongues dripping with sticky saliva zipped in and out of their mouths to sadistically lick the sides of the man's cheeks. The man convulsed and vomited from the stench of reptilian breath.

Then Mark heard the taller captor say in a deep guttural voice with hellish glee, "Which part shall we eat first? Should it be the eyes? Oh yes, the eyes are very tasty."

The other captor chimed in, drooling, "I'm going to rip off your arm, human, and eat it in front of your crude fragile face. But first, let me remind you, puny thing, if you attempt to remember again who you are, then this is what will happen to you."

The taller reptilian bi-pedal demon thrust forward both his long green arms with grasping five-fingered razor sharp claws, ripped out both of the man's eyes and sucked them down his throat off the ends of his bloody fingertips. The tortured man and Mark sitting in the chair simultaneously screamed in agony, as if Mark was actually going through the torture with the man being imaged on the screens all around him. Then, the slightly shorter alien promptly reached forward with both his long sharp-nailed reptilian hands and literally ripped the man's right arm from its socket. Then he quickly chomped and crunched the entire arm down its wide throat through its gaping mouth full of several rows of sharp teeth, until the fingers disappeared. Screams of utter agony rent the air, and the man's head fell forward as he passed into unconsciousness, and Mark's head fell forward with him.

"Mark, it's over," yelled out Sun-deema's concerned voice. "You uncovered the main implants they forced upon you. Now quickly look up at the screens."

Mark reluctantly, slowly opened one eye and then the other to see if the terror might still be there, but instead he was now looking again at the original scene of his own former highly evolved life as a happily married humanoid man on another world with his two children playing upon his knees. All the joy of his enlightened awareness as a highly evolved human type of being from that other world started streaming back into his consciousness and he deeply sighed. Then he started to uncontrollably cry, but they were not tears of sorrow or pain.

He was experiencing indescribable blissful relief, for he was beginning to recall all that was taken from him long ago and he solemnly asked, "How long has it been?"

Monti's kind voice responded, "The terrible events you witnessed took place aboard one of the reptilian battle cruisers that intercepted your Scout ship on your way into Earth's atmosphere thirty-one years ago. You were to carry out a long-planned diplomatic mission to reveal *The Seres Agenda* to several of Earth's top hidden leaders who want freedom from their reptilian overlords that now control Earth's secret second government. Mark, you were to help free them from the mind control that is now twisting their thoughts, and then prepare them for a large-scale arrival of the Galactic Alliance fleet in the near future. Since then, something most extraordinary has happened, and what is now coming to Earth goes far beyond only an open Galactic Alliance presence, something that will unexpectedly permanently alter Earth's destructive direction. It will become an uplifted, benevolent world, and we will invite the populous to join the entire Galactic Alliance. Earth will be taken off the quarantine status, and then the people can freely play among the stars."

Mark looked up, angrily determined and stated, "I will make them pay for what they did to me."

Both Sun-deema and Monti blanched at his angry emotions, but they also wisely understood the pain he was still experiencing.

With a calming voice, Sun-deema said, "Mark, listen to me. This was just the beginning of your full recollection. Do you remember your true name?"

Mark looked forlorn and tired as he tried with all his might to recall what was still lurking just beneath the surface of his awareness.

A moment passed and his eyes lit up, as he breathlessly replied, "I'm a diplomat called Shon-ral from the planet Norexilam in the Starborn cluster, beyond what the people of Earth call the Pleiades star group. Dear Prime Creator, how long have I been imprisoned in this body?"

Compassionately looking on, Sun-deema answered, "In Earth time, thirty-one years has elapsed, but only one year has gone by on your home planet because of the space-time differential that occurred when your ship passed through the Blue Star Meridian vortex. That one is high in the atmosphere above Mt. Shasta in northern California on Earth. After your ship entered the planet's ionosphere, a large Trilotew space ship captured your ship. Do you remember them now?"

Mark was blank-faced at first and then his eyes widened as an angry scowl formed across his face and he bitterly answered, "Yes, now it's all coming back to me. They have been a thorn in the side of the entire Galactic Alliance for over five hundred thousand years. The treaty we signed with them so long ago has been covertly broken by them so many times, it's amazing we haven't gone back to their home world and destroyed their totalitarian madness for all time."

Monti very seriously replied, "My friend, you still have much to remember, or you would know the way of revenge is not our way. The Trilotew were inflicted with their insidious totalitarian subconscious lust for violence, and eating of the flesh of highly evolved sentient beings by their white-winged faction over half a million years ago. These more vile, winged reptilians enslaved their conquered relatives after finally winning a hundred-year-old interplanetary war. During the course of many, many thousands of generations that followed, the subconscious programming drove the reptilian races to carry on their demented behavior wherever and whenever they could get away with it. They still do not realize they have not been in control of their behavior for over five hundred thousand years. However, they were not always this way. When you recall more of yourself, you will remember *The Seres Agenda* implementation also involves the deprogramming of the entire Imperial Trilotew Worlds."

"Anyway, your secret mission was somehow intercepted by Trilotew agents, and we now know a spy must be among our secret ranks on Earth and perhaps even somewhere highly placed within the entire Galactic Inter-dimensional Alliance of Free Worlds. That was how you were so easily captured. They removed your real Atma-self from your body, or what Earth people call soul, using an ancient device outlawed by treaty agreement. Then they implanted the hidden command for you to enter a five-year-old orphaned boy's body, after they forced out its occupant. The Trilotew would also implant a command for you to compulsively reincarnate on Earth as their prized political prisoner. We know your foster parents raised you after that, before they died in that tragic automobile accident fifteen years later."

Mark was now speechless, as more of his former enlightened human state began to surface. Then he remembered his wife back on his home planet and tears began to well up in his eyes again.

He hopefully looked at Monti and hesitantly asked, "Is she... I mean, my wife... is she alright and my children?"

Sun-deema compassionately replied, "Yes, Mark, your wife, Lorun-eral, son Shan-dreal, and daughter Taluna-tala are fine. Of course, they miss you, but they know now you've been found alive."

Monti was not smiling when he hesitantly added, "You should know about one other problem."

Mark apprehensively gazed back at Monti and waited.

Monti reluctantly continued, "After your ship was captured, you were suspended in a powerful electromagnetic field. Then they subconsciously compelled you to enter the selected five-year-old orphaned boy's body with all former memory suppressed. After accomplishing that, they destroyed your adult human body, or devoured it. I'm sorry to tell you this, but the body you now have is the only one you have left."

Mark was crestfallen and his head sadly lowered, for he began to remember the lovely face of his wife and two children, and he dismally thought, *How can I ever return to them now?*

Both Monti and Sun-deema heard his thought and they telepathically replied in unison, *We have a plan to reunite you with your family.*

Mark looked up hopeful and breathlessly waited.

Monti said aloud, "Good... good, now your telepathic ability is starting to come back as well. Welcome back, Mark, or I should say, Ambassador Shon-ral."

Mark, still dismal, did not respond.

Sun-deema sweetly smiled and added, "Once all the implants have been removed from your subconscious mind, we plan to significantly alter the DNA of your Earthly human body. We can reshape it to become the Pleiades body you lost. By utilizing the more complex DNA structure on deposit back on your home world that has not been purposefully toned down or negatively limited by the Trilotew, like all physical bodies on Earth have been, we can restore your former self. But, Shon-ral, we have been instructed to ask if you would be willing to temporarily play the part of Mark Santfield for a little while longer. Our adversaries on and off Earth do not know we have the ability to remove their implants fully, and they will never suspect you could ever be restored to full Galactic Inter-dimensional Alliance status in a DNA-restricted Earthly human body. If you don't look like your former self for now, we can go forward with you in that body to carry out your diplomatic mission to the leaders of Earth's hidden government."

Monti and Sun-deema patiently waited for Shon-ral's response while he contemplated the entire turn of events.

Then he looked up with a hopeful grin and asked, "Are you sure you can eventually transform this body into my former advanced physical human body from the home world?"

Monti and Sun-deema confidently nodded.

Shon-ral's grin widened and he curiously asked, "Can you make the brain of this body function as it should at one hundred percent?"

They both confidently nodded.

It was now Shon-ral that smiled through Mark's body, and the physical eyes appeared to suddenly grow just a little bit larger as he inquired further, "And the lifespan?"

Monti cheerfully answered, "It can be increased to that of our own, well over one thousand years if need be. However, first we must get your memory fully rehabilitated. Then we must promptly send you back to Earth, so suspicions are not raised among others, and you do have a fiancée waiting."

Then the Mark Santfield part of Shon-ral surfaced and he remembered he was also in love with and had committed to marry an Earth woman, and his smile faded.

Once again forlorn, Mark asked, "How can I go forward with her now? I already have a wife and children back home who I treasure dearly."

Sun-deema encouragingly added, "We've already contacted your wife, Lorun-eral, to update her on all that's happened and she wants you to go forward with the mission. However, you should also now know your current fiancée is actually one of us. Can you recall what happened to your cousin, Moon-teran?"

Mark squinted his eyebrows as he struggled to recall something all too familiar, but it was just out of reach. Then his eyes sadly widened.

"Oh, Ancient One, Prime Creator of all, what have I done?" he fearfully replied, as he simultaneously remembered that most of the Galactic Alliance members referred to the primary cause behind all life in creation in this way. Then he lowered his head again and very reluctantly added, "She was my cousin. I was informed right before I left for Earth that she had mysteriously disappeared there after nearly finishing her six-month scientific mission. She was studying the culture and monitoring Earth's dangerously increasing radioactive atmospheric and deep water table pollution levels. Now it's all coming back to me."

Concerned, Sun-deema encouragingly stated, "Shon-ral, do not be ashamed. That feeling is just one of many negative emotions that were implanted in most Earth humans. Before your trip to this ship, we had only recently discovered that Trilotew agents, secretly operating on Earth behind certain government leaders, had captured her. Six months before your ill-fated arrival to the planet, they had already compelled her to forget her former life. Then they forced her into a young female body and destroyed her original body from her home planet. During your full deprogramming, we will arrange to secretly bring her aboard this flagship and she can go through the same process. Then she can also help you with our overall mission objectives to turn Earth around, and save it from being destroyed or completely enslaved by the Trilotew.

"In other words, since both your former home world human bodies no longer exist, each of you could cleverly pose as a married couple until we complete our mission and free Earth's enslaved people. Then you can both go through the biological transformation process and return to your own families on your home world. Your cousin, Moon-teran, also has a husband and three children back on your home planet, but you will remember that soon enough. Mark, I must now ask if you are willing, under these circumstances, to go forward with your original mission?"

He pondered the thought, as he began to recall how fervently he had committed himself to the grand plan to free the people of Earth from the negative subconscious drives implanted in them. Then he recalled the larger plan was to also permanently remove the evil subconscious drives that continue to compel the Imperialistic Trilotew Alliance to make living in the Milky Way galaxy a subtle type of traumatic experience, for all those who must put up with their ongoing terror campaigns.

"Very well," Mark cheerfully replied, "For now, just refer to me as Mark Santfield, and that reminds me of a famous English fictional detective back on Earth named Sherlock Holmes, who would say to his assistant, 'Watson, the game is afoot.'"

He grinned widely at his new found courage, and sense of freedom, now that he had finally remembered who he really was.

Monti and Sun-deema were grinning back at him and Monti confidently asked, "Well then, Mark Santfield, are you ready to get rid of the rest of that awful Trilotew subconscious garbage?"

"Indeed, I am," he eagerly replied and curiously asked, "But how does *The Seres Agenda* create this coming dramatic change?"

Sun-deema solemnly answered, "As you know, the Seres race seeded all humanoid life in the galaxies before they vanished long ago. Recently, they recontacted their first blue-skinned Oceania progeny, presented them with a new consciousness-freeing Ray, and then announced their return to the galaxy."

Mark breathed a deep sigh, pondered her statement, then grinned with a profound new realization and nodded he was ready to continue the deprogramming session.

CHAPTER EIGHT

ESCAPE FROM
REPTILIAN CLAWS

Janice was frantic with worry after she learned that Mark had not returned from his camping trip after the weekend, and she filed a missing person report with the Beverly Hills police.

The ensuing police investigation discovered only a few obliterated tiny shreds of what had once been his tent and the black burnt circle of dirt where it had stood. They also discovered the giant fallen tree near its sheered off stump in the distance behind it, but that had only expanded the mystery further because there was no sign of the missing section of the tree. Her concern deepened after the evening 7:00 P.M. prime-time newscaster on channel seven announced that a forensic team had arrived on the scene. After investigating the bizarre circumstances, they discovered something else very unusual, and concluded that some kind of unknown energy had disintegrated a four-foot missing section of the tree's trunk, because there were no indications of any chainsaw markings or marks from any other type of cutting tools. The following scientific analysis of the finely splintered shreds from the sheered-off tree stump, and from the end of the remaining fallen tree, also revealed a non-analyzable chemical residue in the seared wood fibers.

Janice knew her father had resources to find things out that she had no way to discover, and she went to his mansion three days after Mark's disappearance to seek his assistance. Actually showing concern, which surprised her, he told her he would make several inquiring phone calls and he hurried upstairs to his private study. She anxiously waited on a chair next to the entryway doors and ten minutes later, someone rang the front doorbell. She cautiously opened the door to find standing before her two tall, odd looking strangers staring back at her with penetrating hypnotic gazes that made her immediately feel very uncomfortable. The taller of the two forced an obviously phony smile as he politely asked if Mr. Carter was at home, and she called upstairs to his study. A moment later, Ted appeared at the top of the twin staircases and gazed down with concerned alarm at the two men. Then he hurried down the right staircase to meet them. Janice stood aside as her father walked by to shake their hands, and the taller man whispered something into his ear.

Ted's face blanched as he looked up to briefly gaze into each man's eyes and he seriously stated, "Come up to my study. We can discuss this in private."

Both tall men turned in unison and gave Janice a chilling mistrustful gaze that Ted observed very closely, and the growing concern on his face was obvious.

Then he gazed at his daughter with a reassuring smile and calmly requested, "Janice, dear, I have to meet privately upstairs for a few minutes with both my clients. Perhaps then I'll have more news regarding what may have happened to Mark, because they just informed me they know he's alive, but they don't know exactly where he is right now. They are attempting to track his location. Don't worry, we'll find him. Please wait for me here in the entryway and I'll join you in a few minutes."

He bent forward and kissed her on the forehead, then noticed her rather miffed expression. He did a double take before he hurriedly headed back up the right staircase with his two tall guests trailing right behind him. Janice carefully stepped toward the left staircase in time to catch a glimpse of his two taller guests staring with wide-eyed sadistic glee at the back of her father's head all the way up the stairs. Ted waved his hand for them to proceed into his study ahead of him, and then he pretended to cheerfully smile down at his daughter. As he turned away, Janice couldn't help but notice that his forced smile became a fearful scowl, before he entered his study, closed the door behind him, and forcefully locked the dead bolt with a loud... *clink...* that even she could hear all the way downstairs.

A claustrophobic feeling began to creep over her as she quietly opened the front door and stepped outside. She pulled a cell phone from her purse, hit a speed dial number and moment later a man's voice said, "Hello?"

Janice winced and asked, "Henry, is that you? Oh, thank God you are there. Listen, we have serious problems. The two strange men you told Mark and I about that accidentally surprised you when you attempted to deliver the FedEx package to my father's study just showed up here. I had just asked father to use his resources to locate Mark, and he made a phone call from his study. Ten minutes later, both men arrived and they subsequently informed him they knew Mark was alive but that his location was unknown, and they were trying to track him. Henry, I think his life is in danger."

A kindly mellow man's voice softly stated from somewhere behind her, **Mark is safe and unhurt.**

Startled, with her hand over her heart, Janice spun around but there was no one there.

"Who's there with you?" asked Henry's concerned voice back through her phone.

"I don't know," she nervously replied, "I can't see anyone. Listen, Henry, I must go. Someone may be watching me. I will call you just as soon as I can. Take care."

She turned off the phone, opened the front door, stealthily re-entered the house, quietly closed the door behind her and glanced around the entryway for any spies.

When she turned back around to open the front door again to run from the house as fast as possible, she heard the mysterious stranger firmly state again, **Janice, Mark is safe. My associates rescued him from certain death. You must trust me.**

She fearfully spun back around to confront the voice only to discover she was staring into the kindest human male eyes she had ever seen. A soft golden light briefly flashed off the strange looking pin symbol he was wearing on his right lapel and she discovered her apprehensive fear dissolved away. More than that, she now felt uplifted and refreshed while she gazed back at the six-foot tall clean-shaven man standing before her. He had the most captivating slightly larger than average robin's egg-blue eyes, and shoulder length golden-blond silken hair that she had ever seen. He was wearing blue jeans, a white shirt, leather shoes, and a blue leather jacket with a gold pin attached to the lapel. She began to ponder how it looked like an inch-long fluid form of some kind of ancient Egyptian hieroglyphic symbol or ancient letter. She had never seen anything quite like it or the stranger's slightly larger than average eyes that seemed to be emitting a subtle glowing radiance.

She was already unconsciously smiling back at him when she began inquiring, "Who are you and how did you get here? Did you come in before my father and his two strange guests?"

"Pardon me, Janice. I am Mr. Crystal. My telepathic comments may have startled you, but that was not my intent. I believe Mark told you about me. There's little time left to safely take you to him."

"Oh, thank God," she spouted relieved. "Yes, Mark told me all about you before he left on the camping trip. You're really from... well, you know, from out there?"

"Yes, Janice, I am," replied Mr. Crystal. "Mark is safe, but the two men meeting with your father right now and their associates tried to kill him. One of my people rescued him just in time. Now he's off-world, going through a process to free him from the subconsciously implanted programming he was subjected to before he came to Earth."

"What do you mean... when he came to Earth? What's going on?" asked Janice, becoming apprehensively concerned again.

"You must trust me and quickly before those two meeting with your father detect my presence here. If you are willing, I will take you to Mark and then you will understand everything for yourself. Will you come with me?"

"How will we get there?" she hesitantly asked with certain trepidation.

Mr. Crystal touched the pin on his lapel again and it emitted a brief flash. Suddenly, the churning apprehensive feeling in the pit of her stomach vanished.

With a deep relieving sigh, she confidently looked back at him and gave him a pleased grin.

"We'll be teleported directly to a hidden base located within a mountain cavern inside Mt. Shasta in northern California. From there, we can safely proceed to where Mark is located. You will be pleased to know he learned much more about his quest to discover the truth regarding extraterrestrial life in the universe. Would you like to join him?"

Janice anxiously replied, "Yes, Mr. Crystal. I will go with you now. Those two creeps upstairs looked at me and chills went down my spine. They give me the willies and I am very worried that my father is mixed up in something dreadful. Will you be able to help him too?"

"You'll have answers to your questions soon," seriously responded Mr. Crystal. "But we must leave now. Those two men are about to head back down the stairs and if they catch us here, you would not be glad you're alive."

Janice winced at the thought of their creepy eyes and she replied, "Just having those two look upon me once is all the experience I want of them for the rest of my life. Mr. Crystal, what are we waiting for?" she confidently replied. "Let's get the hell out of here."

Mr. Crystal smiled and touched the golden symbol on his lapel three times. Just as the door to Ted's study opened, they both vanished in a silent oval vapor of shimmering pastel golden-white light that swiftly faded away.

Both tall angry men ran out of the study brandishing the same type of crystalline weapons that the black camouflaged men used to try to kill Mark by his tent in the mountains. Ted fearfully came up behind them grimacing for his daughter's safety, and all three stopped at the railing by the head of the left staircase to gaze below at the vacant entryway. Ted's furious strange guests ran down the stairs lurching with weapons pointing in every direction in the vain hope of finding their intended targets. Ted ran up between them in a panic and stopped, not knowing what to do next, just as both aliens slowly turned around to face him. One was now standing in front of him and the other directly behind him, and sweat began to bead up on Ted's forehead.

A growing fear etched across his face as he watched both intimidating guests reach into their suit coats and touch something. The energy shield illusion surrounding their bodies wavered like a heat wave in the dessert and faded away, revealing their true bipedal reptilian natures. Ted could not hide his revulsion as he watched drool drip from their foot-long, purple-red forked tongues darting several times in and out of their elongated green scale-covered mouths between two rows of sharp fanged teeth. They now appeared to be ten foot-tall, green scale-covered reptilian males, wearing a single-piece body suit made of a silver-gray looking metallic fabric belted at the waist with blue oval buckle. Embossed upon their upper chests were upside-down black obsidian pyramids with the point of a wide vertical curved silver sword touching the middle of the pyramid's square flat shiny bottom. Two double-headed green snakes wound like a braid around the double-edged blade up to their four heads that were arched inward toward each other above the swords mother-of-pearl appearing handle. Their forked tongues, extended out of open mouths, touched together at the space centered between all four heads.

Both aliens were more muscular and solidly built than most weight lifters on Earth, and the strong fingers on each of their hands ended in long, razor-sharp, extendible curved nails. Centered within large pastel-violet oval eyes were vertical cat-like fiery-red pupils. Their reptilian ear holes were located on each side of their heads where human ears would have been.

Grinning sadistically, they both pointed their hand-held weapons at Ted and licked their lips with their long darting forked tongues.

The taller one leaned close to Ted's grimacing face and stated, "It is very lucky for you, Earth human, that we are not hungry now. You told us this Mark Santfield was going to be at his camping location in the mountains, but you failed to tell us soon enough. The Alliance forces now have him, and we must make other plans. Do not fail us again, Earthman, or perhaps we will find another lead collaborator amongst your fellow rulers on the planet that will be more responsive to our requests. Do not forget that we agreed to leave you and your co-conspirators in charge of this planet when we finish helping you possess it. Otherwise, you would end up just like most of the other human cattle on this pathetic world and do not forget that we would not then choose to save your daughter from extinction as well."

The slightly shorter bipedal reptilian sent his long forked tongue out to Ted's face and slowly licked the side of his cheek. Ted nervously quivered with revulsion, but forced a condescending grin.

"Now, now, gentlemen, don't be hasty," he gingerly replied, mocking up some courage, so as not to trigger a more vicious animalistic response from his alien collaborators that could end his life on the spot. "Look, we're allies, correct?"

Both reptilians snickered, sneered a repulsive response, and gazed at each other to share in a private, artificially-created electronic telepathic communication Ted could not hear.

The slightly taller leader sent a silent communication through a thought amplification transfer device on his belt to his associate, *Are you thinking what I am thinking, Gorsapis?*

Gorsapis returned a widening toothy grin and his forked tongue jotting in and out of his gaping mouth between his sharp fanged teeth several quick times before he returned the thought, *Zushsmat, I sure am. If we were not under orders right now, I would rip off his arms and crunch them down my throat, while he watched and slowly died.*

Exactly, mentally replied Gorsapis, grinning and drooling back at him. *But, I would rip out his beady human eyes and pop them into my mouth, and then I would rip off one of his legs and chomp it down before he would have time to fall over screaming. I just hate having to pretend we regard any of them with respect or honor because of that stupid agreement our predecessors made with their former weakling leaders. What a miserable little planet of food stock. I wish we were back home.*

Ted looked on, helpless to do anything other than bide his time to find a way out of the predicament.

Then Gorsapis smiled at Ted and said aloud, appearing to be apologetic, "Oh don't mind us. We're only having a bit of fun at your expense, but it was childish and we apologize."

Frowning, Ted sighed relief and stated, "Well, it wasn't one damned bit funny. We are supposed to be helping each other and I do not like being threatened. Anyway, why is this Mark such a threat to your people? He has no political power here, and most people just think of him and many others like him to be nothing but fascinating crackpots. Besides, he will soon marry my daughter. Can't you just let him be?"

Both reptilian aliens grimaced at Ted's request and they started to become angry, but managed to control themselves.

"He's already been more trouble than he's worth," replied Zushsmat to Gorsapis, mocking-up a consoling grin. "What do you think? Should we back off the hunt?"

Gorsapis thoughtfully replied, "Well, we don't exactly have orders to kill this human, but we will have to ascertain what he knows, and if he's working with our enemies. Mr. Carter, you must let us know if Mark Santfield returns to see you or your daughter. Our entire plan could be in jeopardy if that nosey Galactic Alliance finds a way to intervene with the hidden leaders of your world to end their association with us. Meanwhile, we will use all our resources to discover how he managed to escape our trap. Now we must leave."

Gorsapis touched the sword handle symbol on his belt buckle and they faded away in an upward whirling golden-white teleportation beam that sped-up around their bodies and vanished. Ted looked on, fuming about what he just went through at the hands of his reptilian alien associates. Then he spun around and angrily marched back up the right staircase, headed for his study to make one more very important phone call.

He stopped in front of his desk, quickly grabbed the phone, and punched in a quick series of numbers.

Then he paused until a familiar voice answered and he commanded, "Henry, get your ass over here right now. We have some very serious things to discuss and we don't have much time." The voice on the other end asked something and Ted barked back, "Never mind all that now. Just get here and I'll fill you in."

He slammed down the phone, and then started to pace back and forth in front of his desk nervously rubbing his hands together.

CHAPTER NINE

THE SECRET
MOUNTAIN BASE

Janice and Mr. Crystal rematerialized inside a vast mountain cavern chamber. She grabbed her arms and felt them to make certain she was still in one piece. Then she looked up, both amazed and terrified at the sudden change in surroundings, desperately trying to emotionally adjust to her now greatly altered understanding of reality. Her eyes first focused five hundred feet away toward the back of the huge cavern upon a three-hundred-foot-long cigar or cylindrical shaped silvery metallic spaceship. A faintly detectable wavering blue anti-gravitational energy field was enshrouding the mighty ship while it hovered in a stationary position a dozen feet above the smooth flat green granite cavern floor. Clear convex oval glass-like windows perhaps six feet apart, spread horizontally along the upper half of the hull, appeared to surround the massive vessel.

Mr. Crystal was standing a few feet to her right calmly observing her facial reactions at coming face-to-face with a totally unexpected alien environment, and she slowly turned to face him with wide-eyed bewilderment.

"Stay calm, Janice. You're completely safe now and no longer in any danger," kindly stated Mr. Crystal, and he gave her a warm friendly grin.

Still too stunned speechless to voice a question, she continued to let her eyes naturally rove around the giant, carved out cavern, taking in more detail. She could see the long spaceship moored to a ten-foot-wide walkway ramp with waist-high polished silver handrails. The ramp extended twenty feet to an oval opening in the ship's side from a massive elongated octagon-shaped building made of hundreds of transparent octagon wall panels or windows that were overall twice the width, height and length of the ship. Hundreds of human and humanoid men and women, with varying skin textures and sizes, were moving in many directions on twelve floor levels within the building. Several more were casually walking along the ramp's transparent, rectangular glass-like floor, headed in the direction of the opening leading into the interior of the ship.

She looked up at the center of the domed cavern chamber three hundred feet overhead to behold a four-hundred-foot-wide circular closed door divided equally in half. She mused it must be able to be opened for the ships to come and go on their missions. Set in widening concentric circles around the circular door, and covering the rest of the top of the entire curved dome ceiling, were foot-wide oval-shaped lights radiating an evenly dispersed warm, natural looking sunlight throughout the cavern.

It appeared that she and Mr. Crystal were standing in the center of the gigantic thousand-foot in diameter chamber. Some incomprehensible alien technology had carved out the mountain's interior and smoothly polished it. The walls also appeared to be laced with what she thought must be quartz and gold ore veins. Clusters of emerald colored crystals, glittering from reflected light, were also located in sporadic pockets throughout the cavern. Beyond each end of the long cigar-shaped ship, landed in two groups near the far wall of the cavern, were two dozen much smaller disc shaped silvery metallic spaceships. From her perspective, they appeared to be perhaps thirty feet in diameter and lined up in parallel rows on individually marked circular landing pads. Three semi-spherical pods set in triangular formation were pointing downward from the bottom of their hulls.

Something suddenly drew her attention toward a six-foot-long teardrop-shaped, open-topped ground transport vehicle with no wheels. It was silently speeding in their direction several feet above the cavern floor, after it had just exited a tall oval opening far back in the cavern wall beyond the massive cylindrical ship. Two human beings, a male and a female, were sitting inside it near the front of its wide, rounded teardrop-shaped front end. As the car came to a stop just six feet from where she and Mr. Crystal were standing, Janice could see the two humans who appeared to be in their late-thirties were vibrantly healthy and trim, dressed in familiar casual human attire similar to what Mr. Crystal was wearing. The hover car slowly lowered to the ground and a side door automatically opened. Both occupants stood up, smiling in their direction, and stepped out of it onto the cavern floor. They walked the few remaining feet up to Janice and Mr. Crystal and respectfully nodded their heads with their right hands held across their chests over the heart area as a warm friendly salutation.

For some reason, all trepidation and fear vanished from Janice, and she found herself returning a genuinely warm, friendly smile. Then she gazed puzzled at Mr. Crystal.

"Mr. Crystal," she hesitantly asked, "Wha--... Where... where are we?"

"Please let them explain," he gently interjected, and he turned to introduce the man and woman patiently standing before them.

"This is Commander Tam-lure. He is the planetary Commander of all twelve of our secret bases on Earth, and Una-mala is his wife and Second in Command or First Officer."

They grinned at Janice and nodded.

Tam-lure cordially began, "This station is one of a dozen bases we have located in secret locations on your planet. We built this one over one hundred years ago deep inside the upper portion of Mt. Shasta in Northern California, underneath the extinct volcanic cap of the mountain. This particular type of research facility is here to observe and discretely encourage the ongoing safe advancement of your people while you head toward space travel capability. The facility also functions as a policing or monitoring station to make certain the treaty the Galactic Inter-dimensional Alliance of Free Worlds signed with another totalitarian alliance of worlds is not broken. However, when it was signed back in the Earth year of 1908, our diplomats knew the totalitarian alliance would likely sign it with the ulterior motive to covertly gain dominance over your world, like they have on other worlds in our Galactic history."

Tam-lure sighed and continued, "By treaty agreement, many races from other worlds were allowed to secretly come here for benevolent, non-interfering scientific purposes only, and they were strictly forbidden to make contact with any of your people for some time to come. However, the situation on and off your world has changed much. Off-world totalitarian alliance spies have been caught many times conducting systematic covert operations on your world over the last sixty years. Their treaty breaking illegal contact and subsequent control of your world leaders and your people has altered many things."

"You mean those two strange men back at my father's mansion have my father under their control?" apprehensively asked Janice.

Una-mala chimed in, "Janice, this may be hard for you to understand at first, but your father and the group of men he works with are being manipulated to self-righteously, systematically take over control of all governments on your world. Mark has also been suffering all his life under a type of subconscious hypnotic programming, and he has been struggling in his own way to get free from it by writing about his insights. This despicable deed occurred after his capture on his approach to Earth, when the body he now occupies was five years of age. Janice, dear, things are not as they seem. They also trapped you six months after your arrival on Earth thirty-one years ago."

Janice blanched and her face turned pink with embarrassment.

"But how can that be?" she asked, frightened and shaking.

Compassionately smiling, Una-mala replied, "Janice, tell me how you're feeling right now."

Janice was uncomfortably squirming and fidgeting with her fingers as she glanced around the cavern in hope of finding an escape from the tormenting question.

"I... I'm frightened. Oh God no, I am terrified and a cold chill is running down my spine," she stated with chattering teeth, shaking from head to toe. "What's happening to me?"

"Be at peace, Janice," kindly replied Una-mala. "We're going to free you from the subconscious burden of guilt and fear you've felt all your life whenever you tried to remember what seemed to be just out of reach."

Forlorn and frowning, Janice blanched as a new realization surfaced in her awareness and she hesitantly asked, "You mean my father isn't really my father?"

Tam-lure approached her, gently placed a consoling hand upon her shoulder and answered, "He's your Earth father. He and your departed mother bore your body, loved and raised you. However, they were unaware you were not originally from Earth. You were on a scientific mission to this world when Trilotew agents captured you. Somehow, they discovered your hidden location, and then tracked you when you went out into the world disguised. Then they reprogrammed your subconscious mind to make it possible to eventually get to your father, and his wealthy powerful associates, without your being aware of it. When they had finished with you, they compelled your consciousness or what Earth people call soul to enter the child's body at about two years of age. Then, through your subconscious, they invaded your father's dream state at night without either of you being aware of it. Eventually, they gained a type of hypnotic control over him. However, he is now beginning to see through their masquerade. He is starting to believe they are going to betray all that he and his associates have worked to accomplish. This was discovered when we intercepted a phone call he recently made to Henry, his general council. He's now trying to find a way to extricate himself from their clutches through Henry; but he's up against his own associates who are already dominated by the Trilotew."

"Excuse me, but who are these Trilotew, and do you mean to tell me this is not my real body?" asked Janice, painfully emotionally confused.

Una-mala compassionately replied, "After they captured you, they would have forced your Atma, or soul, from your body to place it in a suspended heavy gravity field by misusing another stolen waveform technology they acquired long ago from their ruling overseers. They would then have compelled you to enter the girl's body your parents bore when it was two years of age, after forcing its former occupant to leave it and seek another one."

Tam-lure seriously continued, "These tyrants call themselves the Righteous Illumined Lords of The Empire Worlds, or Trilotew for short, and they are a very deranged group. Their ancestors were involved in a war over five hundred thousand years ago with even more despicable beings from a parallel dimension that were genetically similar; except they were white and had wings. This white-winged bi-pedal reptilian race called Trilon-Kal, had previously acquired a mind-deprogramming technology designed for healing from a conquered world. Then they perverted it to win that earlier war with their green non-winged and non-carnivorous cousins by first gaining control of their leaders.

"The new Trilotew's white-winged overseers considered themselves superior over all other races, and they subconsciously programmed their captives with deeply aberrant compulsive behavior patterns they could control. The new tyrant Masters could then remain secretly hidden in the background, while they used their captured relatives as remorseless weapons to embark on many terror campaigns, aimed at taking over benevolent world systems. They indiscriminately killed many humanoids, and other races, without a thought of remorse. Sometimes they even ate their human captives alive, or destroyed entire planets if they could not get their way. They acquired most of their current advanced technology through raids back then, and they have become technologically powerful. Yet, they are not as truly telepathic as they pretend. They now use technology to peer into other beings' minds and reprogram their subconscious to bend them to their will."

Una-mala seriously continued, "The Trilotew overseers were finally defeated in a conflict with the Galactic Alliance with the secret help we obtained from friends that inhabit our nearest galactic neighbor you call the Andromeda galaxy. With their assistance, the winged reptilian overseers were defeated, forced back into their own parallel dimension and permanently sealed inside. That war was very devastating to countless worlds, and the remaining reptilian race signed a treaty to avoid further conflict. That gave us time to rebuild the Galactic Alliance. Eventually, we will have to deprogram the entire Trilotew military and their tyrant leaders on their home world systems, in order to end their terror campaigns for all time.

"In fact, we have already made inroads to do just that by utilizing a technology that is unknown and unusable by the Trilotew. What is underway will change the course of Earth from its certain destructive future direction. However, first we must secure the planet from the attempted Trilotew takeover because that outcome would likely lead to the planet's unexpected destruction, like it has on other worlds they infiltrated."

Tam-lure added, "For reasons you will become aware of soon, the destruction of your world would not only cause the loss of all human and other life on Earth, but also great harm would come to hundreds of billions of sentient beings living in parallel dimensions upon many worlds you know nothing about. That would further cause a great imbalance to occur in this galaxy, and the Galactic Alliance will not allow that to occur under any circumstance. Therefore, although we're normally reluctant to intervene in other worlds or their choices, in this case it's well justified, because Earth leaders and the general populous no longer have the free will they think they have."

Janice was worried and still shaking as Una-mala kindly added, "I know this is a lot to take in right now, but once your full memory is restored all that is being imparted to you will make perfect sense. Janice, you must understand the Trilotew agents are still after your fiance. However, since his safe rescue, you become the next best thing to try to capture to use as bait. They will kill or recapture him, if they can, to put him back under their control. For now, if you want to help him and yourself, please go with Boun-tama, or Mr. Crystal, as he is known to you, and he will get you safely to Mark."

Mr. Crystal kindly grinned at her, and then cordially offered his arm. Her shaking suddenly subsided, and her tense shoulders dropped. She cracked a little smile, and then placed her arm through his.

Commander Tam-lure and Second Commander Una-mala smiled, nodded goodbye, and then Tam-lure benevolently added, "We will be waiting here for you and Mark when you return. Then if you wish, you can assist us to carry out a great uplifting change for this planet and its people that has never happened before. In fact, what is about to come to Earth has never happened before in the history of this galaxy. A Scout ship has been prepared for your departure, and do not be concerned. From this base, we can get you to Mark without interference from any Trilotew agents or ships. What we call Prime Creator, or the underlying conscious energy presence behind and supporting all life, will go with you on your journey. Be at peace."

Janice and Boun-tama began to casually walk across the cavern floor, headed toward the closest Scout class ship. It was in the far background landed beside many others beyond the left side of the much larger cigar or cylindrical shaped ship. Tam-lure and Una-mala fondly watched them as they approached and then entered the ship.

A few moments later, the Scout ship lit up, surrounded by a thin layer of blue anti-gravity light, emitting a soft low frequency hum. It lifted straight upward toward the top of the cavern, as the two closed, semicircular launch doors centered in the top of the canopy started to part. Revealed beyond them was the clear view of a rich, star-filled night sky over the mysterious Mt. Shasta. The Scout ship sped up through the opening and paused just on the other side. A brighter blue light pulsed from the hull, and the ship darted straight up in a second at tremendous speed to disappear within the myriad glittering stars of outer space.

Like dutiful parents, Tam-lure and Una-mala lovingly smiled at each other as they clasped hands. Then they turned around and walked away, headed toward the wide octagon-shaped administration building behind the massive cylindrical star ship.

CHAPTER TEN

DESTINED REUNION

Aboard the Scout ship, Janice watched with utter fascination the incomprehensible majesty of the wide panorama of stars in outer space displayed upon the projected transparent energy view screen. Boun-tama (alias Mr. Crystal) was sitting in the white tall-backed chair behind the curved semi-octagon shaped control console with the palms of both hands depressed into the lit up gold quartz guidance controls. The ship was speeding through space the normal way on approach to the gas giant planet Saturn looming ever larger, surrounded by its wide ring system.

Boun-tama looked up at her and commented, "We did not take the more swift direct way of arriving here through an inter-dimensional portal this time because I wanted you to behold the beauty of outer space during our short journey to Saturn."

Spellbound in childlike awe, Janice was unable to take her eyes off the wide rectangular projected view screen, so she just nodded her response. Then, she slowly forced herself to look away to see Boun-tama kindly gazing up at her.

"How did we get here so fast?" she asked amazed. "We've only been traveling for maybe an hour and isn't that the planet Saturn we're

79

approaching?"

Pleased with her astute observations, and that she was keeping her wits about her, Boun-tama grinned wide and replied, "You're correct. That is the planet Saturn, and your estimation of our elapsed travel time is just about right. However, this ship is also capable of travel far beyond the speed of light. An energy warp field created around the hull forms an energy conduit in front of the hull, which literally draws the ship forward through a higher parallel dimension. We can then travel through a parallel universe where the molecular particle flow or time-rate is faster than here. In other words, the ship travels through a higher vibratory reality over a relatively short distance, and that translates to having covered a vast distance when we lower the ship's vibration or molecular time-rate back again. The ship actually travels inside a continuously created, whirling electromagnetic vortex void formed in front of and around the hull. To borrow an old Earth culture analogy, one might say this is like pulling yourself up with your own suspenders, except the suspenders in this case create a type of anti-magnetic vacuum in front of the hull, and the ship is literally continuously drawn forward into it. The intensity of the field created determines the speed of the craft relative to the gravitational focus of our intended destination."

Janice just stared back at him blank-faced and shook her head to clear her boggled mind from attempting to comprehend what he was imparting to her.

She finally sighed and exclaimed, "Wow! I mean...WOW! Well, actually I don't pretend to actually understand what you just told me, so I'll accept you know what you're talking about."

Then she gazed back at the view screen to observe the ship on approach to the mile-long cylindrical flagship stealthily positioned inside Saturn's ring system and asked, "Oh, good heavens, Mark's aboard that thing? It's gigantic."

"That is one of three interstellar, mile-long Emerald Star class flagships stationed in this sector of the galaxy. However, several hundred identical and much larger ships are scheduled to arrive around and on Earth in the near future that make up just a small part of a very vast fleet. After creating the proper conditions, this unprecedented event will take place to bring about a non-destructive, benevolent worldwide disclosure of our existence to the entire Earth population. You will understand how this will be possible after we free you from the terrorizing subconscious programming that was forced upon you."

"I can't wait to see Mark's expression when he sees me walking toward him," Janice fondly stated, gazing dreamy-eyed into an imaginative near future.

Boun-tama smiled up at her.

"You will both discover much that was suppressed from your conscious awareness, and be greatly changed for the better. Know that I wish you only the greatest good will."

He looked back up at the projected view screen, just as Janice stepped up behind him to observe the landing.

She watched their Scout ship slow several dozen feet away from the central section of the mile-long flagship as the massive hull appeared to become transparent, and their Scout ship harmlessly passed right through the transparent metallic side of the parent vessel. In awe, she continued to gaze at the view screen as it switched to reveal the flagship hull turn solid again.

Their Scout ship drastically slowed inside the vast hanger bay and moments later, it gently touched down on a vacant circular landing pad next to eleven other Scout class craft that were already landed in two parallel rows.

Like a child in wonderland, Janice stepped through the Scout ship hatch opening and stopped at the top of the lowered ramp to gaze around the vast hanger-landing bay inside the gigantic flagship. Boun-tama stepped up behind her and stood to her left side to calmly observe her reaction.

"I am a... Well, I don't know what I am anymore," she breathlessly exclaimed, somewhat intimidated by the obviously very advanced technologically surroundings. "Mr. Crystal... oh, pardon me, I mean Boun-tama, when will I see Mark?"

Boun-tama wisely paused to consider how much he should disclose before she fully recovered her true-identity, and then he smiled and replied upbeat, "He's currently undergoing a final therapy session to rid himself of all lingering subconscious Trilotew programming. If you wish, you can see him after that, but wouldn't it be better if you first go on your own experiential journey to recover the suppressed memory of who you are, and where you came from?"

Janice was not smiling at the prospect and she inquired, "What, exactly, will happen to me when I go through it?"

Boun-tama gave her a cheery grin and answered, "In the first five minutes or so, you'll remember a great deal about what was suppressed below your level of awareness and this will startle you at first. I assure you, the experience will also be very uplifting and relieving. There is no need to be afraid. You will not be harmed in any way."

He touched the strange hieroglyphic-like gold pin on his lapel and it softly flashed gold light once. Janice shook her head, took a deep breath, and smiled with the discovery that any apprehensive fear she was experiencing had somehow vanished.

"What does that pin you touch do to me?" she curiously asked.

Boun-tama grinned and replied, "Among other things, it can be used to trigger our teleportation to safety. You just recently experienced that. It can also temporarily emit an energy that can keep your negative subconscious programming from controlling your nervous system. This allows you to be more yourself regarding important decisions you may make for your own benefit. Otherwise, the Trilotew programming in you would likely keep you from accepting the opportunity to be set free of it."

"Well, Boun-tama," she confidently began but hesitated to cordially say, "Oh, I hope you don't mind me calling you that."

He smiled with a shake of his head and she continued, "Please lead the way. I want to be free from this nervous system trauma nonsense forever."

He confidently gestured toward the ramp and they headed down it, walked over to the moving by-directional floor conveyor, and then stepped together upon it, moving toward the same triangular entry hallway that Mark had previously entered.

A short time later, they both walked out of another triangular hallway exit and stepped onto the transparent glass-like floor of the wide spherical chamber with the quartz crystal-lined walls. Janice stopped to stare at a human woman that appeared to be in her late-thirties, who was kindly gazing back at her. She was standing next to the crystalline control console in front of the transparent sided pentagon chamber.

Grinning from ear to ear like an excited little girl, Janice exclaimed, "Oh, good heavens!" Then she began to recall the space observation lounge room she just passed through with Boun-tama and continued, "Boun-tama, perhaps I was just too speechless to say it before, but I never dreamed I'd actually see outer space and Saturn's rings through the windows of this mother ship from right inside it. That was just fantastic."

Then she gazed with a renewed sense of awe at the quartz crystal lined spherical walls. As she glanced down through the transparent floor, a sudden fit of shaking from head to foot took hold, accompanied by waves of nauseous fear. Cold tingling nervous spasms were running up and down her spine and she started to collapse, but Boun-tama caught her arms and held her up. He could see she was going into unconsciousness as her eyes started to roll up behind her eyelids beyond the sockets and he gently laid her down on the floor. He stood back up and touched a spot on the back of the special gold pin on his lapel. A wave of visible golden energy similar to a radio wave shot from it in one quick pulse across her body, which was starting to convulse in an epileptic-type seizure. The golden energy quickly faded as it vanished into her skin. Her body went completely limp, and her breathing instantly returned to comfortable, normal inhalations. Then she opened her eyes to behold both Boun-tama and the woman that had been standing by the console kindly gazing down at her.

Realizing she was lying on a cold surface, she asked mystified, "What am I doing on the floor?"

As they helped her stand up, Boun-tama calmly replied, "You were experiencing another subconscious program triggered to take control of your nervous system in an attempt to keep you from this chamber. It is just an old trick of your former captors. However, this technique will only last for an hour before you may be vulnerable to experience another episode, but do not worry. Sun-deema and I will soon have you free of it. Do you feel strong enough to be rid of that madness?"

"Yes, I believe so," she softly replied.

Boun-tama cheerfully continued, "This is Sun-deema, wife of

Commander Jon-tral. She will be overseeing your session today.

She weakly nodded and stated, "Oh my God, Boun-tama, I never felt so terrible before in all my life. As soon as we entered the room I started having uncontrollable visions of having my clothes torn off, and oh God, I know those two reptilian beings were torturing me to death. The pain was unbearable."

Janice angrily grimaced with new found determination as she firmly grabbed Boun-tama's upper arm and commanded, "You've got to get me into that chamber now. I don't want to experience that insanity again ever."

He calmly removed the firm grip of her fingers unconsciously digging into his skin, tucked her arm through his own, and then waved his other arm toward the clear-sided pentagon chamber in the center of the room. A few minutes later, she was sitting down in the chair and it began to conform to her body shape and size. As he placed the crystal headband around her forehead, a comfortable relaxed feeling came over her body and she confidently grinned.

"Well, Janice, are you ready for Sun-deema to begin the session?" he asked, cheerfully upbeat.

She nodded her consent and Sun-deema extended the palm of her right hand over several faceted crystal controls, lighting them up. The quartz crystals lining the spherical walls in the outer chamber began softly glowing with golden light and the transparent pentagon panels surrounding her instantly lit up, revealing a beautiful human female sitting happily snuggled together with a handsome human male upon violet four-inch-tall grass. Three children, two girls and a boy ages eleven, nine, and seven respectively were playfully giggling while they stood in the near background in a triangular pattern ten feet apart. They were tossing a transparent blue ball to each other. One child threw it underhanded into the air and it darted upward under its own power another fifty feet, then stopped while spinning suspended in place radiating a bright blue light. Then it darted down to the intended child, emitting a blur of rainbow colors behind it, and a pleasant tubular bell tone. It stopped again inches from the child who grabbed it and tossed it back upward. When a child tossed the ball again, it would stop to emit a different steady color before it darted to the next child emitting another stream of rainbow colors and a different tone.

The children's parents, who both appeared to be in their mid-thirties, were remarkably trim and fit. They were all casually dressed in beautiful spring blue and green silken, formfitting attire similar to many of the personnel Janice had already seen coming and going aboard the mile long flagship.

Surrounding the family was a hundred-foot-wide grass covered glade, encircled by gigantic forest trees covered with emerald-green, spoon-shaped leaves. The outer edge of each leaf was emitting a type of self-luminous phosphorescent silvery light visible even in the radiance of the twin setting suns. One radiant orb was higher in the sky and several degrees apart from the second orb, and both were gradually descending to set behind the distant snow-clad mountain range that visibly stretched across the horizon under a light emerald-green sky.

Janice delightfully gasped as she suddenly recalled she was in fact the alien human woman on the grass, and she started to say something when the images surrounding her suddenly changed.

She could now see the same woman standing upright, spread eagle, clasped with coal-colored chains around her ankles and wrists to a crude cavern wall. Lit fiery red torches stuck into spiked metal holders attached along the hard rock wall were casting an eerie shadowy glow that danced across her naked body. Two tall reptilian captors slowly approached her from opposite directions with their sharp-clawed fingers sadistically grasping toward her. She screamed in terror as their long forked tongues licked her torso and face, emitting an appalling stench.

Janice was now also shaking with fear and her forehead was dripping with sweat as her terrified eyes watched the impending doom of the helpless woman that she was experiencing as herself.

Both Janice and the women chained to the cavern wall depicted on the surrounding octagonal view screens suddenly wretched together in disgust. Then they violently jerked their hands and feet to somehow get free, while the taller reptilian began to nastily whisper in the woman's left ear.

"Go on and scream, dainty morsel. No one will ever hear you in here. Remember well, useless human female, what will happen to you if you should try and recall what your fate in our hands is going to be here today."

Her reptilian captors suddenly lurched forward with long arms ending with sharp five-fingered grasping claws. The taller one ripped open her abdomen from her crotch to her throat with one long, knife-like forefinger, while the other one stuffed her right hand all the way down his throat up to her elbow before he viciously ripped off her arm with two rows of sharp fangs. Janice and the chained women screamed together in utter agony and they both dropped their heads forward into unconsciousness as the images of torture on the surrounding view screen panels vanished.

"It's alright now, Janice," announced Sun-deema's kindly voice through the intercom system. "You're safe aboard the flagship. The worst part of their subconscious implanted nightmare is now over."

Janice suddenly discovered she felt safe and relieved as a warm glowing energy began to radiate throughout her body. She slowly opened her eyes to observe she was still sitting in the comfortable chair. Then she apprehensively, slowly lifted her head up to see Boun-tama and Sun-deema compassionately gazing back at her through the transparent pentagon panels. He had joined her and they were patiently standing behind the control console in the outer spherical chamber. She sighed relief.

"Oh God in heaven, Boun-tama, I remember. That was me more than thirty years ago." Tears of sadness welled up in her eyes and she hesitantly asked, "Oh dear prime creator, I remember everything. Did they... actually do that to my body?"

Boun-tama sighed and answered, "We don't know if that was the eventual fate of your body. However, we do know the images and feelings of that nightmare implanted in your subconscious were put there to control you. As you can understand now, any attempt by you to remember this terror would cause your nervous system to replay the event across your conscious awareness as if you were actually going through it, but with no visual memory of what was causing it. In this way, it would be sheer torture for you to try to recall who or what you were, or what you were doing before the time of the implant. Are you clear about this now?"

"Yes, I am," she sadly replied. "I was a scientist and happily married with children back on my home world. I am unable to exactly recall when they captured me, but I do remember it was near the end of my six-month scientific study mission at one of our hidden Galactic Alliance bases in South America, high up in the mountains of Peru. Oh, dear Prime Creator, what has become of my husband and children? Boun-tama, will I ever see them again?"

"Fortunately, they are quite safe back on your home world," he compassionately replied. "However, to them it has only been a year and a half since your disappearance. This time differential occurs because you arrived in less than a day aboard a ship that swiftly traversed vast distances of interstellar space by traveling through a parallel time vortex or inter-dimensional portal. In this way, you could carry out your six month scientific mission on Earth and return after only having left your family on your home world two weeks earlier. Your ongoing family life would then continue with little interruption.

"Your husband, Donum-tuma, daughters Yoral-telan and Vera-tima, and your son Danim-tama now know you are alive. However, they also know your former body from home was likely destroyed or devoured after the Trilotew agents forced you, the being, from it to imprison you in a strong electromagnetic field. After they implanted their control images into your subconscious, they forced you, or what the Earth people call soul, into the young two-year-old female body on Earth. That was how you came to replace the daughter of your Earth parents without you or them ever suspecting a thing. They likely accomplished this by capturing your Earth parent's female child hours earlier to force the being out of it, before compelling it to seek another body. Then they forced you to enter the body with her implanted identity, unconscious of all you were, before they returned you to her unaware parents."

"I'm beginning to remember everything," stated Janice, dismally forlorn. "My real name is Moon-teran. With my original advanced human body destroyed, how will I ever be reunited with my family now?"

Boun-tama grinned and stated, "We have a way. Your original body's four-stranded human DNA is stored back on your home world, the same as is your current fiancé's, who is actually your cousin back home. All Galactic Alliance citizens are protected in this way before they are given the privilege to go out into the universe on a mission."

Her face blanched with shocking realization that she was about to marry her own cousin, and Boun-tama could see her sadness becoming unbearable as she began to uncontrollably sob.

"Quickly, Moon-teran, look back up at the view screens," he urgently commanded, and she slowly looked up with tears running down her cheeks to see new images surround her on every panel.

As Moon-teran, she was back in her specially built six-thousand-square-foot, dome-shaped home swimming with her husband, two daughters, and son in a wide oval pool centered under an overhead transparent oval canopy the width of the pool. The fiber-optic light source, hidden under three overlapping concentric white coverings surrounding the transparent curved dome, was illuminating the pool with natural appearing light like the twin outside suns high in the emerald-green sky.

She suddenly recalled they lived in a beautifully lush country setting not far from a central governing building complex on her home world of Norexilam. She recalled that it circles one of the many suns in the Starborn Cluster beyond what Earth people call the Pleiades star group. Her being lit up with a joy she never knew in her Earth life as Janice, and all fear vanished.

Breathing a sigh of relief, Boun-tama let go his concern for her safety, grinned and confidently stated, "Moon-teran, you will be reunited with them soon. In their time, only a year and a half will have passed when we return you to them. However, thirty-one and half years has gone by while you were growing up on Earth. Please, let me elaborate. The Galactic Council asked me to inquire if you would be willing to play the part of Mark's fiancée to complete a much greater mission the Alliance has initiated for the recovery of Earth's people. They are being entrenched under Trilotew control. Know that Mark, or rather Ambassador Shon-ral remembers his true self again, and he has already agreed to our request. He would like you to join him to help carry out the greater implementation of *The Seres Agenda*."

Expressionless, Boun-tama and Sun-deema patiently waited for the hoped for response, as she closed her eyes to think it over.

Moments later, she opened her eyes and insisted, "I must be free of all Trilotew implants and fully recover from their terrible effects before I could do such a thing, and what about some form of protection for us both if we return to Earth? I mean, don't they know Mark was rescued from their evil clutches?"

Boun-tama thoughtfully looked at Sun-deema and she confidently stated, "Both of you will be provided with a very unique form of protection that cannot be penetrated by any Trilotew agent or weapon. Once they discover it, we must proceed very carefully because revenge upon others will likely dominate their ongoing covert efforts after that."

She angrily grimaced as she thought, *I would dearly love to see those lizards roasted alive for what they have done to many others and to me over such a long period in our Galactic history.*

Boun-tama's eyes widened with concern after he clearly overheard Moon-teran's telepathic anger for the first time and he sent back the thought, *Oh... that is good. Since you are already recovering your telepathic ability, you may also recall that no Galactic Alliance citizen would ever consider acting out of revenge like the subconsciously perverted Trilotew.*

Delightedly surprised, Moon-teran's mouth dropped open and she gasped out loud, "Oh my heavens, you heard me. I wondered if you would get the thought. Yet somehow I just knew I could do it and of course, you are right. Now I remember the Trilotew are following out their evil designs, compelled by a similar despicable subconscious programming they received a very long time ago. They weren't always like they are now." She thoughtfully paused, and then continued with courageous gusto, "I will definitely help anyway I can. We must prevent the populace of Earth from coming under their direct tyrannical control. Earth would become a hellish playground for their madness, and we must not let that happen under any circumstances. We should get this deprogramming done. I want to see Mark, I mean, my cousin Shon-ral, as soon as possible."

Pleased with her new found courage, Boun-tama grinned wide at her and Sun-deema cheerfully said, "Okay, then let's get this done. It shouldn't take more than another hour to get you fully recovered," and she touched two faceted crystals on the console.

Meanwhile, Mark (Shon-ral) was in one of the two command and control centers that were located inside each end of the mile-long flagship. He was now dressed in comfortable silken attire similar to what the ship's personnel wore, sitting next to Monti in one of four comfortable white leather-like chairs positioned around an oval blue glass topped, silver metal conference table. Sitting in one of the two chairs on the other side of the table opposite him and Monti was Commander Jon-tral.

Beyond the oval table nearer to the end of the ship was the front of a fifty-foot wide half-octagon-shaped, ivory textured crystalline control console. Sitting at chairs along its length or standing up were a half dozen other ship's personnel monitoring hundreds of differently sized and shaped luminous pastel-colored crystalline controls. The instrument console's elongated half-octagon shape, constructed along the gradual curve of the rounded end of the ship's hull, was right below a set of twelve horizontally-aligned oval windows or view portals.

A panorama of stars could be seen higher up through the windows, and the rings of Saturn below them appeared to extend into a vast distance as they gradually curved around the massive equator of the gas giant planet.

A dozen wide projected energy view screens, linked together along their vertical rectangular sides above the length of the console, were displaying unknown star systems, beautiful multi-colored nebulae, and two land and water-covered worlds with vast blue-green oceans similar to Earth. On the far left panel, a close up of both worlds revealed pastel green and light pink-colored clouds moving high above their surfaces, while both spheres were slowly turning on their axes. Another view screen on the right was displaying the chart of a dozen naturally occurring, whirling energy doorways or vortexes, mapped out across the solar system containing the labeled planet Earth. One of the whirling, indicated vortexes was located in space near the labeled planet Saturn. A dozen similar but smaller vortexes were displayed as existing at various other locations on the Earth planet's surface, in its atmosphere at varying heights, at two locations at the bottom of the Atlantic and Pacific oceans, and a dozen more just above the planet's outer atmosphere in space.

Red luminous dots indicated the locations around the Earth, and projected luminous English words beside each dot matching the revealed locations. One was marked above the infamous Bermuda Triangle area southeast of Florida. Another one was just outside the planet's atmosphere, positioned directly above Mt. Shasta in Northern California. Another was over the big island of Hawaii in the upper atmosphere directly above the active volcano. Another was depicted somewhere in the mountains of Peru in South America. One was marked in the lower atmosphere above the Mesa airport in Sedona, Arizona. Indicated was another near ground level in the middle of Russia's Siberian wilderness. One was marked at Land's End in Cornwall, England. One was in the atmosphere a mile above the great pyramids of Egypt. Another was in the deepest region of the Himalayan Mountains between Tibet, India, and Pakistan. There was one marked centered on the bottom of the Pacific Ocean, and another centered on the bottom of the Atlantic Ocean. The one Mark Santfield went through aboard Monti's ship above the Earth was marked a hundred miles in space directly above the Sierra Mountain range in central California.

The other vortexes were also indicated, but they were labeled in an extraterrestrial language depicting the following locations: in Spain's mountains; in Russia's Ural Mountains; in the atmosphere over the Gobi Desert; at a mountain location on the southern New Zealand island; and one at ground level in the vast desert in the very center of Australia.

Mark hopefully asked Commander Jon-tral, "When can I see my fiancée, Janice... I mean, my cousin Moon-teran? Oh, forgive me. I guess you can see old habits tend to die hard," and he laughed to shake off the absurdity of all that had happened to him.

"Boun-tama, or who you know as Mr. Crystal, just reported to us that Moon-teran has successfully gone through her first deprogramming session. Like you, we should continue to refer to her as Janice to keep things in line with your original, but now quite expanded, Ambassadorial mission to Earth. She has come out of her most terrorizing repressive implant control session. Now she remembers her own husband and three children back home, and she will soon be ready to join us here."

Mark returned a reticent grin and replied, "Well, that should prove most interesting. Even if she knows what I now know to be true about our past, we were still intimate together and we were going to be married. I've heard of kissing cousins, but this whole thing has already gone way beyond the absurd. It will likely take some time for us to get used to pretending to be engaged, not to mention having to subsequently further pretend to go through with a formal marriage to do our part to implement *The Seres Agenda* on planet Earth."

Jon-tral smiled at him with kind, patient, understanding eyes and encouraged, "You'll both be surprised at how naturally you return to your true selves. The love and respect you have for each other will remain, but each of you will no longer feel an intimate attraction to each other. You should begin to realize that emotion was also artificially programmed into each of you by your Trilotew captors in order to keep you both unconsciously trapped together; too close to each other and unconsciously guilt ridden to ever discover what had been done to you." Jon-tral leaned forward and seriously continued, "Because of what happened to you, we now know a hidden spy is operating somewhere within the Galactic Alliance itself, and we believe we know who it is. This spy would have informed Trilotew agents about your cousin's arrival with a scientific expedition to Earth, as well as the location of her hidden base and your secret, planned arrival six months later. By discretely watching the base from a distance, they would have eventually tracked her leaving its protection on a disguised journey amongst Earth's people. After capturing her, they must have probed her mind to confirm when your scheduled diplomatic mission to Earth's hidden leaders was to take place. They then carefully planned to capture you alive, right before you arrived.

"They could have simply destroyed your ship but that would likely cause an all out war with the Galactic Alliance, which would devastate them all the way back to their home worlds. Instead, they suppressed your former existence and forced you into another body on Earth to stop you from successfully carrying out your mission. They rightfully fear that your mission could possibly not only topple all their evil plans for Earth and its people, but also their ongoing existence as sinister beings in the Galaxy. We only recently discovered the highly placed spy in the Galactic Alliance government compromised your secret mission after Trilotew Agents captured his wife and children during a return space flight back to him on their home world. The Trilotew covertly blackmailed him into cooperating if he ever wanted to see his loved ones alive again."

Monti shook his head frowning and stated, "It has to be someone in the Galactic Alliance governing council itself because they would have been the only other beings that would have known about Mark's secret mission, and its very delicate timing."

"That's what we discovered," seriously replied Jon-tral.

Monti seriously added, "Mark, you and Janice are going to be in grave danger of assassination or torture when you return to Earth, so we're going to provide you both with a very special, unique form of protection that no Trilotew agent or weapon can penetrate. When Janice, Boun-tama, and Sun-deema arrive here in a few minutes, Jon-tral and Sun-deema plan to reveal to both of you something most extraordinary that has never occurred in the entire history of creation itself; something that will end evil as an experiment in the lower worlds and on Earth forever."

Mark's eyes lit up and he curiously gazed at Monti and Commander Jon-tral, and then stated with a quirky, inquiring grin, "It's about damn time the Galactic Alliance showed a little backbone to those tyrannical Trilotew demons. Whether we like it or not, if we don't stop them now, someday there will be another massive interstellar war with them like the one that took place over 500,000 years ago. I know it's not been our way to interfere, but there must be a method to neutralize their evil subconscious drives without killing them or going to war."

Grinning, Jon-tral enthusiastically replied, "Mark, now we have the way to accomplish exactly that."

"Do you mean we can end their rain of terror in the galaxy for good?" shot back Mark, unsure he really heard such good news.

"You heard me correctly," confidently replied Jon-tral. "Before I elaborate, let's wait for Janice to arrive."

"Mark!" excitedly exclaimed the voice of Janice from the background distance.

Mark swung around to behold his cousin with tears of joy streaming down her face, standing beside Boun-tama and Sun-deema twenty feet away by the triangular hallway entryway to the command module.

"Janice!" he excitedly replied and jumped to his feet.

They ran toward each other and she threw her arms around him. He swung her around in several circles before they came to a stop, but this time they did not kiss.

He held her at arms-length and they fondly gazed into each other's eyes, as Boun-tama walked up behind them followed by Commander Jon-tral and Sun-deema.

"Well, cousin," she began to say deeply relieved, and then started to chuckle.

"Good to see you again too, cousin," replied Mark equally relieved and he started chuckling with her.

Shon-ral, I remember everything, she telepathically sent to him with an affectionate grin.

Dear Moon-teran, he telepathically returned, grinning, ***I too remember everything. Maybe now we can do something together that will change the course of galactic history.***

He gallantly took her hand and kissed it.

Second Commander Sun-deema gave them both a joyful smile and said aloud, "Well, I believe we're all glad to see you two have recovered your natural telepathic abilities. That should make carrying out *The Seres Agenda* a little easier from now on."

Commander Jon-tral added, "Please walk over toward the command console and we will reveal what the entire Galactic Inter-dimensional Alliance of Free Worlds has begun to implement. After that, you will both clearly understand why what we respectfully call *The Seres Agenda* is finally moving foreword."

As they approached the command console, Jon-tral smiled at a very attractive young female technician standing near its center and he politely commanded, "Jin-trean, I would say it's time we put *The Seres Agenda* program on the screen for our visitors."

"The program is ready, Commander," she replied with a happy grin, as she touched a violet pyramidal crystal control, lighting it up.

The large rectangular, transparent projected energy view screen directly above and behind the console flashed on, revealing a massive golden-colored metallic pyramid, illumined by a closely encompassing pastel-blue layer of antigravity light. It appeared to be floating in a fixed position somewhere in a mysterious void of outer space, surrounded by a background abundance of radiant blue-white stars.

Jin-trean touched the crystal again, and the image zoomed to a close up of the entire structure. A flagship identical to their mile-long flagship was stationary in space alongside the base of the giant pyramid's side, directly facing the view screen. In comparison, the towering luminous structure now appeared to be twelve times taller and three times wider than the mile-long cylindrical flagship hovering in a nearby stationary position.

A disc-shaped Scout class ship, surrounded by its own thin layer of luminous blue antigravity light, began to gradually appear as it slowly flew right out of the solid, triangular, golden metallic side of the massive pyramid through an invisibly camouflaged, horizontal oval, golden energy shield doorway. It moved above the flagship and slowly lowered, turning transparent before it entered the landing bay within the central section of the mile-long parent vessel.

Jon-tral pointed to the pyramid displayed on the screen and confidently continued his revelation, "As you can see, one of our sister flagships is stationed by this transformational pyramid transmitter. It channels a very special energy from a dimension well beyond what the Trilotew know about that is not part of the dual nature of the physical universe. No positive or negative force, nor any weapon ever devised, can alter or affect these pyramids in any way whatsoever, and they are now beginning to radiate out into the universe in every direction. I'll put an overview of this pyramid network up on the screen so you'll both have a better understanding of the comprehensive nature of what this new structure is capable of creating."

He leaned forward and touched a crystalline control next to Jin-trean. The pyramid and flagship imaged on the view screen began to rapidly zoom into the background until several different stars appeared in a triangular grid pattern. Positioned in between them could now be seen identical radiant golden pyramid devices, and the image continued to rapidly zoom further into the background until an entire quarter quadrant of the Milky Way galaxy could be seen with countless golden dots now present between vast numbers of stars. The image again zoomed further into the background, until the entire galaxy could be seen filled with millions of the pyramid structures radiating as tiny golden lights positioned equidistant between the stars.

Jon-tral's wife, Sun-deema, continued, "What you're seeing depicted here is now taking place all over the entire physical universe within countless billions of galaxies. These pyramids are not comprised of any material known to exist anywhere within the physical universes and we did not build them. I will explain more about this fact a little later. These special pyramid structures conduct or transmit a type of omnipresent energy that can only uplift life in a constructive manner. This energy is something entirely new in creation. It exists for one purpose, and that is to retire evil as an experiment in the same way dinosaurs outlived their usefulness many, many millions of years ago back in the ancient prehistoric period of planet Earth.

"Every living sentient being, every animal, and all matter everywhere are about to be permanently transformed, starting with the most endangered Earth planet, because this energy is now undoing what was created billions of years ago. In other words, evil as an experiment is being permanently retired from creation. Something wonderful is beginning to take its place to carry the now expanding creation forward into the infinite future.

"When we return you both to Earth, you will notice on your way there something new added in outer space. Out in the asteroid belt between Mars and Jupiter, you will discover one of these massive golden pyramids floating in space. With a special device aboard your ship, you will also be able to see the new pulsing waves emanating from all four sides, as well as from the top and the bottom of the pyramid. They will look very similar to repeating pulsating emanations of expanding concentric or circular golden-white radio waves. More of these pyramids are spontaneously coming into existence all the time and they immediately begin to emanate these continuous pulsing waves outward in all directions to interconnect or interlace with the same waves being sent in every direction from identical pyramids. As they interpenetrate each other, they create an energy grid system, and anyone, or anything passing through this normally invisible field of energy will instantly begin to experience an uplifting expansion in their awareness, even the Trilotew.

"A visual energy sphere then instantly forms outside their conscious being that contains all implants, aberrations, and engrams of any negative nature that have been driving their actions from within their subconscious minds. Once done, the conscious energy coming directly from Prime Creator itself will offer the one experiencing the phenomena the opportunity to permanently have dissolved this subconscious nonsense forever.

You must understand that once any being or soul is freed from this karma or subconscious madness, they return to a naturally benevolent state of being that has always been a part of Prime Creator or God itself, as the people of Earth refer to the Supreme Being or the source behind all life."

Mark (Shon-ral) asked, "You mean, this energy field could really change the course of Earth's destructive destiny?"

Smiling wide, Commander Jon-tral confidently replied, "That's exactly what it will do. Because this expanding universal grid system is about to be turned on around Earth, so-to-speak, the Trilotew will not expect this or see it coming, and the process cannot be reversed by anyone living in the lower dimensions of time and space. You might say that the Prime Creator itself has awoken to a new way to operate the entire creation in a far more advanced, benevolent manner to train all sentient beings to become truly free conscious co-creators with it. In other words, the reign of evil as a motivating teacher is being forever retired because a far more advanced way has been discovered to train sentient beings to attain higher states of consciousness than has ever existed before. It's now beginning to be implemented within the omnipresent, omniscient, and omnipotent force that underlies and supports all life, and all creation everywhere, starting with this Milky Way galaxy."

Janice's (Moon-teran's) eyes widened, and she found it hard to respond at first to such unbelievably startling, unexpected revelations.

Then she gathered her wits about her and asked, "Is this real?

Can you really do it? Those pyramids represent a direct threat to the Trilotew totalitarian control of many worlds, and they will try to annihilate them."

Sun-deema patiently answered, "You should both begin to understand now what is being revealed to you. This coming change in creation is beyond any race, force, or science known anywhere by any group throughout the lower multi-dimensional universe. Some people on Earth refer to these dimensions as ever more refined realities ranging upward from the physical through the astral, causal, mental, and etheric planes of existence. However, this very recently created force, brought into existence as a new directive, came down from the much higher pure dimensional realm of Prime Creator that exists well beyond the lower world systems. As we both stated, nothing in the lower worlds can affect the pyramids or the energy they emanate."

"It's true," chimed in Jon-tral, "and, in fact, if any force, weapon, or thought were negatively projected at one of these pyramids the energy would be directly reflected back upon the perpetrator to instantly dissolve or neutralize their weaponry, and suspend their subconscious negative drives objectively outside of their awareness. They would quite literally become part of the solution instead of an evil-oriented, problem-causing source. They would become carriers of this same emanation wherever they went after that, and those that ordered them to carry out such attacks would then go through the same process."

Speechlessly amazed, Mark took a big breath, sighed and exclaimed, "Unbelievably amazing! It's fantastic! Are you telling us that we will become vehicles or channels of such a powerful, transforming energy presence during our mission on Earth?"

Boun-tama jovially replied, "You will both soon know much more because a smaller version of one of these pyramids suddenly appeared within this ship not long ago, and everyone aboard went through a transformation into a new expanded state of awareness. We will escort you to a special chamber where you stand before this radiant energy field to experience this wonderful change for yourselves. When we return you to Earth, you will carry this new liberating energy within you, and it will radiate outward in all directions through your renewed physical bodies. You will also be wearing special gold emblems hung from gold chains around your necks. They will warn you of any pending attack or approach by those intending you harm, and a new perceptive telepathic knowing instinct will begin to operate within each of you twenty-four hours a day. Intuitively, you will both know how to effectively deal with every circumstance that confronts you, while you carry out the diplomatic mission to Earth's hidden leaders and people."

Jon-tral seriously interjected, "But we must also proceed very cautiously, because Trilotew agents have now infiltrated all levels of Earth governments, including the ranks of their top military personnel. They will seek to find ways to maintain their expanding covert control of the planet at any cost. As they have done in the past, if push comes to shove, the Trilotew will likely attempt to destroy the Earth if they are eventually forced to retreat back to their home planets. In fact, that's what we're counting on."

With a sudden realization, Mark grinned and stated, "So, if I'm clearly understanding you, every attempted attack the Trilotew initiate to stop this new energy emanation from going forward would result in a benevolent reversed or mirrored effect upon them. They transform back to their original naturally benevolent natures, and then when they return to their totalitarian home planets their leaders become transformed in the same way. Am I correct?"

Monti replied pleased, "Now you're beginning to see the bigger picture that everyone aboard this ship only recently experienced for themselves. Well, we must get you two fully awakened, so are you both ready to receive the impenetrable protection we told you about?"

Janice was giddy and she chuckled out, "Oh dear Prime Creator, I... Oh my heavens, you mean to tell me that Earth will become a normal human planet like our own home worlds?"

Sun-deema chuckled with her and replied, "That's exactly right, and that will be only the beginning of many vast, uplifting creative changes that will continue to come to Earth, and this Milky Way galaxy. Earth and its people are about to be reborn. Then we will invite them to join the Galactic Inter-dimensional Alliance of Free worlds. Now, if both of you will please go with Mr. Crystal or Boun-tama, he will take you to the chamber where one of these pyramid devices is even now radiating its waves throughout the ship. There you will experience a greatly expanded state of awareness, and like each one of us aboard this ship, you will become more deeply committed to carry out your mission for the benefit of all life. Both of you will know with certainty what is about to take place on Earth, in the galaxy, and throughout all creation."

Boun-tama motioned with his arm toward the triangular hallway exit from the control room. Mark and Janice cheerfully stepped up beside him, and together they casually walked twenty feet up to the exit. They stopped to turn around to gratefully smile back at Jon-tral, Sun-deema, and Monti standing beside the control console grinning back at them like proud dutiful parents. Then Mark and Janice anxiously entered the hallway with Boun-tama in the lead.

CHAPTER ELEVEN

THE CHAMBER
OF
PRIME CREATOR

Radiant golden energy waves were emanating outward in expanding concentric circles from all four sides of the fifteen-foot-tall, luminous gold metallic pyramid that was centered in the circular floor of the chamber. Boun-tama, followed by Mark and Janice, entered the room from another triangular hallway and stopped, amazed. One after the other, the expanding donut-shaped light waves rapidly vibrated their clothing as they harmlessly passed through their bodies to continue unobstructed through the glistening curved ivory walls of the chamber. Their hair was flowing behind their heads as if a mild wind was blowing through the room, and uplifted expressions of pleasure spread across their faces.

Knowingly grinning, Boun-tama turned his head to watch Mark and Janice expressing utter childlike amazement with their mouths unconsciously wide open in awe. Yet, their eyes were glancing back and forth, following the energy waves emanating from the pyramid as they passed through their bodies without resistance to vanish through the circumference of the curved walls behind them.

Boun-tama observed the golden light that started to emanate from the pores of their skin until it created an oval halo of light around their entire bodies. Then the light quickly receded back inside their flesh and their eyes brightened with a profoundly new realization.

Well, now do you two understand how this new conscious wave is beginning to radiate out into all creation and what it does? Bountama telepathically asked them with a knowing chuckle.

Yes, they simultaneously telepathically chuckled back.

They turned their heads with bright smiles of awareness toward him, nodded their appreciation for his guiding them to the experience, and he nodded back. Then he calmly turned to leave the chamber, and they knowingly followed behind him.

A short time later, they were back inside the main Command Bridge control room that was located on the same end of the mile-long flagship, standing before Commander Jon-tral and Sun-deema, his Second in Command wife.

I see you two are now back to your old selves with something new added, cheerfully stated Jon-tral telepathically, and he winked at Mark and Janice.

It's amazing. We simply understand, don't we Moon-teran? cheerfully replied Mark.

Janice looked at him and chuckled out loud, "Yes, now we understand everything." Then she solemnly said, "But I do dearly miss my family back home, even though I know they are fully behind me continuing with the mission. I can feel their radiations of love across time and space. Shon-ral told me he's experiencing the same thing from his family." Then she fondly looked at him.

Grinning at her, Mark replied aloud, "Yes, it's true. I do dearly miss them and they too stand behind me. Although, we now have the opportunity to make a real difference in this universe and on Earth, and we both think it's high time we got started."

He looked toward Jon-tral and Sun-deema for their approval, but it was not necessary.

They were already cheerfully grinning back at them and Commander Jon-tral stated, "I hadn't told you about this before, but you should both know two of these very special massive pyramids now rest at the bottom of two of Earth's deepest oceans and another one is in the Himalayan Mountains. Even now, they are radiating uplifting and transforming energy waves down into the planet's core and upward through the crust. When the waves from the pyramid stationed in the asteroid belt between Mars and Jupiter and the waves from the pyramids on Earth's ocean floor interlace with each other, we'll have a very real opportunity to permanently change the destructive destiny of Earth's people to finally become a normal human planet."

Unusually cheerful, Sun-deema added, "The gift of this new Prime Creator energy, that was passed down to us by the mighty Seres race, who revealed that they live in a higher parallel dimension of the universe, is now with both of you. Therefore, we have arranged for your immediate transport back to Earth. You will be dropped off at separate locations to minimize drawing any unwanted attention to your return."

Boun-tama stepped between them, regally bowed, and stated, smiling, "I'll have the honor of escorting you two back to Earth. I hope that will be acceptable."

Mark and Janice looked at him with a curious smile, and Mark asked, "That would be great, but what happened to Monti?"

"Oh, he was sent back to Earth while you two were in the pyramid chamber," impishly replied Boun-tama, "and he's already managed to beam Henry aboard his ship to enlighten him about our presence in the universe. They did manage to get a message through to your father without tipping their hand in any suspicious manner to Trilotew agents. When you two get back home, he and I will fill you in on how we plan to help you extricate your father from his predicament, and then the entire hidden government personnel from their trap. Well, Mark, are you ready to follow through with your new, expanded diplomatic mission to Earth, and, Janice, are you ready to help him?"

She playfully looked at Mark and answered, "Yes, Mr. Mark Santfield, I will marry you," and then she laughed.

Mark laughed with her and impishly replied, "Yes, Janice Carter, I believe I will marry you too. You know, Boun-tama, I believe we are ready to pull this off. Lead the way."

Boun-tama jovially replied, "If you will follow me, I will get both of you back home in the most expedient manner."

Jon-tral quickly added, "Before you go, we promised to give both of you a very special gift that will provide you with a way to contact us here aboard the flagship, if things get desperate. In the days ahead, you will need to do just that because we will be gradually moving things forward toward the day when our presence in the universe will be openly disclosed to all the people of Earth."

Sun-deema lifted her right arm out from behind her back and clenched in her fingers were two gold chains hanging down a foot to each side below her hand. Two round pendant symbols hanging from the ends of both chains depicted an elegant oval gold pin with an embossed white alabaster pyramid and the elegant hieroglyphic symbol above the apex that Mr. Crystal (Boun-tama) always wears. With a radiant smile, she walked up to Mark and held one of the chains open with the forefingers and thumbs from both her hands to place it around his neck, and Mark lowered his head to receive it. She repeated the ceremony with Janice, and then stepped back beside Jon-tral.

Mark and Janice picked up the gold emblem hanging from the ends of the chains and curiously looked them over.

Jon-tral continued, "You'll be pleased to know these special symbol devices act as telepathic amplifiers that are secretly connected to myself and Sun-deema in a unique way that no Trilotew can penetrate or perceive with any technology they possess. The pendants operate on an unknown frequency within the new Ray that's being emanated from the pyramid aboard this ship, and from all those that are continuing to appear throughout this and other galaxies."

Sun-deema encouragingly continued, "From this ship, we will be able to perceive ahead of time any threat you may encounter. However, you should also both know there will be much dangerous ground to walk over because the Trilotew will try every trick and use any device they have in their arsenal to entrap you one way or the other. If they cannot get to you, they will try to trap and use those who may be dear to you in order to force you to comply with their wishes. However, do not be concerned, for we will be monitoring their movements around the clock."

Jon-tral added, "As Sun-deema said, this new universe-changing wave that comes directly from Prime Creator, also known as the Ancient One, is with both of you. You can now go forward with courage and strength of conviction to carry out the full extent of your mission on Earth. Although the survival of the planet and every living thing on it is a stake, know that several hundred billion of your fellow beings living upon hundreds of millions of worlds within the entire Galactic Inter-dimensional Alliance of Free Worlds in this galaxy are committed to and actively involved in supporting this new effort.

"Also, the one you know as Mr. Crystal or Boun-tama, and of course Monti or Mon-tlan, as well as Sun-deema and I will be available twenty-four hours a day, Earth time, if you need our assistance. In addition, we have a dozen monitoring Scout ships stationed at various secret bases on Earth and another dozen patrolling in orbits around the planet for any emergency back up assistance you may require. Go in peace with Boun-tama, and know our friendship and love goes with you. For now, farewell."

He and Sun-deema respectfully nodded and Mark and Janice respectfully returned the gesture. Boun-tama grinned as he extended his right arm and nodded toward the triangular hallway exit from the bridge.

Jon-tral and Sun-deema compassionately watched Mark and Janice as they walked away behind Boun-tama, until they disappeared down the triangular hallway headed toward the hangar bay to embark on their trip back to Earth.

CHAPTER TWELVE

ATTACKED FROM TWO DIRECTIONS

Janice's concerned thoughts were on her father's safety back home on Earth, while she fondly thought about how he had taken such good care of her all her life. She and Mark were standing behind Mr. Crystal (Boun-tama), who was sitting at the control console aboard the Scout class ship as it lifted off the landing pad inside the flagship's launch bay.

The ship turned transparent and passed through the wall of the landing bay to enter outer space while Janice asked, "It was mentioned my father was secretly contacted by Henry and Monti while we've been away, but what does Henry, or my foster Earth father, know about any of this and will he be kept safe?"

Mr. Crystal looked up from the console with a reassuring smile and replied, "As you know, Henry was aboard Mon-tlan's ship while you two were still aboard the flagship. He knows now extraterrestrials exist, and about the Trilotew threat to your father and Earth. Yet, he was only able to send your father the encouraging message that help was on the way because Trilotew agents are now constantly monitoring him. I understand your concern, but know we are monitoring them. If either of them are threatened with any serious danger, they will either be teleported aboard Mon-tlan's ship or sent to one of the hidden mountain bases."

Listening concerned, with his hand to his chin, Mark silently pondered, *How can we be returned to Earth without being asked questions we can't answer about where we've been?*

Boun-tama stood up, passed his hand over a faceted spherical crystal, and the projected energy view screen appeared in a half-octagon pattern above the control console. Images began to whirl into focus, revealing the forested High Sierra mountain range in Northern California where Monti took Mark off world. The image was continuously magnified until a forested area near a small mountain valley town located at the base of the range came into focus, followed by a quaint white cottage next to a nearby clearing surrounded by dense evergreen trees.

Boun-tama then pointed to the image and stated, "This is my home away from home on planet Earth. My wife, Lean-tala, or Mary Allison Crystal as she is called on Earth, and I live disguised as a married couple in this country cottage. It provides good cover for any mission we embark on across the face of the planet. Both of us can be teleported at any time of day or night to any designated target on Earth, either from a shielded room within the cottage or from the secret Mt. Shasta base, without Earth's military establishment or Trilotew agents being able to detect it. Now that you both understand this, I can answer the question that is foremost in your minds. When we arrive on Earth, I will land the ship in a special hangar near the cottage that is invisible to any outside detection. Then, Janice, you will be beamed to a secret location where Henry is waiting to meet you so that you two can prepare for Mark's subsequent surprise return."

She winced as if she was in pain and asked, "I don't understand how that will work. My father on Earth and the Trilotew know I escaped. Surely, Trilotew agents will be after us again as soon as we arrive."

"Yes, and my situation is even more unbelievable," seriously interjected Mark. "I've been gone a entire week."

Unconcerned, Boun-tama grinned and replied, "On Earth three days will have transpired by the time you, Janice, meet Henry, and that includes all the time you spent aboard the flagship, as well as travel time to get there and back again. This is due to a round trip time displacement phenomenon that occurs every time we travel through one of the inter-dimensional doorways like the one near Earth and the planet Saturn. I believe you both recall now how this works."

They both affirmatively nodded to him.

"Let me explain further," continued Boun-tama. "A short time after we enter the Saturn vortex opening, you will both experience for yourselves the massive golden pyramid that's now stationed hidden in the asteroid belt between Mars and Jupiter. Something extraordinarily new came into creation since the sabotage of your original missions to Earth. The Alliance Council wants you to see the special energy waves it now emanates. Mark, as you recall, Monti brought you to the flagship by entering Earth's high atmosphere vortex that is connected to the vortex opening near Saturn."

Mark affirmatively nodded his head.

"As you also know," continued Boun-tama, "seven days will have elapsed by the time we return you to Earth and land this ship in the hidden hangar, but I have an ideal cover story that will explain your long absence. My wife and I will report to the authorities that we found you wandering along a road near our house dehydrated with memory loss, and we gave you shelter. We will further state that after three days of rest and proper nourishment, you began to recall what happened. When asked, tell the authorities lightning struck the ground a few feet from where you were standing, that threw you twenty feet through the air, knocking you out. When you awoke some hours later, you could not remember your name, where you had come from, or anything else about your former life. Then, after spending the rest of the cold night at your destroyed campsite, you wandered down the mountainside and through the woods to where we found you on our road. When news channel reporters, local police, and any government agents interview you, just relay this story to them. Of course, both state and federal authorities will examine you in a hospital for several days, but don't worry. We'll make certain you are protected from Trilotew agents until your safe release a few days later can be arranged by highly-placed top government officials who are secretly working for our cause to save Earth."

Mark telepathically sent to Janice, *I know we can do this if we work together. Are you with me?*

She smiled with confidence back at him, and then sent back the thought, *Mark, I really miss my family, and I know you miss yours. However, we must succeed, and swiftly, before we can return to our homes to rejoin them and enjoy the many remaining years of our true lives watching our own children grow up.*

The pain on Mark's face was unmistakable as he lowered his head to visualize his own loving wife and children back on their world. Then he suddenly remembered the critical nature of their mission, shook off the depressing feeling, and looked back up at her.

He confidently grinned and telepathically replied, *Dear cousin Moon-teran, I could not have said it any better. However, we should find out what we can accomplish as a pretend married couple back on Earth. Both of us know with certainty that vast numbers of Galactic Alliance worlds will benefit if the Earth people finally join us or they will all suffer negative repercussions if the planet is destroyed. We will not fail.*

She nodded in full agreement and he turned to Boun-tama, who had been patiently grinning while he listened to their telepathic conversations.

He stated aloud, "Looks like we're all in for quite a ride from here on out, but I'm confident with full Galactic Alliance support we can succeed far beyond our original missions. Together we can bring about a new destiny for the Galactic Alliance and the people of Earth." Boun-tama thoughtfully paused and then seriously added, "But I must remind you both again that once we arrive, you two in particular must be very cautious because agents from Earth's hidden military industrial establishment, and the Trilotew, will be after you in full force. They will know Mark's cover story is phony. That's when the real struggle will begin to finally free our fellow human beings on Earth from their covert clutches, or we will watch the planet go down in the flames of annihilation."

"Sounds like quite a plan, Boun-tama," remarked Janice, still uneasy. Then she playfully said, "Oh, pardon me, I must remember to call you Mr. Crystal, and that reminds me, may I ask what your real first name is on earth?"

Grinning at her whimsical upbeat attitude, he nonchalantly replied, "It's Dan, but you two can call me Dan or Mr. Crystal, as long as it doesn't make things more confusing than they are already."

He chuckled at his own comment, and they could not help but join him.

Then Janice thoughtfully asked, "Even though only three days will have elapsed for me when we arrive, how will I explain my sudden disappearance from my father's house?"

"Just tell your father you ran out of the house to look for Mark because you received a phone call with information about his whereabouts. Of course, he will know better, because the brief message Henry sent him will let him know what you say is really a coded message that lets him know you're safe, and that he'll be contacted in a discreet manner very soon. Will that suffice for both of you for now?"

Mark and Janice grinned at each other, and then nodded their heads to Mr. Crystal.

"Very well then," he continued, "we're about to pass through the Saturn vortex that will get us very quickly back to Earth. I will change the view screen so you can see what the ship is doing. After we enter the inter-dimensional opening, we will travel just a short distance and then exit out of another inter-dimensional opening to enter a parallel dimension. It vibrates at a slightly higher molecular time-rate frequency than this reality where the planet Earth exists. From this next higher parallel dimensional, you will be able to observe the pyramid in operation, and you will begin to understand the reason why it is not detectable, for now, by anyone in your parallel reality.

"The normally invisible waves it emits, however, are moving into your parallel dimension from its hidden location to interlace with those waves coming from the pyramids at the bottom of Earth's deepest oceans, and from one hidden in the Himalayan Mountains. Like all the pyramids, it too is currently invisible because they were placed in a higher parallel physical dimension that co-exists alongside the Earth planet. Temporarily, energy shields not only protect them from any possible detection by Earth's military or secret forces, but also from any Trilotew technology that could, under normal circumstances, detect them.

"Like us, the Trilotcw have the ability to travel between numerous parallel dimensions in the normal course of traversing vast distances of outer space. Nevertheless, when they eventually discover them, they will subsequently also discover they are not capable of harming or effecting them in any way, and believe me they will try."

Boun-tama passed his hand over a crystal control and the view screen image changed, revealing the whirling vortex opening in space near the planet Saturn. Then another rectangular, projected view screen turned on beside the first one, revealing the planet Saturn and its ring system quickly fading into the background distance of space.

They watched as the ship darted into the opening heading into the whirling, long inter-dimensional violet tunnel. Boun-tama touched several control crystals, and a view in the distance ahead of the ship appeared, revealing the vortex separated at a junction point into two gradually diverging tunnel directions. The ship passed into the right tunnel. A moment later, it popped out through another whirling opening and stopped to hover near a massive golden pyramid hovering stationary in space, glowing with an enshrouding, thin blue layer of light.

Boun-tama passed his hand over another crystal control and the screen changed to a close up of the pyramid. They could now see it was clearly hovering in its stationary position in space between two massive stable asteroids. The pyramid was emitting wave after wave of concentric circles of white-golden light traveling outward away from the top, the bottom, and all four sides of the pyramid at incredible speed. They were swiftly fading into invisibility in the vast distances of outer space.

"As you can see," continued Boun-tama, "This pyramid is already sending out pulses of uplifting consciousness transforming waves. After they pass beyond the asteroid field, they enter the atmosphere of another Earth-type planet in a parallel dimension that circles the third planet around its sun in exactly the same way as Earth circles its sun. Several of these Earth-type worlds are being prepared for the habitation of the larger part of all humans living on Earth today. They will be relocated to them after the threat has been neutralized."

Mark and Janice knowingly looked at each other, and Mark curiously stated, "Then this pyramid has to be a larger version of the one we both experienced back on the flagship. Is that right?"

"Exactly correct," replied Boun-tama.

Janice was gazing away, deep in reflection about her family back home, beyond what Earth people call the Pleiades star group. Then she snapped out of it and eagerly asked, "Are these pyramids transmitting the same new, uplifting awareness that we both experienced aboard the flagship? Will evil as an experiment actually be permanently retired from creation?"

"Exactly correct again," replied Boun-tama. "I can see you two have just about returned to your normal selves. I also assume you both now recall that most of the worlds in the Galactic Alliance can harmoniously only support about five hundred million inhabitants. Yet, Earth now has nearly seven billion living on its surface. Therefore, the world in this parallel dimension, and several more similar Earth-type planet's in other similar realities, are being prepared to resolve the planet's overpopulation and pollution problems that are beginning to destroy its ability to support life."

Mark and Janice watched in solemn silence. They both understood what Boun-tama has said, as he passed his hand over another crystal control. The view screen revealed the ship heading back into the vortex opening, and then it darted far beyond light-speed into the depth of the whirling, violet tunnel.

Several minutes later, the ship popped out of the other end of the tunnel through another whirling vortex opening, and it was soon hovering in a geosynchronous orbit just outside of Earth's atmosphere high above the northwestern United States. The ship's luminous blue hull brightly pulsed, and the ship darted in a long downward arc to disappear in a large cumulus cloud.

In less than a minute, it was already slowing its descent on approach to land in a circular clearing by the lone white cottage. A lovely, long blonde-haired and blue-eyed woman in her mid-thirties, wearing a simple country dress, was standing on the cottage porch looking up into the sky with an expectant smile.

The occupants inside the ship gazing at the projected view screen could clearly see the cottage looming closer. The small town appeared to be located about a mile beyond the forest tree line, near the base of a part of the High Sierra mountain range in Northern California.

If any people were covertly gazing at the scene from the tree line at ground level, they would most certainly have been quite astonished. Yet, only the woman on the porch knew what to expect, and she smiled as the ship slowly became visible to her. It stopped to hover thirty feet above the center of the circular field nearby the cottage just as slightly brighter light than daylight began to pour upward out of two invisible, widening, rectangular openings. The ship slowly lowered down into the stealthy building, gradually disappearing inside it as the two invisible rectangular doors closed again.

The woman walked down the cottage steps and hurried at a quick pace into the tall grass of the circular field. She stopped a third of the way into it, reached out with her forefinger and touched an invisible spot at eye level. A triangular opening suddenly appeared as the invisible triangular door slid sideways inside an invisible wall, sending slightly brighter light streaming out into the field. Her body vanished from view as she walked inside the structure, and the triangular door dwindled into invisibility as it slid closed to leave behind, once again, the appearance of a vacant field.

Boun-tama's Scout ship, glowing with the thin pale-blue light around the hull's exterior, was just touching down inside the octagon-shaped building as the blonde woman stopped several feet away from the closed triangular door that was now directly behind her. The overhead rectangular launch doors, located in the top center of the gradual curve of the pale-silvery metallic ceiling, were surrounded by four widening concentric circles of brightly lit circular lights. The illumination from them was casting an even, natural appearing, sunlight-like light around the entire octagon-walled building. The oval crease of an opening doorway appeared in the side of the spaceship and Boun-tama stepped through it. He hurried down the steps and into the waiting arms of his loving wife. They kissed and then stood side-by-side to face Mark and Janice, just as they appeared in the opening and headed down the steps.

Boun-tama gestured with his left hand toward the elegant woman by his side and happily stated, "This is Lean-tala, my wife, who is also known here on Earth by the cover name of Mary Allison Crystal."

She smiled at Mark and Janice, placed the palm of her right hand over her heart, and then respectfully nodded to them.

"You are both most welcome to our home away from home here on Earth," she happily stated, as she courteously gestured with a sweep of her hand toward the closed triangular door behind her. "Please, follow us out of the shielded Scout ship hangar facility and be welcomed with refreshments inside our humble home. We can get to know one another better inside while we enjoy a prepared meal to celebrate the beginning of your official mission to finally free the people of this planet from tyranny."

She turned with her husband and they soon passed together out through the triangular doorway opening to step into bright midday sunlight. Mark and Janice followed close behind them.

Outside it was a beautiful mid-summer day near noon, and sweet songbirds were merrily chatting away in the surrounding forest trees. Hummingbirds, bees, and butterflies were busily flying from violet flower to violet flower that covered the tall bushes surrounding all four sides of the cottage. To any casual observer who might happen to walk by the pleasant scene, this setting would appear to be an ideal, dreamlike, fantasy wonderland.

A minute later, Mark and Janice were taking their seats around a wide, oval, glass-topped table in a spacious dinning room. Just beyond their two extraterrestrial human hosts seated opposite them was the open doorway to a large modern kitchen.

While those inside the cottage were beginning to sip their tea, two slightly triangular bat-wing-shaped Trilotew Scout ships, absolutely stealthy with silence and radiating a thin red light around their dark-gray metallic hauls, shot in a blur into view and abruptly stopped to hover sixty feet above the cottage.

Inside the cottage, Boun-tama's golden pin on his lapel began to glow with a pulsing golden light. He clutched the pin in his fist, and both he and Lean-tala jumped in alarm to their feet.

A golden, transparent, spherical energy shield instantly surrounded them, and he shouted out, "Quickly, you two clasp hands. We're under attack."

Mark and Janice nervously jumped to their feet, clasping hands just as both pendants around their necks under their clothes began to glow with a similar pulsing, golden light. The light expanded to instantly radiate an upward spiraling golden energy field that surrounded their vanishing bodies.

They rematerialized from the same upward spiraling golden body-sized light aboard Monti's ship, which was hovering stationary in space, high above the northwestern United States they could see being imaged on the view screens. Monti was grinning at them from behind the control console, while they gazed somewhat bewildered back at him. Then he got up from the chair, and walked around the console to embrace them both with a vibrant jolly hug.

"Welcome to safety, you two. That was a close one, but those two necklaces you are wearing worked perfectly. As you recall, they detect danger ahead of time and send you to safety. In this case, you were sent to my ship because it was the closest place you could be teleported in time."

"Mark shook his head and asked, "What just happened?"

"Yeah, what did we miss?" curiously chimed in Janice.

"The cottage is being attacked by Trilotew ships," solemnly replied Monti. "I'll change the view screen."

Back down near the surface of the planet, the rounded transparent, crystalline front triangular points of both Trilotew spacecrafts hovering over the cottage simultaneously pulsed brightly, and two whirling red foot-wide energy ball weapons darted from them in a high-speed blur down at the cottage. The widening, dome-shaped wave explosion briefly bent back the surrounding forest trees as the entire cottage turned to brilliant white light. The ensuing blaze of searing heat melted every detail of the cottage into a vapor that roared with a deafening hiss before it simply faded and vanished.

The thin red aura surrounding the attacking craft pulsed brighter, and they darted away toward the mountains above the treetops. Two similar blue tracking energy ball weapons suddenly appeared, darting in a blur toward them from the air directly above the invisibly camouflaged launch bay in the nearby field. The two ships darted apart in an attempt to outmaneuver the weapons, but the flaming projectiles matched their maneuver and hit them, one after the other, exploding both enemy ships into disintegrating, blinding balls of golden-blue molecular energy. Only a fine, fiery mist of tiny metallic particles remained to briefly rain down on the ground near the base of the mountain to tell the story of their former existence.

Back aboard ship, Monti continued, "As you both witnessed, the cottage was completely disintegrated, but don't worry. I can assure you Boun-tama and Lean-tala escaped any harm. I was prepared to act swiftly if help was needed, but they handled everything very well."

Boun-tama and Lean-tala remained unhurt back on the ground below where their cottage home once stood. They were still standing holding hands on a small patch of remaining, unburnt ground near the center of the scorched blackened circle of earth. He let go of the gold pin on his shirt and the protective transparent energy shield surrounding them vanished. They turned, gazed into each other's eyes with concerned telepathic knowing, and then looked away to the nearby grass field.

Boun-tama gazed toward the mountainside, looked back at his wife, and stated, relieved, "The hangar's automated defense system worked beautifully. This time we were spared certain death."

Gazing back at her husband, Lean-tala hesitantly asked aloud, "Yes, dear husband, but the authorities of this world will be here soon."

He hugged her, held her at arm's length by the shoulders, and then encouragingly confirmed, "Yes, it's certain they detected the explosions, but we will straighten out the mess once we are aboard the ship. They will also want to investigate the UFO phenomena, and interview any people in town that witnessed what happened to the enemy ships."

She solemnly nodded her understanding, and they took off running side-by-side out into the circular field on the once tall grass, now flattened by the concussive explosion. They stopped a third of the way into the field, and this time Boun-tama touched a place in the air at eye level. The triangular door appeared again sliding inside the invisible hangar bay wall, and they raced inside. The door vanished as it closed behind them.

Once aboard the landed Scout ship, Boun-tama placed both palms of his hands over two faceted, blue, transparent crystalline controls, lighting them up. Two connected projected view screen came to life just above the front of the control console, and the burnt circle where their cottage had stood at the edge of the flattened grass field appeared across them. Then Boun-tama touched a triangular, transparent violet crystal, lighting it up.

Inside the hangar bay, a triangular violet beam projecting out from the disc-shaped front edge of the ship's hull was harmlessly passing right through the hangar bay wall.

Outside, the point of the expanding violet triangular energy emission appeared to be coming out of thin air at eye level from the invisibly camouflaged hangar. The point of the beam touched the very center of the burnt area, and then it began to expand along the ground in a widening circle until it covered the entire burned circle. From the ground up, the vaporized cottage began to reappear molecular layer by layer, while the surrounding air, scintillating with a rushing hissing sound glittered in rainbow colors around it like a small tornado. Within a minute, their entire cottage, the songbirds, hummingbirds, bees, butterflies, and all the tall violet flowering bushes were back in place, as if nothing had ever happened.

Back inside the ship, Lean-tala noticed a blinking crystal on the console and she pointed to it, then stated with calm urgency, "Husband, they are already here."

Boun-tama glanced at the flashing crystal, turned to her and whispered back, "We must be completely silent until they pass far enough away for us to take the ship out of the hangar without being detected."

Two Black Hawk-type unmarked military helicopters, outfitted with full armament and making almost no sound, whooshed over the top of their land. Both of them swung back around several times in wide loops to inspect every inch of area. Finding nothing after a minute, they raced away toward the town at the base of the mountain range. A moment later, two F-22 Raptor fighter jets passed overhead with a booming roar at a slightly higher elevation, also headed toward the town.

Boun-tama looked at his wife and whispered, "It looks like Trilotew agents entrenched in their midst tipped them off. They would also have told them what to look for. It won't be long before they discover the tiny bits of extraterrestrial metal strewn along the mountainside."

Lean-tala seriously added, "But surely our hangar still remains undetectable, as long as the shielding remains intact in the next higher parallel dimension."

"They won't find it," he assured her and thoughtfully paused, then added, "Now it's also clear to me those Trilotew ships didn't have the ability to detect our hangar or they would have targeted it as well."

"You're right, husband, but we must act quickly."

Boun-tama kissed her cheek and said, "We should leave the area for a while, before this country's black-ops personnel search the house for us. When they do, they will not be able to find the shielded teleportation device hidden inside. Not even Trilotew operatives know how that shielding works."

She smiled, nodding at his confidence and added, "We must visit the Mt. Shasta base again, and report what happened here. From there, we can plan a new strategy."

Some minutes later, the roar of the jets' engines were fading into the far distance away from the cottage and field, while the two helicopters remained hovering back and forth like tiny specks along the line of the lower mountainside. Boun-tama's Scout ship slowly appeared, rising in the air above the invisible opening launch bay doors, just as its sleek saucer shape began to quickly fade from visibility. The brighter light gleaming upward into the air below it, coming from the stealthy hangar, rapidly diminished and disappeared as the launch bay doors re-closed. Only the faintly visible transparent outline of the hull remained when the ship briefly stopped to hover fifty feet above the flattened grass field. A widening cone of transparent white light, suddenly emanated from the center of the bottom hull, swept over the circular field and the flattened grass instantly stood back up as if nothing had ever occurred. The beam shut off, the thin, luminous blue aura surrounding the hull brightly pulsed, and then the ship faded to complete invisibility as it darted in a long upward arc away from the direction of the mountainside, and prying eyes.

CHAPTER THIRTEEN

DEADLY
GOVERNMENT ALLIANCE

In thoughtful reverie, President of the United States Martin McCoy was impatiently pacing back and forth in front of the Oval Office desk with his hand to his chin. He was partially African American in heritage, at fifty years of age, and many people considered his appearance youthfully handsome. However, on this day, the anxious stress revealed by his wrinkled forehead and worried gaze could not be hidden from Secretary of Defense Daniel Samuelson, a trim Caucasian about his age with thick, black wavy hair and glasses, as he walked into the office and stopped to await the President's pleasure.

"Daniel, what the hell took you so long? I ordered you here over an hour ago," hotly demanded the President.

The berating he received from the President this time did not faze Daniel because he already had news that would ease his concern and he remained calm, staring unblinking back at the Commander in Chief.

"Mr. President, we now know what happened out there in California," firmly began Daniel.

"Go on, man, out with it," barked out the President.

"It looks like the Galactic Alliance of Worlds the Trilotew warned us about is beginning to intervene more directly," he mysteriously replied, holding back more about the issue.

"Well, what did you find out?" the President impatiently shot back.

"That dangerous author, Mark Santfield, was apparently rescued by a known Galactic Alliance ship just in time, before our joint Trilotew and black ops team could eliminate him."

"Damn it!" shouted the President, turning red in the face as he angrily continued, "How the hell is that possible? We took every precaution. How did they find out about our operation?"

Getting uncomfortable under the collar, Daniel briefly gazed down at the symbol of the Presidential eagle seal woven into the carpet, then confidently looked back up and answered, "It appears this Galactic Alliance, whatever they are, may have become very interested in Mr. Santfield after the successful release of his first book. It's now apparent they have been monitoring him, while he's been gradually uncovering bits and pieces of information about our inner government circle."

Before the President could respond with another sound scolding of the secretary of defense, a small whirling vortex of sparkling golden light appeared between them and a moment later a tall man with very penetrating large green eyes materialized. He was not smiling when he turned to face the President, holding out at arm's length a small-elongated triangular transparent crystal weapon.

Then he pointed it directly at the President's head and commanded, "Tell me now how you failed."

President McCoy hotly shot back, "I'm the President of the United States and I don't take orders from you, Ambassador Grotzil, or any other Trilotew diplomat. Now put that damned thing away, or one second from now the particle beams hidden in these walls will reduce you to a pile of ashes."

Ambassador Grotzil forced a grin as he lowered his arm and stuffed the device into his suit pocket.

"Oh, do forgive my little prank, Mr. President," he cordially responded. "I was ordered to test you to see if you're ready to take out any Galactic Alliance spy if they appear before you, before they take you out."

Still angry, the President replied, "From the stunt you just pulled, it would appear your people have a very sick sense of humor, and I'm becoming increasingly more stressed by the treaty we signed with your Imperial Alliance so many years ago. What assurances do I have you will keep your word when the secret governing council I receive certain special orders from announces their existence to the people of this planet?"

With a sinister grin, Grotzil shook his head and the illusion of his tall human characteristics vanished. He was now standing before the President of the United States in his true form of a tall, dark green, scaly skinned, bipedal reptile. His vertical, red, cat-like slits were centered in his oval, violet eyeballs, and two receding rows of sharp fanged teeth lined the inside of his upper and lower jaws.

His long forked tongue darted once out of his mouth with a hiss, and he calmly stated back to the President, "Have we not been allies for the last sixty years after your predecessors signed the treaty with us? Didn't we provide your military industrial complex with advanced off-world technology and weaponry to put you in the most powerful position on your world?"

The President was not smiling when he replied, "That is basically true, but you also agreed to take off-planet only a few dozen people from around the world to conduct your bizarre genetic experiments. You were to return them unharmed, with no memory of what happened. However, by our latest count you and your associates have now covertly taken several million unsuspecting citizens off-world. To date, fewer than half have been returned with permanent psychological damage, and now they are all starting to remember. Your group has already broken the terms of the treaty many times, and reports are starting to come in from all over the planet concerning intimidation tactics your Trilotew associates are starting to use to control our secret inner government members. Damn it, I want to know what happened to the rest of those people now."

With a wide sweep of the long, sharp, green nailed fingertips of his left hand, Grotzil grinned, diplomatically bowed his head, and then replied, "We will return them right after their training is finished on our home world. If you recall, it was also stipulated there should be an exchange program to orient some of your people to our culture and our ways."

Undeterred and still frowning, President McCoy sternly asked, "Ambassador Grotzil, are they dead?"

Grotzil's phony smile faded and he solemnly replied, "Are you now calling the Supreme Illumined High Lord Ambassador Grotzil of the Righteous Imperial Lords of the Empire Worlds a liar?"

"I want to know what happened to several million Earth citizens and I want that answer now," sternly shot back the President.

Grotzil shoved his long green fingers into his suit pocket and appeared to press something. The President's eyes suddenly softened, and he began to relax into a light-hearted state. Daniel was still stoically standing behind Grotzil observing the President shake his head, and then he suddenly appeared to actually be quite pleased to see the Ambassador standing between them.

"You were saying, Mr. President?" sweetly asked Grotzil.

President McCoy blinked several times and replied, "Oh, that's right. There was an exchange program. Well, may I ask when our citizens will be returning to us?"

Grotzil bowed his head and cordially answered, "They should all be returned to their homes approximately one year from now. Will that do?"

"Yes, yes, of course. Sounds fine," replied the President, and he shook his head again, appearing as if he was trying to recall a now faded memory.

Daniel walked up to the Ambassador's side and cheerfully stated, "Ambassador Grotzil, it's good to see you again. How was your trip this time?"

Grotzil turned his reptilian head toward Daniel and answered, "It was quite pleasant, Mr. Secretary. Thank you for asking. How's the wife and kids?"

Chuckling, Daniel answered, "Oh, they're just fine, although they would like to see their dad more often," and he chuckled.

Suddenly curious, President McCoy inquired, "What brings you to the Oval Office this time?"

"Well, we wanted to make certain your new security weapons system hidden in these walls are adequate to protect you from any

Galactic Alliance threat. They are on the move now, and they will try to make inroads into your secret worldwide governing members to convince them their intentions for your world are benevolent. However, in reality they still want to dominate this planet and make slaves out of all of you. As you recall, we stated to you they had done it before in similar ways on a number of planets that once belonged to our Empire Worlds. Now you, your superiors, and your special forces must be very cautious."

With serious concern, President Martin McCoy gazed back at Grotzil and stated, "We'll be ready. Our reverse engineered spacecrafts are now weapons updated, and with the support of your space fleet we will succeed at neutralizing their plans." He looked at the Secretary of Defense and asked, "Daniel, what have our forces detected on the back side of the moon, and on the orbiting space platforms and ground bases of Mars?"

Daniel proudly smiled and replied, "As we speak, they are observing Galactic Alliance ships in increasing numbers in our solar system, and we recently monitored a number of Galactic Alliance Scout ships patrolling our planet's atmosphere. Several Trilotew ships tried to destroy the one that rescued Mark Santfield, but it escaped through one of those inter-dimensional portals. We think it arrived at another location in the solar system but we are not yet certain where. Our Earth-based Scout ships are now ready to launch from our underground city bases, and a squadron is now on constant patrol within our atmosphere. We'll be ready for them if they try to come at us with any numbers."

"Excellent," confidently replied Martin, now strangely upbeat. "Let me know the moment anything develops."

"Yes, Mr. President," cheerfully replied Daniel, and he walked out of the oval office.

Grotzil silently mused to himself as he turned to confront the President, *Oh, I can't wait to devour this puny human leader when the time comes. My Imperial Lords back home must have had quite a delightful time devouring those stupid human captives.* With a subtle snide grin he stated aloud to the President, "I look forward to my next visit with you one year from today. Then I will have a few surprises for you, and the people of Earth, which will considerably alter your perceptions about many things."

"Well, that sounds like good news, Ambassador Grotzil," replied the President, now apparently quite satisfied with the meeting. "Please give my regards to your leaders, and thank them again for me for all their help over the last sixty years."

"As you wish, Mr. President," cordially replied Grotzil.

The Trilotw Ambassador appeared to press something inside his pocket again and the same whirling golden spiral of light surrounded his vanishing body, and he teleported away.

Martin's smile faded as he glanced down at the eagle symbol on the carpet. Then he looked up puzzled, walked around the desk, and stopped to gaze out through the glass panes at the White House lawn, as a nagging concern about something important he could no longer recall spread across his face.

CHAPTER FOURTEEN

THE SERES AGENDA UNFOLDS

Monti was grinning, pleased with himself, while he mused about how lucky they had all been to escape the covert vile clutches of the disguised Trilotew agents, mixed with Earth's misguided secret black ops special forces. He was also gratefully appreciating the fact that he, Mark, Janice, Boun-tama and his wife, Lean-tala, had survived the attacks because of careful Galactic Alliance preparation, and somewhat superior technology that was, for now, still unknown to the Trilotew. His grin faded as he pondered the thought of what things would be like in the future if somehow the Trilotew were to one day discover how to use any of the slightly superior technological advantage the Galactic Alliance secretly possessed. He knew if they somehow succeeded, the result would once again be great destruction to the universe.

At that moment, Monti, Mark, and Janice were observing the projected energy view screen, watching the Scout ship touching down on one of the landing pads inside the secret hidden Mt. Shasta base. They could see Commander Tam-lure and his Second in Command wife, Una-mala, casually walking side-by-side toward their Scout ship, headed away from the massive elongated octagon administration and command building with the transparent octagon windows. The medium cruiser-sized, cigar-shaped ship that had been hovering in a stationary position in front of it was now gone, as were all the Scout class ships that had been parked on the many landing pads behind and beside Monti's landed ship.

"What happened to the large Transport Carrier that was hovering there?" curiously inquired Mark.

"That's what I was wondering," chimed in Janice, "And what happened to all the other Scout ships that were landed here?"

Monti passed his hand over a crystal control and the oval opening and ladder leading outside the ship appeared behind them.

"I believe they are all out on patrol, invisibly shielded of course. Things are heating up now on Earth between the many disguised Trilotew infiltrators and the entire Galactic Alliance. We must move fast to avoid a major catastrophe on your world. If things get worse, it will be your planet and its people that suffer. For now, let's go out and meet Tam-lure and Una-mala, and they will bring us up to speed."

He cheerfully stood up and cordially waved his hand toward the opening. Mark and Janice respectfully nodded their heads, and then headed down the descended ladder.

Standing on the smooth cavern floor below, Commander Tam-his wife, Una-mala greeted them with a nod and their right palms held over his heart. Then he exuberantly clasped forearms with Mark and then Janice, and Una-mala embraced them.

"Well, you have both experienced direct assaults from the Trilotew and survived," stated Commander Tam-lure. "That is no longer an easy thing to do these days. They are very cunning and vicious."

"They can't help themselves," sadly added Una-mala, with a compassionate shake of her head. "As you both know, they are all suffering from a command program that was forced into the collective subconscious minds of their entire race by their once dominating white-winged reptilian overseers. With the secret help of our very advanced friends from the Andromeda galaxy, the Galactic Alliance defeated them. We drove them back out of this dimension and permanently sealed them within their parallel reality. They cannot return. However, that happened over five hundred thousand years ago, and their remaining non-winged reptilian cousins still arrogantly attempt to carry out that deranged programming as they covertly go about the galaxy terrorizing less advanced species. As you know, when the Trilotew disguise themselves, they must hide a barely suppressible lust to devour alive beings they consider inferior like cattle, and they place humans on Earth in that category. This one thing gives them away."

She paused to respectfully gaze at her Commander husband. He was staring expressionless at Monti, then back and forth between Mark and Janice, and then he firmly stated, "We will all have to be very cautious from now on. The Trilotew and secret United States forces will want to kill you two any way they can, or try to use you and your friends against each other."

"What about my Earth father, Ted?" blurted out Janice, alarmed. "They are already controlling him, and he'll most likely end up as bait to catch us."

Tam-lure calmly interjected, "We are monitoring him twenty four hours a day, and we have been in touch with Henry, who is now ready to fully cooperate with our efforts to save your planet. First, we must get you both back into Earth society under camouflaged surveillance at all times. Mark, you are once again the official Galactic Alliance Ambassador to Earth and the President of the United States, and he most certainly needs your help now more than ever before. Because of current treaty agreements, we could not stop the so-called Trilotew Ambassador from paying a recent visit to him in the Oval Office. We secretly monitored the meeting, but had no authorization at the time to directly intervene. However, now we do, and I can tell you the Trilotew were planning a horrifying future for your world and all humanity."

Una-mala graciously smiled and cordially interjected, "It will be far more comfortable and expeditious to move ahead with *The Seres Agenda* for Earth from inside the command center. Boun-tama and Lean-tala safely teleported here earlier, and they are waiting for us inside. We should join them."

As she and Commander Tam-lure turned together and started walking toward the command center, Monti looked at Mark and Janice, and then stated with an optimistic grin, "It'll be alright. When the moment finally arrives in the days ahead, we now have a way to neutralize the Trilotew threat for all time, hopefully without war or destruction. Please, after you," and he motioned with his hand toward the command center.

Mark and Janice gazed at each other, took a deep breath together and let it out, then boldly walked toward Tam-lure and Una-mala, who were already nearing the base of the command center. Monti smiled at them, proudly shook his head at their courage after all the suffering he knew they had already been through, and then he stepped in place behind them.

Tam-lure and Una-mala walked through the triangular opening at the base of the command center, and Mark, Janice, and Monti walked through it moments later.

A clear oval tubular shaft just inside the entrance whisked them upward utilizing an unseen anti-gravitational force. Their upright bodies quickly slowed to a stop as a transparent oval floor appeared beneath their feet in front of another triangular exit.

They gazed for a moment out through the opening to behold a vast chamber sixty feet high and a thousand feet long. The silvery metallic, octagon framework high overhead, and that surrounded them on all sides, held in place the massive transparent octagon windows lining the entire circumference of the elongated control room. They were now inside the upper third section on the top floor of the command building structure, and six other floors were now below their feet. Hundreds of humanoid personnel from many other world cultures were busy around the room monitoring ten feet wide and four feet high projected energy view screens that surrounded twenty-four octagon control consoles. All the workstations at waist level a dozen feet apart were placed in two parallel rows that extended down the length of the entire oval chamber.

They walked through the triangular opening and headed along the middle of the long oval floor toward a ten-foot-wide octagon control console that had an open space along one side for entry and exit. Hundreds of faceted luminous crystal controls covered the entire surface that surrounded a middle-aged humanoid technician seated behind one of six surrounding projected view screens. His high cheekbones, smooth pale-green skin, ivory-white eyes with red pupils, and long pastel violet hair draped down behind his protruding long pointed ears to his shoulders gave him an elegantly beautiful appearance.

The two commanders, with Mark, Janice, and Monti to each side of them, walked up and stopped at the console by the technician, who looked away from the screens and respectfully stood up to greet them. Then he placed his right hand over his heart and nodded to his superior Commanders, who returned the salute.

"Greetings, Lieutenant Elon-tal," began Commander Tam-lure. "What's the status of the Trilotew war ships hiding above each pole of the planet?"

"Greeting, Commanders," cheerfully replied the Lieutenant. "They remain unmoved in their orbital positions. However, a dozen of their triangular Demon Scout fighters were launched from each vessel an hour ago. They took up positions in the upper atmosphere directly above the Arizona desert where a secret United States underground base is located. Somethings up."

"Well done, Lieutenant," replied Tam-lure with a grin. "Order our fleet ships to approach and surround the planet camouflaged in a higher parallel dimension frequency. Then have them send out two squadrons of Scout fighters camouflaged to surround their demon Scout fighters, and wait for my signal."

"Yes, Commander," replied Elon-tal as he sat back down at the station and touched two crystalline controls that lit up.

Second Commander Una-mala looked at Mark and Janice, and then stated, "Things will speed up significantly from this point onward. The Trilotew know we are massing ships throughout your solar system because we wanted them to. However, they don't know we are about to directly intervene in Earth affairs on a massive planetary scale for the first time in galactic history."

Just then, Boun-tama and his wife, Lean-tala, walked up behind them and Boun-tama said aloud, "Well now, we're all back together again without Trilotew interference."

Lean-tala chuckled and added, "Yes, and perhaps one day we'll actually get to have that casual meal and really good cup of tea we talked about before they rudely obliterated our cottage. Nevertheless, it's good to see we're all in one piece."

Pleased with his wife's upbeat disposition, Boun-tama threw an arm around her shoulder and hugged her close.

"Mon-tlan, why don't you fill them in," cheerfully began Commander Tam-lure, "while Una-mala and I attend to other pressing matters with the Trilotew, and their two battle cruisers covertly operating outside Earth's atmosphere."

"It would be my pleasure, Commander," replied Monti with a playful bow.

The two base Commanders walked away toward another background control station, and then Monti began to fill them in.

"The plan is simple at any rate. You, Mark, Boun-tama, and Lean-tala will be sent back to the teleportation room that is secretly shielded inside the cottage home."

Lean-tala continued, "Then I will call the local police to let them know we found you, Mark, walking around in a daze with amnesia. They will come to the cottage right away and you must then convince them to accept the cover story."

"It'll work," confidently stated Mark. "After all, I did almost get annihilated with their beam weapons, and to that end the story I will tell them is partially true."

"And what about me?" jovially asked Janice, "I have been gone for three days. May I ask exactly how I'm to convince anyone the story I tell them about where I've been all that time is believably valid?"

Lean-tala took her hand and kindly answered, "We've already worked that out with Henry. Monti will take you to rendezvous with him at his estate in Santa Barbara. From there, he will have you contact your father to let him know you rushed terrified away from his home to Henry's home three days ago because of the two odd threatening men you met when you went there seeking his help to find Mark. Through Monti, Henry was able to secretly get a message to your father, and he will know what you say is actually a coded message that let's him know you're safe, and not in Trilotew hands. After that, Henry will arrange to get you both together. At that point, you will have to be extremely cautious because then the Trilotew will have access to you. But don't forget, my dear, you're now wearing a very special pendant that will shield you from any harm, and the Commander and his wife will be watching over you."

Janice was not smiling as she grabbed the pendant hanging from the gold chain around her neck and it lit up, startling her. She held it up to look at it more closely and a warm field of energy shot from it into her heart center. She smiled with relief as all trepidation and fear melted away.

"Oh-h," gasped Janice with pleasure, "Well, that's most intriguing. Now I am truly ready to go forward with Mark to carry out *The Seres Agenda* mission," and she grinned at him.

"Well then, cousin, let's get on with this pretend marriage engagement so we can go back home to our own families."

"Oh, you said it, pretend future husband," and they all chuckled at the absurd nature of their circumstance.

Boun-tama cheerfully jumped in, "I think it's time to go to the teleportation room and get back to our cottage. Janice, I believe you are to go with Monti. He will definitely get you places quickly, and that's certain."

Monti agreeable grinned and asked, "If you will follow me, Janice, we will head to the hangar bay. I can have you back with Henry in about an hour."

Janice hugged Mark, and then she and Monti headed toward the triangular opening leading away from the command center but she turned and waved goodbye before they entered the opening. Then Boun-tama, Lean-tala, and Mark headed in the opposite direction toward another triangular exit on the opposite side of the control room.

Monti and Janice were soon aboard the Scout ship on the floor of the cavernous, hidden Mt. Shasta base. He touched several small faceted crystals in succession, and then looked up toward Janice, who was standing beside him.

"I've just set up a link to Henry's phone. He's back at his house in the Santa Barbara hills. You will hear it ring here just as if I were using a phone to call him."

A moment passed and they could hear his phone ringing as if they were holding a phone handset to their ears, and then Henry answered,

"Hello, who's calling?"

"Henry, my good man, Monti and Janice are on the other end," cheerfully replied Monti.

"Oh, thank God you finally got back in touch with me. I have been pacing the floors for hours. Well, don't keep me waiting. What's our next move?"

"Hello, dear friend Henry," playfully interjected Janice.

"Oh, dear Janice, I'm so glad to hear your voice. Is everything going as planned?"

"Yes, old friend, we're on our way to you now."

"Well, that's relieving news," he anxiously shot back.

"Listen, Henry," interjected Monti. "We will arrive at your estate one hour from now. After I drop off Janice, contact Ted and then take her to meet him at the designated location, and Henry, thanks for your courage. We will need your help to move the plan forward."

"Those are certainly kind words indeed," replied Henry, not expecting a compliment. "All I want is for this sinister covert nonsense to end for all time. I really like Earth, and I don't want to be eaten by one of those overgrown reptiles, if you know what I mean."

"Indeed I do, Henry," replied Monti chuckling. "Take care and we'll make contact again when we arrive. Goodbye for now."

"See you soon, Henry," added Janice, and Monti touched a crystal to disconnect the line. They confidently smiled at each other, and then Monti placed his palms down into the gold quartz guidance controls, lighting them up.

The ship began to glow pale-blue, emitting its usual gently low-frequency hum, and it swiftly lifted straight up and out of the opening launch doors at the top of the cavern ceiling. It faded into transparency as it stopped to hover fifty feet above the extinct Mt. Shasta volcano in the crisp noon air. Then the blue light around the hull flashed brighter, and the ship shot straight upward to vanish in the upper atmosphere in the twinkling of an eye.

CHAPTER FIFTEEN

MISGUIDED SECRET AGENTS

Mark was soon standing with Boun-tama and Lean-tala to each side of him upon a ten-foot-wide and inch-thick circular quartz crystalline teleportation platform. The oval entry opening to the platform chamber across from them was part of a fifteen feet tall and twenty five feet in diameter, transparent glass-like domed enclosure. Three three-inch-thick semicircular crystalline steps surrounding half the platform led down to the smooth ivory-textured floor. A lovely young female technician, with pale blue skin and long silken black hair, was standing by the left side of the first step behind a waist-high, half-moon shaped teleportation console covered with luminous crystal controls.

The technician cheerfully looked up and said, "Safe journey to you Captain Boun-tama, Captain Lean-tala, and Mark Santfield, I mean, Ambassador Shon-ral. The teleportation coordinates are locked onto the higher frequency coordinates of your shielded unit at the back of your cottage home."

"Thank you, Trel-una. We are ready. You may begin the teleportation cycle," replied Boun-tama, and he smiled at her.

She touched a pastel violet, octagon crystal and the chamber was instantly flooded with enveloping golden-white light that dematerialized the occupants and faded away.

They rematerialized from another whirling light that appeared on an identical circular platform. Surrounding it was a normal appearing twenty-foot-square room with satin-smooth white walls. They stepped off the platform and down another set of three crystalline steps to stop beside an identical control console. However, no technician was operating it. The pastel violet, octagon crystal in the center of the console turned off and Boun-tama, followed by Lean-tala, and then Mark, headed for the wooden door at the back of the room.

Boun-tama stopped at the door, turned to Mark, and stated, "The closet room on the other side of this chamber acts as a transformer to lower our molecular frequency down a little to match the time rate frequency of your parallel dimension on Earth. Once we pass through this door, you will feel a little light-headed at first, but that will quickly dissipate. Okay, then, let's go in."

He opened the door, revealing a simple rectangular closet on the other side with clothes hung on hangers from wooden poles that lined both sides of the room. They entered inside and Lean-tala closed the door behind them. The room instantly filled with a faint white luminance that faded away, and Mark shook his head.

"Whoa... that was strange," he exclaimed. "I did feel very dizzy, but only for a moment. Now how is it that if anyone else entered the closet they would not be able see the door on the other side, and then find this chamber?"

Lean-tala answered, "Mark, look behind you."

He turned to observe the door simply fade from view, and try as he might, he could not feel or find anything other than a smooth plaster wall where the door had just been.

Turning back around, he said, pleased, "Now that's the way to hide something. I suppose, in time, I'll remember how it's done but it sure seems familiar, like I should already know."

Boun-tama smiled at Mark and added, "This room is shielded. It's really part of the teleportation chamber designed to look like a simple closet. If a Trilotew or Special Forces team entered here, none of their detection equipment would locate it. Once the frequency modulators inside these walls lower the molecular time rate of our bodies to a slightly slower time rate frequency, the room instantly transforms into a simple closet. It becomes a very real part of the cottage in this reality or parallel dimension on Earth. The room can only be reactivated by myself or Lean-tala after we enter inside, because it's programmed to respond only to our unique life-force-energy signatures."

"Oh, now I remember," stated Mark, suddenly elated. He let out a relieving sigh and said, "It's all coming back to me. Lead the way, my friends. Let's get *The Seres Agenda* moving forward."

Boun-tama opened the outer closet door, revealing the back of their country cottage living room, and the front door on the opposite side of the room. They headed inside, and Lean-tala walked over to a low, glass-topped oval table, picked up the phone handset, and then dialed 911.

A male voice responded on the other end and she calmly stated, "Hello, Sheriff. This is Mrs. Mary Allison Crystal out on Starlight Lane." There was a pause and she answered, "That's right, the cottage home not far from town. I wish to report that my husband and I found a man walking on our property three days ago, dehydrated and starving with amnesia." She paused to listen and then answered, "No, no. He had no I.D. on him, and he couldn't explain that, but thought his wallet may have fallen out of his back pocket when a lightning bolt knocked him backward through the air. He needed our immediate help to survive so we took him in, and then hydrated and fed him. After he cleaned himself up, we gave him a set of my husband's clothes to wear. He was so exhausted after that he fell asleep on the couch. He finally awoke two days later with his memory apparently fully recovered. Then he told us his name is Mark Santfield, and he had quite a story to relate to us. That was yesterday." She paused to listen to the Sheriff, and then replied with pretend surprise, "Oh, he has, for a week? Well, that fits with what we know." Then she listened again and answered, "Well, he said he was standing near his tent when a bolt of lightning struck it, and the force of the charge threw him backward a dozen feet knocking him out cold. He believes he became conscious again two days after that with no memory of who he was or how he got there. He said that he found a circle of black scorched ground but did not recall at the time his tent had been there. Not far from where the lightning threw him, he also discovered the burnt stump of a tree, and the entire giant tree lying on the ground beside it. After the bizarre disorienting circumstances, he remained on the mountain for two more days before he finally wandered down the mountainside and through the woods outside of town. When he walked dazed out of the trees onto our field three days ago, we discovered him and then took him in, or he would not have survived. He may need further medical attention, but he appears unharmed as far as we can tell. Would you send a car over to pick him up?" She paused again and reaffirmed, "Right then, in about ten minutes. We will be waiting. Goodbye." She hung up the phone and stated, "They're on their way."

Boun-tama confidently encouraged, "Mark, you know what to tell them. From here on out you will be on your own. However, Lean-tala and I will also carefully monitor you from our hidden hangar bay in the field, and several invisibly camouflaged Scout ships will also constantly monitor and track your movements. Oh, and do not forget about that special pendant you're wearing. Keep it hidden under your shirt and no harm will come to you."

Mark tucked the gold-chained amulet down inside his shirt, took a breath grinning and replied, "You know, Lean-tala, if you don't mind this time I would actually like to have a really good cup of tea before some other unexpected bizarre thing happens."

"Coming right up, Mr. Ambassador," she cheerfully stated, and then headed into the kitchen to prepare the tea.

Boun-tama further cautioned, "I wouldn't be surprised if more than the local police show up here. I'd better contact the ships scheduled to monitor your movements and alert them to watch over this property for the next hour."

He touched the special smooth edged, gold hieroglyphic pin symbol on his lapel and it flashed three times. Boun-tama grinned at Mark as he faded from view, just as his wife came back into the living room holding a tray with a steaming teapot, a milk dispenser, three cups, and several forms of sweeteners.

"Now where did Boun-tama go to?" she curiously asked.

"As a precaution, he just beamed up to one of the Scout support ships to get them ready in case more than just the local police arrive here."

"A wise move. My husband is always thinking ahead and it's saved our lives many times." She started to pour the tea into a cup for Mark and added, "We've learned to always expect the unexpected in our dealings with the Trilotew and their minions. Other arrangements have also been made to provide security after the police take you away for questioning."

Mark sat down beside her on the comfortable white couch and started to drink his tea when there was three hard knocks on the front door. Lean-tala got up and opened the door to reveal a middle-aged local sheriff, and a much younger deputy standing in the doorway.

"Hello, Mrs. Crystal. I'm Sheriff Pat Donyfield, the one you talked with on the phone, and this is Deputy Alec Johansson."

She invited them in, and they very curiously gazed at Mark sitting on the couch.

"Is he really alright?" inquired the sheriff. "We'll need to question him. Do you think he's up for it?"

"Officers, I assure you I'm fit as a fiddle and ready for your questions. I seem to be no worse for the wear, but a local hospital will no doubt want to run some tests to be sure. Ask me anything you like and I'll tell you what happened."

They approached Mark and the deputy lifted up a note pad he had in his hand, pulled out the pen stuck into the spiral binding, and placed the point on the paper. The sheriff began a long list of questions, starting with what happened to Mark after the lightning struck his tent.

Ten minutes later, Boun-tama came walking up the steps to the porch and entered the house. The sheriff and the deputy, who were now seated in chairs to each side of Mark stood up, and Sheriff Donyfield asked, "I presume you're Mr. Crystal?"

"Yes, Sheriff, I'm Dan Crystal," replied Boun-tama, and they shook hands after the sheriff introduced himself and his deputy. Then Boun-tama continued, "I was just out walking around the circumference of our field to relax from all that's happened when I saw your squad car arrive and I hurried over. I'm certainly glad you're here." He gave

Mark a cheerful grin and asked, "Well, Mark, do you feel ready to get back to your normal life again?"

"Indeed I do, Mr. Crystal, and I thank you and Mrs. Crystal again for all your kind hospitality. I wouldn't have survived without you two."

"It's alright, Mr. Santfield," kindly stated the sheriff, "We can continue the inquiry back at the station."

He nodded toward the deputy, and they both got up and walked out of the front door onto the porch followed by Mark, and then Bountama and Lean-tala. They stopped by the squad car and Mark hugged his hosts, just as two unmarked, gray four-door sport utility vehicles appeared speeding up the dirt road leading to the cottage. They came to an abrupt sliding stop in the dirt, sending clouds of dust into the air. Two well-dressed men wearing dark-blue suits and shades jumped out of each car and quickly surrounded Mark at gunpoint. One of them immediately grabbed one of Mark's hands, then the other one, and roughly handcuffed them behind his back.

As the suspicious sheriff and deputy began to draw their own guns, one of the agents pointed his magnum at the sheriff's head and hotly demanded, "Back off. He's now under federal jurisdiction." Then he reached into his suit coat with his other hand, pulled out a black card wallet, flipped it open, held up his National Security Agency identification card in the sheriff's face and ordered, "He's wanted for questioning regarding a very serious national security matter, and he must come with us now."

Sheriff Donyfield shot back concerned, "But we need to get him to a hospital and have him checked to see if the lightning strike caused any harm."

"That won't be necessary, Sheriff. We will take him to a medical facility where he will receive the best medical care available. We can question him there, and then release him after we are satisfied. Now please step aside and let us do our jobs."

The sheriff threw up his hands and stated, "Go ahead and take him. He would have wound up in our local hospital at any rate, and I am quite certain the press would have had a field day with him there. At least this way he may get some rest."

The agent that revealed his NSA identification turned and firmly gripped Mark's upper arm. Then he began to rudely pull him toward the closest SUV. The other three agents followed right behind them in a triangular position with their guns drawn, pointed at the back of Mark's head.

Boun-tama and Lean-tala were quietly watching the whole episode from the bottom of the steps leading up to the cottage. Boun-tama discretely reached up, tapped the strange gold pin on his lapel, and it blinked once.

The agent gripping Mark's arm let go and grabbed the car door handle, threw open the door, and then started to rudely shove Mark's head down to force him into the back seat. Just then, three Galactic Alliance Scout ships darted into view and stopped to hover fifty feet directly overhead. Faint auras of blue light were radiating around their silver-gray metallic hulls emitting a low frequency humming sound. The agent holding Mark's arm shoved the gun in his other hand back into the shoulder holster inside his suit coat. Then he reached into an inner pocket and pulled out an elongated clear crystal beam weapon. The other agents began firing their guns at the ships, but the bullets just ricocheted off the luminous blue energy shields surrounding them. The agent who had held Mark's arm pointed his alien weapon up at the lead ship and then slowly squeezed the trigger. The lead ship at the front of their triangular formation flashed a widening brilliant golden-white energy beam from the front edge of the hull down over all four agents and instantly sent them away in a blinding whirling golden-white light. A moment later, much more powerful pulsating green beams from all three ships intersected to form one thicker beam that struck both sport utility vehicles. They literally melted into oblivion in an instant, accompanied by a quickly dissipating hissing and upward whirling drafts of fiery vapor. Brighter blue light pulsed from the hulls of the three ships and they darted away in a blur of light. Mark's handcuffs uncoupled themselves from his wrists and dropped to the ground.

The sheriff and deputy were both speechlessly petrified, and they unconsciously slowly began to draw out their guns without really knowing where to point them. Boun-tama and Lean-tala hurried over to Mark, just as two more unmarked, gray four-door sport utility vehicles raced into view coming down the dirt road. They too slammed on their brakes, bringing the cars to a screeching halt that threw more clouds of dust into the air. Four more agents wearing suits and dark sunglasses jumped out of the vehicles, but they cautiously began walking toward Mark without drawing weapons.

Lean-tala urgently shouted, "Mark, it's alright. We requested these men from the NSA for added protection to escort you from here with the local peace officers. Those other men were probably from a hidden faction of the NSA controlled by the Trilotew. They must have monitored my phone call, and then raced here first."

Boun-tama looked over at the sheriff and deputy. Then he touched the gold pin on his lapel two times and it blinked twice. The terror on the faces of both peace officers simply melted away. Then without realizing why, they slowly put their guns back into their holsters, shook their heads as if they were coming out of a trance, and then simply relaxed.

One of the four agents approached the peace officers and sincerely stated, "Thank you, Sheriff, and you, Deputy, for your assistance with holding Mr. Santfield here until we arrived. The United States government will take over from here."

He then vigorously shook hands with both peace officers, who now appeared quite pleased with themselves, for they no longer had any recall of alien spacecraft or the four previous agents and their cars. They respectfully nodded a farewell to Mark, Boun-tama, and Lean-tala, got back into their squad car and slowly drove away.

"What happened to those other four Trilotew controlled NSA Agents?" curiously asked Mark turning toward Boun-tama.

"Oh, don't worry about them. They were not harmed, but they won't be getting their two vehicles back," Boun-tama calmly replied with a mischievous grin. "Those four misguided men are being taken to the flagship to undergo deprogramming that will remove all Trilotew subconscious brainwashing. Then they will be returned to continue as NSA agents who will actually begin to protect the United States, and they will operate as associates of the Galactic Alliance from then on. They will want to after they find out just how deeply duped they have been."

Each of the other three benevolent NSA Agents approached Mark and shook his hand. Then, the lead agent gave him a friendly smile and said, "Mr. Santfield, I'm Special Agent Jacobson. If you are willing, we will safely escort you to an undisclosed hospital location where you will only undergo a simple pretend debriefing and medical inspection for the sake of the news media. In addition, our secret faction of the NSA is aware you are the true Galactic Alliance Ambassador to our planet, and we are very grateful you finally arrived. You can provide your cover story to the press concerning your week-long disappearance at the hospital, and you will receive maximum protection from your people and from us. Will that do for now?"

"Indeed it will, Agent Jacobson, and I am grateful for your help," replied Mark very pleased, "Lead the way."

Mark turned and hugged Boun-tama and Lean-tala, gave them a grateful smile, and then climbed into the back seat of the closest sport utility vehicle. Both cars slowly drove away.

With a twinkle in her eyes, Lean-tala affectionately smiled at her husband, took his hand and said, "I've been wondering how Monti and Janice are getting on with her part of the mission."

"I've been wondering the same thing," replied Boun-tama with an impish grin. "Let's get to the hangar bay and monitor things from there. Come on, I'll race you."

He shot off running out into the field and she darted after him, playfully giggling. They both stopped beside each other a third of the way out in the tall brown grass field and she touched an invisible spot chest-high in the air in front of her. The triangular opening to the hangar silently slid open and he took her hand as they walked inside. The triangular door silently slid closed behind them and vanished, leaving behind the empty appearing circular five-acre field. The tops of the tall brown grass, slightly bent over by a soft summer breeze, were pointing toward the snow-crowned mountain range that towered in the background above the surrounding tall evergreen forest trees.

CHAPTER SIXTEEN

THE HIDDEN GOVERNMENT AWAKENS

Monti touched a crystal control and the projected energy view screen appeared above the console. A tiny image in the center of the blank screen zoomed forward, revealing a clear overview of Henry Throckmorton's mansion estate in Santa Barbara from a hundred feet in the air.

Janice said, "Well, Mon-tlan, it'll be interesting to see how Henry changed now that he knows about us from other worlds."

Monti touched another crystal control and said through the transceiver, "Henry, this is Monti. Please respond."

A moment passed and Henry's voice replied back through the transceiver, "Oh thank God, Monti. I have been so worried. Is everyone all right? Is Janice with you?"

Monti smiled and replied, "Not to worry, Henry. She is standing right here beside me aboard my ship. It's actually hovering above your mansion as we speak, but you won't be able to see it just yet."

Henry was nervously pacing back and forth on the solid oak entryway floor inside his mansion by the double front doors. He was holding a transceiver communicator near his ear, disguised as a normal Timex watch strapped around his wrist. A scintillating rainbow of sunlight color playing across his face was coming through the twin full-body-length stained glass windows. They were set within the surrounding ornately carved twin solid oak door frames. Depicted in the glass were two elegant white swans, facing each other, standing in a still pond near a riverbank under an overhanging weeping willow tree.

Monti's muted voice coming from the communicator continued, "If you come outside, things will become quite clear to you in just a few moments."

Henry held the transceiver watch near his mouth and excitedly replied, "I'm on my way out the front door right now."

Aboard ship, Monti and Janice could hear the opening and slamming of the mansion's front door through the transceiver, and Monti touched several other luminous crystalline controls. From the changing perspective of the mansion on the view screen, Janice could see the ship was now slowly moving in a long downward arc toward the rectangular acre of well-manicured green grass lawn that extended out in front of Henry's mansion estate. Beautiful multicolored rose gardens lined both sides of the long driveway that ran through the center of the grounds. As the ship touched down on the grass on the left side of the driveway, she could see the ship was now level with the rectangular two-story Roman style mansion that was another fifty feet further away. Twin green granite support columns supported a long, curved rectangular glass roof over the entry walkway leading to the twin front doors. Henry was jogging down the six wide blue granite steps that lead away from the long entryway. He continued across the circular driveway and stepped onto the grass, then stopped to speak into the wrist communicator again.

They could hear him ask a little breathlessly through the console transceiver, "When will you arrive? I'm outside waiting at the edge of the grass."

To Janice, Monti's mischievous smile was unmistakable as he touched a small blue faceted spherical crystal.

On the grass far below, Henry's mouth dropped open as he watched the sleek silver-gray disc shaped Scout ship, surrounded by a thin blue luminous aura, slowly materialize into full visibility. It had landed only a dozen feet further out in the grass from where he stood.

He heard Monti's cheerful voice ask through the transceiver wristwatch, "Is that soon enough for you, Henry?"

"Fantastic!" jubilantly shouted Henry back through the wrist device. "That was just fantastic and welcome to my home."

Henry impatiently watched as the oval opening in the side of the ship appeared, and the ramp slid out below it to the ground. Monti and Janice appeared in the opening and headed down the ramp to the grass. Then, Monti touched a spot on the hull next to the ramp and the ship faded from sight. As they started to walk toward him, Henry was already grinning with childlike wonder and he darted off running to greet them.

Monti respectfully bowed his head toward the excited attorney with his right palm held over his heart. Henry stopped in his tracks a few feet away to thoughtfully reflect on the gesture, and then quickly mimicked the cordial salute. Then he excitedly hugged Janice with his right arm, and clasped his left forearm with Monti's forearm.

"I'm so relieved to see you two here," he stated, a little out of breath.

Grinning back at him, Janice said, "Dear Henry, I could always rely on you to calm me down when my father remained stubbornly aloof to answer any of my questions about his strange visitors and odd business dealings."

Henry appeared deeply worried as he looked away and concurred, "He always remained tight lipped, even with me, about any association he had with the hidden second government or their devilish Trilotew sponsors. All those years you were growing up, I was never certain about what I suspected, but now I know how dangerously ensnared he's become in their web of deceit." He shook his head, looked back at Monti, and then added, "I don't know if you can get him free from all this now. Those two Trilotew agents watch over him like a pair of eagles watch over a mouse they can't wait to grasp and then devour."

Monti calmly encouraged, "I think you and Janice should leave that to us from the Galactic Alliance for now. He is being discretely monitored and we will not let anything happen to him. Now I must leave you both here so I can continue to do my part to carry out this mission. Janice, go with Henry back to his house and phone your father to let him know you are safe with Henry. That will be his cue to meet you at the designated time and neutral location right after Henry drops you off there. For now, farewell to you both."

He bowed with his right palm held over his heart again and then began to walk back toward the ship.

Janice and Henry knowingly gazed into each other's eyes, and he boldly stated, "Let's get this done so we can send those Trilotew monsters off planet Earth for good."

"Now you're talking," she replied with equal zeal, and they headed at a hurried clip back toward his house.

They stopped at the top of the granite steps just under the clear canopy walkway to turn around and watch Monti as he placed his right palm on a waist-high spot in the air, and the ship reappeared. He walked up inside it and the ramp withdrew. Then, the opening closed and the seam vanished. The hull lit up with its familiar transparent pale blue aura and the sleek Scout craft lifted off the ground. Then it shot straight up sixty feet and stopped to hover, as it faded back into invisibility. Janice and Henry eagerly grinned at each other, hurried along the long entry walkway, and then entered the large house.

Henry walked over to the phone sitting on the expensive looking stained blue glass-topped, cherry wood living room table, picked up the handset and handed it to Janice.

She quickly dialed a number, listened for an answer, and then stated, relieved, "Daddy, it's me, and I'm alright."

"Thank God," replied Ted relieved in a muted voice, and he waited to hear her anticipated message.

"I've been staying away from you for the last three days because of those two strange men you associate with that sent chills down my spine the moment I saw them. I was worried about Mark, and I had nowhere else to turn. My situation is much better now, and I'll be seeing you soon."

"Understood, dear daughter. I love you," she heard him reply on the other end, a little choked-up, and he added with tears rolling down his cheeks she couldn't see, "I don't know what I'd have done if I lost you."

"I love you too, Daddy. Goodbye for now," she replied and hung up the phone.

Henry urgently stated, "Alright, we better get on the move. I'll have to drop you off at the Griffith Observatory on the Hollywood hilltop overlooking Los Angeles in just under --" he glanced down at his wristwatch, then continued, "--two hours. That should give us plenty of time if we leave now."

They headed across the large living room toward the six-car garage attached to the left side of the ten thousand square foot stately mansion.

Ted placed the phone receiver in the cradle on his desk. Then he took in a deep relieving breath and wiped the tears from his eyes and cheeks. He started to walk toward the open doorway leading out of his office study, but a bright flash of scintillating light coming from behind him raised the hair on the back of his head, and he apprehensively turned around. Standing before him were the same two menacing Trilotew overseers, Gorsapis and Zushsmat, who tried to kill his daughter just one week earlier when she came to see him. Both Trilotew were sporting a sort of growling sneer at Ted, while saliva dripped from the sides of reptilian jowls. The taller one pulled a round, three-inch in diameter black disc device from an inside pocket in his brown leather uniform. Glowering with sadistic glee, he held it in one hand up in front of Ted's face. Then he reached up with the long, sharp-nailed index finger of the other hand and depressed one of the twelve buttons arranged in a circular pattern near the outer circumference of the disc's top surface.

Ted instantly discovered that he was unable to move. The Trilotew inquisitor darted his long forked tongue out of his mouth between the two parallel rows of his sharp fanged teeth. Then he slowly licked the side of Ted's face, and Ted grimaced with revulsion from the stench of reptilian breath. The shorter Trilotew stood close to Ted and stuck his long forged tongue into Ted's left ear. Then, he licked the back of his neck.

"Now, human, you will tell us who just called and what was said," demanded Gorsapis, the taller, senior Trilotew officer, with great obvious revulsion of the human before him that he pretended to respect for so many prior years.

Ted was spellbound by the device, but he was also much stronger willed than either Trilotew suspected, and he struggled to disclose only a partial truth to them as he nervously stuttered, "It-it w-was Henry, my general business attorney. He-he said my daughter went to see him three days ago, because she was terrified after she saw both of you the last time she came here. Where else could she go, and who could she trust after she realized I was somehow covertly involved with both of you? It was you two that compelled her to seek Henry's help instead of mine to locate Mark."

"Yes-s-s-s," sadistically hissed the senior Trilotew, "She should be frightened of us-s-s-s. We would have had our way with her by now if she was not your daughter and that nosey Galactic Alliance spy had not interfered. Now what else will you tell Zushsmat and I, human?" he asked, expressing greater disgust at the human he mistakenly thought was completely under his control.

Ted pretended to hesitate, and both Trilotew menacingly hissed in his face, until he finally added, "She will visit with me here soon, Gorsapis, after she hears any news concerning Mark."

"Very well," scornfully continued the drooling Trilotew interrogator. "After we leave here, order Henry to tell you anything he hears or discovers about Mark Santfield's location. You will then report what you find out to us immediately. Is that understood?"

"Yes, yes I understand," nervously replied Ted.

The superior Trilotew officer sneered at Ted one last time for effect, and then depressed another button on the disc device held in his hand. Ted instantly discovered he was free from the effect, and he rubbed the back of his aching neck.

"Remember this day," angrily added Gorsapis, and then he touched the center of the disc.

A moment passed, and they both vanished in a bright, whirling teleportation light. Ted felt drained as he staggered up against his desk, reached into his sport coat jacket, pulled out a handkerchief, and nervously wiped the sweat from his brow with a shaking hand. He shook his head to clear his mind and then angrily grimaced renewed determination. Then he turned and hurried out of his study, raced down the right staircase, and headed across the entryway toward the ten-car garage.

When Henry and Janice finally arrived in his expensive late model Mercedes Benz four-door sedan at the Griffith Observatory public parking area, he drove the car to the front of the lot, parked it near the entrance walkway, and then shut off the engine. It happened to be a slow day, and only seven other parked cars were in the lot. Henry took her left hand and gave it a squeeze.

"Are you sure about this?" he asked, a little nervous.

"Dear friend Henry," she fondly began, "Thank you for your genuine concern for my welfare. I always knew I could trust you. Don't worry about me. I'll be fine. Besides, I have a special protection those two Trilotew reptilians spying on my father know nothing about."

"Well then, my dear, take special care to watch out for those two because they can disguise themselves as humans, and they are deadly dangerous. If you need me for anything, call my cell phone."

She fondly smiled at him again, squeezed his hand, opened the door, and stepped out of the car. Henry waved at her as he drove away, and she watched his car until it disappeared further down the road beyond the parking lot. A few moments later, she noticed her fathers gold Rolls Royce convertible pass Henry's car, and it turned into the parking lot. He drove the big vehicle up beside her, placed it in park with the motor still running, jumped out, and then threw his arms around her.

"Janice, dear, I'm so glad you're safe."

"Well maybe now we can start to be honest with each other about many things," she seriously replied. "I know about the hidden government and the Trilotew threat. What on Earth were you and your associates thinking? Why did you let those monsters begin to control this world?"

Ted's eyes were now downcast. His saddened expression of guilt and shame was unmistakable, and her compassionate nature took over.

"Father, do you know who I really am?" she quietly asked.

He gave no answer as he kept sadly staring at the ground.

"Father, I know your hidden secret government may have started down its covert road sixty or more years ago for what appeared to be good reasons, but you were all duped. The price this planet may pay, just so you and your greedy members could get your hands on off-world technology none of you are morally or spiritually ready to cope with, may be the destruction of the entire world. The Trilotew will betray and kill you all in the end. They will use up this planet's resources, while they have an all-you-can-eat human buffet."

"Yes, dear daughter, I know who you really are," he sadly began to reply a few moments later as he looked up. "An hour after those two vicious Trilotew overseers left my house the other day, Henry and Monti teleported to my location in the backyard beside the pool. I was startled, but Henry assured me they were there to try to get me out of the mess I was in for cooperating with the Trilotew. Then a moment later, Monti teleported us aboard his ship that was invisibly hovering above my house. There I learned the truth about the Trilotew threat to Earth, and I understand now the extent of the damage many people and their families suffered because we secretly signed a treaty with them. The Trilotew took advantage of my predecessor's lust for power by flattering their huge egos. Those of us that comprise the secret government today inherited our positions from them, and for that I am now truly sorry."

Janice reached up and lovingly lifted his chin up so his sad eyes could meet her loving gaze.

Then she fondly hugged him, rested her head on his shoulder and said, "Oh my dear father, you are the only father I've known most of my life until recently, and you have taken very good care of me." She pulled away to look at him directly and continued, "My true home is located on another planet, and I have a family waiting there for my return. Remember, you are my Earth father, and know that I have always loved you. Now help us to correct this great tragedy before it's too late for all the people of Earth."

"What happened to my own little girl so long ago?" he sadly inquired.

"She was forced from this body by the Trilotew who captured me when I secretly went out among the Earth populous. They also forced me from my own body, suppressed the memories of all I had been, and then projected the memories of your little girl into my subconscious mind, along with their own hidden agenda. After that, they forced me into this body before they returned me unconscious within it to you and mother that same day. After that, they destroyed my own Pleiades body, and your daughter's true essence or Spirit would have moved on to a higher reality. Father, their purpose for this was to work through my unconscious mind to influence you. They also did this on a larger scale to infiltrate your inner government members, after they gained their confidence. They provided only a secret, limited exchange of their less advanced off-world technology for the right to experiment on randomly selected members of Earth's populous they claimed would not be harmed. Actually, they have conducted many damaging genetic experiments on those few they did return. The majority of the several million humans taken off world against their will were likely tortured, and then devoured alive. A small number used as controlled slaves may still be alive.

"To be fair, your reluctant predecessors would have suspected something was wrong with the treaty offer, but the Trilotew blackmailed them into signing it. They inferred it would give them an advantage over other governments, like the former Soviet Union during the Cold War. However, what your predecessors did not know was the Trilotew were also already in Moscow blackmailing them with the very same offer at the same time. After signing the secret treaty, the Trilotew started to implement a direct takeover of certain members inside your secret, government-controlled military industrial complex. They gained control of a few others like yourself through the subtle manipulation of your subconscious minds with devices they carry. However, you, dear father, were a stronger individual than they thought because you recently began to suspect something was wrong. Now you know the truth, and we need your help to get the other remaining members out of this trap before it's too late."

For the first time, he looked at her to see who she really was, and his eyes gradually brightened with the realization of what he must do next.

"Janice, I've got an idea. It's dangerous, and a long shot, but if your friends are willing to help, maybe we can rescue the situation in time. We must get back to my house as soon as possible. From there, I can take you directly to a secret military industrial complex city we have underground in the Arizona desert. With the added protection of your off-world benevolent friends, we must try and awaken the secret government members from this trap. Will you come with me?"

"Yes, of course I'll come with you. Let's get going," she confidently replied and they both jumped into the Rolls Royce and drove away from the famous Griffith Observatory parking lot.

In a little over an hour, they entered the open garage at Ted's sequestered house off Mulholland Drive, high above Beverly Hills, California. They hurried up the twin staircase along the right side of the angel fountain and entered his office study.

"Janice, I never told you about this before because I've sworn an oath to keep it secret to my own organization and the Trilotew. I have a Trilotew teleportation device hidden behind the wall of my study. I plan to teleport us directly to the underground location where an annual worldwide meeting of some of our members is about to take place. They have me scheduled to update them there, and that will be a perfect time for you to reveal to them the elements of the Trilotew betrayal. We can only attempt this if your Galactic Alliance friends will help. Otherwise, we would be foolish to show up together. Trilotew agents will also be present and our lives will be in jeopardy."

She rolled her eyes with a relieved sigh and said, "Well, that explains how you were able to show up here with those sadistic reptilian agents when you were supposed to be in England. It also explains many other unanswered questions I've had about you all my life."

She reached up and touched the pendant hidden under her blouse, and it emitted a quick flash of gold light.

"What was that?" asked Ted, noticing the brief glow.

"It was confirmation we will have help, and that we are to proceed. Now, let's get there and get this done."

Ted proudly smiled at the self-assured woman standing before him, and he placed his hands upon her shoulders. He tenderly kissed her forehead, walked around his desk, and stopped in front of the bookcase shelves on the back wall. He started to reach for a particular book, but froze with fear of a well-known flash of golden-white light behind them. Then, he spun around to confront Gorsapis and Zushsmat. They finished materializing in their tall, non-camouflaged Trilotew bodies, holding two elongated triangular clear-crystalline weapons pointed at them. Gorsapis sadistically sneered, and they both pulled the triggers. The two inch-thick green beams ricocheted off a thin transparent golden energy shield that instantly appeared, emanating from the glowing pendant under Janice's white blouse, and both beams struck the two Trilotew agents in the chest. The expressions of terrified shock on their faces lasted but a second as their bodies disintegrated into vanishing white dust, along with their fading, echoing screams. The glowing energy emanating from the pendant shut off, and the protective energy shield surrounding them vanished.

"Oh my God," gasped Ted. "That was too close. We could have been killed."

"And we would have been, if it hadn't been for the protective pendant I'm wearing," she fondly stated in grateful recollection. "It was Commander Jon-tral and Sun-deema, his Second in Command wife from the Galactic Alliance flagship who gave me the gift, before I was returned to Earth."

"Well now, that gives me more confidence to go forward with this plan. But what happened to those two monsters?"

"They were destroyed by their actions toward us. The new Ray coming from the pendant reflected their exact intent and weapons back upon them. It could have simply spared their lives and neutralized their weapons. However, in their case in particular, maybe it decided to remove their bodies and send them into another incarnation to experience what it's like to be on the other side of their evil natures."

"You mean you're telling me those two monsters are now permanently removed from ever intimidating me again?" he cautiously asked.

"Yes, Father, they are," she solemnly replied. "But it wouldn't have been my choice to kill their bodies. That decision was way out of my hands."

Ted shook his head and shoulders to throw off the emotionally frightening experience. Then he reached toward the bookcase and grabbed a book that was partially sticking out between two others. A moment later, the appearance of a wall lined with bookshelves vanished, revealing a short hallway leading to a strange, smooth, blue-metal door with no handles. They walked up to the door, and Ted placed his right palm with spread fingers on the center of the door and removed it, leaving behind his luminous hand impression on its surface that faded as the door silently slid open inside the left wall. The fifteen-foot in diameter dome shaped room beyond the opening was made of polished silver-like metal. A waist-high semicircular control console centered in the room was covered with different colored illumined semi-spherical controls. Ted indicated for Janice to walk around the console and stand upon the six-foot-wide, transparent quartz-like circular platform. As she stepped up onto it, Ted touched the largest semi-spherical control centered on the console's surface, and it lit up blinking. Then he hurried around the console and stepped onto the circular platform next to her. The control brightened as it stopped blinking, and they both dematerialized into an upward whirling golden-white molecular light that swiftly faded away.

They rematerialized from inside another upward whirling light upon an identical circular platform next to another control console. They stepped off the platform, down three steps, and onto the smooth quartz-rich, milky-white granite floor. Janice stopped to look around, amazed at what she thought must be a huge hangar bay the size of an enclosed football field. A few feet to their left was another three steps leading up to a longer platform. A six-foot in diameter, transparent, glass-like tube with a rounded end, filled with radiant transparent turquoise-blue light began a dozen feet from the far end of the platform and continued into the distance along the smooth rock floor another five hundred feet, before it entered a round opening in the center of the back wall of the huge hangar bay.

Fifty feet directly overhead were two massive, closed polished silver metal doors centered on the long curved rectangular solid rock cavern ceiling. Bright halogen lights lining both sides of the metal doors extended in six parallel rows across the entire ceiling to brightly illuminate the interior of the hangar bay. The light was also curiously reflecting off the dark-gray metal surfaces of four Trilotew triangular Demon Scout ships landed just twenty-five feet further away from where they were standing.

"Be cautious about what you say here, Janice. We're being met," seriously stated Ted, and he looked toward the far end of the cavern along the length of the luminous blue tube.

She began to hear a soft, low frequency humming that was gradually growing louder, and then she saw a very sleek, double terminated (double ended) clear crystalline-shaped transport vehicle speeding toward them inside the tube that extended out of a round opening in the bottom center of the far back wall. It appeared to be about twelve feet long as it sped in a blur down the length of the tube and dramatically slowed, revealing two human occupants riding inside. Both pointed ends of the vehicle were rapidly changing color from red, to blue, and to green every few seconds. Janice surmised that some type of very advanced anti-gravity or gravity suspension propulsion must have been powering the transport vehicle. She could now see it had traveled down its entire length suspended inside the tube by the radiant blue light without touching the inner circumference of the tube's wall. It came to an abrupt stop at the end of the transport tube, and the blue light illuminating its interior suddenly vanished. Then its rounded end silently swung open upward, and the double-terminated vehicle slowly moved forward out of the tube until its entire length was alongside the platform. Janice could now clearly see the human passengers were actually two U.S. Air Force military police sitting in the two front seats under the transparent teardrop-shaped canopy. The canopy opened upward from the side of the car facing them, and the two MPs jumped out and stood at attention.

Ted grabbed Janice's hand and they briskly walked up the three steps to the blue-granite platform, and then along its length to the waiting car and the two MPs.

"Good evening, Mr. Chairman," respectfully stated the taller MP, and both men formally saluted Ted military fashion.

Ted saluted them back and replied, "Thanks for your prompt arrival, Lieutenant Thomas, and you too, Sergeant Walker."

"We've been expecting you for over an hour," continued the Lieutenant. "We came as soon as we detected your teleportation arrival, but our orders were to pick up only you."

"Gentlemen, this is my daughter, Janice. She has no security clearance, but I will personally vouch for her this time because she just brought to my attention important critical information the Council must know about at once."

She gave both MPs a courteous smile, but artfully hid her mystified curiosity as she whispered into her father's right ear, "Mr. Chairman? Chairman of what, may I ask?"

He softly stated back, "It's a long story, Janice dear, but here I'm the Chairman or President of the second hidden government that runs this planet in some ways that direct the President of the United States to make certain decisions, and take certain actions apart from his usual duties. However, do not be concerned with that now. We have far more important critical matters to address at this time."

"Yes, of course you are right, Mr. Chairman," she respectfully acknowledged for the sake of the two service members looking on in wonder of what they were discussing.

"Has the Council started the session?" inquired Ted.

"They are all now gathered together awaiting your arrival."

"Okay, Lieutenant, we're ready to be taken directly to the central Council chamber. My daughter and I will address the members as soon as we arrive."

The Lieutenant grabbed a walkie-talkie clipped on the side of his belt, lifted it to his lips and said, "This is Lieutenant Thomas. The Chairman and his daughter have arrived. Please have your security people waiting at the lobby elevator to escort them inside the main Council chambers. We should arrive there in a few minutes."

"Acknowledged," replied a female voice.

The Lieutenant placed the communicator back on his belt, and then both MPs saluted the Chairman. They assisted Ted and Janice to step into the back of the hovering transport car, and then they strapped them securely into the two leather-lined seats. The MPs then jumped into the front seats and buckled up. The canopy closed, sealing them in with a swift sucking sound, and the transport car slowly moved back inside the open tube. The rounded tube end swung down and closed with a swift air-removing *s-s-sip* and the entire inside length of the tube instantly lit-up with the same turquoise-blue luminescence. The car suddenly shot away in a blur at tremendous speed to vanish back inside the round tunnel opening at the far end of the hangar.

A short time later, the transport car came out of another round opening already slowing on approach to another long blue rectangular granite platform. It also had three wide steps leading from it down to a smaller platform level. The car came to a stop, the blue radiance within the tube turned off, and the rounded tube end opened upward. The MPs stood up as the teardrop shaped canopy swung open upward, and they both hopped out to assist Ted and Janice step out of the car onto the platform landing. The MPs then stepped behind Ted and his daughter as they headed down the few steps to the smaller platform and up a few more steps to a much larger blue granite platform. A ten-foot high rectangular structure that looked like an elevator made of transparent glass-like walls with horizontally opened doors was at the center of the platform floor a few feet further away. They walked over to it, headed inside, and the doors closed. A blue luminance began to emanate from underneath it, and it silently levitated up several inches above the floor. Then it smoothly moved sideways a dozen feet toward the end of the platform. It slowed and came to a stop inside a rectangular opening below an enclosed rectangular, clear-glass elevator shaft that continued up through the twenty-foot-high, long curved rectangular green granite ceiling. Then the elevator swiftly levitated up the shaft and vanished beyond the ceiling.

The elevator appeared again coming to a stop at the top of the shaft, several floors above the hangar bay and transport tube station. Before exiting the elevator, Janice could see they were about to enter a short hallway with polished green granite floors, and her first impression was it looked very much like the elevator hallway of a modern hotel. As they walked out of the elevator, she noticed the hallway actually lead to a main lobby area, just as two men wearing expensive Italian suits walked up to them and nodded, and the MPs walked away.

"Welcome, Mr. Chairman," respectfully stated the taller man. "I was instructed to meet you here and take you directly to the central Council chamber, but no one else has been cleared to come here with you."

Both men dubiously eyed Janice because her presence there was certainly a breach of protocol. Janice sternly stared back at both men with her hands defiantly on her hips, and the men took a cautious step backward.

"You have questioned her presence here and both of you are precisely following correct protocols, but there is no need for concern. That was well done. I will put in a good word for each of you. This is my daughter, Janice. I brought her here to speak directly to the entire World Council to deliver new critical information for our survival. Now, please lead us to the main Council chamber."

The two men nodded compliance to the Chairman's wishes, and then headed into an adjacent carpeted hallway. They had not gone far when they came upon a set of large golden doors. Centered on both doors was the symbol of a radiant eye over a white alabaster pyramid. To Janice, it looked like very similar to the symbol that is on the back of a one-dollar bill. The taller man opened the doors and they walked inside. The eyes of a hundred men dressed in expensive suits, varying in age from thirty-five to eighty years old, turned to stare unsmiling at Ted and Janice. Then angry scowls for her presence among them immediately registered on all their faces. Ted protectively took her hand and they boldly began to walk together down the lush blue-green carpeted aisle between the austere men. He remained confidently staring straight ahead, while he walked up the three steps that led to a podium centered on a small stage area. Then he turned around with Janice at his side to face the secret government Councilmen. They were all sitting in lush brown leather chairs as he began to address them in a serious somber tone through the flexible microphone attached to the top of the podium.

"Fellow Council members, and any Trilotew associates that may be present, I came here today to inform you of some very critical information that has come to my attention from my daughter, Janice. I brought her here without going through normal security clearance procedures due to the very stark nature of what I just learned from her. I will now give the floor to her, and she will enlighten you so that each one of you can make new constructive choices that will alter the direction we've set for the future of this planet."

The men now appeared quite nervous as they restlessly stirred in their chairs, not quite knowing what to make of Ted's comments. Several tall men in the back seats suddenly jumped to their feet, just as Janice approached the podium to speak into the microphone. One of them pulled out a small device from his suit pocket hidden in his palm and put it to his lips. Both men appeared to be very nervously anxious about something as he lowered the device, stuck his hand back in his suit pocket, and then firmly grabbed something else. He appeared to tighten his grip around it, as an angry sadistic sneer formed on his face.

Janice calmly looked over all the men in the chamber with the certain knowledge she was among a den of vultures ready to pounce on her, and then tear her to pieces. Their actions did not deter her as she reached up and touched the pendant hanging from its gold chain around her neck hidden inside her blouse.

She let her hand go and firmly stated, "Gentlemen, if I can call you and your predecessors that, you have all been lied to for over sixty years."

The following uproar in the room was deafening as the members stood up shouting their indignation at her.

One rotund elderly bald man yelled out, "What the hell is she doing here, Chairman?"

"How dare you address us in that tone, insolent child!" shouted another angry middle-aged man.

"Young lady, do you know who you're talking to?" arrogantly yelled another angry younger man.

Another yelled out, "What does your daughter have to do with our plans, and how does she know what we're planning?"

Ted stepped between her and the microphone, then sternly shouted, "Shut up, all of you. She may just save all your lives today, and that of your families, from a fate worse than death."

Still fuming, they remained standing but shut up to listen as she calmly continued.

"The treaty your predecessors signed with the Trilotew to gain certain off-world technologies is a fraud. They promised them the power to rule this world, but they are merely using all of you to take over this planet. When they determine your usefulness to them is over, you and your families will be sadistically tortured to death as they devour your bodies alive. Then, Trilotew agents disguised to look like you will replace you. Each man in this room, who still has his own human wits about him, has suspected for some time that several of your other members no longer act quite like their normal selves. After the Trilotew take over your positions worldwide, they will use all humankind as either slaves or a food source. Even now, the secret waveform transmitters they carry in their coat pockets are subconsciously influencing all of you. I suspect Trilotew agents disguised as two of your former human Council members are the taller two men standing at the very back of this room. If I'm right, they just contacted their ships, and when they arrive here they will annihilate this place to cover up any evidence of their breaking of the treaty they signed with the entire Galactic Inter-dimensional Alliance of Free Worlds."

The two tall men at the back of the room angrily grimaced, and then darted down the isle toward the podium. They reached inside their suit jackets, pulled out long triangular clear crystal hand weapons and pointed them at Janice and Ted. Two undisguised Trilotew agents, wearing their own off-world tight-fitting brown leather uniforms, with the symbol of a white-winged bipedal reptilian emblazoned upon their chests, suddenly materialized in the back of the room. They were holding longer crystalline weapons pointing them in sweeping maneuvers at all the men gathered there. The startled Council members were aghast with disbelief upon seeing their supposed off-world Trilotew reptilian allies pointing weapons at them, while expressing menacing, sadistic sneers on their green scaly faces.

Janice grabbed the pendant hidden under her blouse in her closed fist and it flashed to life, brilliantly lighting the room through her clenched fingers. Ted instinctively threw her to the floor and covered her with his arms, just as two sizzling beams of green radiant energy blasted a round hole in the wall, directly behind the podium, with fiery disintegrating atoms of green light. The energy emission coming from her pendant instantly expanded into the room with a thousand rainbow colors that harmlessly passed right through the bodies of everyone to continue in every direction through the walls, floor, and ceiling of the chamber. All four Trilotew agents were suddenly stopped in their tracks, and they fearfully discovered they could no longer move, except for their eyes, which gazed down to see their crystalline weapons harmlessly drop from their limp hands to the carpeted floor. The human illusion disguises covering the two Trilotew agents wearing suits melted away in quick puffs of vanishing smoke, openly revealing their true bipedal reptilian nature. For the first time, the oval violet eyes with cat-like red pupils of all four reptilians were expressing real terror.

Ted helped Janice to her feet, while she remained clutching the glowing pendant. Then she approached the podium again and calmly continued, "This new energy Ray that was recently given to the Galactic Alliance comes from a higher realm that is many, many dimensions far above the entire physical universes. No force utilized by beings residing in the lower dimensions can stop it, and no type of weapon can affect it in any way. This new energy Ray is not here to harm any of you. As you feel it penetrate your chests, you will also begin to perceive a projected transparent white sphere of light above your heads filled with all the negative implanted control images that were deep inside your sub-conscious minds. Then you will once again know the truth about your original celestial natures: that of being exhilarated loving beings filled with the passion to create new things, and new ways of living for the well being of all life everywhere. Please, all of you take your seats. Then make the right choice. Determine right here and now to have those awful false torturous sub-conscious memories dissolved forever, and this new gift Ray will erase them. Finally, you will be set free once again to live as you were always meant to live - in harmony with all life."

The force that was holding the four Trilotew from any movement vanished and they shook their heads. Then they cautiously picked up their weapons but did not point them at Ted and Janice. All hardened expressions on the faces of the power-mad men in the chamber, and the sinister expressions of sadistic glee on the four Trilotew agents began to soften. Expressions of childlike wonder and real joy gradually took their place for the first time in their lives. One by one, transparent white spheres appeared above all their heads filled with images of horror, torture, suppression, sadistic cruelty, and every other imaginable demented type of experience. As each individual in the room silently made the correct true free-will inner decision for the first time, all the horrifying scenes inside the transparent spheres hovering above their heads dissolved into pure white light, and the spheres faded away. Many astonished childlike murmurs began to spontaneously come from the mouths of the Council members.

"Oh dear God, at last," cried out one, greatly relieved.

"This is unbelievable! Finally, I am free of this terror," breathlessly said another, as tears began to pour from his eyes.

"I didn't know. I just didn't know," lamented another older man, and then he began to smile from the warm expansive feeling he was beginning to experience.

The most senior representative gasped with a new realization and asked, "Oh my heavens, what have we done to our people and our planet? Oh no, no, we must turn this around."

Then many more uplifted expressions of sublime surprise continued to come from all of them.

The facial features of the four Trilotew had now completely changed. Their coarse reptilian scales had morphed into beautiful smooth green scaly skin. Humble smiles now appeared upon their faces, and their eyes began to emanate a kindly nature. Their true selves, genetically buried below their level of awareness, had surfaced for the first time. They began to slowly walk together toward the podium respectfully holding their arms extended away from their chests with open palms up toward Janice and Ted, while repeatedly bowing their heads.

Their mystified apparent leader stopped a few feet away and humbly asked, "You set us free. Why would you do this for us?" Before now, we would have gladly tortured you to death by ravenously eating your bodies."

Janice kindly smiled at them and replied, "You couldn't have stopped yourselves before if you had tried. The sub-conscious control implants, genetically placed inside your ancient ancestors by their former ruthless white-winged reptilian conquerors, was continuing to drive your negative passions before today. The Great War we had with your ancient winged overlords ended over five hundred thousand years ago, after our secret allies forced them back into that hellish parallel dimension from which they came. However, all of you, their non-winged reptilian cousins from this galaxy, had to deal with us to end all hostilities. We only recently discovered this long past genetic programming is still controlling your entire ancient race, and your current Emperor. Even now, he continues to order you to terrorize and conquer other races through deception, blackmail, and sadistic intimidation. This is how you have covertly operated to avoid another open war. The Galactic Inter-dimensional Alliance of Free Worlds did notice your many attempts to disguise your covert breaking of the treaty. I can see in your eyes that all four of you now know this to be the truth."

The Trilotew leader humbly nodded back that he did, and she continued, "I presume you are the senior officer of the other three Trilotew agents." He nodded again, and she cordially inquired, "May I ask your name?"

He lowered his now saddening eyes and replied, "I am First Officer Zorbok, but I'm unworthy to gaze upon one such as you. You set us all free from this terrible curse, and we will be eternally grateful to you, and the entire Galactic Alliance for this miraculous change."

"First Officer Zorbok of the Trilotew, I didn't bring about this change. Even now, this Ray emanating to everyone here is continuing to accomplish that miracle. I must also tell you this process of changing you back to your true original natures is irreversible. From now on, no Imperial Trilotew technology, or any other technology, will be able to negatively affect or control you ever again. After you return to your ships, each of you will discover you have awakened the innate desire to help change the course of history in a benevolent way. You will actually become consciously aware, contributing conduits for this new gift Ray. Eventually, this uplifting, transforming new energy will spread to all your people on all the Trilotew-dominated worlds, including to your Emperor himself. You will be the first Trilotew to begin to repair all the damage your combined races have caused over the last five hundred thousand years. Be at peace, for each of you are no longer enemies of the Galactic Alliance, and I for one can now call you friends."

The four Trilotew soldiers began to uncontrollably grin from the effect of her completely unexpected kind comments, and utter relief began to show on their astonished faces.

Zorbok smiled wider as he nodded, and then replied, "I will signal our ship to beam us back aboard. Know this, Janice and Chairman

Carter, we will always fondly remember and treasure this momentous day."

She boldly walked down the steps and extended her forearm to the Trilotew officer. He looked even more amazed back at her entirely unexpected friendly gesture, and then cheerfully but gently grasped her hand. She graciously shook it, and then repeated the gesture to the other three Trilotew. Then Ted did the same, giving each one a warm genuine smile.

Zorbok reached into a pouch strapped to the side of his brown leather uniform, pulled out a flat triangular ruby-red crystalline device, and he was about to touch a concave depression in its center with his thumb when the back wall of the council chamber suddenly exploded, sending debris flying through the room.

A warning siren began to loudly clang, and the panicked Council members raced for the nearest exits located on each side of the chamber. Two dozen more Trilotew soldiers carrying long triangular crystalline rifles rushed into the chamber through the wide gaping hole, just as heavily armored defending base soldiers raced into the chamber from both side exits pointing similar crystalline weapons back at the Trilotew.

"Council members, hit the floor," forcefully yelled the squadron commander, as the Trilotew infantry opened fire at many of the fleeing Council members and their defense infantry.

The many radiant green energy beams shot from the tips of their weapons vanished several feet away into the neutralizing power of the new Ray still radiating throughout the room. The military soldiers returned fire but the new Ray also neutralized those sizzling light beams. The opposing forces desperately tried several more times to open fire at each other with the same effect, and then they gradually began to recover from the immediate shock of the ineffectiveness of their weapons. The Trilotew infantry standing behind the four Trilotew nearest to Ted and Janice tried to open fire at them again, but the green beams also vanished inches away from the tips of their weapons. The bewildered Trilotew frantically shook the rifles, and then pulled the triggers repeatedly with the same result.

Janice grabbed the glowing pendant again under her blouse with her fist. This time, Commander Tam-lure and Una-mala, his Second in Command wife from the hidden Galactic Mt. Shasta Alliance base materialized directly behind her and Ted. They just simply appeared without the necessity of getting there by the energy vortex of a teleportation beam. A transparent, golden, protective bubble instantly formed around all four of them, and the angered Trilotew soldiers repeatedly opened fire. The green beams ricocheting off the protective energy sphere instantly dissolved several feet away in the neutralizing rainbow colored energy still radiating throughout the room.

The Trilotew soldiers and the base security forces finally began to relax their fear; but they remained nervously pointing their weapons at each other. Then Commander Tam-lure began to clearly speak to them through the protective transparent barrier.

"Cease all hostilities," he kindly commanded. "I promise no harm will come to any of you."

As they all reluctantly began to lower their weapons, one of the Trilotew soldiers standing hidden behind several others lifted a wrist communicator to his reptilian jaws to quietly warn his fleet about the events taking place in the chamber.

"I am Commander Tam-lure and this is my wife, Second Commander Una-mala of the Galactic Inter-dimensional Alliance of Free Worlds. We wish you no harm. You must realize by now any weapons used here will be completely ineffective."

Una-mala then kindly added, "You will each begin to experience a change in consciousness from the effect of the new energy Ray emanating in this room, and you will soon discover your suppressed original natures as the deranged terror implants that were programmed into your ancestors' genetic codes so long ago are removed."

All of the soldiers' faces on both sides suddenly began to soften, and then their facial features began to morph into non-aggressive kindness, while they continued to gaze amazed at each other. Each of them began to look up to behold transparent golden-white energy spheres appearing above each of their heads. Upon seeing images of terror, torture, and sadistic vengeance appear inside them, they all started to fearfully back away. A moment later, the images dissolved and the spheres vanished. The soldiers on both sides then began to gaze for the first time at a former enemy with humble respect and awe.

Tam-lure continued, "If you wish, all the Trilotew here may go back with us to our Mt. Shasta base to undergo a full deprogramming. You will become what your ancient ancestors were before they were perverted by their white-winged overseers. They were benevolent then, highly intelligent, non-carnivorous in nature, and at one time long ago, they were also very giving, constructive members of the Galactic Alliance. After we return you to your own ships secretly stationed around Earth a day later, you will discover this new Ray will continue to emanate through each of you toward your fellow Trilotew. Then they too will begin to experience the awareness that your long conflict between us is now headed toward a permanent peace."

The one who had tipped off his superiors by lifting a wrist communicator to his lips was now also gratefully smiling back at the humans standing on the stage, and he reached to touch the same button on the communicator again but thoughtfully hesitated.

Concerned, he loudly stated to Tam-lure, "I am Second Officer Razjewl, and right before the transformation I contacted my superiors to tell them of your presence here in this base. They will want immediate revenge."

Commander Tam-lure kindly smiled and nodded his thanks for the information.

Then he looked at First Officer Zorbok standing near him and he stated, "We will be ready for them, and you all need to know they will not be harmed if we can help it."

He looked over the two dozen other Trilotew soldiers and asked, "Will you let us help you return to your true selves?"

All the Trilotew soldiers looked toward their comrades for confirmation, and then Zorbok answered with a relieved grin, "We are all tired of this conflict and we will go with you now."

Tam-lure smiled at each one of them, touched the crystal on his sleeve three times, and all the Trilotew present in the room vanished from sight before the astounded eyes of the Council members, and the perplexed base soldiers guarding them.

The protective transparent bubble surrounding the four humans on the stage vanished, and the relieved Council members began to stand back up with astounding dazed expressions upon their faces.

Then they began to move closer together toward the center of the room like bees drawn to flowers.

Tam-lure kindly continued, "Each one of you in this secret government knows the truth about what happened to your predecessors and to you. The vicious covert control over you is now gone. If you wish, we can send you all to our secret Mt. Shasta base. There you can also experience a more complete deprogramming of any other subconscious implants that remain in the way of a full re-awakening to your original highly intelligent, benevolent natures. After we return all of you back here a day later, you will have one great task. You will be passionately inspired to benevolently utilize your control of the military industrial complex, and the hidden wealth you have stolen from the world's hardworking populous, to right all the past wrongs. You will have help to correct what your predecessors, you, and the Trilotew have done. We understand there are many other prominent men belonging to your organization who are not present here at this meeting. They will need your help before we can implement the full disclosure of our presence to all the people of Earth. Know that when you contact your fellow members worldwide, or their Trilotew overseers, this new uplifting and transforming Ray will begin to operate through you. It will help them make the same transition back to their true benevolent natures. In the near future, many of our representatives in every field of endeavor will be coming to Earth to advise and assist you all with this transitional process. Then all humanity on Earth will have the opportunity to become a full member of the entire Galactic Inter-dimensional Alliance of Free Worlds. Will you and those soldiers who are present here come with us?"

The one hundred former members of a hidden world government on Earth, finally liberated from the sub-conscious effects of their former Trilotew overseer's wrist devices, were now smiling with childlike wonder for the first time in their lives. Their soldiers were also now greatly uplifted. Yet, for the most part, they had previously blindly followed the orders of their superiors, who they had mistakenly thought were official representatives of the elected leaders of the United States government. They were also beginning to experience a rapidly expanding conscious awakening back to their suppressed benevolent natures, and each one wanted more. They all nodded their approval to Tam-lure, and then Tam-lure touched the small crystal on his other sleeve three times. All one hundred Council members, along with the several dozen soldiers guarding them, vanished from the room in an upward whirling light. A moment later, a soft beeping sound coming from his wrist communicator interrupted Tam-lure.

He lifted the device to his ear to hear an urgent young adult male voice state, "Commander, we just monitored the launch of two dozen Demon Scout fighters from those two Trilotew battle cruisers that are in synchronous orbits over each pole of the planet. They are on their way toward your location. What are your orders?"

Tam-lure put the device to his lips and replied, "They know we're on to them. They will very likely attempt to destroy all evidence of their treaty-breaking, covert influence on this planet, starting with this hidden government base. Lieutenant Dun-tal, I believe the time has come for us to reveal to all the Trilotew the beginning phase of *The Seres Agenda*. Have they detected our fleet in orbit?"

"No, Commander," replied Dun-tal's younger sounding voice back through the transceiver. "They show no signs they are able to detect our ships, while we're operating in the higher parallel dimension frequency. We remain invisible to them."

Tam-lure sternly commanded, "Before their forces arrive above this hidden underground location, order our four medium cruisers stationed in the upper atmosphere to descend to a mile above us. Have them prepared to neutralize all power aboard the Trilotew medium destroyers. Then have them launch four Scout fighter squadrons frequency phased to remain undetectable. When the Trilotew Demon Scout fighters attempt to launch their matter annihilator weapons, have our Scout squadrons surround and neutralize them as well. Do it quickly, and keep me updated."

"Yes, Commander, I'm already on it," confidently replied the young Lieutenant.

Ted's face had also now softened, and he was smiling with joy at the new state of consciousness he was experiencing from the energy emanations that were continuing to pass through his body, coming from his daughter's off-world pendant. Then, for the first time, he began to experience concern for the fate of the monstrous Trilotew, without regard for his own safety.

He found himself silently musing, *After all, they couldn't have stopped what they were doing. Implanted subconscious programming created by their sadistic winged overlords was also driving their sadistic behavior.*

Ted came out of his reverie and asked Una-mala, "Well, what happens now?"

"That's what I'd like to know," chimed in Janice.

"A battle is coming," Una-mala compassionately replied, "The first battle that may be openly witnessed by average Earth citizens, and I don't think the Trilotew will be able to cover up the truth about their covert involvement with Earth's secret leaders for much longer. There are other powerful people in hidden bases like this one around the world who are also a part of the hidden secret government cover-up, and their controlling Trilotew overseers could still destroy this planet out of sheer meanness, if they believe their plans for Earth are about to be neutralized. For the first time, I am very optimistic about the eventual outcome. All four of us should now beam back to the base to help with the full deprogramming of all those just sent there. Then we will see what tomorrow brings."

Commander Tam-lure grinned at his wife, and then cheerfully said to Ted and Janice, "Are you ready?"

They eagerly nodded, and he touched the crystal on his sleeve three times. Then, they too vanished from the room.

CHAPTER SEVENTEEN

A PUBLISHER
EXPERIENCES TRUTH

Mark Santfield had now fully recovered all memory of his original off-world Pleiades origin as Ambassador Shon-ral, and he was about to be released from the University of California Medical Center where he had just undergone a fictitious health observation. The local police and select members from the NSA faction secretly operating with the Galactic Alliance had debriefed him for the benefit of the press. He had been inundated non-stop for three straight days by reporters from all the major television networks and newspapers. They had accepted the fabricated cover story Mark relayed to them about how he had suffered from amnesia for nearly a week, after surviving a lightning strike while camping in the mountains.

Agent Jacobson, the special NSA agent that took Mark from the Crystal's cottage home to the hospital, was standing next to him handing back his wallet and other personal effects that were kept safe to make the amnesia cover story about his temporary loss of identity convincing.

"What's your next move?" he cordially asked Mark.

"Hmm, that's a good one, but I think I should first let my publisher off the hook by showing up alive, and give him the long overdue manuscript of my next book. What's contained in its pages could help prepare the public for the day when Galactic Alliance representatives show up here in great numbers to help this world make the transition to become one of its members. Can you imagine how this negative world will be transformed?"

"Mr. Ambassador, I can only speculate," he respectfully replied. "But there is one thing I've always wanted to do since I was just a boy. Can I go to the stars and visit other worlds?"

Mark nodded smiling, finished straightening his tie, slipped on his new suit coat, and then enthusiastically replied, "I can promise you this, Agent Jacobson. Over the next few years, the transformation of the Earth back to a normal world of benevolent human beings will take place. Then, you and the rest of Earth's human population can visit our worlds in many exchange programs of learning. You will be involved in uplifting exploration, and new enlightening experiences. Yes, Agent Jacobson, you will get to live your dream far beyond even your wildest expectations. Well, I deeply appreciate and thank you for all your help. I know you will be monitoring my movements for security reasons from now on, so I hope we cross paths many times over the next few years. Now, I have to catch a cab. Good bye, my friend."

Grinning with childlike wonder, Agent Jacobson shook Mark's hand, and then escorted him out of the hospital room. A few minutes later, they walked side by side out of the hospital lobby, and Agent Jacobson waited until Mark caught a cab. Then, he took a special cell phone from his pocket and said something into it. A moment later, a dark blue late model four-door sedan pulled up beside him with a fellow female agent at the wheel. He jumped into the front passenger seat and they pulled away.

A half-hour later, Mark walked into a modern fifty-story building in Beverly Hills with the manuscript tucked under his arm. He took the elevator to the fiftieth floor and entered the Waymeyer Publishing Company offices through the double-wide ornate oak doors. Chairman and CEO, Dan Waymeyer, was impatiently standing in front of the receptionist's desk with his hand out palm up, to insinuate that Mark should immediately hand over the manuscript. The very pretty receptionist in her mid-twenties looked up and cutely smiled at Mark from behind her boss's back.

"Mark, it's about damn time you came here to deliver that manuscript," he cheerfully stated, eyeing him with an expressive mild rebuke. "I watched the news about what happened to you, how you were found and finally recovered your memory. Damn lucky break if you ask me. I'm relieved to see you in one piece."

Mark reached to place the manuscript in Dan's hand, playfully yanked it back just to see the grimace on Dan's face, and then dropped it. Dan grabbed it out of the air, read the title page, turned it over, and then scanned down the list of chapter titles before he looked back up concerned.

"Now wait a damn minute. Do these chapter titles actually reveal what they imply?"

Mark seriously stated back, "You bet your ass they do, and there's much more to it than what's on the pages of my second book. I plan to considerably expand it through the editing process before it's finalized and released."

"Mark, please come into my office," respectfully requested Dan, and he nodded with a roll of his eyes toward the pretty secretary sitting behind the reception desk. "There's something important I need to discuss with you in private."

Mark could not help but also notice an unmistakable concern deepening on Dan's face that was beginning to show signs of fear as they walked to the end of the long polished solid oak wood floor hallway. They stopped in front of a set of the double-wide clear glass doors with bold gold letters painted across them that read: Waymeyer Publishing Group – Mr. Dan Waymeyer, Chairman & CEO. They headed through the doors and stopped again to face each other, beside two lush blue leather guest chairs that were arranged in front of Dan's huge, very expensive looking dark wood desk. The taller, more lavish leather chair was behind it. Mark looked away to gaze through the floor to ceiling corner office windows at the expansive overview of the city of Beverly Hills and the mountainous hills beyond it, and then looked back.

"Mark, are you out of your mind, or do you just have a death wish?" blurted out Dan, suddenly hot under the collar.

Mark did not flinch, while he continued to confidently stare back at his senior editor and publishing company owner.

"Don't be concerned about the content, even though every word in it is true and there's more, ever so much more you need to know. When this book is published, you, your wife, your offspring and their children, as well as every employee working here will be protected from any harm in ways you couldn't possibly imagine at this moment."

Dan nervously inquired, "What ways could possibly protect us from the tyrants you claim are operating a powerful second hidden government with the assistance of their diabolical extraterrestrial allies?"

"Dan, listen to me," Mark calmly replied, "I'm not who you think I am. I'm not from this world, although this body is."

Dan flushed red in the face, cleared his throat, and angrily replied, "Damn it, Mark, are you telling me you're now on some kind of psychic mumbo-jumbo kick, and you're actually a walk-in from outer space?"

Mark still did not flinch, while he steadily gazed at his fearfully apprehensive publisher, and then he replied, "There isn't time for me to try and convince you of anything I'm telling you. Only direct personal experience of your own will convince you, and answer all your questions. Do I have your permission to prove, without a shadow of doubt, that everything I'm telling you is the undistorted truth?"

"What do you mean?" nervously snapped back Dan.

"Will you come with me to discover for yourself just how deeply everyone has been lied to on this planet?" seriously shot back Mark. "Do you want to safely know the real truth behind all this for yourself?"

"You're kidding, right?" replied Dan, even more perplexed than before. "Are you saying you can get me aboard a flying saucer or something like that?"

"That's exactly what I'm saying," confidently replied Mark. "Wouldn't you like to know you're about to publish a book that's part of a vastly greater plan to free this world once and for all time from the madmen who have been running things from behind the scenes, while unconsciously heading our world to destruction?"

Dan looked at Mark with deep worried lines of consternation etched into his face, as Mark reached up and touched the pendant hidden under his shirt and it flashed once. Dan's tight shoulders suddenly dropped, and he relaxed as he shook his head. Then he looked at Mark with new found confident courage.

"Mark, you better be right about this," he firmly stated, pointing his finger at Mark's chest.

"My friend," replied Mark grinning, "you're about to go on the greatest adventure of your life."

Mark reached up and grabbed the pendant hidden under his shirt in his fist and it instantly lit up, radiating subtle rainbow-colored rays throughout the office. Dan's face began to show he was being deeply uplifted, as a childlike expression of wonder began to form. A moment later, both of them were encased in a bright upward whirling vortex of light, and they vanished from the office.

They rematerialized aboard Monti's Scout ship and Dan looked around the control room amazed, before his eyes came to focus on Monti, who was just starting to stand up from behind the console.

"Welcome, Mr. Waymeyer. I'm known as Monti," he cordially stated. "I am a human being from another world that belongs to an ancient benevolent organization known as the Galactic Inter-dimensional Alliance of Free Worlds, and we're the good guys."

Dan was grinning back spellbound by Monti's slightly larger than average appearing blue eyes, and from the uplifting vibrations emanating from his benevolent face. He was also surprised he now innately understood that Monti was benevolent, and that was that. Then he looked to Mark for more answers.

"As I said, you're about to go on the greatest adventure of your life," cheerfully restated Mark.

Dan was speechless at first and then, without realizing he was actually expressing his thoughts aloud, he blurted out with gusto, "Wow! I mean... oh my God, wow! You were telling the truth the whole time, and I thought I was just publishing another money making conspiracy theory novel. Oh my God... oh my God! So uh, well, what do we do now?"

Monti very kindly replied, "How would you like to visit one of our mile-long flagships hidden in the rings of Saturn? There you can discover for yourself the truth about what is covertly happening hidden behind the scene on your world, and what's about to take place there for the great benefit of all your people."

Mark looked at Dan and winked, giving him an encouraging nod and added, "Monti can have you back here in half a day, but you will be a completely different, far wiser person by then."

Dan rubbed his sweating palms on his pants, but he was no longer concerned for his own welfare. All fear had left him, and he felt better than he had felt at any time in his entire life.

He looked at Mark and Monti, then courageously replied with the excited zeal of a ten year old going on his first camping trip, "Oh my God, I would like that very much. Let's do it."

"You'll be in good hands for the next six hours. Then, Monti will see to it you are discreetly returned to your office back on Earth, and do not be concerned about your secretary Suzanne. She will not realize the hours have passed so quickly when you walk out of your office before closing time. I promise, you will never forget the wonder of the experiences you are about to have, and thanks for trusting me. Now Monti will send me to an important, destined meeting with the President of the United States."

Dan gazed at him greatly concerned, but Mark reassured him, "Dan, remember I said I'm not who you think I am. Officially, I am actually Ambassador Shon-ral from the Galactic Inter-dimensional Alliance of Free Worlds to Earth's leaders and people. Now I need to get the President permanently free from the Trilotew Ambassador's control, and the hidden second world government. We'll meet up after that momentous deed is done."

Monti calmly interjected, "Mark, you should know I received an update an hour ago from Commander Tam-lure and Second Commander Una-mala regarding Janice and Ted. They said Henry took Janice to meet Ted at the Griffith Observatory. Then she and Ted drove to his home and teleported to a secret government underground installation in Arizona. However, the members did not accept the message Janice gave them, and when two Trilotew agents disguised as known members attacked them Janice used the pendant, but don't worry, they are both safe. One hundred members of the secret hidden worldwide governing Council and several dozen attacking Trilotew soldiers are now permanently free from the terrorizing influence of their former perverted subconscious programming. Implementation of *The Seres Agenda* is now underway."

"That's wonderful news, Monti, although I really expected it to go well."

Monti continued on an up note, "You should also know that Janice and Ted are assisting Tam-lure and Una-mala with the full rehabilitation of the Council members and the Trilotew soldiers. Perhaps you would like to join them there after your mission to the President is complete."

Mark smiled and nodded for Monti to proceed. Before Dan could ask another question, Monti touched a crystal on the control board and Mark was dematerialized in another bright upward whirling teleportation beam. Dan looked at Monti to ask him a question, but changed his mind with a shake of his head, and then smiled childlike trusting acceptance.

"Well, Monti, my good man, take me to your leader," he jovially commanded and laughed, feeling extraordinarily good.

"That's supposed to be my line, friend," shot back Monti, and then he laughed with Dan.

Dan shrugged his shoulders, and agreeably nodded. Then Monti touched several other crystal controls and the projected energy view screen appeared above the console.

"I thought you would like to experience a perspective of Earth from where we are now aboard this ship," added Monti with an impish twinkle in his eyes.

Blurred images cleared on the screen, and Dan was amazed to discover he had become an astronaut aboard an extraterrestrial spacecraft orbiting high above the beautiful blue-green water covered jewel of planet Earth. He could see far below through a break in the clouds all of California, part of Oregon, and all of Nevada and Arizona.

Monti grinned, when Dan looked back amazed with childlike wonder. Then he placed both hands, palms down, into the hand impressions set within the gold quartz guidance controls.

The Scout ship had been hovering invisibly camouflaged in a slightly higher molecular frequency or parallel dimension in a stationary orbit just outside Earth's atmosphere. It gradually faded back into full visibility, the luminous blue aura surrounding the saucer shaped hull pulsed brighter, and the ship darted in a blur of light into the depths of space.

CHAPTER EIGHTEEN

THE PRESIDENT AT CROSSROADS

President Martin McCoy of the United States was standing by the curved Oval Office windows gazing out over the well manicured green lawn and rose bushes, when a golden-white flash of light brightened the room from behind him and he jumped around startled to behold Mark Santfield smiling back at him.

"Who the hell are you?" nervously demanded the President.

"I'm called Shon-ral. However, I am actually the official Ambassador from the entire Galactic Inter-dimensional Alliance of Free Worlds to you, and the rest of the duly elected world leaders. In other words, Mr. President, I'm here to help you out of the jam you're in with the Trilotew, and with all the dominated misguided secret world government members."

A moment later, the beam weapons concealed inside the Oval Office walls at twelve different locations suddenly opened fire on Mark with radiant thick green beams of energy. The pendant hidden under his shirt instantly flashed to life, emanating a transparent golden spherical shield that surrounded him. The sizzling green beams hit the luminous sphere, deflected back to the walls and vaporized all the concealed weapons into oblivion. The smoke quickly faded and vanished leaving burned round foot-wide holes in a dozen places around the room and ceiling.

The energy shield surrounding Mark suddenly vanished, just as the Trilotew Ambassador Grotzil materialized behind him slowly reaching out to strangle Mark with the long sharp nailed grasping fingers of both his reptilian hands. Then he suddenly lunged forward to grasp Mark's neck and the glowing pendant hidden under his shirt immediately emitted two fiery rays that darted around both sides of Mark's body to instantly burn the Ambassador's hands into blackened stumps at the wrists. The shocked Trilotew Ambassador backed away screaming in agony, while Martin helplessly looked on aghast at all that was unexpectedly happening before him. Mark spun around, grasping the pendant under his shirt with his clenched fist, and two blue widening beams of energy darted from it to envelope the Ambassador's entire body in a halo of rainbow colored light. Still screaming, the Ambassador's hands miraculously rematerialized unharmed. He gazed astounded down at them and grinned great relief. Then he looked up at Mark and gratefully bowed before him.

He was beginning to delightfully discover his subconscious evil nature was miraculously gone and he asked very much amazed, "What did you do to me?"

"I didn't do this to you," shot back Mark benevolently. "The special Ray that accomplished what you are experiencing is a gift to the entire Galactic Alliance, the Trilotew, and all life. It comes from a far, far higher dimension beyond the entire physical universes. You are now experiencing your true nature. If you are willing, after you return aboard your mother ship, you can discover the suppressed truth about how your white-winged relatives from a parallel dimension captured your entire culture so long ago. They genetically perverted all of you to carry out their evil intentions throughout this galaxy, before the Galactic Alliance stopped them. Are you willing to be completely set free?"

Ambassador Grotzil started to cry, while he was also blissfully smiling for the first time in his life, and his hardened facial characteristics softened before Mark's and the astounded President's eyes.

"Wait a minute," interrupted President McCoy, "I recognize

you. You are the Mark Santfield that wrote that conspiracy theory book. How did you get into this office, and what are you doing to the Trilotew Ambassador?"

Mark turned, kindly smiled at the President and replied, "Mr. President, I was sent here by the Galactic Alliance to make you aware that you have been under the subversive technological brainwashing of the Trilotew to carry out their mission to not only enslave this planet, but to utilize the world's populace as a food source. This is the same kind of perverted genetic programming another more monstrous race used to capture the ancient Trilotew ancestors over five hundred thousand years ago. Since then, the Trilotew have been automatically carrying out that subconscious program without awareness of the fact that back then our friends of the Galactic Alliance from the Andromeda galaxy permanently removed that terrible race from this galaxy. Mr. President, you are suffering from the effects of a subconscious projection control device this Trilotew Ambassador is carrying in his pocket at this very moment."

Martin's mystified face revealed this was beyond his understanding and his skeptical fear was unmistakable. Try as he might, he also discovered that he could not make his body move. Mark boldly walked up to the Trilotew Ambassador, reached into his pocket and pulled out an elongated triangular metallic device with several multi-colored luminous buttons on its polished surface.

Mark handed the device to the Ambassador and calmly stated, "Now, do the right thing and set President McCoy free from the effect of this vile thing."

To the President's dismay, Ambassador Grotzil graciously accepted the device. Then he touched several buttons on its surface that flashed on, and Martin blinked several times shaking his head, as if he was trying to clear a fog from his thoughts.

Amazed, he looked up and said, "Oh dear God, I remember."

He angrily gazed at Grotzil and hotly demanded, "What the hell did you do to the several million citizens of our planet when you took them off-world?"

The dejected Ambassador was askance with embarrassment as his green face actually turned beet-red, and he lowered his head in an agony of despair. Mark stepped toward the President and stopped again to patiently wait while he continued to hold the pendant under his shirt in his clenched fist. A moment passed, and the pendant lit up, projecting a widening beam of transparent rainbow light that enveloped Martin from head to toe. His angry expression melted away as he became aware of a new surfacing, knowing understanding of all that was done to the Trilotew so long ago by their wicked invading white-winged cousins. Then he discovered he could move again, and he gazed at the despairing Ambassador with real compassion for the first time. He fearlessly walked up to the Trilotew invader and placed a friendly hand on his shoulder.

Ambassador Grotzil slowly lifted his head up and proclaimed as his sad reptilian eyes looked down to met President McCoy's benevolent stare, "I was not in control of what we were doing to your people. In the name of the great Ancient One, I now remember everything. How could we have become such monsters?"

He looked away toward the windows overlooking the White House lawn as tears continued to freely flow down the now softer features of his reptilian face.

Mark reached over and placed a consoling hand on Gritzil's shoulder, then kindly stated, "Now you're once again your true self, and that's all that will be required of you from now on. Return to your ship orbiting the planet and you will discover something new has been added there as well."

Grotzil looked up with a slight glimmer of hope in his forlorn eyes as Mark continued, "You will find a very special golden pyramid is now aboard your vessel. Your crew is already starting to go through this same experience. Join them, and then pay a visit to all the other Trilotew aboard all your other ships and in your hidden Earth bases. You will then experience for yourself how this Ray will go with you and be passed onward, until your entire race on all your collective worlds are freed forever from the awful ancestral genetic programming they have endured for so many thousands of generations. In a short time, your race will become a benevolent boon to the entire Galactic Alliance, and your citizens will be welcomed to join us in our efforts to free up many other world systems from this type of madness."

Grotzil actually found himself grinning at the possibility, and then he humbly replied, "We would deserve under any other circumstance to be destroyed for all the evil we've done. Yet, now I realize, even as you do, that we too are to accomplish something far more constructively contributing in the great collective of life in the universe. I will never forget this meeting, and your kind words to me. I owe you my eternal allegiance to help emanate the new energy Ray that comes from those mysterious pyramids you spoke of, and I will dedicate the rest of my life to that end. You have my undying thanks."

He looked at the President, who was now standing before him with kind eyes, and he sadly stated, "Mr. President, most of those humans who were taken off-world are probably dead, and to that end I am truly sorry. Yet, I am certain some are alive, kept as slaves or for other evil deeds. I promise you on my life that I will find any survivors, and return them to you. Please trust me in this."

As the now greatly changed Supreme Illumined High Lord Ambassador Grotzil of the Trilotew slowly looked up with hopeful eyes, President Martin McCoy reached out to clasp forearms with him in friendship. Compassionately smiling, the President nodded again, and Grotzil clasped forearms with him.

"Please do that as a priority before you do anything else," insisted Martin. "It will not satisfy the great loss to the families who will never see their loved ones again but if I'm reading Mark correctly, all of the people of Earth will receive this new enlightening energy coming from these pyramids in the very near future. No doubt, the anger and hatred they will all aim toward your race when they first learn the truth about your hidden existence on this planet, and what was done to some of their relatives and friends, will quickly be replaced with knowing benevolent understanding by the wondrous new Ray."

For the first time, Ambassador Grotzil smiled with great relief.

President McCoy then hopefully looked at Mark and asked, "Ambassador Shon-ral is it?" Mark nodded and the President continued, "Please accept my deepest apology for having conspired with the Trilotew to have you killed. As you know, I did not realize what I was doing. From now on, I will do all I can to see to it no one will interfere with your latest novel upon its publication, and you have only to ask any favor of me. If it's within my power as President, I will see that it is done."

Mark grinned, shook the President's hand and replied, "It wasn't your fault your predecessors got caught in their own lust for supremacy, secrecy, and dominance over the rest of humanity after World War II. The Trilotew were manipulating their budding thirst for power to make inroads to bring the secret second world government under their seductive control. If you understand this now, all is well. The benevolent neutralization of the misguided looming annihilation of the Earth has begun. Mr. President, you must also understand that if the Trilotew had been allowed to continue their secret operations the consequence, known without a shadow of doubt from galactic history regarding past similar situations on other worlds, would eventually have resulted in the unexpected and unanticipated misuse of your secret weapons. The subsequent destruction of the entire planet Earth would have been the result. The Trilotew would simply abandon this planet to embark on a quest to conquer some other world. Now, all that has changed forever.

"Our next big problem will be to safely extricate the remaining hidden world government members from the hypnotic control they are under, and then send home any remaining Trilotew who are present among them. With your permission, I will leave you now. Remember, you will have an unseen protection around you, as will Trilotew Ambassador Grotzil. From this moment on, both of you can go forward doing what you know to be right, and the dark forces will have no power to stop you in any way. Will that meet with both your approvals?"

"Yes, indeed it does," exuberantly replied Martin, and Grotzil smiled, affirmatively nodding. "I've been so depressed lately," continued Martin, "now everything has changed for the better and you will always have my grateful thanks. You will be welcomed back here at anytime. Goodbye for now, my friend."

Mark graciously nodded at President Martin McCoy and Trilotew Ambassador Grotzil, and Grotzil gratefully nodded back.

The newly benevolently transformed Trilotew Ambassador then reverently bowed before the President and humbly stated, "I will return now to our command ship and contact the fleet commander of our hidden bases under the great Amazon jungle in Brazil and deep in the Congo jungle of Africa. I believe my Trilotew warriors there will need some changing before they rejoin our ships orbiting the poles of your planet."

Then he touched a button on his hand-held device and a moment later, a whirling upward spiral of bright energy surrounded him and he vanished inside a teleportation beam.

Mark gazed at Martin and cheerfully stated, "It's time for me to return aboard a Scout ship to visit a good friend. I will be in touch. Farewell."

He grabbed his pendant again, touched it six times, and he too vanished before the astonished eyes of the President.

Mark reappeared aboard Boun-tama's (Mr. Crystal's) Scout ship pleased with his recent accomplishment and declared, "Boun-tama, my friend, now President Martin McCoy of the United States and Trilotew Ambassador Grotzil are finally freed from tyranny. *The Seres Agenda* is now officially underway on Earth."

Already jubilant, Boun-tama stood up from behind the console grinning, walked over to Mark and clasped forearms with him.

"Well done, Ambassador Shon-ral. Well done indeed," he enthusiastically proclaimed. "A new day is finally dawning throughout the universe. I will relay your success to Monti, Janice, and the others. However, we must also remember that a spy remains hidden somewhere within the ranks of the Galactic Alliance. Once this news gets out the Trilotew will make their next move, and we will discreetly watch them to expose the spy."

"Boun-tama, that is a relief. Everything is proceeding as planned. Now if you would be so kind, perhaps it would be good if I was returned to meet up with Janice to carry out our supposed romance and marriage back on Earth, and I must get my next book published. Do you think Mrs. Crystal, I mean, Lean-tala, would mind your being late for dinner?"

Mark chuckled with Boun-tama over his own seemingly trivial, lighthearted statement, just to vent relief from all that had recently happened to him.

Then Boun-tama added, "Janice is back at the Mt. Shasta base with her foster Earth father, Ted. We can be back there in under a half-hour and I'm certain they will both have their own stories to tell."

"You can be sure of that, my friend," cheerfully replied Mark. "From what I heard, they also had a long day."

Back at the White House, the now gratefully transformed President Martin McCoy turned away from gazing out through the Oval Office windows at the verdant, well kept grounds. He picked up the phone handset on the desk and paused grinning to briefly reflect on all that just happened.

Then he punched a button, put the receiver to his ear, and commanded, "Susan, contact all the Joint Chiefs and the entire cabinet, and have them come to the White House immediately. Then get my wife on the phone."

"Yes, Mr. President, right away," respectfully replied his younger sounding secretary on the other end of the line.

THE
TRILOTEW ARMADA
TRANSFORMS

Two massive, oval-shaped, charcoal-black Trilotew Medium Galactic Destroyer Class mother ships nearly half a mile long, with the characteristic luminous red ionized layer of antigravity light surrounding their hulls, were rapidly moving down through the upper ionosphere of Earth's atmosphere. Far below them hidden somewhere in the Arizona desert was their intended target: one of a dozen hidden combined classified United States government and Trilotew underground bases. Each parent ship was being escorted by their slightly bat-wing shaped and slightly elongated triangular escort fighters with their characteristic red glow tightly hugging their hulls.

The Trilotew command flagship in the lead position that had been stealthily stationed in orbit over the North Pole for the previous two years, and the other identical command vessel that had been stationed over the South Pole were about to try and cover-up their sinister presence on Earth.

Aboard the flagship was the arrogant High Divine Imperial Commander Yalgoot sitting in his wide, high-backed obsidian textured command chair. His long forked tongue was anxiously darting in and out of his slightly elongated jaws between double upper and lower rows of long sharp fanged teeth. Six other subordinate Command Officers, four males and two females, were sitting at stations around the outer circumference of the circular command console that surrounded their superior Commander. They were busy monitoring flat vertical view screens suspended at eye level from the end of long black metal poles that extended down from the arched ceiling twenty feet above their heads. Sharp nails at the ends of long reptilian five-fingered hands were deftly touching many illumined multicolored Trilotew symbols displayed underneath the entire length of the clear touch-sensitive LCD-type control board.

Commander Yalgoot was gazing steadily at the younger male warrior sitting opposite him with an intimidating air of dominating power.

Then he angrily yelled out in the Trilotew guttural growling language, "Lieutenant Shogmot, order our escort fighters to disperse in a wide staggered pattern thirty thousand feet above that desert base, and have them ready to launch the Matter Disintegrator bombs on my command."

The cowering thinner green scaly-skinned Officer instantly lowered his eyes, bowed his head, and loudly yelled back, "At once, oh Most High Divine Imperial Commander Yalgoot."

Then he touched a lit Trilotew hieroglyphic symbol on the console in front of him, set amongst a dozen parallel vertical rows of varying sized luminous control symbols.

The group of fifteen escort demon fighters, slowly moving in triangular squadron formation alongside each of their massive parent vessels, turned downward in unison at a forty-five degree angle toward a wide desert area located in the southwestern United States. The luminous, red ionized light surrounding their hulls flashed slightly brighter and they sped toward the Earth, leaving swiftly dissipating spectral light trails in their wake.

Back on one of the two bridge command control rooms, located at each end of the Galactic Alliance flagship still hidden within the ice crystal rings of Saturn, unique events were also quickly unfolding. Commander Jon-tral and Sun-deema were standing in front of the fifty-foot wide half-octagon shaped, ivory textured, luminous faceted crystalline control console. The ship's half-dozen other personnel were still sitting to each side of them along the length of the console that curved along the rounded end of the ship's hull. They were intently monitoring the glowing crystalline instrument panels below the twelve horizontal oval view portal windows. The dozen rectangular projected energy view screens linked together along their vertical rectangular sides above the entire length of the console were on, revealing a wide interlinked continuous view of the upper atmosphere of Earth. The two Trilotew command warships were clearly visible descending below the light cloud cover fifty thousand feet above the State of Arizona. Monti and Mark's publishing company CEO guest from Earth, Dan Waymeyer, had arrived aboard and they were standing just behind them to observe unfolding events.

Dan nervously inquired, "You mean you people are about to attack those ships?" and he looked to Commander Jon-tral for confirmation.

"Their attack on the hidden underground base has started, but our four much larger undetected command ships are now beginning to surround those two Trilotew command ships," Jon-tral firmly answered. "However, we do not intend to cause them harm or destruction if it can be helped." Then he kindly stated to Sun-deema, "Please change the mode to the split-screen view."

She nodded and touched a lit golden faceted spherical crystal on the console in front of her. The six rectangular view screens to the right of the evenly divided central point of the wide curved control console changed to a view of the thirty slightly bat-wing shaped triangular Trilotew Demon Scout fighters. All thirty Scout escort ships were beginning to break from their triangular formations, and then each ship spread out over a wide area. They stopped to hover approximately thirty thousand feet above a desolate desert area in Arizona.

"The time has come for us to swiftly move the flagship back to Earth," calmly stated Commander Jon-tral. "However, Mr. Waymeyer, after this emergency operation we are beginning that is about to take place above your own home world is resolved, you can personally undergo a very uplifting and enlightening experience aboard this ship. But first, you can bare witness to the kindness we will impart to the Trilotew, even though they would not have hesitated to viciously annihilate all humans and their own warrior soldiers in that secret base under the floor of the desert." He looked down at the man sitting behind the console directly to his left and kindly commanded, "Pilot Shul-non, take the ship through the vortex to Earth and establish a high orbital position in the atmosphere above the battle area."

The long blond-haired Caucasian man, who appeared to be in his early thirties, enthusiastically looked up and replied, "We're already moving, Commander."

Dan hesitantly tried to grin; but he couldn't hide his nervousness about the seeming unreality of his off-world experience with extraterrestrial human beings, and he stuttered out, "Uh... Wha-wha-what are you going to do with me?"

"Do not be at all afraid, Dan," replied Sun-deema with a deep kindness that made Dan unconsciously grin back at her. "You will become aware of all that was purposefully kept from you, and remember who you really are beyond just this one lifetime. Your intelligence will also greatly increase, and you will be uplifted in many other ways."

"Oh, well then, that is uh...that's a good thing," he replied and smiled as best he could under the profound circumstances.

The massive mile-long cylindrical ship was already moving up out of its stealthy hiding place among the icy rings of Saturn. The luminous blue anti-gravity aura tightly surrounding the hull brightened and the ship moved swiftly away from the planet. It quickly disappeared inside the nearby invisible inter-dimensional vortex opening in space.

Several minutes later, the massive ship was already reappearing emerging out the other end of the protected secret coordinates of the invisible vortex opening located high above planet Earth. It quickly settled into a geosynchronous orbit above the Southwestern United States the occupants could clearly see beyond the observation windows far below through a break in the cloud cover.

The two half-mile long cylindrical Trilotew command ships came to a sudden stop side-by-side high in the desert atmosphere directly over the secret underground desert base.

At that moment, Trilotew Commander Yalgoot was sternly eyeing his respectfully intimidated younger officer and he angrily shouted, "Lieutenant Shogmot, order our Demon Scout fighters to attack that base with Matter Disintegrator bombs timed to go off a mile below ground in the central meeting chamber. We must immediately destroy any evidence of our Trilotew presence there."

"At once, oh most High Divine Imperial Commander," sharply shot back Shogmot standing up at strict attention behind the other side of the console.

He reached to touch another Trilotew hieroglyphic luminous control symbol but hesitated and ever so humbly cautiously inquired with downcast eyes, "Oh Most Supreme Imperial Commander, what about our soldiers down there? Should we beam them out first?"

"Do as I command at once or you will experience the agony of dying in a fiery blaze of heat and light along with those stupid humans," growled back Yalgoot, menacingly squinting his violet eyes with red vertical cat-like slits burning with anger.

Then he began to hiss between sentences as he continued, darting his long forked tongue in and out of his jaws, "Do not question my orders ever again...s-s-s-s. Do you clearly understand me, Lieutenant...s-s-s-s-s?"

"Yes, most Supreme Divine One. I will order the attack at once."

Shogmot respectfully snapped his jaws shut, and slumped down in his own smaller high-backed black chair positioned behind his station on the opposite side of the control console. Then he reached over with his fearfully shaking long sharp nailed reptilian forefinger and touched an illuminated control hieroglyphic symbol causing it to blink.

He leaned slightly over to speak into some type of transceiver and crisply stated, "This is Lieutenant Commander Shogmot. By order of Most High Divine Imperial Commander Yalgoot, set your Matter Disintegrator bombs to explode at a one-mile-depth below the ground, cluster-targeted for the main meeting chamber, and launch them immediately. Do it now before beaming out our warriors or your lives will also be forfeit."

The pale red light halo surrounding all thirty Trilotew Demon Scout fighters suddenly brightened, and they simultaneously fired red whirling balled-light energy projectiles from the rounded clear quartz tips at the front points of their slightly elongated triangular hulls.

An instant later, thirty blue energy beams coming from invisible sources in a surrounding spherical pattern interspersed between the Trilotew Demon Scout ships, and from above and below them, ripped through the air and penetrated each red fireball weapon, melting them into swiftly vanishing vapor. Before the attacking Trilotew Scout ships could fire again, they were suddenly encompassed by sixty Galactic Alliance disc-shaped Scout ships swiftly materializing into visibility. The blue light surrounding all sixty Galactic Scouts brightened, and green beams suddenly shot from the outer edge of their hulls harmlessly passed directly through the center of the hulls of all thirty Trilotew ships. The beams interconnected with each other beyond them and swiftly formed a green spherical grid pattern in the atmosphere enshrouding the enemy attackers. Within a second, the space between the green luminous grids filled in with green light creating an encompassing transparent luminous green sphere. Several of the enemy ships started to move to flee their captors but all the red anti-gravity light surrounding their triangular hulls suddenly shut off, leaving them suspended in the air.

"No, it can't be," nervously stated a female Trilotew warrior pilot aboard the lead Demon Scout fighter, located in the center of the thirty horizontally spread out armada of triangular Demon Scout ships. She touched one of the hieroglyphic symbols on her console and shouted, "It's a trap! The enemy was waiting for us and they cut off our power. We cannot maneuver. What are your orders?"

Higher in the atmosphere aboard the primary Trilotew command ship, Commander Yalgoot was now beside himself with anger standing up frothing at the mouth with his tongue nervously darting in and out of his jaws.

"Both command ships open fire immediately on those puny Galactic Scouts...s-s-s-s-s-s. Destroy them all now...s-s-s-s-s-s."

Both half-mile long cylindrical command ships hovering parallel to each other began firing massive red fireball energy weapons at incredible speed down out of opening circular portals along the entire bottom length of their curved hulls.

The roaring sizzling energy balls had not gone a hundred feet when wide golden energy beams intercepted all eighty of them, and the red energy ball weapons faded and vanished. Four mile-long Galactic

Alliance Command ships materialized in positions surrounding the enemy ships from above and below their parallel positions, emanating the wide golden energy beam weapons. Before the enemy command ships could return fire the golden beams emanating from the four much larger Galactic Alliance ships were re-directed to hit each end of the hulls of both enemy mother ships. Like liquid light, the golden energy roared over the entire hulls of the enemy vessels to surround each one in a single wide transparent oval light. Then the golden beams began to widen the oval spheres of light until they joined and encompassed the Trilotew command ships, and the red anti-gravity power halo tightly surrounding their hulls shut off.

Froth with venomous anger, High Commander Yalgoot screamed, "First Lieutenant Shogmot, self-destruct our ship immediately and order our second command ship to do that same. We will take them all out with us. Do it at once."

Shogmot hesitated and started to open his mouth to speak when Yalgoot screamed louder, "Perish then, cowardly fool!"

He yanked out an elongated clear crystalline hand weapon from a holster at his side and fired it at Shogmot. The Lieutenant screamed in agony grasping his head with both hands, while the molecules of his body burned away into fiery vaporizing atoms. The astonished remaining officers jumped up from their chairs, and Yalgoot menacingly waved the gun at them.

"Do any of you wish to ignore my orders?" he viciously growled, and the closest female officer walked up to Shogmot's station, touched several luminous symbols on the control console, and the lights dimmed inside the bridge command room.

Yalgoot deviously smiled and stated, "Now those Galactic Alliance meddlers will be extinct in five more seconds. Do not fear, warriors of the Empire. We will be well-remembered with high honor back on the home world, and the Emperor himself will honor our families."

Yalgoot then closed his eyes to wait for annihilation but nothing happened. He slowly opened his eyes again just as power to the entire bridge went out.

A three dimensional projection of Galactic Alliance Commander Jon-tral appeared above the circular command console between all the remaining Trilotew officers, and he kindly stated, "Do not be afraid, Trilotew warriors. We will not harm any of you. The time has come for you to be set free from the terrible subconscious programming you are suffering from that was genetically forced upon your ancient ancestors long ago."

Commander Yalgoot was almost hysterical with angry venom as he fired his laser weapon at the projection. The beam harmlessly passed through the image to blast a foot wide burning hole in the control panel at the back of the room.

Inside the special chamber in the center of the Galactic Alliance Flagship, the large luminous golden pyramid flashed an expanding circle of golden light the shape of a donut out through the hull of the flagship. The radiant expanding energy hit the hulls of both Trilotew command ships and slowly dissolved inside their hulls.

Yalgoot was about to fire at the projection again but stopped, terrified and unable to move as he reluctantly watched thousands of tiny golden teardrop shaped lights appear softly dropping from the ceiling like gently falling golden snow. Most of the drops passed through everything in the bridge control room and vanished through the floor. To his great astonishment, and that of his remaining officers, the luminous drops hitting their bodies vanished inside their reptilian flesh and their more coarse physical features gradually softened. Their scale-covered torsos transformed into smooth scaled skin, and Commander Yalgoot's anger washed away. Then he actually smiled, appearing quite pleased for the first time from a deeply pleasure-full experience.

"Now you know, Trilotew Commander," kindly continued Galactic Alliance Commander Jon-tral through the holographic projection. "You and your warriors are now freed from the vile subconscious programming your white-winged cousins had forced into your ancient ancestors to genetically suppress and control your entire race over five hundred thousand years ago."

Just then, large spheres of white transparent light appeared above all the Trilotew officer's heads, and they all knowingly looked up to observe scenes of horror, murder, and every imaginable terror depicted within them.

"You must each choose now if you want that monstrous

brainwashing removed from you for ever. Know that this new Ray of energy is a gift from a reality far beyond the lower worlds of time and space. The transforming uplifting effects you are each experiencing, and what you are beginning to remember, cannot be reversed by any power or being residing in the lower worlds systems."

Yalgoot and his other officers groaned in terror of what they were seeing, just as the torture images inside the transparent energy spheres over their heads dissolved into pure white light, and the surrounding transparent spheres faded away.

With a humbly lowered head, Commander Yalgoot asked the projection of Commander Jon-tral, "You mean, we are no longer under the dominating power of the Emperor or his secret terror soldiers?"

"You are all now free from any outside control by anyone, including your Emperor. Even the twisted technology his ancestors left him to brainwash you all under his control will no longer effect any of you. During your journey back to your home world other officers and soldiers aboard their ships will contact you. Know that this energy Ray will pass through you into them and they too will be set free. On the day that you arrive back on your home world, your Emperor and his staff will undergo this very same great change. From now on, I will call you friends of the entire Galactic Inter-dimensional Alliance of Free Worlds."

The once mighty High Commander Yalgoot actually started to cry with real emotional relief from the complete removal of the subconscious tyranny he and all Trilotew have been suffering from since the most ancient of times in their racial memory.

Aboard the lead-Trilotew Scout fighter, suspended without power in the atmosphere, was a now greatly transformed captain. She was sitting down in the black chair behind the circular control console humbly smiling with softened and more refined reptilian features. The same projection of Jon-tral, only smaller in scale, was also before her. She too was experiencing and hearing all that his commander was going through.

Back aboard the primary Trilotew command ship, Yalgoot was still crying tears of joy when he looked up at Jon-tral's projection to ask, "You would do this for us when you know we would have destroyed you all without mercy?"

Jon-tral replied, "While I'm speaking with you, what is now becoming known throughout the membership of the entire Galactic Inter-dimensional Alliance of Free Worlds will surface within your own innate awareness. This great truth is that the Trilotew and other totalitarian regimes aligned with you in this galaxy had no choice but to follow the subconscious terrorizing programming that was placed in them by your distant white-winged relatives. After they discovered a way to cross over from their own very negative parallel dimension to this dimension of the Galaxy they conquered your race. Then they had your ancestors initiate a long destructive war with the Galactic Alliance. Eventually, the Galactic Alliance forced them out of this galaxy and permanently sealing them back inside their own hellish dimension with the aid we received from our more highly evolved friends that reside in our neighboring galaxy or what the Earth people call Andromeda. Subsequently, your ancient Emperor had to sign a treaty with the entire Galactic Alliance members to end the very destructive war he had started. However, it was only recently that we discovered, from the gift of this new Ray you just experienced, the enlightening understanding that your entire collective races were left with the programming running on automatic deep inside your subconscious minds. They had reprogrammed the DNA of your race so their twisted diabolical nature would be passed-on from generation to generation.

"Our own ancient ancestors mistakenly thought the Trilotew were only using this outlawed brainwashing technology to dominate the races they conquered. They did not realize the same misused technology had also reprogrammed your DNA. A very long line of your Emperors have continuously reinforced this tyrant nature upon your entire race because they were also genetically subjected to it generation after generation. As you can now understand, that twisted insanity is about to permanently change for the great uplifting benefit of all life in this galaxy. In fact, this is beginning to take place throughout the vast creation of the multi-dimensional universe."

Yalgoot humbly looked up to see what only moments ago he thought was merely an enemy that was only good for enslaving or eating, and his green face reddened with shame, but it did not last long. A wave of golden light suddenly appeared coming through the metal walls of the bridge control room that appeared like golden expanding circular radio waves. They harmlessly passed right through the Trilotew officers' bodies and continued out through the hull of the ship into space.

"Commander Yalgoot, that shame you feel being dissolved away was also part of the original suppressive genetic programming that is being removed from you as we speak. You will soon remember that your entire race, long ago, was not carnivorous. In fact, they were once highly evolved, loving beings that were our friends and great constructive contributors to the entire Galactic Alliance."

"Now I know," replied Yalgoot as he confidently looked up to gaze directly into Jon-tral's eyes within the holographic projection. What you have done for us will never be forgotten. We owe you an eternal allegiance of friendship."

Jon-tral's image nodded smiling, and he cheerfully added, "We have another surprise for you and your warriors, Commander. If you and your officers are willing to discover more, I request that you all beam yourselves into your largest storage bay near your launch bay facility ten feet away from the center of the room. There you will all find something extraordinarily new in all creation has been added for your uplifting benefit."

Commander Yalgoot's eyes eagerly widened with the enthusiasm of a fascinated child, and he looked questioningly for the first time at his male and female warrior officers gathered in the bridge control room to seek their permission to proceed. They were already eagerly grinning, affirmatively nodding their heads, and the once mighty terrorizing Commander Yalgoot now grinned wide with them in the Spirit of true friendship.

Then, he turned to reply to Commander Jon-tral and stated with another wide grin of relief, "We will meet with you there."

The holographic projection of Jon-tral shut off and Yalgoot nodded to his remaining once intimidated Officers, who were now standing confident and fearless before their Trilotew Commander. Yalgoot leaned down and touched several lit teleportation LCD-type symbols on the console, and a moment later everyone on the bridge vanished in an upward whirling golden light.

They reappeared from another bright whirling light standing near the center of a large rectangular storage facility. Directly behind them was a closed wide oval entry door located in the bottom center of the long right sidewall of the rectangular storage bay. Sealed three feet tall gray plastic-like containers with smooth rounded ends, tied down with red synthetic woven ropes, were neatly stacked in a dozen parallel rows against all four walls. The open free-space centered within the storage bay was unused, and sitting in the exact middle of it was a fifteen feet tall luminous golden pyramid. Its seamless walls made out of a solid gold material appeared to be translucent to all the gathered Trilotew. They began to unconsciously grin with pleasure, while they continued to gaze with childlike mystified wonder at the new addition to their storage bay. The faint golden light radiating into the room from the top, the bottom, and all four sides of the pyramid was uplifting them.

Commander Jon-tral and his wife Sun-deema simply appeared standing between them and the pyramid kindly smiling with the palms of their right hands held across their hearts in a respectful salute. Yalgoot boldly stepped forward and returned their salute with a nod and his hands held crisscrossed over his chest. The other Trilotew soldiers gathered behind him repeated the salute.

"Commander Yalgoot, my wife, Sun-deema, and I would like introduce you and your fellow Trilotew gathered in this now sacred chamber to the new Ray that comes from a pure dimension far above the physical worlds. The radiant energy emanating from this device has already liberated each one of you from the tyrannical control that has subconsciously haunted your race to be destructive for over five hundred thousand years."

Sun-deema kindly continued, "This great gift will now take us all into our true form as energy beings of light with knowing awareness that is, and always has been, beyond the physical nature of things. Are you all ready for the greatest adventure beyond imagination?"

Yalgoot eagerly grinned at his fellow Trilotews, who were just as eagerly grinning back, and he replied, "We are all beyond ready. Please, let us remember who we are once again."

Jon-tral nodded in the direction of the mysterious radiating pyramid, and the light coming from it intensified ten-fold causing them all to shield their eyes from the powerful golden illumination. Then expanding golden donut shaped energy waves, similar in appearance to thick repeating radio waves, began to emanate out into the room from the top and from all four sides of the pyramid. The golden energy, comprised of millions of pastel golden particles of teardrop shaped light, was harmlessly passing right through all their bodies and out through the walls of the storage bay chamber. Each one of the Trilotew, including Jon-tral and Sun-deema, were now wearing expressions of sublime uplifted freedom and knowing bliss.

A moment later, an eight-foot-tall statue of a bare-chested man standing in the center of a wide white granite bowl supported by a foot-wide by four-foot-high round white granite column became visibly outlined inside the pyramid through the front triangular wall. The bald human appearing bronze-skinned male was wearing two golden bracelets on each of his strongly built upper arms. Only a white skirt extended from the waist down to just above his bare feet. He was standing upon a raised disc centered in the bottom of the white granite bowl with an ornately carved rim. The radiant glow emanating from his face rendered any distinct facial features not clearly discernible. His arms held down at his sides with palms held facing forward were pouring from them an even brighter, glistening golden-white liquid light to continuously keep the bowl filled. The luminous liquid pouring over the entire rim in a smooth sheet was harmlessly vanishing through the metal floor, headed for unknown destinations.

It was similar to the welcoming drawing power of bees to honey and the Trilotew found they were already slowly walking toward the fountain when they heard Jon-tral kindly state, "My fellow beings living within our great Prime Creator, know that this liquid light may look like glowing water. However, it actually is a new expanding consciousness liberating Ray that comes from the higher worlds down into this physical universe. The process is beginning to permanently remove all fear, and thereby emotional suffering from all the worlds of creation. A new way has finally been found to take the place of fear or evil as a way to prod beings to evolve into an awakened co-creative place amongst the great Ancient One or Prime Creator of all."

Sun-deema compassionately smiled and encouraged, "Real truth within this golden field of energy cannot be kept from you. You are all now feeling the natural pull to drink from this nectar. Once you do, you will forever leave your dismal tortured past behind you. Then each one of you will remember your benevolent constructive place amongst the stars. Now fearlessly go forward, my friends, and remember all of who you really are."

Commander Yalgoot approached the fountain first as it passed right through the pyramid wall and sat itself on the chamber floor. An ornate golden cup appeared in his hand and he grinned with wonder. Then he carefully dipped the cup into the fountain, lifted it to his reptilian mouth, opened his jaws and poured the luminous liquid down his throat. The effect was immediate as the radiant liquid visibly moved throughout his body until it began to softly emanate a golden aura. Then the other Trilotew drank from the fountain with the same result.

Sun-deema added, "Now, fellow beings from afar, the time has come for you to remember what was taken from you so long ago. Countless lifetimes were lived by you in repetitive rounds of births and deaths with no memory each time of who you were or where you came from previously."

Jon-tral kindly added, "Now it begins."

Then all their bodies simply began to dissolve into identical looking transparent bodies made of thousands of radiant blue teardrop shaped lights. A moment later, brighter foot-wide energy spheres appeared rising out of their heads, and they stopped a foot above their bodies radiating a light as bright as the golden light coming from the pyramid. Each Atma, soul, or pure spherical energy being was comprised of a white central core, surrounded by luminous colors spanning the spectrum from the white core to a violet exterior in successively widening concentric spheres or layers of teardrop shaped lights. A golden outer layer was softly glittering around them. However, the true selves of Jon-tral and Sun-deema hovering above their transparent physical bodies appeared slightly larger and brighter than the Trilotew.

Then, all the Trilotew began to clearly hear Commander Jon-tral elegantly telepathically state, *My fellow beings living within the great*

Prime Creator or most Ancient One, here in this state of true being truth can no longer elude any of you. Look about you and you will discover you can now clearly see in any direction or in 360 degrees all at once, if you desire. Commander Yalgoot, do you now remember?

Yes, yes... Yes, yes, yes, we all remember now, excitedly replied Yalgoot's telepathic voice, sounding almost breathless with enthusiasm. *Oh great Prime Creator, how could we have lost so much? Oh, this is beyond anything any one of us ever hoped for or imagined. We are finally free and now we remember who we really are. Like you, in our true form we are eternal energy beings experiencing lifetimes often in differing forms to discover our true destiny: to become consciously aware co-creative benevolent lords of creation in harmony with the one omnipresent radiant source of all life and all that is. We are here to creatively contribute new ways for Prime Creator to constructively expand through our personal journeys of exploration and experimentation in the grand universe.*

Sun-deema's sweet telepathic voice chimed in, *Yes, my Trilotew brothers and sisters, now you know the truth again. Except, this time no force or beings that exist anywhere in the vast multi-dimensional creation within the Great Ancient One can ever take this from you again. What took place here today is irreversible. The constructive expansive change coming to the entire creation is permanent. This great awakening of the One behind all life to expand creation again is now taking place within each one of us.*

Then Jon-tral added one last true blessing to the Trilotew's extraordinary unexpected and unanticipated event.

This change is now complete; however, you will all be remembering ever so much more in the days and months ahead each time the inspiration wells up within you to drink from this fountain.

The fountain then literally lifted up a few inches off the floor, floated up to the front face of the four-sided golden pyramid, and then it passed right back through the translucent wall to slowly fade from view. For a moment, they could all see its faint glowing outline within the pyramid, before the golden side facing them brightened to hide what was inside.

The Atma or true spherical energy beings of everyone, moved back down inside their transparent physical forms, and the bodies returned to their normal solid physical appearance. Everyone in the room was now literally glowing with faint pastel golden auras that swiftly moved inside their bodies.

Commander Jon-tral smiled back at Yalgoot and said, "You and your men aboard your two command ships, and those warriors aboard your Scout support fighters are now considered friends of the Galactic Alliance. Contact your fellow Trilotew in the hidden bases on Earth and this new Ray will also transform them. They will go through the same experience that each of you just went through. In essence, you will take this new freedom and greater awareness with you back home. We will now release your ships from the power neutralizing effect of this Ray. As you may have guessed, the ability for us to neutralize your weapons and the power aboard your ships did not come from any new weapons technology we developed. This all happened by the direct grace of this new gift to all life coming directly from Prime Creator operating through our activated weapons consoles. This new way of things comes from those realms that exist in parallel dimensions many, many levels beyond time and space. This is not now, nor will it ever be a power that any race can use at any time to control or dominate any other race. No thing or any being in the entire creation can change or control this new Ray. No doubt, you will find this out on your own."

Sun-deema added, "What you have all experienced here today is freedom for the first time that comes directly from the awakening and consciousness expanding new way of the Ancient One or Prime Creator. The source of all life is beginning to administer creation for the far greater good of all that is. Now be at peace, gather up your fellow Trilotew soldiers, and then take your ships home. Along the way, this new Ray will set free all other Trilotew you contact. Then, as each one of you now inherently know, one day even your Emperor will go through this same experience. We did not harm your soldiers already stationed at the secret desert base or those you had sent there. We safely sent them to our mountain base located in northern California, and they have already gone through what you are experiencing. I will now have them sent back to your ships."

Jon-tral smiled and touched the golden pin symbol attached

to the right chest area of his single slip-on command suit. It flashed once, and a moment later, he and Sun-deema simply vanished from sight. Commander Yalgoot then touched a button on his wristwatch-like device, and all the Trilotew were sent away from their now sacred pyramid storage chamber in an upward whirling teleportation light.

They re-materialized back inside the bridge control room, and then Yalgoot casually walked over and sat down in his command chair. Then he took a deep breath, smiled, and gazed with humble gratitude at his patiently waiting grinning officers and warrior soldiers.

Back deep inside the Galactic Alliance Mt. Shasta base, Commander Tam-lure and his Second in Command wife Una-mala were standing near a much larger central teleportation station. He looked down at a blinking light on the control console next to the female technician and then looked back up at the several dozen lined up Trilotew soldiers who were continuing to pass by them to briefly clasp forearms in committed friendship. Then each Trilotew soldier walked behind the console to take their place near others who were already standing upon the larger sixteen-foot in diameter teleportation pad. Ambassador Shon-ral's (Mark Santfield's) cousin Moon-teran (his pretend fiancée Janice Carter), and her foster father Ted Carter, Chairman of the entire secret second World Government, were standing side by side just behind Tam-lure and Una-mala to observe unfolding events. They were both now smiling compassionate understanding toward the Trilotew warriors who would have either killed or eaten them alive a short time earlier. After all twenty-four Trilotew soldiers had stepped onto the pad, both base commanders saluted them with their right palms held across their hearts, and the highest-ranking Trilotew squadron commander saluted them in return. Jon-tral nodded his head again toward the female teleportation technician. She grinned and touched a faceted crystal control. A moment later, all the Trilotew soldiers were teleported away.

One dozen of the Trilotew soldiers suddenly materialized in High Commander Yalgoot's bridge control room between the waiting Trilotew Officers and the other bridge command personnel. Then Commander Jon-tral's holographic projection appeared before them above the circular control console again.

He kindly stated, "Commander Yalgoot, the other dozen of

your soldiers that were in our mountain base have been sent to your sister command ship. When you are ready, you can meet diplomatic members of the Galactic Alliance by standing before one of the golden pyramids, and then just ask to make contact. Please go in peace with the friendship of the entire Galactic Inter-dimensional Alliance of Free Worlds. Farewell for now."

Jon-tral's holographic project faded away, and the now truly grateful High Trilotew Commander Yalgoot gazed at his men, who were peacefully grinning back at him for the first time. They too were free and aware of all that he now knew.

Outside the atmosphere, the golden halo of light enshrouding both Trilotew command ships and the green light encompassing all thirty slightly bat-wing shaped triangular Demon Scout ships vanished. The red halo of their own anti-gravity power reappeared around their hulls, and they separated into two squadrons with fifteen ships in each group. Each group flew back up to their respective command ships and broke formation to enter, one at a time, through an opening rectangular launch bay centered in the bottom of their parent ship's long oval cylindrical hulls. Then both command ships slowly moved straight upward another thousand feet and darted off in different directions, headed toward stealthily hidden bases somewhere under the Earth's surface.

The four much larger Galactic Alliance ships remained in place, while all sixty of their disc-shaped support Scout ships separated into four squadrons that flew back up beside the central hull of each parent vessel. One at a time, each Scout ship turned transparent just before it entered the launch bays of their four mile-long cylindrical command ships. Then the four mighty Galactic Alliance Emerald Star cruisers darted up out of the Earth's atmosphere to join the flagship far above them in space moving in a geosynchronous orbit.

FROM TYRANTS TO ANGELS

Base Commander Tam-lure was standing beside Una-mala, and Moon-teran was standing to the right of them in front of the half octagonal-shaped crystalline control console and teleportation pad. They were deep inside the secret Mt. Shasta Galactic Alliance base in northern California.

The female teleportation technician, Trel-una, still seated behind the console looked up at them and eagerly stated, "Commanders, Ambassador Shon-ral just triggered teleportation back to us from the Oval Office of the President of the United States."

A moment passed, and Mark appeared out of the whirling bright beam standing upon the circular platform confidently smiling back at them. Moon-teran ran up the three steps to the platform and they joyfully embraced, then parted. They walked arm-in-arm back down the platform steps and up to the base Commanders.

"Well, Mr. Mark Santfield," she diplomatically began looking up at Ambassador Shon-ral with a coy grin, "How will you juggle being married to two women from the same planet at the same time?"

"Well, Janice Carter," he fondly replied with a wry grin back at his home world cousin Moon-teran, "I guess we'll both have some very careful explaining to do when we get home to our own families," and they both rolled their eyes chuckling.

"You two have had quite a busy day," remarked Second Commander Una-mala with an appreciated smile. "Perhaps now would be the right time for you both to journey back home for a short time to become reunited with your true families again."

Proudly grinning, Commander Tam-lure added, "Yes and we can arrange for both of you to undergo the DNA replacement therapy we told you about to transform your Earth bodies to your original Norexilam four-stranded DNA bodies, before you are reunited with your spouses and children. This can be accomplished once you arrive back in orbit around your home world aboard the Transport Carrier ship. Then your homeworld DNA samples can be sent up to the ship and you can both go through the transformation onboard. It will only take twenty-four hours to complete, and then you will be reunited with your loved ones."

Too moved for words, Mark and Janice nodded their anxious consent. They were holding back tears of joy over the prospect of actually reuniting with their own dear ones after so many terrifying years. At the same time, they were telepathically picking-up on the intense but disciplined emotional longing to be reunited that was emanating from their families across a distance of more than five hundred light-years.

Now fully aware of his true identity disguised as author Mark Santfield, Ambassador Shon-ral thoughtfully told Commander Tam-lure, "We both came to help in whatever way we can with the uplifting transformation of Earth's hidden government leaders, and the Trilotew soldiers you beamed to this base."

"We already perceived you both felt that way," kindly replied Tam-lure. "However, they already stood before the radiant pyramid gift from Prime Creator, and now they know who they really are."

Una-mala chimed in, "You would be amazed at the complete transformation they went through to gain back their true benevolent natures. Their former terrible subconscious fear-based implants, engrams, and aberrations are no longer driving them to dominate and destroy. And now, all the Trilotew here are eager to get back to their respective worlds systems to witness how this transforming Ray will manifest upon their home planets to set free all the rest of their people."

Tam-lure added with an alluring smile, "Come with us for a short time and you can both experience this amazing event for yourselves. Then we will send you two back to your home-world Norexilam."

"Lead on, Commander," eagerly agreed Mark.

Janice curious added, "They had already started going through the transformation back at the hidden desert base, but I would really like to experience them as they truly are."

Tam-lure and Una-mala smiled at them, and then they headed out of the teleportation chamber through the triangular exit. Ambassador Shon-ral and Moon-teran simultaneously recalled how they recently falsely believed their identities were the Earth humans Mark Santfield and Janice Carter. They gave each other a knowing glance and eagerly followed the Commanders.

They soon entered the main conference room inside the secret Mt. Shasta base walking behind the base commanders, and they stopped to gaze at the multitude gathered there. To them it was now a truly odd sight to witness one hundred of the former self-righteous tyrant leaders of Earth's hidden covert government freely mingling with several dozen of their own black ops protection soldiers, and nearly the same amount of Trilotew officers and soldiers. Everyone appeared to be radiantly happy, openly sharing in excited bubbly conversations that permeated the entire room with vibrantly uplifted transformed life.

First Officer Zorbok of the Trilotew, who first walked up to Janice and Ted after her special pendant suspended his terrorizing aggressive nature back inside the secret underground Arizona base, approached them. He respectfully bowed with both his long clawed hands held crisscrossed over this chest.

"I see now that you two are actually non-Earth humans," he curiously cordially stated.

"You are quite correct," kindly replied Moon-teran. "Both Ambassador Shon-ral and I come from a planet beyond what Earth astronomers call the Pleiades star group. Seven of these stars are visible from Earth in the night sky away from city lights."

Zorbok's violet reptilian eyes lit up surprised for the first time and he asked, "You, Mark Santfield, are actually the Ambassador for the entire Galactic Inter-dimensional Alliance of Free Worlds?"

Mark smiled and nodded.

"But, we tried with all our might and resources to kill you, and that I truly regret."

"You are now free from all that subconscious evil programming that was controlling your conscious will," cordially replied Mark. "Know that I look forward to serving the Galactic Alliance in the near future as a negotiator between your worlds and the entire Galactic Alliance."

The Trilotew Officer grinned and bowed again at Shon-ral and Moon-teran. Then he turned and walked away to join several other Trilotew soldiers who were engaged in a jovial conversation with base Commander Tam-lure and Una-mala.

Mark looked at Janice to say something but three of the approaching former tyrant leaders of Earth's secret hidden second government interrupted him. All three men were wearing expensive suits with a golden pin symbol of their secret organization attached to their lapels – a rectangular gold pin embossed with a raised white alabaster pyramid and a single radiant eye suspended above the apex. Two of the men were of medium height, one aged around forty with his black hair swept back over the top of his head, and the other older slightly rotund bald man appeared to be aged about seventy years.

The third taller middle-aged dashingly handsome man with wavy brown hair and a handlebar mustache stepped closer to Mark and Janice, and then respectfully stated, "Hello, my name is Harold Van Tipton. This is Jameson Rockefeller," and he nodded toward the older bald man, "And this is Jason Armontel," and he nodded toward the black-haired man. Both humbly smiling men standing behind him nodded and Harold continued, "We wanted to thank you for freeing us from the terrible subconscious implants the Trilotew placed in us to arrogantly dominate others. We also want you two to know we will use all our financial resources and our positions within the secret government to heal the Earth. Please believe that we are very sorry for having conspired with the Trilotew to command our combined agents to have both of you killed. We would have deserved it if the Trilotew had succeeded in taking over Earth, and then viciously killed us. That you would subsequently care to liberate us from the sinister control they had over us has taught us a great lesson. What really matters is our reawakened true nature to respect all life."

As Ambassadorial Shon-ral, Mark smiled and said, "I believe each of you now know why we endeavored to free you without harm, and I will now confirm what you recently discovered yourselves. Your already warped passion for covert power and monetary control over your fellow Earth inhabitants twisted your Spiritual reason. That made all of you easy targets for the Trilotew agents. First, they subconsciously fanned your lust for power to artificially bloated heights. Then it was relatively easy for them to get you to consider creating an alliance with them by promising that your covert group would eventually gain total control of the entire Earth and all its citizens. They further encouraged compliance with their wishes by using their hidden handheld brainwashing devices to misdirect your intuitive insight to determine right from wrong. In other words, they shut down your intuitive perceptions that would warn you of their treacherous covert motives to take over the Earth with absolute ruling terror. The Trilotew probably killed many members of your secret organization that were not present at the hidden desert base when Janice and Ted arrived. They would have replaced them with Trilotew disguised by a device to make them look, act, and talk like them. Each one of you would have been next in line to be eaten alive and replaced with Trilotew lookalikes, probably within just a few more weeks if we had not intervened."

Relieved, Harold smiled at Mark's words, for the malevolent aspects of his former-self were no longer in his subconscious to make him feel ashamed or embarrassed, and he extended a hand.

Mark gladly shook it, and Harold added upbeat, "Ambassador Shon-ral, know that from now on you and the entire Galactic Alliance will have at your disposal our committed grateful assistance to help free up the rest of the world leaders, and all the people of Earth." He looked at Janice and compassionately added, "Moon-teran is it?" She nodded and he continued, "I can't imagine how horrible it must have been for you to grow up on Earth with all memory of your true self from another world suppressed."

Janice kindly smiled and replied, "All of us are now who we really are once again, and that's good enough for me."

"Thank you, Moon-teran," he replied with a relieved grin. Then he looked at Mark and humbly asked, "How can our entire organization and resources help you now?"

"When you and your associates here are returned to your desert base, call all your members worldwide to come together for a meeting of extreme importance. Many will come. However, the Trilotew who already took over the identities of some of your secret members will refuse, and they will plan your demise. Know that there is no need to fear them. Each of you is now an emissary of the new consciousness freeing energy Ray that is emanating from the special fountains within the luminous golden pyramids. Two are already in operation on the bottom of two of Earth's deepest oceans, and a third one is hidden inside a mountain deep in the Himalayas. Wherever you go from now on, and whatever or whomever may cross paths with you will go through the very same transformations each of you just went through. This will always occur before they could harm you or your families."

Base Commanders Tam-lure and Una-mala approached and Tam-lure cheerfully added, "All of your members that we brought here will be watched over by Galactic Alliance observers from now on. We are dispatching many more Scout reconnaissance ships to monitor the Trilotew that remain hidden in various locations on Earth. We will be ready for them when they attempt their next move."

Una-mala graciously smiled at the three greatly transformed men and added, "We have already assigned a number of Galactic Alliance representatives to discretely watch over your families when you are engaged in any future government activities. Once each of you have finished the complete deprogramming, you will have full use of your innate benevolent intelligence, and you will remember the many lives that it took for you to be standing here today. Then we will beam you back to your desert base. Know that from now on Tam-lure and I will be in constant contact in one form or another."

The three men were now beaming gratitude as they shook hands with Commander Tam-lure, Second Commander Una-mala, Mark and Janice. Then they walked away to give the good news to their ninety-seven other associates that were standing in various places around the chamber.

Una-mala smiled at her husband, he smiled back, and then she turned to Ambassador Shon-ral and Moon-teran and said, "And now, at least for a short time, you two have the opportunity to return home to go through your DNA transformations to regain your former original physical natures. We can have you back at your home world in under a day's travel time."

Mark and Janice knowingly gazed at each other and simultaneously telepathically replied, *Finally!*

Both Commanders grinned and Tam-lure added, "The smaller three hundred-foot cylindrical Transport Carrier ship you saw stationed in front of the command complex when you first arrived has returned. I have instructed the Captain to leave within the hour. Will that be acceptable?"

Mark and Janice anxiously replied aloud in unison, "We are in your hands. Lead the way, Commander."

Tam-lure chuckled at their enthusiasm and added, "I have other matters to attend to with Commanders Jon-tral and Sun-deema aboard the flagship regarding Earth and our approaching fleet. Thousands of Galactic Alliance Emerald Star cruisers, including a number of the ten-mile-long inter-galactic class cruisers are already on their way here. More will arrive in a second wave behind them. This should give you two at least several weeks to be reunited with your anxiously awaiting families, before you will be needed back here. Una-mala will escort you to the ship. For now, my friends, farewell."

He held his right palm over his heart and nodded. Mark and Janice returned the fond respectful gesture, and he walked away.

Janice suddenly heard her foster Earth father Ted's voice excitedly calling from behind them, "Janice, dear daughter, it's so good to see you."

She and Mark turned to see him walking into the conference and recreation room at a hurried clip. He looked more vibrant and many years younger as he walked up to his daughter and stopped to fondly gaze into her eyes.

To her amazement, she heard him telepathically continue, *Dear daughter from far away, it's me. I remember more about my true self. As you have guessed, I also recovered some telepathic ability after they turned back on several of my genetically suppressed genes. It is just so amazing. My God, Janice, all of Earth's people are asleep. They have no idea how suppressed the entire human race has been for so many thousands of years.*

With tears trickling down her cheeks, Moon-teran threw her arms around her foster father, and they hugged long and tenderly.

She let him go, smiled up at him and telepathically stated, ***Dearest foster father in the entire universe, this is beyond words for me. You look ten years younger.***

He lovingly gazed at her for a moment, and then turned toward Mark to say aloud, "Mark, I mean, Ambassador Shon-ral, I... Well, I don't know how to say this. Because of you, I have been set far more than free. I also remember a number of other lifetimes I spent on this planet, blindly seeking power and fortune but I did not originally come from Earth. Like you, I too came from the stars during another colonization period after one of the earlier polar shifts a million years ago."

Mark was fondly smiling at him when he kindly replied, "Well, I'm not who you should credit for that miracle. The gift of the special Ray emanating from many dimensions far above this physical universe accomplished that. If my own people had not located me on Earth after the publication of my first book, we would not be having this conversation. Now that you are back to who you really are, I am quite gratefully satisfied about how you so carefully raised Janice, I mean, my cousin Moon-teran. Now we can finally be returned to our former home planet human forms, and to our own families very soon."

Grinning like an imp, Una-mala winked and said, "If you will be so kind as to follow me, we will get you two back home to your families, and the long wait will be over. Ted, you may wish to go through more thorough past life awakening aboard the flagship before you return to Earth. Then you will be prepared to help awaken your fellow hidden government members."

"Commander Una-mala, I would like that very much," cheerfully replied Ted, "And thank you for all the kindness you have shown me and all the others here in this amazing Mt. Shasta base. My colleagues and I are quite anxious to get back to the business of freeing all the people of Earth with Galactic Alliance guidance and assistance, of course."

Una-mala graciously nodded and added, "Then by all means, let's not keep any of you waiting a moment longer."

She courteously waived her hand toward the exit from the chamber but before she could take a step, Tam-lure came running back up to them concerned and announced, "Dear wife, I regret to say our friend's trip back home will have to be temporarily postponed. Our monitoring ships have picked up Trilotew conversations coming from their hidden base deep in the Amazon jungle. It has been confirmed the Trilotew now have control over both the Chinese and the Russian leaders, and they have just compelled them to arrange a coordinated preemptive nuclear strike against the United States."

"Oh, my husband," replied Una-mala blanching, "They must have been contacted by that Trilotew General we set free aboard one of their fleet cruisers. My understanding is that this new consciousness-freeing Ray emanating from the pyramids cannot work through a communication link or transceiver. A freed being has to be present before the Ray can pass through them to create a benevolent change in others."

Tam-lure seriously added, "After being set free, the Trilotew General and their own Ambassador must have contacted the other Trilotew on Earth. If they tried to arrange a face-to-face meeting without their tyrant Emperor's direct order, they would refuse to allow it. Knowing the Trilotew, they would conclude that somehow the General and the Ambassador were driven insane or forced to become traitors, and the remaining Trilotew Commanders operating in other countries would have immediately called for reinforcements from home. Most certainly, an armada of Trilotew warships is already on the way. We will have to work fast if we want to avoid much destruction."

"I have an idea," confidently stated Mark with his eyes lit up. "Janice is still wearing her pendant under her clothes, and I'm authorized to transmit the Ray from the pyramid on the flagship through my pendant directly to anyone standing before me." He eagerly gazed at his cousin but she appeared sad, and he asked, "Dear Moon-teran, I know this delay will be hard but we must practice patience for the benefit of all. Are you willing?"

She sadly looked away for a moment in reverie, and then looked back suddenly cheerful.

"Mr. Ambassador, forgive me," she began courageously upbeat. "I let myself indulge for a moment in a selfish yearning to see my family once again but I let the feeling go. I'm with you."

"Oh good, that's a relief. I felt the same thing, but we are so close to freeing the people of this planet. Many of them trapped here for countless lifetimes are actually our own people who came to explore this world long ago. Dear cousin, we must see this through to completion. Otherwise, how could we rest in bliss with our families back home?"

She nodded her agreement, and Mark confidently continued imparting his plan to Commanders Tam-lure and Una-mala, "Of course, we'll need the consent and cooperation of fleet Commanders Jon-tral and Sun-deema aboard the flagship. Can you also arrange to have the four Emerald star cruisers invisibly operate over the Russian and Chinese Capitals?"

"Of course we can," enthusiastically answered Tam-lure. "I'm certain fleet Commanders Jon-tral and Sun-deema will agree."

"Then I believe, no I'm certain, we can bring to a permanent end the Trilotew role and presence on this planet," continued Mark with a mischievous grin. "When the time is right, your base personnel and all the ships we have on or around the Earth will have to be coordinated for one well timed move."

Tam-lure and Una-mala both grinned at the direction his plan was heading, and she asked, "What do you have in mind?"

"You must be prepared to beam the remaining controlled world leaders, and the Trilotew thugs controlling them, to one place at the same moment, even those already disguised as the humans they probably killed to take over their identities. Moon-teran's special pendant will shield us from any initial attacks they may try, while the transforming Ray that will pass through my pendant can free them from the subconscious terror that drives their hideous behavior. Can you do it?"

"Yes, yes we can certainly do that," eagerly replied Tam-lure."

"Can Janice and I use the smaller Inter-stellar Transport Carrier ship you have landed outside this complex as a temporary base of operations?"

"Indeed you can," enthusiastically answered Tam-lure.

"And we will need someone to oversee any beaming we will have to accomplish with great precision at very precise moments."

Tam-lure confidently replied, "We already have that covered. I asked our friends Boun-tama and Lean-tala to join us here in case their assistance is required, and they have probably already beamed to the base from their cottage home. I'll have them meet us at the ship and they can oversee everything you require."

"Then, once again," enthusiastically replied Mark, "As the genius character detective Sherlock Holmes in the old classic Earth novels would say to his assistant before starting a crime solving adventure, 'Watson, my good man, the game is afoot.'"

"And I'm your Watson, Mr. Ambassador," confidently announced Janice.

"Indeed you are, dear cousin," regally agreed Mark. "Indeed you are."

Then Ted hesitantly asked, "How can I help?"

"You, Ted, my good man, should first get more deprogramming freedom aboard the flagship. However, before that you will want to experience a first hand overview of what is about to take place around the planet. Then you can later telepathically communicate what took place to your fellow associates back on Earth."

Satisfied, Ted grinned, and they walked away at a fast clip.

A few minutes later, they walked out of the football field-sized, elongated octagon-shaped command structure. They crossed the boarding ramp and stopped in front of a trim muscular middle-aged man standing in front of the open hatch leading inside the Transport Carrier ship. He was clean-shaven with high cheekbones, shoulder length wavy brown hair, and clear robin's egg-blue eyes, typically slightly larger than the eyes of Earth humans. He smiled and acknowledged the Commanders and then Mark and Janice with his right palm held over his heart, and they acknowledged him back.

Then he cheerfully stated, "Mr. Ambassador and Moon-teran, it will be my pleasure to escort you back to your home world."

"For now, Captain Zin-tamal, that will have to wait," seriously interjected Commander Tam-lure. "Something has come up, and we must use the Transport Carrier ship as an emergency base of operations for Ambassador Shon-ral and Moon-teran. I will fill you in on our way to the flagship."

"As you wish, Commander," respectfully replied the Captain. "If you will all come aboard, we can get to the flagship in orbit around the Earth in about ten minutes Earth time."

As he turned and headed toward the oval entry hatch, Boun-tama and his wife, Lean-tala, approached from behind them at a good clip. They were very cheery as Mark greeted them with a warm bear hug. Then he turned and gallantly waved his arm toward Janice.

"This, my good friends, is Janice, or more correctly, my cousin Moon-teran from our home world.

Janice grinned at them and said, "I've heard a lot about you two and what you did for Ambassador Shon-ral's survival."

"Well," replied Lean-tala grinning, "It's what we do."

"Indeed it is, dear wife," chimed-in Boun-tama.

Commander Tam-lure urgently interjected, "I have filled them in and they are ready to assist you. Now, we must get to the flagship as soon as possible."

As they walked through the oval entry hatch of the Transport Carrier ship, they could hear the soft deep frequency humming of the inch-thick pale blue anti-gravity energy field and see it surrounding the ship's massive cylindrical shaped hull. A golden light grid pattern appeared across the opening behind them rapidly filling with materializing solid silvery metal, until the hull appeared seamless with no apparent door.

A moment later, the light surrounding the hull brightened and the three hundred-foot-long cylindrical ship lifted straight up above the landing pad. The two semi-spherical launch bay doors far overhead began to open at the top of cavern base, and the massive ship turned vertical as it began to fade into invisibility. Then it shot straight up and out of northern California's mysterious Mt. Shasta's extinct volcanic caldera to vanish in the brilliant star-lit night sky.

CHAPTER TWENTY-ONE

OBLIVION
OR
PARADISE

In just under ten minutes, the medium-sized Transport Carrier ship was already slowing its approach to the mile-long Emerald Star Galactic Alliance flagship. It dwarfed the three hundred foot-long Transport Carrier as it slowed to a stop to hover in a parallel position several thousand yards from the central section of the massive interstellar parent vessel.

Tam-lure and Una-mala, Mark and Janice, Boun-tama and Lean-tala, and Ted were standing on the teleportation platform as Captain Zin-tamal nodded his head to a trim, well built technician with curly brown hair that appeared to be in his late-twenties. The technician grinned, nodding back, and touched a luminous faceted crystal on the control board. A moment later, their seven bodies were dematerialized and whisked away in the bright whirling teleportation beam.

At the same moment, they reappeared on an identical pad deep inside the flagship of the Galactic Inter-dimensional Alliance of Free Worlds. With warm welcoming smiles, Commanders Jon-tral and Sun-deema were standing up to greet them directly behind a very pretty long brunette-haired female technician in her mid-twenties.

They walked down the steps from the pad and up to the flagship

Commanders, then respectfully acknowledged them with their right palms held over their hearts.

The flagship Commanders returned the respectful gesture, and Jon-tral asked, "This flagship and our other four Emerald Star cruisers are now stealthily orbiting the planet. We are prepared to act on a moment's notice."

Mark smiled and nodded his appreciation.

Jon-tral waived his arm toward the triangular exit from the teleportation chamber and said, "If all of you will follow us to the bridge command center, we can monitor the Trilotew movements before we engage Ambassador Shon-ral's plan."

Jon-tral and Sun-deema walked out of the room followed in order by Mark, Janice, Ted, Boun-tama, Lean-tala, and then Tam-lure and Una-mala.

They walked into the command bridge through the triangular hallway entrance and continued until Jon-tral and Sun-deema stopped in front of the waist-high central command station, centered in the half octagon-shaped control console that curved like a half-moon below the horizontal oval space view windows.

Jon-tral kindly asked the gracefully beautiful young female technician, who was sitting in front of the console diligently gazing down at the crystalline control board, "Jin-trean, please activate the surrounding view screen."

Like a graceful swan, she lifted her head up on a long slender neck, turned to face the Commander and cheerfully replied, "As you wish, Commander, and welcome back everyone."

She turned back around and touched a luminous crystal control, and the eight horizontal oval energy view screens connected end-to-end appeared projected along the top length of the curved control complex. All of Asia, including Russia and China, appeared as a single large image spread across the series of screens that provided the overview from a hundred miles above the planet. The image zoomed closer to gradually focus on China and continued to zoom downward until a large government complex in Beijing came into clear focus. Then the image switched to a large interior office within the government-building complex. A slightly rotund sixty-year-old Chinese President with gray streaked hair, black-rimmed glasses, and an expensive three-piece blue suit was standing behind his large cherry wood desk. A tall thin Chinese man with glaring black eyes, black wavy hair, and wearing a dark-blue suit was standing right behind him. The Chinese flag with a single red star draped down from a golden metal pole was behind them. A stiff, fully extended plastic Chinese flag on a small wooden stand was sitting on the middle front edge of the desk. The taller man pulled his right hand out of his suit pocket holding in his clenched fist one of the Trilotew subconscious programming devices. He pointed it at the back of the Chinese President's head, pushed a button, and then quickly stuffed it back into his suit pocket.

Then he sneered at the back of the President's head, mocked-up a smile and stated in Mandarin Chinese, "Mr. President, you know what we must do now that we have the full cooperation of the Russian President."

The translation into English simultaneously appeared across the bottom of the view screens back on the Galactic Alliance flagship, and the silent observers continued to watch. The Chinese President blinked several times and his blank expression transformed into a devilishly cunning grin. Then he nodded his agreement as he reached down and touched one of ten buttons on the back edge of the desk with his forefinger. The yellow wall to their right slid up into the ceiling, revealing a turning on rectangular twenty feet wide and ten feet high LCD-type television screen. The solidly built Russian President in his sixties with gray hair parted on the side wearing a black suit came into focus. He was standing behind his large dark wood desk somewhere in the Kremlin government complex in Moscow. Standing behind him was a taller lanky Caucasian man with penetrating dark brown eyes and short brown hair, wearing a more modest dark suit. He was staring at the back of the President's head with malicious glee, while he was just stuffing another subconscious programming device back inside his suit coat pocket.

The Russian President's blank look suddenly transformed into devilish glee as the taller man mocked up a respectful smile and stated in Russian, "Mr. President, you know what we must do to stop the United States President from threatening our plans. We know he has left our worldwide hidden organization. Now he will attempt to destroy us with his new Galactic Alliance allies."

The translation from Russian to English also simultaneously appeared across the bottom of the view screens in the bridge control room aboard the Galactic Alliance flagship, and the Russian President asked, "Are you ready, Mr. President of the great Chinese nation?"

The Chinese President smiled back with equal malicious intent and replied this time in English, "Yes, Mr. President of the proud Russian republic. My generals are now in communication with your generals. The time is set for eight P.M. tonight. We are ready to launch our entire ground and space based nuclear missile arsenals."

The Russian President proudly confirmed, "We also have our orbital platforms and ground based missile units ready for launch."

Back on the command bridge of the Galactic Alliance flagship, the very serious facial expressions of everyone said it all without words.

Then Mark's eyes brightened with a sudden realization and he asked Jon-tral, "Commander, how much time does that give us?"

Jon-tral looked at the console in front of the technician, looked back, and replied, "That gives us just under two hours to stop this madness."

Mark enthusiastically continued, "Can you have two of the large fleet cruisers invisibly hovering over Moscow, and the other two invisibly hovering over Beijing within the hour?"

Commander Jon-tral curiously replied, "Yes, we can arrange that, but what are you suggesting?"

Grinning like an imp, Mark asked, "Can they be ready to beam up the Russian and Chinese Presidents, along with those two disguised Trilotew thugs controlling them at the same instant? Can you then beam them to the Oval Office in the White House in Washington, D.C.?"

"Yes, we can certainly accomplish that," more curiously replied Jon-tral.

"Can you also neutralize their launch computers both on the ground and in space?" eagerly continued Mark.

"Yes, of course," he confidently replied. "But we don't need to accomplish that from the ships. A device with that capability was installed long ago back at the Mt. Shasta base," and then he nodded at Commanders Tam-lure and Una-mala.

Tam-lure confidently added, "Mark, that device back at the base can neutralize any power system or computer device worldwide, if the emergency need should arise. In fact, we were compelled to secretly use it twelve times on Earth through our Scout Class ships during the Cold War between the United States and the former Soviet Union, after the fools on one side or the other actually pushed the button to annihilate the planet. During those times, we had no authorization to directly interfere with the affairs of Earth governments according to strict treaty regulations with the Trilotew. Yet, we all knew how often over hundreds of years the Trilotew have broken that treaty to try and gain control of one planet or another. Because of that, we at least had permission to stop the world super powers from destroying themselves through their uncontrollable negative passions the Trilotew artificially fanned into flaming heights. The nuclear destruction of the planet's surface would have caused harm to several hundred billion beings living in a number of parallel dimensions the Earth scientists know practically nothing about. Of course, every time either government tried to push the button to engage in nuclear war mysterious extraterrestrial Scout ships would appear over their key launch control facilities and shut down their launch computers. Our Scout ships would then simply leave without interfering in any other way. Then we turned back on their launch computers with the launch ready modes deactivated. When we're ready, this same neutralizing beam can be transmitted through our four Emerald Star cruisers hovering over Moscow and Beijing."

Second Commander Una-mala continued, "To clarify several other points, both sides soon realized some power beyond their control was not going to allow them the insane use of their new nuclear toys. Of course, both governments, and in fact the governments of thirty-three other countries as well, soon agreed to keep most highly classified their awareness of far more advanced extraterrestrial beings, and what they knew about their capability to intervene in their insane affairs. Subsequently, at great secret expense nearly all of Earth's people have been kept in the dark for more than the last sixty years."

Mark and Janice knowingly gazed at each other, and Mark

anxiously continued, "We must be ready to act the moment the Chinese and Russian President's attempt to actually launch their missile arsenals."

Commander Jon-tral looked at Mt. Shasta base Commanders Tam-lure and Una-mala and suggested, "You two should now beam back to the Mt. Shasta base to prepare the Energy Field Dampening Device. The Russian and Chinese launch computers must be shut down the moment you receive the signal from Ambassador Shon-ral."

Both base Commanders nodded their acknowledgment to his request with their right palms held over their hearts, and Jon-tral returned the gesture. Then both base Commanders respectfully smiled at Mark and walked away.

Janice's foster Earth father, Ted, had remained silently observant of all that was transpiring and he anxiously stated to Commander Jon-tral, "I would like to return to Earth with my fellow freed second government associates as soon as possible. With the assistance of Henry, my General Council, I can do far more good down there than I can from up here."

"You should first finish your full deprogramming, and there is another important matter we have not told you about regarding Henry," replied Second Commander Sun-deema with an alluring smile.

Ted gazed puzzled back at her and asked, "What's happening with Henry?"

"Look behind you," she impishly replied, and Ted spun around to see Henry walking into the command bridge through the triangular entry hallway. His beaming smile from ear to ear was unmistakable to everyone as he approached and stopped a few feet away to regally bow with a comical wide sweep of his arm.

"Henry!" excitedly exclaimed Ted and Janice simultaneously.

With a chuckle, Henry shot back, "Well, what did you expect? I've been through the complete deprogramming and, Ted... I've got to tell you, it's just beyond amazing how expanded your awareness of everything comes clearly into focus for the first time. I understand you have yet to finish your full deprogramming. Let me recommend you go through it right away if you really want to be effective back on Earth."

Ted, Janice, and Mark jubilantly walked up to Henry, and Ted gave him an unexpectedly vigorous brotherly bear hug, swept him off the floor, and then spun him in a circle before he set him back down. Then Janice kissed him on the cheek and hugged him. Mark cheerfully extended his arm, and Henry clasped it with his forearm as if long lost brothers were just reuniting.

"Henry, my good man," continued Ted elatedly, "It looks like our association has permanently changed for the better. Now that we know who we really are, I can only thank you for all the years of loyalty and brilliance you gave to me. Please know that I now deeply regret having kept you, my most important friend, in the dark regarding the trap I was getting myself into ever more deeply."

"Not to worry," calmly replied Henry grinning. "That's all behind us now. If you go through the rest of the deprogramming, that takes only about an hour, you will remember ever so much more about yourself - your true self. Sun-deema has informed me after that we can both return to Earth to help liberate the other hidden government members worldwide. That is something I can really sink my teeth into, so to speak. What do you say?"

"Henry, dearest friend, I will listen to your wise council now, and do exactly that if Sun-deema will accompany me," happily replied Ted and he looked to Sun-deema.

She was already smiling back at him like a loving mother as she walked up and confidently stated, "It would be my honor to help set you free. First, we must remove the remaining veils that are keeping you from knowing who you really are, even those that occurred before this one familiar lifetime. If you will follow me, I'll escort you to the liberation chamber, as some of us now call it."

Ted questioningly gazed with raised eyebrows at Jon-tral and asked, "Well, Commander, would you mind if I borrow your wife, Sun-deema, for about an hour?"

"Go with her and get it behind you," replied Jon-tral. "When you return, Mon-tlan or the one you know as Monti, who is on his way here, can safely escort you both back to Earth. We will also send your other associates gathered here back to the Arizona base. Will that do for starters?"

Ted grinned and eagerly smiled at Sun-deema. She very courteously motioned with her hand toward the triangular hallway exit, and he gallantly offered her his elbow. Pleased by his gesture, she regally stuck her arm through it and they walked side-by-side out of the command bridge.

"Well what do ya know?" stated Henry surprised. "Now that's a brand new side of Ted I've never seen before."

He looked at Jon-tral and inquired, "Commander, do you mind if I go with them? I would really like to be there when the completely rehabilitated Ted shows up for the first time. I have a feeling we will have a lot to talk about."

"Go ahead and join them, but you will not be allowed to attend the actual session unless Ted wants you there," replied Jon-tral chuckling, and then his smile faded. "Some of the things a person discovers through this process can be really shocking, and many people don't want others to know about it."

"Understood, Commander," anxiously replied Henry. "I'll offer to be there for him as a friend, if he wants one."

Henry anxiously spun around and walked at a quick clip toward the triangular hallway exit. Commander Jon-tral gazed after him until he disappeared down the hallway, and then he appreciatively grinned at Henry's newly awakened wisdom.

Boun-tama and Lean-tala, known by the cover names of Dan and Mary Allison Crystal on Earth, also remained silently observant of all that had transpired during the last half-hour.

They gave each other a knowing glance, and then Boun-tama urged Mark and Janice, "If we must get you two to the White House in Washington in time to succeed with this plan, we must return now to the Transport Carrier."

Janice commented with a wry grin, shaking her head, "There's never a dull moment around here."

"That's an understatement if ever there was one," added Mark as he threw his arm around her shoulder, gave her a squeeze for courage, and then confidently stated, "Well, friends, let's get this done once and for all time. Please, lead the way."

Mark respectfully acknowledged Boun-tama and Lean-tala with a cheerful grin and they nodded back. Then Boun-tama kindly gazed at his lovely wife, offered her his arm, and they walked at a quick pace out of the control room, followed closely by the eager Interstellar Diplomat, Shon-ral, and his equally eager Prime Scientist cousin, Moon-teran.

A few minutes later, they were in a cheerful mood as they rematerialized back aboard the Transport Carrier ship standing upon the teleportation pad. Captain Zin-tamal was waiting to greet them with a welcoming smile, standing behind the semicircular octagon control console.

He nodded and confidently stated, "Welcome, travelers. Maybe now we can take the ship to a place where we can actually accomplish something. I assume we are heading to Washington, D.C., invisibly frequency cloaked in our special parallel dimension."

They walked off the pad and up to Zin-tamal, and then Boun-tama stated, "Yes, Captain, it's finally time. We must get this ship hovering over the White House as quickly as possible."

"I can have us there in a stationary hovering position in under ten minutes if the need is great," confidently replied the Captain.

Mark stepped toward him and urgently added, "Captain, once the ship is in position, Boun-tama and Lean-tala will coordinate our beaming to the President's Oval Office in the White House. When his military advisers tell him the Russian and Chinese homelands are about to launch an all out nuclear war against the United States, I'll make certain he doesn't prepare a retaliatory strike." He took a deep breath, looked to Boun-tama and Lean-tala, and then continued, "I will keep the transceiver pin on my coat lapel open so you two can monitor events as they unfold."

Janice added, "I hope after this day is over there will be some sort of worldwide peace to build upon in the coming months. Lean-tala, may I ask when the massive open disclosure and worldwide landing of the Galactic Alliance fleet is scheduled to take place?"

Lean-tala looked at her husband for approval, he nodded his consent, and then she looked back at Janice and Mark and eagerly answered, "After all the Trilotew secretly operating on Earth are transformed, and they are ready to depart for their own world systems, the much larger aspects of *The Seres Agenda* will be openly brought into operation. Via a worldwide TV transmission, the President of the United States will stand beside the person they know as Mark Santfield and announce that you are actually Ambassador Shon-ral from the Galactic Inter-dimensional Alliance of Free Worlds. He will state you are here to officially announce to the world that extraterrestrials exist. After that, sparks will fly all over the planet."

Boun-tama confidently interjected, "After the TV broadcast, you two will be free to take your vacation back on your home world to finally be reunited with your anxiously waiting families. The Galactic Alliance Grand Council also hopes that you will both return to Earth as emissaries of this new consciousness transforming Ray. Your presence on Earth will help to safely bridge the great constructive changes that will happen to the people all over the planet at an accelerating rate. Enormous benevolent environmental and political transformations will also be taking place worldwide. I believe you get the big picture."

Yes, dear friends, we do, telepathically replied Janice and Mark in unison with solemn nods of their heads.

"Captain Zin-tamal, get us hovering over the White House," firmly commanded Boun-tama.

The Captain eagerly spun around and headed off toward the bridge control room, and they followed close behind him.

The Transport Carrier arrived to hover in a slightly higher frequency or parallel dimension five thousand feet above the White House. It was radiating its usual pale blue antigravity aura around the cylindrical hull but no radar picked them up, and no one on the ground could see anything in the clear blue sky that day over the capital of the United States.

Lean-tala was standing next to Boun-tama behind the crystalline teleportation control console. Smiling encouragement, they placed their right palms over their hearts and nodded their best wishes. Mark and Janice standing on the pad returned the gesture as Lean-tala touched a golden glowing faceted crystal on the console. The crystalline control brightened and the two emissaries to President Martin McCoy of the United States were dissolved in the upward whirling teleportation light.

They rematerialized from the same upward whirling light standing upon the official eagle symbol woven into the rug in front of the

President's desk, just as the astonished President Martin McCoy was getting up from his chair behind it. Repairs to the burned holes in the Oval Office walls were completed.

"Oh my God, Ambassador Shon-ral, what's happened and who is that with you?" blurted out the nervous President.

Mark motioned with his hand for the President to calm himself and replied, "Mr. President, the United States is about to be attacked by the combined nuclear forces of both Russia and China, but do not be afraid. We are about to neutralize their launch capabilities."

At that moment, there was a loud, frantic knock on the Oval Office door and Secretary of Defense Daniel Samuelson barged into the room out of breath. He stopped surprised in his tracks to see Mark in particular and Janice, and he very distrustfully asked, "What in blazes is he doing here?"

"Daniel, don't worry about him. I invited him. Now tell me quickly why you're here," ordered Martin.

"As you wish, Mr. President. Our early warning satellites have detected that both the Russian and Chinese nuclear missile arsenals have been placed in a launch readiness mode, and our primary agent in Russia just informed us the Generals have been ordered to make a preemptive strike against the United States at any moment."

"Daniel, for your own well being, I want you to remain here to experience what's about to take place. Now make sure the door is locked behind you," calmly commanded the President.

Though confused, Daniel summarily turned around and walked back to the Oval Office door, then locked it. Then he turned around for some answers.

Janice carefully observed Daniel's nervousness as he began to slowly back up against the Oval Office door. She touched her pendant under her blouse and it briefly flashed. Daniel suddenly stopped in his tracks and shook his head as if he was coming out of some kind of trance.

He gazed amazed at Janice, Mark, and the President, and then asked, "What's happening to me? I suddenly feel so good and now, I remember that I never trusted the Trilotew Ambassador every time he came here to visit you, Mr. President. However, whenever I endeavored to speak out, I suddenly found myself agreeing with whatever he was saying. He must have done something to me, I mean to both of us."

"It's all right, Daniel," calmly reassured Martin. "Now you are also free from the brainwashing they put us both through."

"But I thought we were supposed to be allies with the Trilotew," shot back Daniel, still mystified.

Janice compassionately gazed at him and asked, "Daniel, what does your heart tell you now?"

"It's clear that we were being manipulated by those reptilian monsters. They meant to do us all harm. I'm certain of that now," angrily answered Daniel, and then his anger suddenly transformed into compassion. "The Trilotew must also be compelled to behave that way by subconscious drives they cannot control or stop." He curiously looked to Mark to confirm his suspicion and asked, "Could that be correct?"

Mark put a consoling hand on Daniel's shoulder and answered, "My friend, you are beginning to gain back your own innate intuitive wisdom. Just go with it. Now we must leave."

"Daniel, trust your own feelings while you patiently observe what is about to happen," quickly insisted Martin, and Daniel nodded he understood.

"Mr. President and Secretary Samuelson, please let me introduce my cousin Moon-teran from our home planet. She is here to assist me with the events that are about to unfold around the world but we must act quickly."

"I don't follow you," replied President McCoy concerned. "What must we do?"

Mark calmly continued, "With your permission, I must now contact the Galactic Alliance flagship to stop the Russian and Chinese launch computers in time. May I proceed?"

Before the President could answer, the pin on Mark's lapel flashed three times. He reached up and touched it. Then he began to hear a telepathic communication.

Ambassador Shon-ral, can you and Moon-teran hear me? This is Commander Jon-tral aboard the flagship.

"Yes, I hear you," replied Shon-ral.

CHAPTER TWENTY-ONE

"We both hear you," confirmed Moon-teran.

Commander Jon-tral telepathically continued, *In thirty seconds it will be 8:00 P.M. – the designated time for Moscow and Beijing to launch their missiles. Both the Russian and the Chinese Presidents have just given the green light for their top military generals to order the combined preemptive nuclear strike. I just ordered the Emerald Star fleet cruisers invisibly hovering over Moscow and Beijing to stand ready to receive the energy-dampening beam from the Mt. Shasta base. We are ready. Stand by to hear Tam-lure's voice.*

A moment passed and both Mark and Janice telepathically heard, *Can you two hear me? This is Commander Tam-lure. Una-mala is standing here beside me cheering you on.*

Mark and Janice grinned at each other, and he cheerfully replied out loud, "Yes, we both clearly hear you. We are ready to receive our unexpected guests. I will count down from five. Then, activate the device to shut down their launch computers, and signal the fleet Commanders to teleport them all here in shielded energy spheres. After the Ray has neutralized their subconscious negative drives, Moon-teran will signal you to release them from their surrounding shields. I'm beginning the count now... five... four... three... two... one."

At that moment in Moscow and Beijing, both Presidents simultaneously ordered their top generals to launch their missiles through a special direct phone link. Standing behind each man was the taller human disguised Trilotew, scowling with devilish glee at the back of their heads.

The top generals deep inside the command and control bunkers of both countries simultaneously reached to turn a single gold firing key to launch their entire missile arsenals stationed on the ground and on orbiting satellite platforms.

However, one finger just a second ahead of them was already touching a clear red triangular luminous crystal on the central control board deep inside the Mt. Shasta base.

High atop Mt. Shasta, an identical triangular red crystal atop a silver pole extended a dozen feet above the extinct volcanic caldera floor turned on. A six-inch-thick beam of red wavering light shot from it up through the sky into space to hit an identical crystal extended from a pole out from the curved hull of one end of the mile-long Galactic Alliance flagship. As the beam passed through this crystal, it split into four beams that darted at the speed of light back down into the atmosphere. They passed through identical crystals extended from poles at one end of all four Emerald Star cruisers that were hovering above Moscow and Beijing and continued down into the Russian and Chinese underground launch command facilities.

The two generals in their respective bases did not see the red beams, invisibly vibrating at a higher frequency, as they penetrated their launch control computers and instantly shut them down. Both frustrated angry generals picked up a phone to contact their Presidents.

Having overheard both General's flustered messages to their respective Presidents, the two disguised Trilotew were frothing venomous anger. They simultaneously ripped the phones from the hands of both Presidents, and they started to gleefully strangle the back of their necks. Their hands suddenly went limp and let go with terror etched across their faces.

Both Presidents in their respective countries, and their disguised Trilotew overseers, found themselves suddenly encased in transparent golden energy bubbles that faded away.

In France, England, India, Pakistan, and several other nuclear capable countries, the same phenomenon was taking place. Transparent golden energy bubbles instantly surrounded their stunned leaders and their equally stunned disguised Trilotew overseers, just before they faded from sight.

Back in the Oval Office of the White House, many transparent golden energy bubbles containing the now angrily fuming leaders were reappearing all over the room. The human disguises camouflaging the Trilotew hovering in bubbles next to each of them suddenly melted away in vanishing puffs of black smoke, revealing their true bi-pedal reptilian natures.

Janice stepped up beside Mark. They both reached inside their clothes and pulled out their special pendants hanging from the gold chains. They held them up at chest level and respectfully lowered their heads just as both pendants lit up with radiant white light. Waves in repeating concentric circles began emanating from them that harmlessly passed right through the beings encased inside the energy bubbles, through everyone else in the room, and out through the walls of the Oval Office. The angry expressions of the Presidents of Russia, China, and the other leaders transformed into uplifted joy, a bliss none of them had ever experienced before in their lives. The coarse green-scaled skin of the Trilotew began to soften, and their facial features became more elegant and benign. Noticeably apparent to everyone else in the room, the devilish glare of their vertical cat-like red slits in their horizontal violet oval eyes actually transformed to gentler loving natures.

President Martin McCoy walked around his desk and stood equidistant between Mark and Janice.

He raised his right hand in a peace gesture toward the other eight transforming government leaders and the Trilotew encased in their transparent golden energy spheres, and then calmly stated, "Fellow leaders from around the world, and their Trilotew associates, be at peace here in the Oval Office. As you must know by now, no harm will come to you. All of you are being set free from the terrible subconscious implanted programs that were driving you to act in an insane, destructive manner."

The Chinese President gazed back at him and timidly replied in Mandarin that everyone heard translated into their own language by the mysterious uplifting Ray, "But we were trying to annihilate you and your country. Now this makes no sense to me, and I don't understand how could we have acted this way."

"Yes, he's quite right," enthusiastically chimed in the Russian President in Russian that everyone also heard clearly stated in his or her own language. "We were driven to annihilate you by the hideous Trilotew we stupidly trusted to gain more power."

A general agreement was voiced in a mix of rambling chatter excitedly coming from the other world leaders hovering a foot above the floor in their individual energy spheres. The sad downcast eyes of their former devilish Trilotew programmers were now very apparent to Mark, Janice, and President McCoy. They waited for the general clamor to die down, and then Mark touched his pendant hanging from its gold chain again. One pulsing radiant soft golden light poured out of it like an expanding waterfall. It was comprised of tiny golden self-effulgent teardrops that penetrated and dissolved inside everyone in the Oval Office. They were all greatly uplifted to a momentary speechless state of profound insight and understanding. The Russian President was the first to speak with a new found compassion to his former Trilotew controller floating next to him.

"Shaoulnoom, it wasn't your fault. You could not stop what you were doing; what you knew was wrong with every fiber of your being."

Shaoulnoom's deep regretful sadness suddenly lifted, and his newly freed consciousness gazed for the first time through benevolent eyes at the Russian Earth human he had wanted to eat alive the moment he finished using him.

"You would say that to one that would have destroyed you only moments ago without remorse?" humbly inquired Shaoulnoom.

The Russian President kindly smiled at him and replied, "Do you now know the true nature of your being as I do my own?"

Shaoulnoom thoughtfully lowered his reptilian head, then looked back up grinning and confidently answered amazed, "Yes, yes, I see it now."

He looked to Mark and asked, "Why did you give us all this great gift of freedom?"

Mark kindly smiled back at all the world leaders and the Trilotew, and then answered, "No, my new friends, this special uplifting and transforming Ray does not come from me. This gift comes to all of us from a reality that exists in a far, far higher dimension above the entire physical universe. The liberation of consciousness you are all experiencing is now beginning to spread throughout creation. It is not just for the Earth humans, the Trilotew, or any one planet or people. Each of you will soon further awaken to all that is within you, suppressed in a lifetime so long ago. You will begin to innately know that evil, an experimental artificial emotion brought into creation in the great distant past to prod beings to evolve, is being permanently retired and replaced with this wondrous consciousness liberating energy Ray. Now it is time to retire the protective energy shields that surround each of you. They were only there for your protection during this change."

Mark nodded at Janice and declared, "This is my cousin Moon-teran from my home world. Here on Earth you all know her as Janice Carter, the daughter of your hidden second government Chairmen Ted Carter. She is also here to assist you as a channel of this wondrous transforming Ray."

Janice nodded smiling at everyone in the room. Then she touched the gold pin on her lapel three times. A moment later, all the transparent golden energy shields surrounding the world leaders and their former Trilotew captors dissolved away, and their feet suspended a few inches above the floor gently touched the carpet.

The freed government leaders were immediately inspired to gaze with compassionate knowing eyes at their former Trilotew tormentors, only to discover the Trilotew were also gazing in a knowing compassionate manner back at them. All subconscious terror, hate, and lust for dominance over others was now gone.

President of the United States Martin McCoy stepped forward, indicated Mark with his hand and stated, "Since our true benevolent natures have been returned to us, let me introduce Ambassador Shon-ral to you, who is also known as the author Mark Santfield here on Earth. He is the official emissary of this new consciousness-freeing Ray to Earth and to all Trilotew everywhere. The entire Galactic Inter-dimensional Alliance of Free Worlds he represents will be assisting all of us from now on to straighten out this damaged world. If this new Ray had not been brought into existence as a gift from far beyond the physical universe, we would most certainly have destroyed this planet with the compulsive insistence of our former Trilotew associates."

The coarse, hardened scaly-skin characteristics of all the Trilotew were continuing to transform, becoming more appealing, and their sinister violet eyes with red cat-like vertical slits were actually now radiating clearly apparent benevolent natures.

The gentle face of the Trilotew Shaoulnoom blanched and he exclaimed to Mark, "Ambassador Shon-ral, our superior Commander Gonshockal, hidden in an underground base complex deep in the jungles of Brazil, will quickly discover he can no longer command any of us to be destructive or act in any sinister covert manner. He will assume the attempted control of Earth has somehow failed, and you should know he most certainly would attempt to set off a special bomb he brought with him to this planet in case of failure. Our Supreme Emperor himself ordered this. Such a device would blow the planet apart from the core outward, and it would become another asteroid belt circling in the orbit of a planet like the one between the planets you call Mars and Jupiter. He will set a delayed timer, and then attempt to escape the planet aboard the special interstellar transport he has stationed at the base."

"Thank you, Shaoulnoom, for telling me this," kindly replied Mark. Then he touched the gold pin on his coat lapel and asked, "Boun-tama and Lean-tala did you get that?"

Their telepathic voices responded together, *Yes, we have it all recorded.*

Boun-tama telepathically continued, *The information has been sent through to base Commanders Tam-lure and Una-mala, and to Commanders Jon-tral and Sun-deema on the flagship. They report they have tuned into this Supreme Commander Gonshockal in the Brazilian jungle, and they are moving the flagship to invisibly hover above the hidden base.*

President McCoy looked surprised at Mark and stated, "Wow, I could hear them in my head."

The Russian and Chinese Presidents simultaneously chimed in, amazed, "Yes, I heard them too."

Then all the others gathered in the Oval Office proclaimed amazed they all could telepathically hear them in their heads.

Mark benevolently gazed at them and confirmed, "I see your natural telepathic abilities are already resurfacing. "That is excellent. Now you will all be able to help vastly improve this planet and its people in the days to come. Before we send all you world leaders back to your respective countries, I have a surprise for the Trilotew that are present here." Mark touched his gold pin on his lapel two times and stated, "Okay, Commander Tam-lure, send him here."

He's on his way, replied the clear telepathic voice of the Mt. Shasta base Commander.

A moment passed, and then Supreme Illumined High Lord Ambassador Grotzil materialized from a whirling teleportation beam directly in front of Mark, Janice, and President McCoy. His benevolent gaze swept the room and came to rest, one at a time, upon the other transformed Trilotew.

"My fellow Trilotew, our entire race has been suppressed for over five hundred thousand years. As a result, we have been one of the worst tyrant races in the galaxy. Now that is all behind us. I have gone through a more thorough deprogramming, and certain genes purposefully turned off in our race long ago are now on. This process is beginning to take place within all of you here. Come with me now back to the Mt. Shasta base, and each of you can experience the great return to our true kind generous natures. Will you come with me?"

The other Trilotew standing in the room beside their former world leader captives solemnly nodded and grinned.

Grotzil turned to Mark, Janice, and the President of the United States and said, "Now that we Trilotew have been set free from the subconscious over-control of our perverse tyrant Emperor, we will always be ready to assist the Galactic Alliance from now on in any way that we can. There is only one more problem to solve and that is our still vicious Imperial Overlord Fleet Commander Gonshockal in Brazil. However, I understand from Commanders Tam-lure and Una-mala that Commanders Jon-tral and Sun-deema aboard the Galactic Alliance flagship are en route as we speak to resolve that problem. Once that is accomplished, all the Trilotew in this Earth sector will return to our home planet. There we can observe first-hand how the mysterious fountains of light within the golden pyramids that appeared aboard our two main battle transport ships can transform our more powerful overlords, and then the Emperor."

He reached out his reptilian arm and Mark firmly clasped it. Then he repeated the friendly gesture with Janice and President McCoy, and then respectfully bowed to them with both of his long sharp nailed reptilian hands crossed over his chest. All three returned the respectful gesture. Then Grotzil turned around to face his fellow liberated Trilotew and bowed in the same manner to them, and they sincerely returned the salute.

As Grotzil stood back up tall, he confidently stated, "Now you will soon know what I know, and each of you will remember just how many lifetimes you have already lived in tyranny to finally come to this point of freedom. Now, my brothers, come with me."

He touched a watch-like device on his wrist and all the Trilotew in the Oval Office faded away in another whirling teleportation beam.

Mark gazed at the world leaders, who were staring back at him with childlike wonder, and he stated, "Okay, now it's time for each one of you to be returned to your own countries. Please have your respective military leaders stand down, and tell them what happened was only a test. Know that a Galactic Alliance representative will soon be in contact with each of you and your top military personnel. Then you can all go through the complete deprogramming back at the Mt. Shasta base. None of you will be gone more that a day to complete the procedure. When you return, you will discover a much deeper profound wonder of life has surfaced that is beyond what you can now imagine. Know that I wish you all only the very greatest goodwill. Farewell."

Mark touched the gold pin on his coat lapel five times and the world leaders faded away in another bright beam of light.

Gazing at the President, Janice stated, "President McCoy, a number of Galactic Alliance specialists have arrived at the Mt. Shasta base. If you can spare a day off from your busy schedule, we can take you with us back to the base, where you can go through your own complete deprogramming. Other genomes in your DNA that were genetically turned off long ago in your ancient ancestors will be turned back on there. You will have a hundred percent use of your brain, and much that was buried spanning many lifetimes over millions of years will resurface. This will greatly help you to bring about the same wondrous change in the rest of humankind in the days and months ahead. Then I believe you and Mark, as well as the Trilotew Ambassador, will want to deliver the truth to the entire populace of the planet via a worldwide television broadcast. From now on, you will be able to count on the combined support of your fellow hidden world leaders."

President McCoy sighed, took a relieving breath, and then replied, "Yes, I gathered that from what just happened here, and I would like to get this full deprogramming thing done."

He looked over at Secretary of Defense Daniel Samuelson, who had wisely remained silent during the entire episode in the Oval Office.

He was grinning with childlike wonder back at them. The President walked up and threw his arm around Daniel's shoulder as if they were actually close brothers.

"Well, my friend, we won't be able to look at each other in the same way from now on. What I mean by that is now we both know that I'm actually not your superior. My guess is, in a relatively short time we won't need governments on Earth anymore like we have today, or money for that matter."

"I was hoping you were also seeing what I was imagining," replied Daniel relieved. "We will have a lot to do from now on."

"Daniel, I trust you can handle things for a day without me," cheerfully stated the President. "Please let my wife know I will be away on a special mission for the night, and that I will be back tomorrow. Now, I will go with Mark and Janice, and when I come back it will be your turn."

Daniel respectfully smiled and nodded.

President McCoy looked at Mark and confidently stated, "Well, I'm ready if you two are."

"We will have the Commanders at the Mt. Shasta base return the President sometime tomorrow," cordially stated Mark, and then he touched the gold pin on his lapel six times.

A moment passed, and then Mark, Janice, and the President were dematerialized in another bright beam, leaving the astonished Secretary of Defense alone but greatly changed. He grinned like an excited imp and hurried out of the Oval Office of the President of the United States.

They rematerialized back on the pad aboard the Transport Carrier ship, and Boun-tama and Lean-tala graciously greeted them.

"What's the status of the remaining problem in South America?" asked Mark concerned.

"The flagship is now invisibly hovering five thousand feet above the hidden Trilotew jungle base complex in the remote Brazilian jungles," seriously replied Lean-tala. "Rolling, lush, tree-covered mountainous hills and waterfalls surround the underground facility in the most dense jungle area, and there is no outward sign of any entry or exit to the base. It is well camouflaged."

Boun-tama touched a transceiver crystal on the control console and reported, "Captain Zin-tamal, they are now safely back aboard ship, along with the President of the United States. How fast can you get us to rendezvous with the flagship hovering above the Brazilian jungle?"

"We will arrive there in approximately fifteen minutes," answered back Zin-tamal's voice. "Come up to the bridge and all of you can watch the arrival."

Boun-tama then curiously stated, "Mr. President, Ambassador Shon-ral, and Moon-teran, I sense it is important you are all present over Brazil when things unravel. Please, follow me."

Boun-tama appeared confidently cheerful as he took Lean-tala's hand, and they all walked out of the teleportation chamber.

CHAPTER TWENTY-TWO

TICKING
TIME BOMB

Commander Jon-tral had his hands full back in the bridge control room of the Galactic Alliance flagship. Utilizing the secret Galactic Alliance Deep Penetration Observation Magnifyer, he was monitoring the enlarged image of the angry Trilotew Imperial Overlord Fleet Commander Gonshockal. The image being displayed extended across the entire inter-linked projected view screens in a gradual curve above the semi-circular control console. Gonshockal appeared to be taller, more muscular, and more vicious looking than the hundred officers and warrior soldiers under his command, who were feverishly moving back and forth behind him. He was standing in front of his circular command station at the back of the football field-sized underground cavern base, exuding an arrogant air of dominating power. A hundred-foot-long, oval shaped, Trilotew Fast-Attack Destroyer Class spacecraft, supported by four cup-shaped support struts, had landed a hundred feet away in the center of the smooth cavern floor. Four parallel rows of twenty blue-white triangular shaped lights pointing downward, hung from foot-long metal poles attached to the rough rock ceiling, were brightly illuminating the ship and the interior of the cavern.

Two merry men's voices approaching from the background broke

238

Jon-tral's concentration on the view screens, and he turned around to see Ted and Henry merrily chatting as they walked side-by-side into the bridge command section from the triangular hallway. Second Commander Sun-deema, following close behind them, quickened her pace and passed them by to walk up and stop next to Jon-tral. Then she carefully gazed with her husband at the enlarged image display of angry Trilotew Overlord Commander Gonshockal, spread end-to-end across the projected holographic view screens.

Ted and Henry eagerly hurried around the long curved command control console to gaze through the vertical oval observation windows. They were instantly spellbound by the wondrous, breathtaking overview of lush green equatorial rainforest covered rolling hills that receded to the horizon in every direction five thousand feet below the hovering flagship. Jon-tral smiled at Sun-deema, took her hand, and they returned their gaze to the view screens, as Ted and Henry walked over to them to observe continuing events taking place inside the underground Trilotew base.

The irate Overlord Gonshockal began to rant at four shorter Trilotew officers who were now standing at strict fearful attention before him.

"You, Lieutenant Trondshopa, were responsible for capturing back our Ambassador Grotzil, and my two generals, so they can be reprogrammed away from Galactic Alliance interference," venomously spouted Gonshockal with his long forked tongue flailing in and out of his mouth, sending spittle into the face of the terrified warrior before him. Then he screamed out, "Miserable human lover, the sentence for failure is death!"

Gonshockal leveled a long triangular clear crystalline beam weapon at Trondshopa and pulled the trigger. A searing green energy beam hit Trondshopa in the chest and he screamed as his body melted into a puddle of evaporating atoms on the floor. The other three officers stood back aghast at Gonshockal's actions as he leveled the gun at the one to his right side.

"Why should I spare any of you miserable failures, especially you, Lieutenant Skondrilm?" demanded Gonshockal, still irate.

With sweat dripping off his green scaly brow, Skondrilm timidly replied, "Oh most glorious leader, they used some kind of new weapon upon our advance scouts. It turned them into human lovers on the spot. If we had not retreated back here, we would never have returned."

Gonshockal angrily pushed the pointed transparent barrel of the weapon into Skondrilm's face to pull the trigger, but just managed to contain his outrage and backed off.

"You speak the truth. I tried to talk Ambassador Grotzil and my two fleet battle cruiser Generals out of their insanity when they contacted me. They tried to tell me some Galactic Alliance gibberish about subconscious compulsive drives our distant white-winged cousins placed into our ancestors in the ancient past. I was so irate at their voices coming through the transceiver I leveled my gun at it and melted the com-link into oblivion. Now, you three get down below and set the timer on the Matter Implosion Bomb to go off in one hour. I want this miserable planet turned to rubble five minutes after we take the transport into space to join our reinforcements. They are already on their way here from the home system. Now get moving and report back to me when it's done."

The three remaining terrified Trilotew Officers bowed and saluted him with their long clawed hands held palms down crisscrossed over their chests. Then they hurried a few feet over to a staircase and descended below the cavern level.

"Sir," elegantly inquired Ted aboard the Galactic Alliance flagship, "how could I have ever done other than I did back there on that psychologically and genetically imprisoned planet Earth?"

Then he just shook his head amazed at how he could ever have been the way he was before his true self and true benevolent nature had fully re-surfaced.

I thank Prime Creator that you and the gracious Sun-deema were here for us, telepathically continued Ted deeply grateful, trying out his new wings of freedom. *We would have been lost without your intervention.*

Jon-tral grinned and commented aloud, "Oh, that was very clear. Your natural telepathic ability has been fully restored."

"He had quite a rough session," stated Sun-deema. "But as you can see, he came out of it just fine.

Ted grimaced as he briefly recalled his full deprogramming experience, and then he smiled with the realization of his new liberated state of consciousness.

He calmly telepathically continued, *Yes, it was wild. Long ago, I was from the planetary group you two came from beyond the Pleiades. Those white-winged devil cousins of the Trilotew captured me on my way to Earth during one of our colonizing scientific expeditions to the planet. Back then I was the Commander of one of our medium-sized reconnaissance and exploration vessels when it was attacked by overwhelming forces. The white-winged Trilon-kal, as they called themselves, captured alive the few of us they did not kill at once during the brief encounter. First, they subconsciously implanted us with terrorizing control images. Then they took us to Earth to operate as their slaves to maintain the secret bases they had established in the equatorial jungles that far more abundantly surrounded Earth at that time.*

They were planning long-term slavery for the future of all political prisoners they had captured by implanting them with the compulsion to incarnate over and over again on Earth, completely unconscious of all that came before in previous lifetimes. I learned from Sun-deema that those monsters turned off certain genomes on our DNA, leaving us with only six to ten percent use of our brains, and our lifetimes were shortened to grow old and die before ninety or at maximum slightly over a hundred years old. Well, anyway, thank you for letting me share this with both of you. I needed to get it completely off my chest by relaying part of what was uncovered during my final session. My dear friend Henry was there to help me through it all. I know he went through his own hell because he was my best friend back then, and one of those captured alive who was put on Earth to be a long-term slave.

Then he continued aloud, "Commander Jon-tral, may I say the wonderful loving being that is your wife really helped me get through all the terrorizing vicious death implants those cruel reptilians put me through. From now on, my new friends, I will forever be available to help both of you and the Galactic Alliance."

Having also telepathically overheard Ted, Henry was proudly

grinning at his employer from Earth, as Sun-deema graciously bowed with an exuberant joyful smile and said, "It was an honor to help set you free, my fellow traveler through time, space, and so many lifetimes."

Commander Jon-tral breathed a relieved sigh and then stated, "We will help both of you recover much more in the coming days and months, and over the next several years, while all of Earth's people are being liberated. Many of them are like you and Henry. They originally came to Earth during past colonization experiments to reseed human beings and other life forms after one of the planet's many cyclic polar shifts. The planet is due for another one, but this time it will not take place. The new Expansion Ray and a host of many mighty beings you know nothing about, are in the process of changing the mechanics of Earth and this solar system. Earth's polar shift cycles are being permanently retired, along with evil as an experiment in the lower worlds of time and space."

Henry's eyes perked up and he asked, "Do you mean our world and its people will begin to experience normal human life again with thousand year life-spans, just like you do on your worlds?"

"Yes, that, and much more," cheerfully replied Sun-deema. "You two may not realize it yet, but you are both now able to use one hundred percent of your Earth human brains, and the genomes in your DNA that control normal human longevity have been permanently turned back on. You will naturally serve as prototype channels of this new transforming energy or consciousness liberating Ray that is now continuously radiating from the special fountains within the golden pyramids. Your first mission is already a part of your natural benevolent natures.

"Mon-tlan should be here any moment. His new assignment is to assist you two with the endeavor to liberate all your hidden secret second government members from their Trilotew programming. Then all the combined financial and political power you collectively have amassed can help liberate all the other human beings living on Earth today, and repair the damaged ecology of the planet. We will transform all automobiles and other devices that utilize dangerously polluting fossil fuels, as well as all radioactive nuclear materials. Teleportation stations and a completely non-polluting source of energy in the universe will take their place. This energy source is never actually used. It simply passes through the advanced devices to motivate travel, and for other needs."

"Hello, everyone," came the cheerful voice of Mon-tlan (Monti) from behind them as he walked into the bridge control room.

"We were just talking about you, Special Officer Mon-tlan," cheerfully commented Sun-deema.

"Oh really? That bad, huh?" replied Monti, refreshingly elated," and they laughed at his elevated sense of humor.

Monti gazed at Henry and Ted, and then added, "It's good to see you two again. I mean, who you really are. We are not so much different now as human beings, are we?"

Ted curiously gazed back at him and stated, "I remember you now. You were one of the Captains under my command way back toward the end of that terrible war with the white-winged Trilon-kal."

Monti briefly blushed and replied, "In that lifetime I was one of the few that escaped in a Scout ship that was out on patrol when the overwhelming attack on our reconnaissance and exploration transport ship began. I am sorry to say those of us who survived believed everyone else was killed. After the Trilon-kal were finally defeated, they were compelled to return to their hideous parallel dimension, and they were locked within it with the assistance of our secret friends from Medulonta, or what Earth people call the Andromeda galaxy. I lived to a little over one thousand one hundred years in that lifetime. I have been reincarnating ever since on my home world with all memory of my former lives intact. You and Henry now know this is the way for normal human beings to continue to evolve, to expand their consciousness toward one day becoming a truly capable co-creator with the one source behind all life we call Prime Creator."

Commander Jon-tral interrupted, "It's good to have you back Mon-tlan, but I must curtail the amenities for now. Time is very short before that Trilotew Overlord Commander down there tries to destroy Earth and escape. He just set the timer on their Matter Disruptor Implosion bomb located on a lower level of the jungle base. We have less than an hour now to destroy it and capture him or the Earth will be gone. I have explained to Ted and Henry that you will take them back to Ted's house, and remain with them to assist with the deprogramming of the rest of the hidden second government leaders around the planet. It is now time to proceed."

Sun-deema cordially added, "Ted, you and Henry should know that Mark and Janice, and the United States President Martin McCoy are en route to us now. The President will finish his full deprogramming aboard this flagship and we will return him the next day. Mark and Janice are coming to assist us with the split-second timing that must take place in just under an hour."

"You mean I won't get to see my daughter before we go?" asked Ted, frowning.

"There isn't enough time for that now," kindly answered Jon-tral. "However, you will see her again after the Trilotew problem is resolved on Earth. Then Ambassador Shon-ral and Prime Scientist Moon-teran will return to their home planet to be re-united with their own families for a short vacation. I trust you understand they are also all anxiously waiting to see them again."

Ted thoughtfully lowered his head, and then lifted it up again to reply elated, "Yes, yes I understand perfectly what must happen now. It's all so clear."

"It sure is, my friend," confirmed Henry on a cheerful supportive note.

"We want you and Henry to wear a special pendant suspended from a gold chain tucked under your clothes," sweetly continued Sun-deema. "It connects directly to the pyramid aboard this ship. You will know what to do with them when the time comes."

She reached into a pocket on the side of her uniform and pulled out two golden pendants. They depicted a golden pyramid above a silver galaxy, with three blue stars set in a triangular pattern just above the pyramid's apex. She handed them to Ted and Henry. They placed them around their necks and grasped the beautiful pendant symbols to fondly gaze at them, before they stuffed them down inside their shirts.

"Well, new friends Ted and Henry," cheerfully encouraged Monti, "it's time to get aboard my Scout ship and race back to your estate, Ted."

Ted and Henry hugged Commanders Jon-tral and Sun-deema,

and then Ted wiped his joyfully tearing eyes before he confidently said, "Monti, my good man, take us home."

Monti placed the palm of his right hand over his heart area nodding to Jon-tral and Sun-deema, and they nodded back.

"Gentlemen, shall we," encouraged Monti with an elegant sweep of his left hand toward the triangular hallway exit, and they walked away just as Ted excitedly initiated a rapid-fire conversation.

"Well, Monti, my friend, will we be trained to pilot the Scout ships? I would really like that. That would fulfill an old childhood dream of mine to pilot spaceships to the stars."

"Oh right, me too," chimed in Henry. "I've been wondering about that ever since I remembered my true self."

Monti chuckled back, "As a matter of fact, that will be part of your further training curriculum in the months to come. You are in good hands. We will have a lot of fun mixed with business, as you Earth people say. On the way to Ted's estate, we can discuss what to accomplish next with your new mission."

They disappeared down the triangular hallway, while Jon-tral and Sun-deema briefly gazed after them like pleased parents, before they turned back to observe the view screens.

A few minutes later, Monti's Scout ship had left the launch bay and it was fading back into visibility as it lowered its molecular vibration just outside the central section of the flagship. The pale blue light enshrouding the hull pulsed brighter and the ship darted in a long upward arc headed away from the Brazilian jungle back toward the North American continent and Ted's mansion estate located high above Beverly Hills, California.

The Galactic Alliance Transport Carrier with Mark, Janice, Boun-tama (Mr. Crystal), his wife, Lean-tala, and United States President Martin McCoy aboard darted into view from the distant sky rapidly slowing and fading into transparency as it headed toward the flagship. It stopped to hover alongside the giant vessel, and then it passed right through the massive ship's hull to land on the launch bay floor.

The anti-gravity glow around the craft blinked and went out. The five occupants were soon hurrying down the ramp extending from the middle of the hull below the open hatch. President McCoy briefly glanced back to notice how the Transport Carrier was very similar in appearance to the mighty flagship but much smaller in scale as they continued walking at a hurried clip over to the bi-directional walkways. They stepped upon the one moving toward the far left triangular exit from the launch bay and it whisked them away.

Back on the command bridge, Jon-tral touched a crystalline control on the curved console located between two seated technicians. The displayed image of Gonshockal walking toward his dark-gray oval fast-attack ship landed in the middle of the cavern floor switched to the clear image of the lower underground level of the base. The three Trilotew Officers that Gonshockal ordered to set the timer on the outlawed off-world bomb were working around a solid, four-foot square green granite cube. Sitting atop it was a barrel-shaped blue metal canister. Dozens of different colored lit controls curved across its middle circumference in three concentric rows. The taller officer touched a series of them and they began to blink in a repetitive series that gradually began speeding up. All three nervously sweating reptilian officers looked askance at each other, then raced out of the laboratory and back up a nearby spiral black metal ladder.

The three officers appeared climbing up the top of the ladder, stepped one-by-one back onto the main cavern floor, and then stopped in a sudden panic. They could see the pale-red anti-gravity light already surrounded the fast-attack ship and they bolted in a frantic race toward it. The last one hundred of the base personnel ran up inside the ship and the wide boarding ramp withdrew up inside the hull. The wide oval door slid closed, just as the three frantic officers stopped a few feet away. They watched in horror as the ship lifted off the floor of the cavern and sped toward the camouflaged thick vine-covered oval opening exit from the hidden base. The thick jungle growth disguising the opening dropped toward the jungle like a doorway and the ship raced out of it gaining speed as it darted in a long upward curve into the sky.

"The miserable murderous coward," exclaimed Sun-deema. "He's leaving behind his own officers just for spite at the loss of his despicable mission to Earth."

"Yes, dear wife, that has always been their way. I am beaming the three officers to the Chamber of Prime Creator aboard the flagship."

The three bewildered Trilotew Officers standing in the cavern base were suddenly beamed away in whirling golden light.

They reappeared standing in front of the glowing golden pyramid aboard the Galactic Alliance ship. Before they could react, the pyramid began emitting pulsing concentric waves of golden-white energy that harmlessly passed through their bodies. Their terrorizing fear vanished as smiles of exhilarating joy began to register on their softening reptilian features.

Back on the command bridge, Jon-tral seriously said to Sun-deema, "Now, let's bring an end to the Trilotew reign of terror on planet Earth. The rest will come later."

She confidently gazed at him and then touched a faceted deep-blue spherical luminous crystal.

Down in the sub-level of the jungle cavern base the three concentric rows of lights across the timed barrel bomb resting on the cube shaped stand suddenly sped up.

"I've locked on our Matter-To-Energy Conversion Beam," stated Jon-tral. "This is it, dear wife. On my mark, neutralize all power aboard Gonshockal's retreating ship. It's just exiting Earth's atmosphere. Ready... and now."

She nodded and touched the luminous triangular crystal on the control console next to the spherical faced targeting device and it brightened, just as Jon-tral touched the faceted spherical crystal again and it pulsed once.

The massive Galactic Alliance flagship slowly materialized into view from its stealthy higher frequency, and a radiant blue beam of light projected from one front end of the giant cylindrical ship seared down through the air to the thick jungle growth to vanish into the ground. At the same instant, a thick yellow beam shot from the opposite end of the mighty ship up into the atmosphere.

The three concentric rows of colored lights around the circumference of the ticking barrel bomb sped up again, and then topped. A moment later, the bomb imploded into a brilliant fiery white light that started to violently explode back outward, just as the blue beam shot from the flagship hit the top of the explosion. The beam then literally sucked the expanding force of the blast backward into itself and then it rapidly widened, turning the entire underground base into melting molecular white light. All materials used to build the sinister base became pure whirling energy that swiftly transformed the entire cavern in moments back into the original natural state that existed there before the perverted Trilotew took it over.

The beam then withdrew from the jungle back up into the hovering flagship, and the pale blue light enshrouding the giant ship's hull brightened. The mighty ship turned vertical and darted straight up into space, following the yellow beam it was still projecting from the other end of its rounded hull.

Gonshockal's oval transport with its red light aura hugging the hull had stopped in space high above the equator of the planet. An inter-dimensional whirling energy escape conduit, or portal to a parallel dimension, opened several hundred yards in front of the ship. The ship started to move inside it just as the radiant thick yellow energy beam darting up out of the atmosphere struck the middle of the hull. The golden light spread in seconds across the hull of the escaping Trilotew fast-attack ship, and the luminous red anti-gravity power surrounding the hull vanished in the encapsulating golden force field. The open vortex to another dimension dwindled to a point of light and faded from view, leaving Gonshockal's dark gray cylindrical ship suspended powerless in space.

The Galactic Alliance flagship darted out of the atmosphere and dramatically slowed to a stop to hover in a parallel position alongside the Trilotew ship. The yellow beam emanating from the end of the flagship shut off, leaving in place the yellow luminance surrounding the Trilotew warship.

Gonshockal was now beside himself with drooling anger. He was hissing with his long forked tongue darting in and out between his sharp teeth, as he tried repeatedly touching the LCD-type controls on his circular command console but everything was dead. He gazed at his helpless bridge command crew and pointed his hand weapon at them in a sweeping gesture. Then he pulled the trigger, but some mysterious force suddenly yanked the gun from his tight grip and it stopped suspended in the air several feet in front of his face.

It turned around to face the triangular point of the clear crystalline barrel at his head to fire itself, and Gonshockal threw his long claw tipped fingered hands in front of his face in dire panic and screamed out, "No, no, please don't kill me."

The gun vanished just as the oval images of Commanders Jon-tral and Sun-deema appeared within a projected holographic view screen image between Gonshockal and his bridge support crew.

"How dare you," spouted Gonshockal, mocking up courage to counter his obvious cowardly behavior. "Do you know who I am? What happened to our power? Let us go or face all out war with the Trilotew Empire worlds."

Jon-tral compassionately responded, "I am Commander Jon-tral of the Galactic Inter-dimensional Alliance of Free Worlds. Cease all hostility and you will not be harmed."

"I know who you are, human devil," venomously shot back Gonshockal, while the dozen male and female Officers and warriors at various command stations on the Trilotew bridge stood watching dumbfounded at what was taking place.

"In a moment, you will all understand the error of your ways. We will help set you free," kindly stated Sun-deema.

Jon-tral continued, "Your outlawed Matter Disruptor Implosion bomb has been neutralized, along with your illegal base in the jungle. As of right now, all Trilotew activity on or about planet Earth is being permanently retired. We have neutralized the bomb you set off in an attempt to destroy the Earth and you have failed. However, we will not harm any of you for your vial deeds. Although, I can't say that for your own officer you murdered back there in the jungle base."

Viciously frothing at the mouth, Gonshockal screamed at his bridge personnel, "Do something now or you will all be sent to the frying pits back home."

The others in the bridge control room did not move.

At that moment, Ambassador Shon-ral (Mark), his home world cousin Moon-teran (Janice), Boun-tama (Mr. Crystal), his wife Lean-tala, and President McCoy walked onto the flagship command bridge from the triangular hallway. They hurried up to Jon-tral and Sun-deema and Mark anxiously inquired, "What's our status?"

"The bomb this mad Trilotew timed to destroy the Earth was neutralized back into pure harmless energy the moment it detonated. Then we turned their base back into the original pristine jungle state it was in before they arrived, and Gonshockal's escaping transport is now suspended in space without power. As you can see, one irate reptilian lunatic is helpless, along with a hundred Trilotew on his ship. Now it's up to the new Ray emanating from the pyramid in this flagship."

Mark nodded and addressed the Trilotew Overlord Commander, "Gonshockal, I am Ambassador Shon-ral from the Galactic Alliance. Your presence on Earth and in fact any future Trilotew presence on this planet has been permanently retired. Although it is certain you would have killed everyone on the planet without remorse or care, we will not harm you or the warriors under your command. In fact, what's about to happen will set you free from a tyrant subconscious program that has been dominating your race for over five hundred thousand years."

"No, no, no, let us go or war is upon you all," fearfully spouted back Gonshockal, who never showed signs of any fear before in his life for anyone or anything, other than in front of his far more sinister Emperor back home.

Mark nodded at Janice, they both reached up and touched the pendants hanging from the gold chains around their necks, and the pendants simultaneously flashed a bright golden-white light.

Deep inside the flagship, the radiant golden pyramid began to pulse concentric waves of donut shaped circles of golden white light, made of thousands of tiny teardrop shaped self-effulgent lights that passed like a thick radiant rain out through the walls of the chamber. Outside the mighty ship, the concentric energy waves passed into the hull of the Trilotew carrier and vanished.

The metallic walls surrounding the oval control room aboard Gonshockal's ship began to rain the tiny droplets of tear drop shaped lights from every direction until the entire bridge was filled with them. Then they shot into Gonshockal and all the other Trilotew standing in a transfixed state of bewilderment throughout the bridge. A warm pastel pink radiance began to glow in their chest areas that spread throughout their entire bodies, before it turned white and moved above their heads to form into transparent spheres of golden-white light. Many subconscious controlling death implant memories began to appear within the spheres, compelling all the Trilotew to gaze at them. Their coarse reptilian characteristics softened, and Gonshockal himself breathed a sigh of pleasure-full relief. For a reason none of them understood, they all just simply knew to give permission to this new Ray to have those demonic implanted false natures turned into pure white light. Then, one by one around the room, starting with Gonshockal, the decision to have the dark terrifying images of torture and terror vanished was made. All the transparent golden spheres then faded away, but that was not the end of their beginning transformations.

"What's happening to us?" nervously stuttered out Gonshockal, voicing the same nervous concern the other Trilotew had thought as they stood around the oval bridge room.

Jon-tral answered from his projected image still present in front of Gonshockal, "You are beginning to rediscover your true selves and your original true natures. This is the way you were before your ancient white-winged cousins genetically altered your true Trilotew form. They diabolically implanted the subconscious minds of your distant ancestors over five hundred thousand years ago, and then used them as slaves they compelled to terrorize many races on other worlds for their selfish ends. If any refused, they would horribly suffer from the subconscious controlling images they had programmed into them."

Mark nodded to Janice again, and they touched their pendants. This time they emitted a bright white flash and Gonshockal and the hundred other Trilotew simply vanished.

They instantly rematerialized standing in concentric circles around the special pyramid chamber aboard the flagship. Gonshockal found himself closest to the pyramid as Jon-tral, Sun-deema, Mark and Janice appeared between him and the other Trilotew who were now free of fear, terror, and any desire to harm others.

"Behold," stated Mark, and he waved his hand toward the glowing pyramid.

A moment passed, and the faint outline of a brighter radiant statue fountain began to appear within the pyramid through its sidewalls that were becoming transparent. The fountain levitated right through the front pyramid wall, and it expanded to fifteen feet high. Now wide-eyed with childlike wonder, the Trilotew were too uplifted to be afraid. They could see the statue of a bronzed bare-chested bald man, wearing a white cotton-like skirt that extended from the waist to above his bare feet, and two gold bracelets around his upper muscular arms. He was standing in the center of the curved white granite bowl set upon a round granite pillar. The golden-white liquid light, issuing from his open palms held at his sides facing forward, was pouring down into the full bowl to continue to evenly drop over the entire bowl's rim like a smooth radiant curtain, before it vanished through the floor.

A Ray of light suddenly shot from the heart area of the majestic statue being right into the heart area of everyone. A moment later, all the Atma, or true spherical Soul forms of the Trilotew and the humans, lifted out of the tops of their heads. They were comprised of tear drop shaped golden droplets of light built in layers from a white central core through the light spectrum to a violet exterior, surrounded by a pale-golden aura.

Jubilant cries of amazement issued from the telepathic voices of all the Trilotew, and the telepathic voice of Gonshockal cried out elated, *Oh Prime Creator, I remember now. How could we have fallen so far? Yes, we all remember. I was trying to destroy all of you. For you to show such compassion for us is beyond my understanding. I thank you, Commander Jon-tral and the Galactic Inter-dimensional Alliance of Free Worlds, for setting us free from our diabolical leaders back home.*

The true Atma-self of everyone then vanished back inside their bodies, and Shon-ral (Mark) replied aloud, "Now that you are all your true benevolent selves again, I can officially welcome you as friends instead of enemies of the entire Galactic Inter-dimensional Alliance of Free Worlds for the first time in five hundred thousand years."

Sun-deema kindly added, "You are all welcome to meet with us and many of other personnel aboard this Galactic Alliance flagship in our main reception and observation lounge. Know that each of you have a very bright future ahead of you."

Gonshockal and the other Trilotew respectfully crisscrossed their hands over their chests and bowed as they vanished from the pyramid chamber of Prime Creator.

They reappeared again standing in more spread out positions around the Galactic Alliance flagship reception and observation lounge. The North American continent on the beautiful blue-green ocean covered planet Earth loomed large through the oval observation windows in the near background of space. Several dozen of the flagship's personnel entered the lounge through the triangular hallway and spread out to walk up and introduce themselves to the Trilotew, who were cheerfully waiting to greet them.

Meanwhile, as Monti's Scout ship sped further down into Earth's atmosphere, it began to fade into invisibility and vanished as it briefly punched a downward whirling hole in a fluffy cumulus layer of clouds. It was soon slowing its rapid descent as it headed toward the high mountainous hills above Beverly Hills, California.

Displayed on the projected view screen above Monti's control board was the Los Angeles metropolis and surrounding suburbs. Ted and Henry were utterly fascinated by the images of the city they were seeing that appeared to be zooming ever closer as the ship slowed, until it stopped to hover above Ted's ten acre estate. Then, it slowly lowered down again and stopped just above the well-manicured lawns and flowering plants nearby a large swimming pool at the back of Ted's estate.

The Scout ship faded back into visibility hovering just a foot above the early morning emerald-green dew-covered lawns. The well-manicured grass continued another hundred feet up to the Olympic sized swimming pool and poolside bungalow located in backyard of the Tudor style mansion, surrounded by Greek style green granite pillars. Then it lowered and softly landed upon the three triangularly positioned semi-spherical pods that extended down from under the ship's hull. The pale blue anti-gravity light surrounding the ship shut off, the seam of the oval door appeared, and the opening door retracted inside the hull. The ramp slid out of the hull below the oval opening and lowered to the grass just as Monti stepped out of the ship. He headed down the ramp, followed by the very exuberant Ted and Henry. Then they walked a few feet away from the ship's hull and stopped to talk.

"Monti, I have a plan I want to run by you and Henry," stated

CHAPTER TWENTY-TWO

Ted, expressively raising his eyebrows.

"What you are imagining will work," confidently answered Monti to Ted's surprise.

"Oh, you saw what I was imagining," remarked Ted with a chuckle.

"So did I," cheerfully added Henry.

"Do you think it's now safe to use the Trilotew teleportation device I have hidden in my office?" curiously asked Ted.

Monti thoughtfully replied, "Yes, we can use it now that the remaining Trilotew are being transformed. Do you know what the capacity is of that teleportation unit?"

Ted looked away, then answered, "I was told by Gorsapis and Zushsmat it could send up to twenty five individuals at one time. We could bring all four hundred remaining hidden government members in the world to my grand reception room in the mansion. They can comfortably stand together inside it, and with our new link to the pyramid's transforming Ray they too can be set free to be benevolent evolved human beings once again." Then Ted looked at Henry and instructed, "Monti and I will get to the teleportation unit to begin beaming each group to the reception room, and you could remain there to greet them with the Ray coming through your pendant."

Grinning enthusiasm, Henry nodded acceptance of his part in the plan.

Ted curiously gazed at Monti and asked, "Can you help me lock the teleportation unit onto them at various places around the Earth, if I give you their names and approximate locations?"

"I'm already ahead of you, Ted," confidently replied Monti. "My ship's sensors can pinpoint their individual vibrations, and their coordinates can be telepathically relayed to me from the ship's central computer intelligence. We can input them into the teleportation computer in your office and transfer them to the reception room."

"Dear friend Henry, you must be ready to activate the pendant Sun-deema gave you to link to the pyramid Ray the moment they arrive. They will be bewildered and angry, and some of them will have Trilotew hand weapons. Their subconscious implants will compel them to attack first and ask questions later. Each arriving group of twenty-five must be treated the same way, until we get them all gathered together at one time."

Monti interjected, "I'll telepathically contact Commanders Jon-tral and Sun-deema to update them about our plans on our way to the house."

"Well then, my friends, we better get moving," encouraged Ted, and he started walking over the grass headed toward the right side of the pool walkway to get to the double wide French glass doors located at the back of his two story mansion.

Henry and Monti picked up their pace to walk to each side of him. On the way, Monti touched the gold symbol pin on his coat lapel three times and he began to send a telepathic communication.

Commanders Jon-tral and Sun-deema, I'm reporting in with an update. I will now send you the complete visual of our plans to liberate the rest of Earth's hidden government leaders.

He heard Jon-tral's telepathic response, *Well-done, Mon-tlan. Sun-deema and I have clearly received your plans. Proceed and let us know the moment the first phase of their transformation is complete. We will be ready to take them to the next level after that.*

Sun-deema kindly telepathically added, *Mon-tlan, dearest and oldest of friends, you have our thanks for all you've done.*

Back on the flagship, Jon-tral, Sun-deema, Ambassador Shon-ral (Mark), Moon-teran (Janice), and President Martin McCoy were now beginning to cordially entertain the once tyrant Overlord Gonshockal, and his one hundred officers and warrior soldiers in the flagship's large reception and observation room. Over four dozen of the ship's personnel were already jubilantly discussing many topics with their former Trilotew reptilian enemies.

Gonshockal respectfully crisscrossed both his hands over his chest and bowed before Commander Jon-tral, Sun-deema, Ambassador Shon-ral, and Moon-teran. As he rose back up, he was smiling with joyful tears streaming down his green face.

"We are now free to once again be the benevolent beings we were so long ago." His now softer facial features, with smoother reptilian scales and skin tones, began to express remorse and he said with downcast eyes, "I mercilessly destroyed one of my best officers down there in the jungle base. He didn't deserve to be the target of my insanity."

Sun-deema reached up and compassionately placed a gentle hand on Gonshockal's shoulder then stated, "That could not be helped, for your actions were beyond the control of your true nature that was still suppressed. You can best serve all your people now and help repair the damage they have caused through history by walking amongst them. Be filled now with the joy of your awakened true self, and this wondrous consciousness liberating Ray will travel with you."

Jon-tral was compassionately smiling as Gonshockal lifted his head back up with pure joy now radiating from the softer features of his reptilian face and eyes.

"Commander Gonshockal," he cordially continued, "this is the official Galactic Alliance Ambassador Shon-ral. This is his scientist cousin Moon-teran, and this is President Martin McCoy of the United States of America."

"Oh yes, I know of you, Ambassador, but you were known to me as Mark Santfield. I had my agents monitoring your movements in hopes of having you captured or killed. Now I truly regret those actions."

Mark smiled and replied, "We are no longer enemies, Commander Gonshockal, and now I can sincerely call you a friend. I also look forward to assisting with our future relationship as the Galactic Alliance Ambassador to your home world systems."

Gonshockal nodded his thanks, looked to Moon-teran, and stated, "I also know of you, Moon-teran. Yet, I knew you as Janice Carter, the daughter of the Chairman of Earth's hidden government. We were using you to get to him over the years, and for that I am also truly sorry."

She compassionately replied, "As terrorizing as this whole thing has been over many years, I know now it was all worth it. I do not hold you personally responsible. Shon-ral and I will be reunited with our own families soon, and for that alone I could not be more grateful."

"Thank you, Moon-teran, from all of us. We will forever be in your service wherever and whenever you may need us," replied Gonshockal and he grinned wide, then bowed and turned to face President McCoy.

"Mr. President, let me say that I'm truly happy you are now free of all our Trilotew terrorizing brainwashing. You probably know I did not know what I was doing. I was unable to stop myself."

"That's all behind us now," replied Martin, cheerfully grinning back at him. "We are once again free to be our true selves. I am quite pleased with our new relationship, and equally relieved the old one is gone forever."

"You are most kind, Mr. President, to say that to me now, for I would have had you killed when we were done with you. Now I am unable to imagine contemplating such a twisted thing for any other living being. For that, I will always be grateful."

"Wherever you go," added Jon-tral with an encouraging tone, "You will experience this gift Ray beginning to free all those who come across your path. You are now considered my friend, Sun-deema's friend, and a friend to the entire Galactic Inter-dimensional Alliance of Free Worlds."

Gonshockal grinned wide at them all, respectfully nodded, pondered a new thought, and then urgently remarked, "You should all know a fleet of a hundred battle cruisers are on their way here. I signaled for them as emergency back-up before I was set free."

"Thank you for sharing that with us in trust," kindly replied Jon-tral. "Our own massive fleet is monitoring their movements. Thousands of ships stationed throughout this solar system are now invisibly operating in a higher parallel reality, and many more are on the way. All the fleet cruisers are carrying the new pyramid and the new Ray it emanates. They will free your fellow Trilotew aboard those one hundred ships before they can cause any more damage or harm to life. Now we will send all of you back to your ship. After you arrive back aboard, you will discover something new there. One of the new golden pyramids is appearing aboard your transport as we speak, and you will all intuitively know where to find it. The special Ray it emanates will go with you on your return trip. It will benevolently neutralize any weapons technology or harm that your own people or your Emperor himself may attempt to employ against you, your crew, or your families on your home worlds. Depart knowing that each of you will experience for yourselves how the golden pyramid aboard your ship will multiply itself. At the right time, they will appear aboard all one hundred of the ships that are on their way to this solar system with the intent to cause harm. Several Commanders from our fleet will contact you on your way to rendezvous with your approaching ships. Now go in peace with the friendship of the Galactic Alliance."

Several dozen of the other jubilantly grateful Trilotew Officers and warriors in the room drew close to Gonshockal and they bowed together with their hands held crisscrossed over their chests. Gonshockal gratefully offered the same respectful gesture, and then he and all one hundred Trilotew sincerely repeated the respectful salute.

Jon-tral, Sun-deema, and the many Galactic Alliance ship's personnel returned their own respectful gesture with their right hand held over their hearts and a gentle nod of their heads. Then Jon-tral and Sun-deema raised their right hands up with the palms open at shoulder level facing the Trilotew, and all the Trilotew simply vanished from the room.

CHAPTER TWENTY-THREE

A FREEDOM SO RARE

Ted opened the back door to his mansion, flicked on the living room lights, and walked inside with Monti and Henry. They walked across the living room and through a doorway leading inside the front entryway. Then, Ted and Monti hurried over to the female angel figurine fountain standing on the raised square granite platform in the center of the three-foot-wide blue granite bowl between the twin staircases. Water spewing down from her palms was reflecting the light coming from the overhead chandelier like sparkling diamonds, and rainbow colors were radiating out into the room. To Henry, the hundreds of glittering faceted teardrop shaped lead crystals, hung from diminishing downward in size concentric circles of chained together gold metal frames, appeared like a glittering upside down Christmas tree. Ted and Monti glanced at each other and headed up the right staircase. Henry continued to watch them until they entered Ted's office through the door centered at the back of the balcony hallway between the staircases. Then he hurried into the Grand Reception room through the twin set of folded-back accordion style French glass doors. He walked across the deep blue granite floor and stopped at the left side of the large green granite fireplace to await the teleportation of the first group of hidden government members to the royal sized room.

Up in Ted's office, Monti was already entering the first set of coordinates into the Trilotew teleportation control console hidden inside the room behind the now wide open camouflaging bookcase.

"Okay, Ted, I have the first group of twenty-five members locked into the teleportation unit's computer memory," stated Monti and he gave Ted a thumbs up sign.

"Well then, here we go," courageously replied Ted and he grabbed the gold pendant symbol suspended from the gold chain around his neck.

Down below in the Grand Reception room, Henry's gold pendant hanging from its gold chain around his neck flashed a gold light once, and he grabbed it in his right fist.

Back up in the office, Ted's pendant flashed a gold light once through his tightly closed right fist and he nodded to Monti, who then touched the illumined semi-spherical teleportation trigger control on the Trilotew console.

Henry's eyes anxiously opened wide in anticipation as his pendant began to emit a steady faint golden glow and twenty-five of the worlds remaining fearfully astonished hidden government members comprised of mostly men and a dozen women, ranging in age from their mid-thirties to late seventies, appeared huddled together in a tight circle a few feet away from him. Then, his eyes lit with recognition of one of the taller women in the group. It was none other than Cynthia Piermont, the snobbish and very wealthy member of the secret governing Council he had been asked to escort to Ted's party before he discovered that Ted was actually the Chairman of the entire secret government.

Two of the taller men in their late forties suddenly pulled Trilotew crystalline beam guns from their suit coat pockets. They aimed them at Henry to fire and instantly discovered they could not move a muscle as concentric circles of golden-white light began to emanate into the room from Henry's brightly glowing pendant. The pulsing energy waves, comprised of the tiny golden teardrop shaped self-effulgent lights like thousands of horizontal raindrops, harmlessly passed right through the bodies of all the men and women, and their fearfully astonished expressions transformed into childlike grins of wonderment. The two taller men holding the Trilotew guns out at arm's length watched astonished as the weapons turned into white light and vanished in a puff of dissipating mist. Suddenly, everyone could move again. The two taller men lowered their arms and gratefully gazed at Henry.

"Welcome to your Chairman's house everyone," stated Henry, proudly grinning back at them. "You are all being freed from the twisted, negative drives the Trilotew implanted into your subconscious minds. Your distorted behaviors, created by your tyrant Trilotew overseers, caused you to act as their emissaries to negatively dominate your fellow human beings on Earth. They would have killed all of you and your families after they were finished covertly using you. You should know now that your former Trilotew mentors, who were responsible for that brainwashing, have been transformed back to their true original benevolent natures by this same special energy Ray that each one of you are now experiencing for yourselves. In fact, they are headed back to their home worlds as we speak, and our planet is about to be permanently, dynamically transformed."

Transparent golden spheres appeared above all their heads, and Henry watched them all look up to behold the many terrorizing deadly images appear inside each sphere that had been driving their diabolical actions from the subconscious implants. Then, one by one, the vile images within each sphere dissolved into white light and the spheres faded away.

Henry touched his glowing pendant, and then he began to send an enthusiastic telepathic message to Ted upstairs, *The first group has successfully arrived, and they have experienced the new Ray. It removed the controlling subconscious implants, and they are now returning to their true, naturally evolved, benevolent human natures right before my eyes.*

That is good news, cheerfully replied Ted telepathically.

I have received the coordinates for the next group, confidently interjected Monti. *Are you ready to have them beamed over?*

Quite ready, Monti my friend, enthusiastically replied back Henry.

Monti telepathically continued, *Have the first group remain standing where they are near you and I will send the second group of twenty-five Council members to you. They will arrive standing in a tight circle to the right side of the fireplace. Here they come.*

The successful teleportation of all four hundred worldwide hidden government Council members to the Grand Reception room in Ted's mansion was soon completed. Then Monti and Chairman Ted Carter, with his pendant still faintly glowing, walked side-by-side back down the right staircase and into the Grand Reception room to join all the arriving transforming worldwide members.

Ted placed his hand over his heart, respectfully nodded his head beaming a benevolent smile at all of them and stated, "Fellow governing Council members, you are all now aware of the reason you were brought here with no forewarning. We most certainly could not ask your permission while the Trilotew subconscious terror images controlled you. Here in my home, you are all welcome now that you are beginning to experience your true human natures, your true selves that have been deeply suppressed for years beyond count going back into the distant past far beyond this one lifetime."

While Ted was talking, Henry was fondly gazing at Cynthia. Though middle-aged, he had to admit that with her shapely figure and long silken-black hair, Cynthia was still quite lovely. Then he noticed she happened to be again wearing her expensive diamond and emerald necklace hanging down over the open front of her low-cut blue and black silken dress. She stepped away from the older shorter white-haired woman standing at her left side to speak to the Chairman.

"Mr. Chairman, how could this have happened to all of us? We started out with such good intentions for the planet, and then those demon reptilians twisted everything we were originally trying to accomplish."

"Cynthia Piermont, you have been a good and loyal Vice Chairman, and a good friend. I know it's hard to accept at first, but you know it's all true," solemnly answered Ted, and he glanced around the room at the entire group of men and women. "Now I can reveal the truth to all of you because you will be able to perceive it in a knowing manner through the new consciousness liberating Ray. If the Galactic Alliance had decided not to intervene at this time in the perverted affairs of our world, the treaty-breaking interference of the Trilotew would eventually result in the destruction of the entire planet. My fellow Council members, do not go back into hate, anger, and other misguided negative ways for all the Trilotew stationed on or around the Earth have already been transformed back to their original benevolent natures. That nature is the same as their ancient ancestors expressed before their white-winged Trilon-kal cousins suppressed them over five hundred thousand years ago.

"We now have the great opportunity to accomplish wonders working alongside the specialists who are on their way here from the Galactic Alliance. When they arrive, every man, woman, and child on our planet Earth will know without a shadow of a doubt that human and other highly intelligent forms of life exist throughout the galaxy. Highly trained Masters of every specialized skill will assist us to completely transform the entire surface of the planet by using a form of non-polluting, limitless energy in the universe. They will also help free the human race from all known diseases, and they will turn back on certain genomes in the DNA of all Earth humans to enable them to once again use a hundred percent of their brains, instead of the usual six to ten percent. In addition, they will significantly expand our lifetime to a thousand years or more, after they turn back on several longevity age-clock genomes; those purposefully suppressed in our ancient ancestors and then genetically passed on a very long time ago. The one hundred Council members that were convening with my daughter Janice and I back at the underground Arizona facility have already experienced this Ray. Now at last all the other worldwide members are being set free."

Cheers from everyone present went up like a rolling tide of liberation across the room, and Vice Chairman Cynthia Piermont standing closer to Henry blissfully remarked, "It's just beyond amazing. I am actually beginning to have insight into the deeper, hidden, co-creative purpose for life. I'm simply astounded I couldn't see it before now." She paused to muse about something, and then timidly tried sending out the telepathic thought, *Can you hear me, Chairman Carter? I want to help any way I can with all the wealth and position I have to free up all the people of Earth, and I already know all the others feel the same way.*

Ted grinned and telepathically replied, *I most certainly can hear you, my friend.* Then he continued aloud, "I'm delighted that you, Vice Chairman Piermont, and the others are already gaining back your natural telepathic ability. That will make what we must do in the days to come much easier and far more efficient. We have a lot of work to do together to prepare the world for a joint worldwide broadcast that will take place at the appropriate time by duly elected President of the United States Martin McCoy. Ambassador Shon-ral, representing the entire Galactic Inter-dimensional Alliance of Free Worlds will be present, the now benevolently transformed Ambassador Grotzil of the Trilotew will return, and I will also be there as Chairman of our secret second government Council to present the truth to all the people of Earth.

"Together from the White House we will reveal the truth about our secret second government members and how we came into existence by the unethical actions of our forebears. More details than that are not necessary to disclose at this time. You can all now understand the significance of what I am saying to you. We are about to be fully exposed. However, be aware that the people of Earth will swiftly come to know your former tyrant natures are gone. With Galactic Alliance assistance, they will come to know we are now irrevocably dedicated to utilizing our great combined financial and political resources to completely transform the entire Earth, and set free everyone living on it in vastly improved ways. In addition, do not forget that this special liberating Ray each one of you are experiencing will be made available throughout the world to all our fellow human beings, and to all life on the planet. We will not be alone."

Ted gazed at Monti and elegantly stated, "This, my fellow Council members, is Mon-tlan or who we like to call Monti, and he is my new trusted friend. Monti is a Special Mission representative of the Galactic Alliance from a star system beyond what we on Earth refer to as the Pleiades star group, and he is here to help us through this worldwide change."

All the transforming members gazed at Monti with grateful childlike wonder.

He smiled back at them and stated, "Well, I sense now it is safe to say that both myself and the normal extraterrestrial humans that live on far more elevated pollution free worlds no longer appear to be much different than yourselves, now that your true natures have been liberated. As we speak, several thousand ships are on their way here. After they arrive, each of you, and all the people of Earth, will receive assistance from off-world beings that have become very adept at every imaginable advanced discipline. Cures for every disease, greatly extended longevity, anti-gravity outer space and parallel dimension travel technology, as well as very advanced ecological and geological sciences, to name a few, will be available. We will help prepare this world and its people for official admittance into the Galactic Inter-dimensional Alliance of Free Worlds. Will that do for starters?"

Vice Chairman Piermont cheerfully replied, "I know I speak for all of us when I say that we are now, oh how can I put this, well... beyond passionately committed to free up the entire world. We actually have a true creatively constructive purpose in life now and most importantly, the fear and dread for the future has vanished from us. We are looking forward to once again being benevolent contributors to this vast and wondrous universe we live in."

Delighted, Monti placed his right palm over his heart area and slightly bowed.

Then Ted gazed at Henry and added, "I believe you all know Henry Throckmorton, my general Council. He will be my trusted right hand to all of you to help us carry out this new, most important mission we all now share together."

Henry smiled toward the group, and Cynthia found herself fondly gazing at him. Then he found himself fondly gazing back at her. Ted immediately noticed their affection and smiled his approval with a subtle, slight nod.

"In the days and months to come," cordially continued Monti, "you will all be taken aboard the Galactic Alliance flagship to go through a more thorough deprogramming of the Trilotew brainwashing. After that, each of you will remember ever so much more about the nature of your true selves as spherical energy beings, or what you Earth humans refer to as Soul. You will also begin to realize just how many lifetimes were already spent evolving in order to be in this room at this moment to go through such an unexpected dynamic change for the better."

Ted added, "We wish you and your families only the very best, and now we better send you all back to your various locations around the world before it becomes any more strange to those who may have witnessed your sudden departures. Trust me as I now tell you that each of you will simply intuitively know what to say and do from now on. Henry, Monti, or I will soon be in touch with each of you in one form or another. By the grace of the special liberating Ray itself, we will now send you all back to your respective locations in a more direct manner. Farewell."

Ted respectfully placed his right palm over his heart area and slightly bowed. All the other Council members in the room sincerely returned the gesture. Then Ted and Henry simultaneously touched the gold pendant symbols hanging from the gold chains around their necks and they both flashed once. A moment passed, and then all four hundred secret government Council members simply vanished from the room without having to use the hidden Trilotew teleportation device up in Ted's office.

"Well, my friends," jovially commented Monti, giving Ted and Henry the thumbs-up sign, "We're in the thick of it now."

Both Ted and Henry paused to ponder the meaning of Monti's odd statement, and then they just started chuckling with him as they both telepathically picked-up on the constructive, uplifting nature of his dry sense of humor.

CHAPTER TWENTY-FOUR

THE MIGHTY SERES RETURN

Mark's publisher, Mr. Dan Waymeyer of Waymeyer Publishing, was sitting behind his desk atop the fifteen-story Waymeyer Publishing building gazing out through the large surrounding corner windows at the small mountainous ridge line above Beverly Hills, California. He was nervously tapping a pencil on top of Mark Santfield's latest book manuscript he had just finished final editing when the phone on his desk rang.

He was irritated when he picked up the handset and snapped out, "What is it, Suzanne?"

She politely replied, "Pardon me for interrupting you, Mr. Waymeyer, but Mathew McConnell is holding for you."

Dan rolled his eyes and said, "Go ahead and put him through," and he paused, then asked, "Yes, Mathew?" He listened and hotly shot back, "No, we've already been over this. I want Mark Santfield's new book set for worldwide release on the first of next month." He listened to Mathew's beginning response and then cut him off, "Yes, yes Mathew, I'm well aware we have to spend several million more for the marketing campaign at such short notice than probably any other book in history. I ordered it. Were you listening back at the book release scheduling meeting? Look, as I stated then, this book will be the most monumental, ground shaking success of any publishing company on the planet. What's that? No, I can't elaborate now, but like I told the entire Executive staff, what will officially be revealed worldwide regarding the truth about what's coming that's revealed in Mark's second book will put sales right through the roof. Hell, we'll be very hard pressed just to come up with ways to keep books supplied to the retail stores and online. I just finished the final manuscript edit and I'll send it down to you in the next few minutes. Then finish the final galley proof and get the print ready draft on my desk by tomorrow evening. Trust me on this, Mathew. Don't think about it, just do it. Use the entire editing staff to get it done if you have to, and I'll authorize any overtime." He listened more intently and then replied, "Good, good, alright then. Call me here or at home at anytime just as soon as you have it ready. Remember, I want the television ads, the trade magazines, and the Internet campaigns tied together like clockwork for release to the public in two weeks. With the unique full-sized LCD video display monitors and video promotion about Mark's second book, we will provide all the book retailers at no cost to them, they have already committed. Now, get on it, Mathew, and there will be big rewards and promotions for everyone working here." He paused to listen and anxiously replied, "Yes, yes, inform all the employees their efforts will be well worth it. Okay then, call me later."

He hung up the handset, got up and impatiently walked over to the wide, surrounding corner windows to thoughtfully gaze out over the city and up at the rolling mountainous hills along the Mulholland Drive crest line. Then he softly stated, "This world and all the people on it are in for quite an unexpected shock. There will be no turning back now, thank God."

Up on the Galactic Alliance flagship stealthily hovering in orbit above the North American continent, Mark and Janice were standing next to each other gazing down through the oval observation windows at the beautiful planet they knew most people living on its surface took entirely for granted.

"You know, dear cousin, I suppose I'll miss this world of strife and constant turmoil while we're gone," stated Mark, a little melancholy.

"I was feeling the same way, but I remember my husband and children now as if I had left them only yesterday," thoughtfully replied Janice.

In reverie, Mark continued, "Having lived the lives of two people from two different worlds at the same time has at the very least expanded our creative horizons beyond what anyone would have expected."

Janice turned to him, gently placed a hand on his arm and impishly added, "You know, Mr. Ambassador to the whole incredible unexpected universal change for the best in all creation, there will be no returning to the way things were. By the grace of Prime Creator our loving natures have been expanded to encompass the entire Earth world, our own home planet, and it's beginning to embrace the whole of creation."

Mark solemnly nodded and looked back at the Earth silently, slowly spinning on its axis.

Then he voiced his thoughts aloud as he began to imagine the tremendous changes coming to the entire Earth planet and its people, "We should bring our families from the home-world to Earth while it's being completely liberated and transformed. They would have profound experiences of a lifetime."

Telepathically picking up on Mark's vision, Janice began to see Earth's new future unfolding and she thoughtfully commented, "All the suffering and all the pain of our former tortured lives seems so unimportant now compared to what we have become. Yes, we should bring our families back here to see the entire planet and people transformed from utter unconscious terror to the brilliant light of a new day."

Commanders Jon-tral and Sun-deema walked up behind them already smiling. They too had tuned into the future vision for Earth's transformation coming from the mysterious liberating Ray that now filled their lives with ever expanding awareness. In truth, at that very moment the limitless overflow of its luminous liquid light presence was passing through them to all life for the great uplifting benefit of all.

Sun-deema sweetly said, "*The Seres Agenda* is beginning to unfold across the face of the Earth, and in fact everywhere else in the universe."

Jon-tral elegantly added, "We are in the very heart of the greatest expanding benevolent change in what the Earth people call God, or what we know as the Ancient One or Prime Creator. None of us can yet see all the incredible uplifting events that are now coming. Yet, at least we know this is the end time for evil as an experiment and not the Armageddon of destruction so many of the Earth people are hell-bent on seeing happen. Those perverse attitudes will melt away like a fog in the morning sun when the Expansion Ray also touches their lives. Now that we are all on the same page in this story of dynamic change I believe the time has come for Captain Zin-tamal to finally take you two back home to be reunited with your families. The captain, crew, and ship are waiting in the launch bay."

Mark and Janice didn't reply, for the moment was too real and too profoundly deep in truth, trust, love, and joy for what all life would soon be experiencing, and they just hugged both commanders in turn - like the true brothers and sisters of the one Prime Creator they had now fully become in their hearts.

Both Commanders placed their right hand over their heart area and respectfully nodded. Mark and Janice returned the true gesture of wise understanding and they started to walk away.

They had not gone ten feet when Sun-deema's sweet voice called to them, "We'll be awaiting your return with your families to help out with the great many changes the Earth humans are about to go through."

Mark and Janice stopped and turned chuckling before Mark curiously commented, "You both already know about our family planes."

Grinning like an imp, Sun-deema continued, "And you will both need to be here when the President of the United States makes the worldwide announcement about all that was covered up."

Chuckling, Jon-tral added, "Well, you should both know by now we were not spying in on your private conversations. With the new Ray, truth is true for all or it's not true at all."

The four of them softly laughed, knowing there were no more secrets, no covert thoughts, imaginings or negative scenarios left within their beings, for they no longer had subconscious minds in their now greatly expanded benevolent human natures.

Farewell! sent out Mark and Janice in telepathic unison, expressing deep compassionate understanding.

Farewell! replied Jon-tral and Sun-deema in telepathic unison, expressing the same depth of expanding love for all life.

The cousins turned around and solemnly walked out of the observation chamber.

Jon-tral began to gaze into Sun-deema's loving eyes as only a true lover can for his beloved trustworthy wife, and she gazed in knowing union back at him. He threw his arms around her slender waist, drew her near and they passionately kissed long and tenderly. When they parted, they looked together through the wide oval observation windows upon the lovely blue-green water covered Earth planet in contemplation of its future. Then they turned around and walked hand-in-hand out of the main gathering and observation room of the mighty Galactic Alliance flagship.

Captain Zin-tamal cheerfully greeted Mark and Janice at the boarding ramp that led into the medium sized inter-stellar Transport Carrier, and he cordially escorted them inside.

A minute later, the glowing three-hundred foot-long cylindrical ship lifted up above the launch bay floor and turned transparent as it moved right through the hull of the massive flagship.

It momentarily stopped in space several thousand yards away from the mile-long parent vessel, and the pale blue light enshrouding the ship flashed a white swirling spiral of light from the front of one end of its curved hull to open an inter-dimensional whirling, violet vortex tunnel. The ship shot in a blur far beyond the speed of light into the mysterious energy tunnel and the vortex whirled closed, then vanished.

Mark and Janice were reclining in comfortable, white, form-fitting chairs similar to the one they both sat in inside the deprogramming chamber aboard the flagship. Their conversations were jovial now, mostly about their excitement at the prospect of being reunited with their families at last. They had been traveling through the inter-dimensional vortex for nearly a full day and the ship was now more than five hundred light years from Earth beyond the Pleiades star group. It was nearing their home planet Norexilam in the Starborn

271

Cluster.

Another whirling violet vortex appeared opening in a far distant space amidst a brilliant cluster of several dozen young hot blue-white stars. The Transport Carrier shot out of the opening and almost instantly slowed to a stop, as the vortex behind it whirled closed and vanished. The luminous blue hull pulsed brightly and the ship sped away toward a nearby planet that was similar in appearance to the blue-green water covered jewel of planet Earth.

It was soon orbiting the planet in a geosynchronous orbit above the equator. Three large mountainous continents centered over the equator extended a considerable distance above and below the planet's northern and southern hemispheres. Two more continents were over the north and south poles, but they also appeared to be lush with verdant plant life with no polar icecaps covering them. Deep emerald green oceans separated all the landmasses.

Several dozen large saucer shaped transports were flying in and out of the planet's turquoise-blue atmosphere from numerous points around the globe, headed in many different directions. One approached the Transport Carrier turning transparent and it moved through the hull into the central section of the ship.

Captain Zin-tamal approached the cousins, who were merrily chatting away, and he courteously stated, "Ambassador Shon-ral and Prime Scientist Moon-teran, we have arrived at Norexilam. One of the larger Courier Scout Class ships has docked in our launch bay. Your original DNA samples are with one of the advanced biology scientists. She will assist both of you with the DNA reversion process."

Mark and Janice got up and Mark replied, "Thank you, Captain Zin-tamal. We are grateful for your assistance."

Janice gave him a grateful kiss on the cheek and said, "You told us your family is also waiting for your return down on the planet. Will you be able to go see them now as well?"

Smiling, Zin-tamal replied, "I have planet leave coming, if that's what you are asking, and I'm anxious to see them but not as anxious as you two must be after all the years of separation you went through on Earth. Fortunately, the time-space differential that occurs when we travel through the inter-stellar vortex from Earth to here means they only had to wait a relatively short number of months since your departures. Know that I will be standing by with the Transport Carrier whenever you need me. Farewell, my friends."

Farewell Captain, thankfully replied Mark and Janice in telepathic unison, and they walked with Captain Zin-tamal out of the lounge area.

A short time later, a trim middle-aged woman shorter than Janice with long brunette hair and a striking adorable smile was walking toward them down a long light beige oval corridor.

Captain Zin-tamal stopped and said, "There she is now. I have something to attend to, so please introduce yourselves."

He smiled at her and walked away in the opposite direction.

So, you two have finally returned to us from the land of the lost. Somehow I knew one day you would turn up, stated the woman telepathically, as she walked up and stopped by them in the center of the long corridor carrying a small rectangular silver case clutched in her left hand. "I'm Prime Biologist Shanal-teal," she cordially continued with her voice. "It was my privilege to be selected to bring the samples of your original DNA that we fortunately preserved before either of you departed on those dangerous missions to the Earth planet."

"You look very familiar to me," curiously stated Janice. "Have we met before?"

Smiling up at her, Shanal-teal replied, "Why of course, dear Moon-teran, we have. I was one of the lead development biologists on your parent's team that spearheaded the DNA reversion procedure. Your parents, Prime DNA Biologists Kantal-teran and Fimala-tanis, were best friends to me and my husband, before they tragically translated from this life in that unexpected meteor collision with their exploration ship. I understand the ship was hovering stationary with the shields coincidentally down for repair when that meteor hit. To this day, I believe the Trilotew had something to do with it. You were very young at the time."

Janice appeared dreamy-eyed as she responded, "Yes, I remember you now. You came often to our home in the Jubilanton Forest after my parents did not return from that particular week-long journey away from me. My father's brother and his wife had no children, and they raised me after that."

Shanal-teal kindly commented, "They are great scientists in their own right today, advancing the speed and efficiency of our inter-stellar cruisers."

"I never knew my parents," interjected Mark, a little forlorn with a shrug of his shoulders.

"I know, but I did know them," solemnly relied Shanal-teal. "Your father was one of the greatest Ambassadors the entire Galactic Alliance has ever known. That is, until that previous terrible Trilotew Emperor betrayed and killed him and your High Council member mother. She traveled with him to their awful ruling planet on the fateful day under a flag of peace."

"I remember the story now," said Mark, looking away in reverie, and he winced at the memory. "Our flagship orbiting the planet retaliated and destroyed the Emperor and half their capital city, before it retreated back to Galactic Alliance territory. The brief but devastating battles that began after that nearly plunged the galaxy back into an all out inter-stellar war like the one we left behind five hundred thousand years ago."

"Ambassador Shon-ral, the Galactic Alliance owes you a great debt of gratitude," encouragingly interjected Shanal-teal. "You are most certainly taking it beyond your father's footsteps now. After you took his place, I know that Ambassador Shon-dema and your mother Coral-shana would have been very pleased with how you orchestrated our current treaty with the new Trilotew Emperor. Now you are the official Galactic Alliance Ambassador to prepare the way for our fleet to arrive and save the Earth and its people from certain annihilation. It was a sore loss to all of us when you vanished without a trace en route to Earth, but now we are beyond delighted that you have returned safely to us."

Mark smiled kindly at her and said, "Thank you for that Shanal-teal. I can see you are exactly the right Norexilam scientist to take us through this process. How long has it been available?"

"We were nearing completion of the DNA reversion process after Moon-teran disappeared, and shortly after you vanished we succeeded," she curiously replied. "We were driven because too many of our citizens were being covertly intercepted over the years by those Trilotew monsters to be used as programmed tools for their vicious missions. Many of the citizens we retrieved were operating unconsciously in suppressed human bodies on other worlds, and we were able to successfully change them back to their original advanced human physical forms using the new DNA reversion procedure. Since then, we have installed special chambers aboard our large Scout ships, medium and large inter-stellar transports, and the very large Emerald Star cruisers.

"As you know, a traitor in the Galactic Alliance high up had been tipping off Trilotew spies. On your way here, I received a report from the Galactic High Council in the central Novissam system. They finally discovered the traitor. It was one of the High Council members. His wife had been captured by the Trilotew, and they used her as bait to get him to reveal the travel schedules of very select Galactic Alliance citizens like you, Ambassador Shon-ral, and you, Moon-teran, or they promised to devour her alive while he watched. They made him secretly meet with their disguised spies, and afterward he was under their control through those outlawed brainwashing devices.

"We secretly liberated him from their control, and caught the spies that captured his wife. They experienced the liberating Ray, and then helped us track down his wife with Special Forces that raided their hidden base on a remote world where a dozen Trilotew had imprisoned her. The captured Trilotew soldiers were then set free from their subconscious brainwashing. The High Council member's wife found chained to a crude wall was badly mistreated and near death, but the new Ray saved her life and liberated her from their vile brainwashing.

"Dear Moon-teran, my team was only able to finish the DNA reversion experiment shortly after your disappearance because of the brilliant advances your parents had already completed before their so-called accidental demise. When we get enough of the Trilotew liberated from the madness that directs them, we will likely discover they were actually behind your parents deaths as well."

Janice solemnly nodded her thanks to the kind words.

"There is much more to this tale, dear friends," seriously continued Shanal-teal. "After the pyramids started to appear on many

Galactic Alliance worlds, a ten-foot-wide glowing sphere of radiant light appeared in the main Council Chamber on the central Galactic Alliance world of Zetranami in the Novissam system. It appeared as thousands of teardrop shaped self-effulgent lights built in layers of the spectrum from a white central core to a violet exterior, surrounded by a subtle golden glow.

"Before anyone could speak, the radiant sphere transformed into one of the eighteen-foot-tall humans from the ancient Seres race. He was elegant beyond any being anyone had ever witnessed with his glistening long blond hair, slightly pointed ears and blue eyes, emanating a subtle radiant wisdom so deep words fail to describe it. Like a legendary Greek God of old from Earth's history, he was wearing a golden knee-length gown and simple sandals. Tucked under his long right arm was a three-foot-long, by two-foot-wide, by two-inch thick blue metallic covered book with golden-white pages.

"No one had seen one of the Seres in over a billion years, and he was described as being radiantly beautiful beyond any concept of handsome with a soft golden light radiating around his body. His presence alone transformed the Council in under a minute, and they understood the purpose of the pyramids and this liberating new Ray emanating from the fountains inside them that is bringing about the great change coming to the galaxy."

She reached inside her gown with her other hand, pulled out a small clear spherical crystal with a red faceted gem in its center, held it out in her open palm and continued, "This crystal storage unit was sent to the most wise leaders of all the Galactic Alliance worlds. Then one came to me. It contains the visual and voice recording of that event with the Seres Ambassador. The odd thing is I understand he began to speak in Galactic Standard; however, those in the meeting chamber could all simultaneously hear him speak in their own native tongue. There is no explanation for the phenomena at this time. I'll play it now and you will both be brought up to date."

This new revelation deeply moved Mark and Janice, and Mark remarked, "I knew they were behind this to some degree. I had sensed they were returning but could not be sure. This changes everything for the better. It is my honor to be the Galactic Alliance Ambassador in this galaxy, and I know that one day my destiny is to meet the Seres Ambassador. He will have much to share with me and everyone else as well. We are most fortunate to be alive at this moment in eternity."

Shanal-teal nodded at the crystal and a cone of golden light shot into the hallway, revealing a three dimensional projection down the corridor. The Milky Way galaxy appeared and the image zoomed closer, revealing the labeled Norexilam Planetary System located near the galactic center. The image zoomed closer to the fifth planet from their sun labeled "Central Planet Zetranami." Then the massive circular High Council Chambers on Zetranami appeared. Tall Greek style white granite-like pillars surrounded the inner circumference of the deep blue granite-like walls of the chamber. Five thousand Council members were wearing white silken slip-on footwear, and their customary white robes with the gold sash around the waist. They were sitting down in their comfortable white leather-like chairs arranged in the fifteen circular tiered seating levels under the wide clear overhead dome below a golden cloudless sky.

A radiant sphere of light appeared before them hovering above the round key-speaker stage centered below the fifteen tiered circular levels, and all the Council members jumped in alarm to their feet. Instantly, a soft golden light briefly emanated from the sphere causing them all to be at peace, and then an eighteen-foot-tall human male formed from the sphere. With a deep melodious voice, he began to address all five thousand Council members that represent over four hundred and fifty million advanced benevolent space-faring world systems.

"This benevolent High Council has done all it could for so many hundreds of thousands of years to bring sanity and truth to all those who are living in your member worlds since our departure from your dimension so long ago. This new consciousness expanding Ray from Prime Creator also recently elevated our awareness in our higher protected purified parallel dimensional reality. The pyramids first started appearing among us and we began to realize that we had a responsibility to help you in this reality become free from evil as an experiment in the lower worlds for all time. Our old selfish view to leave you all behind to struggle through your own way to a higher expanded awareness has been washed from our beings. Since then, much more of our true benevolent characteristics has surfaced.

"The gift of this new Ray from the lofty dimensional realm of Prime Creator or the Ancient One in a fineness of vibration far above our own is permanently retiring evil as a prodding tool for growth throughout creation. Something far better is now in creation to take its place. The lower universes that have been fixed and finished with good and evil concepts dominating them are about to become unfixed and unfinished. They are about to finally become reflections of the more greatly expanding love for all life that is also now taking place above the void and well beyond even the fifth main creative dimension in that lofty ocean of majestic Light and Sound where dwells Prime Creator or the Ancient One.

"I am Torellian, the Seres Ambassador to your physical universe and this prototype galaxy where the golden pyramids and the fountains within them emanating the Ray are first being manifested. I brought *The Seres Agenda*, a gift of new directions for this mighty change that is taking place. In the days to come, it will help transform all that exists. You are all destined to become true creative co-workers with Prime Creator or Gods amongst the great one itself, even as we are. The time has finally come for this great expansion to all life.

"Know that the Seres race is about to return to this galaxy and to that planet referred to as Earth by its inhabitants, for it was one of the first worlds where we seeded human life over fifty million years ago, after their dinosaur age had come to an end. Planet Earth's cycle of one hundred and eighty degree polar shifts every one hundred thousand years that usually destroys most of the life on its surface has made it necessary to constantly reseed that world with human beings from other planets. Unfortunately, this has resulted in it being the most suppressed of human worlds for far too long. That planet's cyclic polar shifts are about to permanently end with the help of far more advanced beings than we are, who we know as the Silent Mentors. They will help the new Ray make this great transformation in this and other galaxies. Now I must apologize for our race having been so long away from assisting you to greatly expand your awareness. It is now time that you all began to play in the far higher realms, where the pyramids and the Ray only recently began to appear. We will contact you again when we are ready. Farewell."

The mighty Seres Ambassador placed the large blue metallic covered book on the floor of the Council chamber. Everyone there could clearly see *The Seres Agenda* title etched upon its surface in large golden letters. With a benevolent smile, Torellian nodded to all five thousand members, transformed back into the radiant sphere, and it simply faded away.

Even through the recorded projection, Shanal-teal, Ambassador Shon-ral, and Moon-teran were profoundly moved by the Seres Ambassador and they simultaneously took a relaxing breath, let it out, and then blinked several times from the amazing revelation presented by the ancient majestic being.

"Well, I believe you two will agree," continued Shanal-teal on a cheerful note, "that was the full update of the recent most momentous historical event that was missed during your absence. Now, let's get you both back to your original physical natures. Then you can rejoin your families, who happen to know you are on this ship in orbit above them right now. We must not keep them waiting a moment longer than necessary. Please follow me to the medical bay."

Mark and Janice eagerly followed Shanal-teal with a barely subdued renewed zeal for life as she began to walk further back down the corridor in the direction she had come from.

CHAPTER TWENTY-FIVE

THERE'S NO PLACE LIKE HOME

They walked together into the fifty-foot-long, smooth white walled cylindrical Medical Bay that contained unfathomably advanced crystalline control panels, diagnostic instruments, and reclining bed chambers. They stopped halfway inside the facility and Shanal-teal turned aside to enter another room through a triangular doorway opening. Inside the semi-spherical chamber were four empty transparent oval containers, built waist-high parallel to each other at a ninety-degree right angle to the nearby surface of the far curved white wall. A curved four-foot-wide, faceted crystalline control panel lined the adjacent quarter of the semi-spherical shaped wall, and another three curved medical diagnostic control panels lined the other three, quarter sections of the room. Although the light in the chamber was bright, there was no apparent light source.

Shanal-teal knowingly grinned at Mark and Janice, and then stated, "This is where you will be renewed or returned to your original true human bodies. We call the device that controls the horizontal enclosures a DNA Transverse Molecular Reconstructor and this is the transverse procedure room of our newly designed Medical Bay.

"You will both be suspended floating in one of these anti-gravity suspension and DNA reversion tubes, and a highly oxygenated fluorocarbon emulsion converted into a specially designed breathable gas is injected into them. A precise sonic or sound frequency is then sent through the gas that compels you, the true Atma or spherical energy form, to leave your physical Earth bodies. Then from above the chambers, you will both be able to witness the transformation of your Earth human bodies to your original advanced human Norexilam DNA characteristics and capabilities.

"We do this to eliminate the intense pain you would otherwise experience over the next twelve hours if you remained inside them. The change occurs on a sub-atomic molecular level at one time, including turning back on the genomes that will allow both of you to live the normal advanced human lifespan of a thousand years or more. You will also regain one hundred percent use of your brains, recover your natural photographic memory ability, and many other more advanced characteristic of your former Norexilam lives.

"Now, please step into the individual dressing closets you can see to the left side of the four oval chambers. Take off your Earth clothes and slip into the special flexible form-fitting body suits that are inside. Inside the chambers, they conduct the Transverse Carrier Waves containing the imprinted patterns of your original advanced four-stranded DNA genome codes inside your Earth bodies. Then a golden checkerboard patterned light-grid or matrix will surround your bodies, and the process will begin as the two-stranded Earth human DNA helix is recombined into the genomes of your original four-stranded DNA helix. You will both observe the Earth human bodies being restructured into your more advanced Norexilam human forms."

"I'll see you, Cousin, on the other side," whimsically stated Janice, but she still appeared a little nervous.

"Right, let's get this done, Cousin, and behold each other as we once did before this whole Trilotew madness intervened," confidently replied Mark, and they followed Shanal-teal up to the two dressing closets.

She opened the oval doors and the cousins stepped inside. They emerged a few minutes later wearing the sheer formfitting, single-piece slip-on gowns that shimmered with changing iridescent colors as they moved in the light.

Shanal-teal touched a luminous blue rectangular faceted crystal on the console and the transparent canopy top halves of the closest two oval transverse chambers swung up and stopped parallel to the wall and at a ninety degree angle to the floor. The containers lowered down for easy access, and then Mark and Janice stepped inside them and laid down face-up. The lids closed over them and sealed with a soft suctioning *hiss-s-s.*

Shanal-teal cheerfully asked, "Are you both ready?"

They both nodded and Shanal-teal touched a lit pink faceted rectangular crystal and it brightened. The subtly pink transparent gas quickly filled both containers, while Mark and Janice continued to breath normally in the new atmosphere. Shanal-teal then turned on several square faceted golden crystals and the inside of both chambers were instantly filled with seven horizontally stacked, rectangular layers of small checkerboard patterned light grids. The layers then harmlessly interpenetrated their entire physical bodies remaining extended another four inches from their torsos, as Mark and Janice began to drift off into a trance-like sleep state. The encompassing golden light grid pattern then suspended them up to float in the center of the chambers.

Shanal-teal opened the small silver case she was carrying and lifted out from the molded sockets in the bottom two sealed transparent glass vials containing a clear liquid. She opened the square lid on the console and inserted both vials into two of the four silver cylinders that projected up out of the compartment. The cylinders automatically lowered back down and the lid swung closed. Then she touched a small blue triangular crystal next to the vial compartment and it turned on, radiating a pulsing blue light. The grid light patterns encompassing the bodies of Mark and Janice began to flash on in very complex light patterns that began to speed up until it was just a brilliant blur.

A moment passed, and the true luminous spherical Atma energy selves of Shon-ral and Moon-teran appeared exiting upward out of the heads of both bodies. Thy moved upward and passed right through the clear lids of the chambers, then stopped to float side-by-side above them.

Moon-teran? telepathically asked Shon-ral.

Yes, I'm here, Shon-ral, she telepathically replied.

Can you hear us, Shanal-teal? anxiously asked Shon-ral.

Yes, I hear both of you but my physical eyes cannot see you. Then she telepathically continued on an up-note, *The screen monitor on the instrument panel is now showing me your true energy forms hovering above the chambers. The DNA transverse procedure will now automatically begin.*

The skin covering the faces of Mark Santfield and Janice Carter began to slowly ripple like tiny ocean waves, first up and down, and then from side to side. Their craniums, eyes, facial bones, jaw lines, ears, noses, hair color and texture, skin color, and other discernible characteristics began to morph into the recognizable forms of Shon-ral's and Moon-teran's original far more advanced radiant Norexilam human body characteristics - which they both gratefully treasured before the Trilotew viciously destroyed them.

Time for them swiftly passed, while they temporarily existed in their true Atma energy spheres outside or beyond their physical forms. Then they turned their focus down on their suspended sleeping bodies to discover they were looking at the exact physical characteristics of their former destroyed but far more advanced human Norexilam bodies.

At that moment, Shanal-teal walked back into the DNA Transverse laboratory and confidently stated, "The process has finished and you two should now get back into your new home world bodies."

The golden grid light pattern lowered their sleeping bodies to the bottom of both chambers and shut off. Then the subtly pink gas was instantly drawn back out of both oval chambers. The true Atma forms of Shon-ral and Moon-teran lowered back down inside the transparent oval chambers and faded away inside the heads of their advanced human bodies. A moment passed, and both of them opened their eyes, just as the lids to their chambers unsealed with a quick *s-s-sip* sound and opened up.

Shanal-teal cheerfully grinned at them and then helped them climb out of the lowering chambers. When they were both standing on their feet, they looked at each other and their gaze of astonishment was unmistakable.

"Moon-teran, is that really you?" asked Shon-ral, delighted to hear his own forgotten elegant and more deeply attractive vibrant male home world voice.

"Shon-ral, is it true? Are we really back?" she asked, amazed at the return of her original angelic home world voice.

They embraced and then held each other at arm's length, smiling from ear to ear. Of course, their more radiant clear eyes were now slightly larger than most human eyes on the Earth planet, and their own original voices sounded more elegantly resonant than most Earth people ever experience.

"I told you two we perfected the technique," jubilantly proudly proclaimed Shanal-teal. "Now your are both fully ready to rejoin your families."

Shon-ral and Moon-teran looked at each other to share a private thought, and then Shon-ral elatedly stated, "Shanal-teal, you are a saint. It's truly amazing."

Moon-teran added equally elated, "You have saved our marriages and our families from much suffering."

"Nonsense," she humbly shot back, "I was just doing my job, you know, what I love doing anyway. It was my privilege to do this for you both and damn it, utilizing an old Earth slang word properly, I would do it again in a heartbeat."

They both cracked up laughing at her quirky sense of humor, while Shanal-teal opened one of the cabinets and pulled out two sets of new clothes.

"I thought you would be more at home with your own home world clothes. I had your families provide these for your momentous return. Now get dressed you two and the joyous reunion can begin. Then I can return planet-side to rejoin my husband, Tamal-shan. You would like him. He's Prime Scientist in inter-stellar vortex and parallel dimension physics, and he's even more of a kidder than I am."

She grinned wide, picturing him back in their home somewhat impatiently awaiting her return. Then she headed out of the Medical Bay and the Norexilam cousins eagerly followed.

Ambassador Shon-ral and Prime Social and Historical Trend scientist Moon-teran, now fully conscious of their restored true natures were soon dressed. He was wearing the exact same Galactic Alliance Diplomat's single formfitting silky-white attire he was wearing the day he left on that ill-fated mission thirty-one Earth years ago. Moonteran was wearing the same beautiful casual spring blue and green silken formfitting dress, and the blue silken slip-on comfortable shoes she wore thirty-one and a half years earlier, just before she left on her supposed six-month scientific mission to Earth.

While en route to the ship's teleportation beaming platform, they were telepathically sending picture memories to each other of all they recalled about what their advanced normal human planet was like compared to the deranged functioning of the suppressed and misguided people of Earth.

Long ago, the advanced human civilizations living on over eighty-seven worlds circling their parent stars in the Starborn Cluster had disbanded their centralized cities. They actually had the cities dissolved on a molecular level and restructured back into the natural harmonious environments that existed before the cities were constructed. The vast areas of remaining terrain were then arranged with gorgeous flowering gardens and natural pathways that all citizens could enjoy. The buildings they did manifest were architectural works of art made of special non-corrosive alloys, large naturally appearing laboratory grown crystalline spires, and organic fibrous materials that were all created from combining various molecules together under controlled conditions. None of the materials came from mining the land or harvesting the verdant forests and abundant fauna around their world.

The individual home of each family was an expression of their artistic imagination with at least twenty acres of land allotted per family dwelling. They each had their own power supply device to furnish all their needs, and teleportation beaming units to send food, trade goods, and people to and from the science and manufacturing facilities, and to visit friends anywhere on the planet. No fences between properties existed on these worlds systems, and no one sought to possess another person's property or station in life. Their governing Council members were selected from only the most wise and enlightened people to act as the planetary citizen's representatives in the small government complexes that were built within the art, science, cultural, and manufacturing centers. However, no one lived in these small centralized city complexes. Everyone teleported to and from a given destination from homes that were ecologically built in harmony with the environment, and freely spaced around the planet. Since the people were telepathic and only worked for the pleasure of creating that which would be of benefit to all life, their governing Council members truly represented the combined decision of all their people when it came to implementing any change to their society or way of life.

They long ago solved all their non-polluting energy requirements, after they discovered an unlimited power source woven through the magnetic fields around their planets and the galaxy to drive their spacecraft. They invented ways to pass this latent energy through their devices and out the other end without depleting anything or causing harm to the environment.

This unlimited energy source, coupled with the citizen's lives being free from the drudgery of working in ways to survive that were contrary to their creative natures, resulted in great leaps forward in medical sciences. Environmental pollutants of any kind were neutralized, and the various genetic genome controls on the four-stranded helix of their human DNA discovered to be responsible for any disease were simply switched to different settings. Eventually, they eliminated the possibility of the occurrence of any kind of disease. All microscopic life on their worlds that preyed upon more evolved life forms were swiftly neutralized, and their human life spans were increased to well over a thousand years or longer if the individual had a purpose for extending the vitality of a particular body. Though rare, any failing organs could be grown from a person's own DNA and replaced in their bodies without invasive surgery. Matter transformation consoles took care of that by the instantaneous removal of the failing organ and replacement of it with a healthy one.

As a race, they had finally collectively attained their full higher sanity as naturally evolving benevolent human beings. War had been retired over five hundred thousand years earlier at the end of the last official inter-stellar conflict with the Trilotew. However, after that the tyrant totalitarian race, and a few space faring civilizations aligned with them, continued to be a thorn in the side of the Galactic Alliance.

They remained a constant reminder that aggressive insane beings still roam the stars. In some ways, the ever-present potential for conflict also held back the entire Galactic Alliance from attaining higher states of consciousness. Now the citizens were joyously relieved the potential threat was finally coming to a neutralized permanent end with *The Seres Agenda* introduction.

They had discovered the key to this greater expansion was intertwined with the survival and uplifting transformation of the distant suppressed people on planet Earth. They also found that many of their own people had been subconsciously trapped and put on Earth in long past ages and compelled to reincarnate there, while they remained completely unaware of their once former higher human existence on other planets. However, until *The Seres Agenda* and the new pyramids emitting the liberating Ray from the luminous fountains within them came into their lives, they had no way to safely liberate the Earth world. They did their best to maintain an ongoing treaty policing action to keep the diabolical Trilotew, and other associated space faring cultures, from dominating or destroying the people of Earth.

Of course, the Galactic Alliance had remained fully capable of defending itself with advanced weapons capabilities they kept state of the art out of the sheer necessity to continuously police any tyrant threats. However, their strict use was for self-defense purposes only. In fact, they were able to develop certain capabilities far beyond what races like the vile Trilotew reptilians could imagine. Yet, they had not deployed them out of their compassionate love for all life. Even so, the Trilotew and their allies still represented a serious threat because of their use of the subconscious healing technology they had stolen and perverted from a peaceful culture they dominated long ago. After the signing of the treaty, they constantly sought to raid any world not already a part of the Galactic Alliance to retrieve any advanced weapons technologies they could find. The Trilotew scientists were forced to become devoted to refining more deadly weapons but the combined sciences of the Galactic Inter-dimensional Alliance of Free Worlds managed to keep one step ahead of them. They held them at bay with a constant surveillance they maintained to keep the treaty enforced for over five hundred thousand years.

Therefore, most of the benevolent human, humanoid, and other beings living on more than four hundred and fifty million inhabited Galactic Alliance worlds had never been prey to the evil practices of the totalitarian monsters from other world systems. They were able to safely develop past their earlier industrial stages by expanding their collective consciousness to experientially know the purpose for their benevolent existence as beings. They had crossed over into that higher vibration or threshold of expanded understanding that allowed them to respect the freedom of others to explore how they wanted to creatively contribute to the betterment of all life. This they practically accomplished by collectively encouraging and supporting each individual from the time they were infants. They encouraged something uniquely creative to develop within them, so that as adults they could present new creations of great benefit to their societies.

Permanently removed from their subconscious minds were all conflicts over territory, personal wealth, and dominating drives for individual glorification and gratification at the expense of others. The collective free choice of well over four hundred billion human, humanoid, and other benevolently evolved races living throughout the Galactic Alliance had agreed. They reached a harmonious unselfish way of thriving with each other by refining and expanding their conscious awareness of all life, and they continued to create more efficient ways of doing things for the well being of everyone.

Eventually, anything that was needed for the fulfillment of their lives toward greater enlightenment, artistic development, scientific inventiveness, personal housing wishes, clothing, clean healthy food, and any other necessities for living an abundant life were taken care of by the very refined development of highly efficient automated facilities.

No one had to make a living just because of their birth on those worlds, and there was no taxation of any kind. They were all raised from the cradle into adulthood being genuinely encouraged to excel only at what they loved doing. As adults, those citizens that worked in any particular field of endeavor volunteered to supervise their own area of expertise. They would actually only engage in any necessary manual labor with others of like creative natures, because of their passionate love for what they were working to accomplish.

It was to this kind of normal human world that Ambassador Shon-ral and Prime Scientist Moon-teran finally returned; a place the people of Earth would certainly see as paradise. Two golden-white upward whirling teleportation beams whisked them from the pad aboard ship down to two different specific locations on the planet's surface. They were now beaming as pure energy to the smaller matter teleportation chambers located in each of their family homes. Every family enjoyed this wondrous interconnected worldwide transportation system on the advanced human planet of Norexilam, beyond what the Earth astronomers call the Pleiades star group.

Moon-teran materialized from the whirling teleportation beam standing on the pad in the back of her special six thousand square-foot, smooth ivory-white textured geodesic style home. Her strikingly handsome middle-aged husband, Donum-tuma, with his long brown hair touching his shoulders and slightly cleft chin was a few feet away standing with their two daughters and son to each side of him. Yoral-telan, the slightly taller eleven year old with wavy blond hair and dimples, and Vera-tima, her nine-year-old sister with wavy brunette hair and a contagious smile were gorgeously beautiful girls that would grow up to be beautiful women who would rival even their lovely mother. Although, they would never express their beauty in competitive ways as adults so frequently do back on the Earth planet to obtain what they desire. Danim-tama, their seven-year-old boy was handsome like his father with identical long brown hair, and no covert nature existed in his being.

Tears spontaneously poured down the cheeks of both parents, coming from a joy so deep in knowing the connection that existed between them. It stretched even beyond time and space to finally reunite them again as she stepped down off the pad, and the children ran up to her and threw their arms around her waist as she squatted down, embraced, and repeatedly kissed each one.

"Mother... Mother... Mother," the three ecstatic children excitedly repeated.

"Dearest Yoral-telan, Vera-tima, and Danim-tama, I have missed you so," replied Moon-teran, crying tears of joy.

Then they huddled together in the depth of their hearts that now beat as one. When she finally stood back up the children remained hugging her waist. Her patient husband stood there staring in wonder at her radiant beauty he so much missed during the vast time and space that held them separated for a year and a half in his time, and thirty-one and a half years Earth time for her. Not quite knowing what to do next, Donum-tuma gently approached his wife.

Then he telepathically stated with caring respect, *Beloved Moon-teran, I can't imagine what it must have been like growing up again in another life on that planet, but know that your loss to me was far greater than all the treasures of the universe.*

With tears streaming down her face, Moon-teran's widening joyful smile, expressing an agony of anticipation of being in his arms once again, connected to him. His widening matching smile of anticipation beamed back an almost palpable loving energy that even the children could perceive as they stepped back from them in awe. They observed both parents hesitate for a moment, before they leapt into each other's arms crying and laughing. He lifted her up and swung her off the ground in circles, and the children started to spontaneously jump up and down giggling with delight and clapping their hands. Then Donum-tuma passionately kissed Moon-teran for the first time since their long separation from each other.

That kiss was one for the history books. The sweetness of their committed dedication to each other, and their gratitude for life was about to go far beyond their physical bodies. Their true spherical Atma or Soul energy forms suddenly floated up out of the tops of their heads, while their bodies remained below in a kissing swoon. The enlightened children stopped their excited play to gaze above their parent's heads, for they could see their parents' true selves. The children's pure wide-open eyes in a deep gaze of profound awe and wonder of the special moment would stun almost any human being living on Earth, had they witnessed it. The white light radiating between them began increasing in intensity and their two separate Atma spheres gradually moved into each other to become one slightly larger and more luminous sphere. The tiny teardrop shaped self-effulgent lights that comprised the structure of their spheres built in layers, from a white central core through the spectrum of colors to a violet exterior surrounded by a pale golden aura, was doubled inside the one sphere they had become.

Waves of the finest golden energy mist began to pulse from the larger sphere out into the room. The three children stood there bathing in the profound experience their fully illumined parents were sending them as an example of a true parental bond, and the intrinsic value it held for all life because of its committed experiential nature. They were expressing their well being now to all life and not just for their own family members. The elevated awareness of their true eternal natures was now emanating the new Ray of unsuppressed love that is always for the uplifting benefit of the entire universe.

The wonder of their united sphere slowly separated again, and they remained for a moment hovering a few feet apart before they re-entered their kissing swooning bodies by fading back into the tops of their heads.

The children suddenly broke out giggling and performing jubilant dancing antics, and they laughed with delight clapping their hands as the blissful tightly embraced parents stopped kissing. They turned their heads to lovingly gaze at their three children with opening arms and the children ran into their closing embrace.

Mother... Mother... Mother, shouted all three ecstatic children this time in telepathic unison.

Oh Moon-teran, my heart was left so yearning in an empty room without you here, telepathically stated Donum-tuma much-relieved with his deeply melodious quivering inner voice.

She smiled through tears of joy and telepathically replied, *My heart was glowing ever warmer in an agony of anticipation the closer we came on our return to the home planet and to you, my husband.*

Donum-tuma wiped tears of joy from his eyes and sweetly telepathically replied aloud as he fondly gazed down at the smiling upturned faces of their children, *Beloved young ones, your mother has finally returned to us. She is home at last.*

She sighed, wiped the tears from her eyes and sweetly added with gratitude deeper than the sky, *Dear Donum-tuma, there is no place like home. Oh Prime Creator of all, there just is no place like home.*

He took her hand and she tightly squeezed his fingers to express the solid firmness of their inner connection, and they suddenly thought in unison that their kindred but still suppressed fellow human beings back on Earth should be experiencing what they now knew about their true natures. Then she rested her head on his shoulder as they walked through an oval opening at the back of the teleportation room to enter the main living room.

Their three vibrantly happy children rushed past their parents, who stopped to gaze at the large wide oval indoor swimming pool. Moon-teran fondly looked up through the gentle curve of the transparent semi-spherical canopy that crowned the top third of their luxurious home in the country, and he followed her gaze. She stood there drinking in with her eyes the magnificent vibrations of peace and harmony, and then her gaze slowly swept around the pool and living room area of their tranquil home.

On the far side of the pool centered in the surrounding living room under the overhead dome were several steps that led up to a modern open kitchen. A number of other rooms extended from each side of the kitchen around the circumference of the upper half of the dome. Living room sofas, chairs, and transparent glass-like topped tables adorned the wide blue granite-like stone floor surrounding the pool. The bedrooms on the second level were also accessed from the lower floor by four spiral metal staircases positioned at four equidistant points around the interior circumference of the dome. An advanced form of fiber-optic lighting, recessed underneath three overlapping concentric circles of foot-wide ivory-colored panels, surrounded the lower half of the clear overhead canopy. Everything was illuminated as if they were outside under the natural light of their planet's twin suns.

Moon-teran returned her gaze to her happy husband and rested her head on his shoulder again. Just then, the children, who had changed into bathing suits, ran together and jumped into the beautiful pool with the surrounding rim set with glistening faceted gems of many colors. They began a happy splashing play of throwing a floating ball back and forth in appreciation of each other. Competitive natures for gaining or winning over another were not apparent in their loving gentle actions, for they truly appreciated the great gift from Prime Creator of knowing they were together for each other's benefit.

Then Moon-teran began to thoughtfully reflect on how fortunate they were to live on a normal human world. With her inner vision, she recalled how they resided in a beautifully lush country setting not far from one of the twelve worldwide governing complexes with their science labs, art, and cultural buildings that all citizens enjoyed on her home world of Norexilam. Then her being lit up with an overflowing joy she had never imagined existed in her suppressed life growing up as Janice Carter back on Earth.

Having also envisioned all she was seeing, Donum-tuma gently took her hand and kissed it. Then they casually walked together outside their home through a round transparent glass-like door that automatically opened by sliding into the surrounding circular eight-foot high smooth ivory colored wall.

They had stepped into a botanical garden paradise of multi-tiered waterfalls laced with wonderfully landscaped flowering rock gardens. Trees far bigger than the great Redwood and Sequoia trees of northern California back on Earth were growing in well-selected places interspersed through the wonderland of nature in harmony with itself. The lush gardens extended into the distant acreage toward the snow crowned blue-gray mountain range. Perhaps twenty miles away, they curved like a half-moon across the horizon under the twin golden-bronzed suns. The slightly smaller radiant orb was just above the top of the crest of the mountain range, and the radiant larger orb was to the right of it higher up in the deep turquoise-blue sky. Faintly crimson and lavender tinted clouds, slowly moving from west to east, were laced between them on several levels.

There were plants the size of an adult person with broad green leaves like prehistoric giant Earth ferns, and wide gold and violet flowers blossoming from ten feet tall dark green stalks. Soft bright-green moss covered the many paths that wound throughout the garden splendor.

Small chirping birds singing complicated beautiful tunes through long thin beaks extended from lovely violet heads looked similar to birds on Earth. They were merrily fluttering back and forth, briefly stopping to hover over a large flower to dart a long sticky tongue down behind the shimmering phosphorescent six-inch tall stamens dripping with nectar. The smooth, curved, emerald-green, four-inch-wide teardrop shaped overlapping flower petals spread around the stamens like a fan. The full spectrum of iridescent pastel feather plumage on several dozen birds flying by overhead were subtly blended together down their twin, long fan-shaped tail feathers, and across the two sets of their beautifully elegant wings that were beating together one above the other like a dragonfly. Their aerodynamically streamlined bodies became more apparent when a mated pair briefly landed on a branch to sing a different beautiful melody to each other. The slightly smaller female exhibited her more delicate feminine characteristics by spreading out her two slightly longer tail feathers like twin Japanese fans, and the pair flew away again with their two sets of wings rapidly beating as fast as a hummingbird back on Earth.

Later that night, after they had tucked their three children into their soft oval beds in their individual rooms on the second floor and snuggled them close, Donum-tuma and Moon-teran climbed into their own big oval bed ideally located centered at the top of their living dome between the smaller rooms that surrounded the second floor level. They lay side-by-side to appreciate the breathtaking celestial view of the night stars under the clear overhead canopy. If any Earth person suddenly arrived to see the radiant depth of colorful stars and numerous nebulae that adorn the night sky of their world, they would be stunned beyond words. They would not believe their eyes as they watched the three moons orbiting the planet at different positions across the heavens. One was faintly tinted pale bluish, another was faintly tinted pale green, and third was faintly tinted red. It would all seem like a dreamy fantasy after their instant arrival back on Earth.

The two reunited lovers were soon reaching the peak of their intimate passionate ecstasy, when their Atma or true radiant spherical selves unexpectedly propelled out of their bodies to hover side-by-side above their swooning physical bodies. Their telepathic cries of release began to create a blinding white light that pulsed outward in all directions like concentric radio waves. The waves then quickly faded away, just as a whirling golden-white inter-dimensional tunnel opening appeared above them. Their two radiant spheres merged into one brighter and larger sphere that darted into the tunnel of light.

A third of the way around the planet, on one of the other three equidistantly spaced continents centered over the planet's equator, stood another elegantly designed domed home. It rested on several dozen lush, green moss-covered acres. The nearby light green mile-high waterfall, illumined by the phosphorescent mineral rich water with a soft moonstone-like sheen, was tumbling over the top of the crescent valley below the rolling lush forested snow-free mountain ridge. The powerful water was cascading down across a three-tiered cliff face to the river valley that wound like a snake off into the distant countryside. The twin setting suns were high in the sky above this mountain range. It just happened to be located on the same latitude as that of the taller snow covered mountains that were on a continent a third of the way around the planet's equator near Moon-teran's home.

This unique home was made up of a three geodesic-domed complex built in a triangular pattern interconnected by transparent glass-like triangular walkways. Crowning two of the domes were clear transparent canopies. The third one had a smooth ivory-white, smaller turret type dome topping it that looked like it might conceal some kind of advanced astronomical telescope or other stellar observation equipment.

Assortments of multicolored vegetables cultivated in crisscrossing rows beside many bushy fruit trees were growing inside the triangular area between the three domes. The acreage surrounding the domes was immaculately well-landscaped, and laced with many circulating multi-tiered rock garden waterfalls. Verdant flowers much larger and more prolific than any Earth garden were artfully growing in and around them.

The interspersed forest trees were ten times larger than the tallest giant Redwood or Sequoia trees back on Earth, but the resemblance to Earth varieties was uncanny. Some of the tree trunks with crimson-red bark were seventy-five feet wide at or near the ground and several thousand feet tall. The eight to twelve feet thick branches near their base extended straight out from the massive trunks nearly twenty feet before they gradually curved up at almost ninety-degree angles.

In the distance beyond this particular home spread out a thick forest of the giant trees with more geodesic-domed homes built upon the massive branches in gradually ascending levels. Spiraling upward transparent triangular corridors connected them together, like those that linked together Shon-ral's three geodesic-domed home complex back in the valley nearby the mile-high waterfall.

It was to this house that Ambassador Shon-ral arrived as he fully materialized on the teleportation pad chamber within the primary living dome under the clear overhead canopy. His trim, elegantly beautiful wife, Lorun-eral, who appeared to be in her mid-thirties was standing nearby with her long golden blond hair flowing down her back. She was wearing the very same soft white dress, shimmering like a moonstone, that she wore before he went to Earth on his ill-fated mission. She had been anxiously awaiting his return with their two eager, lovely children for a full year, undergoing the agony of dearly missing his absence from their lives.

Their two children, the handsome eight-year old boy, Shan-dreal, and beautiful ten-year old girl, Taluna-tala, who resembled their parents' characteristics to a fine point, ran to him as he stepped off the pad and squatted down to embrace and kiss them.

"Father. . . Father. . . Father," the ecstatically happy children repeatedly cried out.

"Oh, my beloved Shan-dreal and Taluna-tala, I have so dearly missed you," exclaimed Shon-ral through raining tears of joy.

While they both hugged his neck and kissed him back, he gazed up at his wife just as she stepped up to them with tears running down her cheeks through a smile of anticipated joy deeper than the clean clear sky around their planet, and he was awe-struck. Her radiant beauty now surpassed his deepest recollections of their previous bond of love for each other, and for the gift of their two wondrous children. The tears finally sprang from his eyes as he stood up and embraced his graceful wife, who rose up on her tiptoes like an Earth world ballerina. Their two children hugged their hips, and then stood back in wonder with their mouths open to observe the deep reunion that was taking place.

Shon-ral picked her up a foot off the floor and swung her around kissing her. She placed the long slender feminine fingers of her hands behind his head and neck to tenderly cup his head in her palms. At that moment, their children broke out joyfully clapping and giggling, and then they began jumping up and down.

Father... Father... Father, shouted the two ecstatic children this time in telepathic unison.

Their parents continued to passionately kiss even as he gently set her feet back down to the floor. To the children, time suddenly appeared to stand still as the pure Atma, the Soul spheres, or the true inner selves of their parents appeared ascending above the tops of their heads. The children stood back in wondrous awe of what they were witnessing. The eternal essences that are the real Shon-ral and Lorun-eral, hovering above the heads of the physical bodies, gradually moved toward each other until both spheres perfectly blended into one slightly larger more radiant sphere of light. The white luminous cores of their beings began to radiate with increasing intensity until a warm golden energy mist pulsed out into the chamber. It uplifted the children, impressing them with the refined honest nature of their parent's pure love for each other, for them, and for all life everywhere. The children's wide joyful eyes grew larger with anticipation, and then they broke out with more giggles, laughter, hand-clapping, and jumping up and down. The radiant spheres of their parents gradually separated and hovered back over the heads of their kissing bodies, before they faded back down inside the tops of their heads.

The parents parted to fondly gaze down at their knowing children, and the youngsters happily ran into their opening arms. A few minutes later, the family finally reunited in harmony and grace walked together through the oval opening leading into the living room area of their home under the overhead transparent canopy. Shon-ral began to appreciatively survey the majestic home and loving wife and children he had to leave behind thirty-one Earth years earlier.

Then the entire family calmly walked past the large oval pool and smaller hot tub-type pool to walk through the triangular opening leading into a twenty-foot-long transparent sided triangular walkway. Along the way, they gazed in at their vibrant food garden. It was growing outside in the triangular plot of land located inside the triangular space between the walkways that connected the three domed structures of their home complex together.

They passed through another oval opening at the other end of the walkway to enter their kitchen dome that was filled with very advanced appliances, granite-like appearing counter tops, sinks and food preparation areas that had been built into the octagon shaped cabinetry under the dome's inner circumference.

They continued to the other side of their kitchen dome to pass into another triangular hallway, and they were soon walking into the third dome. There Shon-ral paused to gaze with zeal up through the transparent round second floor level to fondly appreciate the very special tube-shaped astronomical telescope device attached to the center of the floor. It was two feet wide and twenty feet long, pointing at an upward angle toward the curved closed sliding hatch to the outside. A horizontal and vertical axis mounting system supported the telescope. Mounted on a three-legged gold metal tripod atop the upper end of the tube was a double-terminated one-foot-wide by two-foot-long flawless clear quartz crystal.

Shon-ral looked away and they walked together over to a transparent round doorway, similar to the one in Moon-teran's home. It automatically opened, silently sliding inside the eight-foot-tall ivory white wall that surrounded the lower level of the dome. The two children playfully ran out through it to the outside, and their cheerful parents walked out after them.

They stopped again just outside the astronomical dome to fondly gaze at the nearby mile-high luminous waterfall, and the giant forest trees with the many domed homes built ever upward in its massively strong branches. Their astronomical dome was facing the direction of their delighted gaze at the waterfall, and their running children playing before them in the glorious landscaped garden paradise.

As Lorun-eral lovingly looked up into his eyes, she telepathically stated to him with great relief apparent in her every word, *Oh how I thank the great Prime Creator behind all life for your return, my dear husband. You are finally home with us.*

He kissed his wife again and replied with sublime humble gratitude, while gazing lovingly back down into her beautiful green eyes, *Dearest wife, all I can say is there is no place like home. Oh dear Prime Creator of all, there just is no place like home on any other world in the universe.*

After their two children were put to bed and snuggled close in their individual rooms on the second floor of their living dome, Shon-ral and Lorun-eral climbed into their own big round bed in their round bedroom that was centered under the top of the clear curved sleeping canopy. They lay back to view the breathtaking celestial view of the night stars, colorful nebulae and the three slightly tinted bluish, green, and red moons orbiting their planet. They thought about how elevating their simple experience at that moment would be for any of the people back on Earth, after such a liberating gift of life is freely available to them.

They were soon intimately entwined for the first time in one year for Lorun-eral, and the first time in thirty-one Earth years for Shon-ral now that he was back in his original advanced human body. Just as they reached the peak of their intimate passionate ecstasy, they propelled out of their bodies to hover close together above the bed in their true spherical Atma energy forms. Their telepathic cries of release filled the air that no one but they could hear, and then their two radiant orbs merged into one larger brighter sphere creating a blinding white light that pulsed outward in all directions like concentric radio waves. As the waves faded away, a whirling golden-white inter-dimensional opening suddenly appeared above their united sphere, and it darted up into the tunnel of light.

A mighty ocean of brighter whirling light filled with millions upon millions of orbs, identical to what they had become, soon appeared before them moving like a galaxy around a more brilliant massive bulging nucleus in the immense deep blue surrounding void of some ethereal space. They were now in a far, far higher reality, and their sphere shot into the immense distance toward the galaxy-like nucleus center of the mighty ocean of light. They were being moved forward by a deep humming sound mixed with a hauntingly beautiful alluring ocean of male and female voices singing in round whole drawn out tones the word "HU" on many harmonic levels in perfect pitch. Their united sphere soon reached the center of the massive light and vanished deep inside its thunderous power.

Together as one light they began to telepathically speak to each other, just as their light sphere emerged inside another deep blue void with one massively larger sphere of light that was identical in structure to their own but a hundred times larger. It was peacefully hovering before them in the very center of the mysterious void.

Oh Shon-ral, where are we? humbly asked Lorun-eral with her quivering telepathic voice creating a pulsing light within their sphere that matched each uttered word.

Shon-ral replied with his own quivering telepathic voice, *Lorun-eral, dear heart, we are now in the high realm of Prime Creator itself. I don't know how I know this, but it is true.*

She replied frightened, *Oh my, what's happening to us?* Shon-ral projected back to her with his light sphere continuing to pulse with each word spoken, *Feel my courage, my love, and do not be afraid. We are exactly like Prime Creator, but on a much smaller scale, and we are here to learn.*

The voice of the Ancient One or Prime Creator was deeply melodious and filled with the secrets of the center of eternal creation itself. It too pulsed from within its massive center but each word created ecstasy in the combined light sphere of Shon-ral and Lorun-eral, and they separated back into two spheres hovering close side-by-side.

Beloved ones, began its smooth elevating voice of utter benevolence, *You have come home at last. You are here to understand more about the purpose for the new Ray that has been sent to your physical universe, and what this means for the far better enlightenment of every Atma or Soul throughout the many mansions or multi-dimensions of creation. You will be imbued with this new understanding now.*

A wave of misty white light so high in hue that the finest tinge of gold could just be made out laced throughout it shot from the center white core of Prime Creator to the center white cores of Shon-ral's and Lorun-eral's true selves. Both spheres expanded slightly larger, and their light intensity increased several times greater as the misty wave continued into the distance beyond the deep blue void.

Now you know, spoke Prime Creator or the Ancient One's majestic vibrant voice once again.

Yes, dear Prime Creator, now we know, solemnly proclaimed their inner voices in perfect unison.

Be at peace, and freely create with this new liberating Ray for it will forever bring constructive change to all the lower dimensions. All fear or what many beings refer to as evil is being forever retired from all the worlds of time and space. Return now and enjoy this moment in eternity. Know that your futures are very bright indeed.

Can we return here one day? asked Shon-ral and Lorun-eral in telepathic unison.

You will both return here many times to learn and expand your awareness capabilities throughout the eternity that is flung into your ever more creative futures. Now, you should return. To stay here any longer would result in the loss of your physical bodies back on your home planet, and you would not be able to carry out your part in the unfolding Expansion Ray mission that is uniquely yours to enjoy by right. All is well.

Their two separate spheres merged into one again and it shot downward in a blur of light at incredible speed. A moment later, the sphere sped right back down out of the open whirling inter-dimensional vortex to hover above their bodies that were now peacefully asleep with arms wrapped around each other. The vortex vanished as the radiant sphere separated back into two slightly smaller orbs. Then both spheres descended back down inside their bodies, and grateful smiles appeared on their bodies' sleeping faces.

CHAPTER TWENTY-SIX

THE CALL
TO
EXCELLENCE

The weeks went by for the cousins on their beautiful home world of Norexilam. Their normally highly refined human love for their world had been significantly elevated, evolving into a deep abiding love they knew was a privilege to express in waves of good will to all life throughout the multi-dimensional universes of Prime Creator. Their fellow citizens knew where this uplifting energy was coming from, and they knew why it was now radiating across the face of their world. They had all known about the loss of Ambassador Shon-ral and Prime Scientists Moon-teran, and about their amazing recovery and return from their devastating ordeal on the troubled Earth planet. Now they were all silently rejoicing, for they were beginning to go through an ever-greater transformation after a dozen of the mighty golden pyramids appeared in the botanical parks located within each of their twelve government, cultural, and science development centers. Within several days, the Ray radiating from them had refined every man, woman, and child on their world even further. They had all become dedicated together in their collectively awakened good will to see that Earth was finally set free from the tyranny that had plagued it for countless ages. The collective energy coming from each of them was emanating back through the chain of pyramids stationed across time and space all the way to planet Earth. That alone they knew would do more to uplift that planet's suppressed people than anyone could possibly imagine in the days, weeks, months, and several years that were to follow.

Then one day, the fountains hidden within the pyramids emerged from them to permanently sit themselves down in the very center of each botanical wonderland. Pouring from the palms of the mighty male statue standing in each of the wide granite bowls was that irresistible liberating white-golden light in the form of a drinkable liquid. What happened to the people on Norexilam after that can be best revealed by the phenomenal event that took place after the eighteen-foot-tall Seres Ambassador Torellian unexpectedly contacted Ambassador Shon-ral and Moon-teran one bright twin sun-filled day.

They were both puttering around alone outside in their home gardens on their respective continents, just for the pleasure of the solitude and peace it afforded them, when the mighty being appeared before Shon-ral radiating a clearly visible soft golden light from around his entire body. His wife and children had teleported away earlier to visit the nearest art and science center that was several hundred miles away from their home.

I knew that one day we would meet, telepathically stated Shon-ral, feeling rather more elated than usual at that moment, as the very tall majestic ancient immortal being towered above him that day.

Although he appeared like a youthful male in his thirties, Shon-ral knew the Seres race had immortalized their physical bodies before they disappeared from the galaxy so long ago. At that moment, he recalled they had originally seeded all human and humanoid life throughout the many galaxies of time and space, before they vanished from the lower dimensions over a billion years earlier. He knew the Seres had long ago evolved to greater heights than those refined humans who presently lived within the Galactic Inter-dimensional Alliance of Free Worlds.

You are now one of us, even though you may not yet be aware of this fact, telepathically replied the deep melodious inner voice of the Seres Ambassador with a loving nature that almost literally lifted

Shon-ral off his feet.

Shon-ral was about to say something but held back as Torellian continued to enlighten him with the purpose of his visit, *We are not now so different. You are about to begin to discover you have an eight-stranded DNA helix structure to your molecular make-up instead of four. You, your wife, Lorun-eral, and your cousin Moon-teran and her husband Donum-tuma, are gradually being transformed. This great change will not be noticeable to your fellow citizens on Norexilam just yet. However, this new body type will allow the Atma that is the real you to operate through it in ways you cannot yet imagine. I am committed to helping you and Lorun-eral through the transformation of this great gift given to you by Prime Creator during your recent trip. The full awareness of this will come in time.*

I am also here on another matter. I have spoken with the Galactic Alliance High Council and they wish me to ask you and Moon-teran if you would return to Earth this day. The President of the United States on that world, the newly liberated Trilotew Ambassador Grotzil, and Chairman Ted Carter of the secret second worldwide government are about to announce to all the people of Earth the truth at last about all that has been kept from them. There will be great unrest and perhaps even rebellion among the confused masses, and you and Moon-teran's presence there will be necessary to transmit to them all what you both went through to awaken from the torturous suppression you suffered under for so many years. Your experiences will emanate from the pyramids that will begin to appear right after the most important speech in Earth's entire history is given, and both you and Moon-teran will be inspired to share what happened. When this is taking place, you two will serve as examples for all the people of Earth. You will emanate your prototype as the advanced human beings you have become to give them a glimpse of what they will experience in the near future. Once they have the understanding of what you went through, all fear, anger, hate, and any other subconscious negatively driven emotions or thoughts that were running their lives will be given up and turned back into the pure primordial omnipresent force that supports and sustains all life and all that exists.

Shon-ral was smiling for he began to actually visually see the tremendous worldwide transformation that was coming to the entire Earth planet to keep the people from otherwise destroying themselves in the very near future.

He looked up at the graceful Seres Ambassador and said using his own voice, "Now I clearly see what you have been saying about the entirely unexpected events that are coming to the people of Earth."

"Will you return?" humbly asked Torellian using his vocal chords, and he unassumingly waited for Shon-ral's response.

"Yes, of course I will," replied Shon-ral without hesitation, "And I am certain Moon-teran will agree."

Torellian grinned and the soft angelic light emanating from around his entire body brightened.

Then all is well, he telepathically stated, as if he were actually relieved. *The truth you and Moon-teran will radiate through the pyramids to all the people of Earth will help them remain peacefully balanced through the tremendous changes that their planet must go through to purify the environment. However, this will not be the destructive method of cyclic planetary polar shifts used to accomplish this in the past. You can also communicate to them all about the coming return of our Seres race to the universe. However, we will not make our presence known to the Earth people until after the planet's transformation, and they have accepted being part of the Galactic Inter-dimensional Alliance of Free Worlds.*

Moon-teran will contact you now, for I have appeared before her during this same time while she stood alone outside in her home garden. Her husband is also away with their three children on a day trip to the mountains. The ability to be in more than one place at the same time will be awakened in you when the time is right. You will shortly both discover that I have already spoken with your mates and they are comfortable with the plan to temporarily return you to Earth. Shon-ral, you will soon realize that you do not need a spaceship to return this time, and Moon-teran will be the first to utilize the important ability that is beginning to awaken within each of you. Then you will understand. For now, know that you have the good will and friendship of the entire Seres race, and the gift of grace from Prime Creator. Now, I must depart. Farewell.

The majestic angelic Seres Ambassador began to sparkle like a million tiny glittering blue stars and faded away. Ambassador Shon-ral walked back inside his living dome and went into the teleportation chamber to see a blinking yellow faceted crystal on the console, and he touched it. An energy projected view screen appeared above the console and Moon-teran came into focus on it radiantly happy.

She cheerfully stated, "Dear cousin, it looks like we're headed back to Earth already. I understand what Ambassador Torellian meant. I no longer need the teleportation unit to join you now. Behold!"

The image on the view screen of her standing in the outside garden by her domed home simply vanished from view, and she just as simply instantly reappeared standing beside Shon-ral in his teleportation chamber an ocean and a continent away. He began to express amazement, but stopped as he grinned wide with his own sudden new understanding, and he grasped her hand. Then, they both simply vanished again and reappeared standing side-by-side back outside in his garden, giddy with childlike wonder.

"Cousin dear," began Shon-ral elated, "I perceive the President of the United States is about to give that scheduled speech to the people of Earth."

"Yes, I see the liberated Trilotew Ambassador Grotzil standing beside him," replied Moon-teran also elated.

"We're already discovering new abilities with our transformed eight-stranded DNA helix bodies," curiously added Shon-ral. "We can project ourselves anywhere now just by visualizing the destination, and the new liberating Ray will send us there bypassing the laws of physics that rule the lower dimensions."

"Perhaps we should contact the President first before we just show up unannounced in his office," cautiously inquired Moon-teran.

"You're right," thoughtfully replied Shon-ral and he added, "I must try something I'm beginning to sense we are both also capable of doing or he won't recognize either of us."

"Yes, yes, you're right, cousin. I was just sensing the same thing," she curiously shot back.

Shon-ral dreamily looked away and a transparent energy wave passed down over his body, similar to a heat wave in the desert, and his molecules swiftly rearranged themselves back into the body of Mark Santfield.

"Well, cousin, how do I look?" he impishly asked and bowed.

Chuckling back at him, she replied, "Oh, it's perfect. You look exactly like Mark Santfield. Okay then, here goes."

She dreamily looked away and her body transformed in the same way back to Janice Carter.

Chuckling, Mark stated, "Oh that's just superb. Now how are we going to explain this to our families?"

She winked at him and replied, "We don't! At least, not for a while, if we're wise."

Grinning, Mark wisely nodded his agreement.

Back in the Oval Office at the White House in Washington D.C. on planet Earth, President Martin McCoy and Trilotew Ambassador Grotzil were standing in front of the President's desk when they both clearly heard Mark's telepathic voice respectfully inquire, *Excuse my interruption, Mr. President and Ambassador Grotzil, but can you both hear me? This is Ambassador Shon-ral, who you also know as Mark Santfield.*

Startled but unafraid, they both replied in unison, "Yes," and the President asked, "Where are you?"

On our home world of Norexilam, replied Mark. *Moon-teran or the one you know as Janice Carter and I would like to join you to add our voices to the momentous announcement you are about to make to the people of Earth. I perceive that Chairman Ted Carter is not with you now. It's important that he disclose the truth about his hidden organization as well.*

"He'll be arriving any minute with Monti and Henry," commented the President. "I've been very anxious to hear from you. Know that you are always most welcome. It would not be a complete announcement without you two."

Outside Ambassador Shon-ral's home on planet Norexilam in the garden, he and Moon-teran smiled and they both telepathically replied to the President, *We're on our way.*

CHAPTER TWENTY-SIX

Grinning, Shon-ral asked Moon-teran, "Are you ready, cousin?"

She smiled, nodded and cheerily replied, "I'm more than ready."

Shon-ral confidently extended his elbow to her. She placed her arm through it, grabbed his hand, and they both looked up into the sky with widening exhilarating smiles. Then they simply vanished.

They both reappeared an instant later standing upon the elegant rug with the official Presidential eagle seal beautifully woven into it right in front of President McCoy and Ambassador Grotzil.

"How did you get here?" curiously asked Grotzil. "There was no teleportation beam."

"All I can say for now is we have acquired some new abilities. A moment ago, we were more than five hundred light years away on our home planet Norexilam and now we're here," impishly replied Mark.

Grotzil thought about what he said, and then his eyes lit-up with a profound realization.

"You can project between worlds now on your own?" he curiously inquired.

"Yes, and I suspect when the time is right, after all your fellow Trilotew citizens living on your combined world systems are set free from their subconscious nightmare, they too will discover how to accomplish this. The ability will not function if the intent is negatively covert or if it is intended for conquest or the domination of others."

The Trilotew Ambassador thoughtfully reflected on Mark's words, nodded smiling and said, "I understand. It is as it should be."

There was a knock on the door. Secretary of Defense Daniel Samuelson opened it and walked in but stopped to stare amazed to see that Mark and Janice had somehow arrived in the Oval Office without going through the front door.

He curiously gazed at them and sincerely stated, "Welcome back, Mark and Janice. We've been wondering if you two would show up." They both smiled and nodded their appreciation for his warm welcome, and then Daniel looked at President McCoy and announced, "Mr. President, Chairman Carter just telepathically informed me that he, Henry, and Monti are about to arrive."

"Thank you, Daniel," calmly replied Martin. "You should join us. Now we can begin the news conference. Is everything ready to go?"

Daniel smiled and confidently answered, "Yes, Mr. President, we go live worldwide in fifteen minutes."

At that moment, a bright whirling beam appeared behind Mark and Janice, revealing Chairman Ted Carter and his general council Henry Throckmorton in business suits, and Monti standing close together as the beam faded away.

"Janice, dear daughter," cried out Ted delightfully surprised, "I so much missed you."

He and Janice ran into each other's arms, and he gave her a long fatherly embrace. Then she looked up at him and said, "Dearest foster father from Earth, I have also missed you."

Henry walked up, they hugged each other, and she said, "Dear friend Henry, I am so very glad to see you too."

"This news conference is going to be most interesting," he declared smiling at her and he gazed at Mark, "Well Mark, or I should say Ambassador Shon-ral, what's going to happen on this planet after all the frustrated people in the world learn the truth about just how much they were lied to over the decades? They will have every right to get really pissed off."

"I was thinking the same thing," curiously concurred Ted.

Mark gazed back at both men, at the President, at Ambassador Grotzil, and then at Monti, who appeared quite cheerful and he asked, "Monti, my friend, will you join us?"

Monti cheerfully replied, "Not this time. I must return to the flagship to assist with the changes that will be taking place all over the Earth after you conclude your announcement. Know that I will contact you when I can. Farewell, my friends."

He touched the gold pin on his lapel and vanished in a whirl of teleportation light.

Then Ted curiously asked, "If the people do get really pissed off as Henry said, how are we going to handle that?"

With a compassionate smile, Mark replied, "That foreseen difficulty has been taken care of, and you will all see events take place on this Earth that will stay vividly impressed within your new expanding state of awareness for eternity." He confidently looked at the President and stated, "It's time for Janice and I to reveal our true off-world natures and physical characteristics. Our Earth bodies have just undergone a genetic transformation back to our original extraterrestrial human bodies, even though the Trilotew destroyed them long ago. This took place through a special process that utilized our original DNA stored back on our home world. What you are seeing before you now are the temporary molecular DNA reformations from our original extraterrestrial human bodies back to the Earth physical bodies that are familiar to you."

Mark looked at Janice and she nodded. Then he looked at Ted, who was gazing back at her in wonder and they both looked away in their imaginations. The desert-like heat wave effect appeared flowing down over their bodies, and it turned their molecular DNA compositions back into the true original human appearances of Ambassador Shon-ral and Prime Scientist Moon-teran. Everyone else in the room was awestruck by the change. However, they could not help but notice they also had slightly larger than average human eyes, and their general physical characteristics appeared to be much more youthfully refined. Then, the amazed observers began to realize that an invisible energy radiating from Shon-ral and Moon-teran was actually uplifting them.

"Janice, is that you?" apprehensively asked Ted.

She smiled with deep affection back at him and replied, "Yes, I'm the same being you knew while I was growing up, and ever so much more. Do not be concerned. In a short time, it will be clear to everyone here why we are now all together."

"I believe the time has come for me to use our morphing device," interjected Ambassador Grotzil, "To camouflage my reptilian features until the time comes toward the end of my speech to reveal my true appearance to Earth's people. We use a device that projects an electromagnetic field that tightly bends light around our bodies to make us appear like normal human beings wearing appropriate attire. I've per-selected one stored in its memory that I like to use, but it doesn't actually change my molecular structure."

He touched the symbol on his belt buckle and his body took on the appearance of a taller thin human male with oddly penetrating eyes, wearing a dark blue suit.

Then he looked at President McCoy and asked, "Will this do, Mr.

President?"

Martin grinned and replied, "It will indeed, at least until you reveal what you really look like as agreed toward the end of your disclosure to the people of Earth."

The Trilotew Ambassador grinned and nodded.

Daniel Samuelson looked down at his wristwatch and urgently stated, "We've got to get moving. We go live in the conference room in ten minutes.

"Lead the way, Daniel," courteously replied Martin, and they all began to head out of the Oval Office. Then the President stopped to relay to Ambassador Shon-ral, "I'm scheduled to speak to the nation and the world at large first. Then Ted will go on, followed by Trilotew Ambassador Grotzil. After that, things will really heat up. You and Moon-teran will address the people of Earth last as channels of the new Ray to prepare them to go through their own coming transformations."

"Understood," calmly replied Shon-ral. My Cousin Moon-teran and I will deliver to all the people of Earth our entire experience of what we went through: from the time we were both captured by the Trilotew to finally being liberated from their suppressive subconscious programming that freed our true hidden natures. Then we will reveal our purpose for coming to Earth, and the far greater awareness we both now share. But first, I believe it would be best if Moon-teran and I changed back to Mark and Janice because the people will initially be able to relate to us far better as recognizable fellow citizens."

Shon-ral and Moon-teran looked at each other, and the transparent heat wave energy effect rippled down over their bodies to instantly transform them back into Mark Santfield and Janice Carter right before the gaping eyes of the entourage.

Mark kindly smiled and nodded encouragement to the President, who nodded back grinning before he turned and walked out of the Oval Office behind Daniel. Then, Mark turned to Janice, gallantly offered his arm, and she threw her arm through his as they confidently walked out of the Oval Office. The amazed Trilotew Ambassador, and the equally amazed Ted and Henry followed close behind them.

CHAPTER TWENTY-SEVEN

THE EARTH WORLD TRANSFORMS

President Martin McCoy walked into the White House press room and up behind the podium, but there were no reporters gathered there this time. Mark, Janice, Ted, Daniel, and then Ambassador Grotzil appearing as the tall lanky normal man wearing a dark blue suit stopped beside each other along the sidewall. President McCoy nodded he was ready at the lead TV camera operator. The operator nodded back and touched the headset on his left ear. He listened for a moment for timing instructions from the control booth, then held up three fingers on his right hand and silently mouthed out, dropping a finger each time, "Three, two, one," and he pointed at the President to let him know he was now on live television to the entire world.

"Good evening, my fellow Americans. Tonight I am here to address you and all the citizens of Earth. This will be the most important speech that any President or any leader has ever given to the people of this world. A great uplifting transformation is coming to our world, and it is finally time to reveal what the misguided leaders of many countries have purposefully kept from you for far too long. It may be difficult at first to hear this, but we came under the control of a misdirected small elite group of financially powerful men who had orchestrated the creation of a second secret hidden government after World War II. They did this with good initial intentions to create an inner government that could run the country if the elected officials were killed in a nuclear war with the former Soviet Union. However, after its creation the power-mad ambitions of this group, who could operate completely outside of the law with the creation of the National Security Act, rapidly gained control of the military industrial complex.

"A short time later, they gained influential control over the true elected officials in our country and the leaders of many other powerful nations, after they secretly signed a treaty with a visiting cunning totalitarian extraterrestrial race called the Trilotew. This race offered to provide certain advanced alien technology and weaponry to the United States in exchange for being permitted to conduct supposedly harmless DNA experiments on a number of unsuspecting world citizens they claimed would not be harmed; but they lied. Once the power hungry men started down the covert path of classified secrecy to gain an elite power status over all humankind, the alien race began to take over their minds without them realizing it. They did this by using a far more advanced subconscious terrorizing control technology. Tonight, I formally announce their sinister designs upon our world have miraculously ended.

"I am also deeply sorry to report that several million citizens from our planet were secretly abducted by the Trilotew over the years, and they have never been returned. We know the Trilotew killed many of them, but some will be returning they kept alive to do their bidding. The alien threat to this world was very real and it threatened the very existence of every man, woman, and child on the planet. If something quite unexpected had not stopped their inroads to controlling our world, their continued influence would likely have resulted in the complete destruction of our planet. However, a great benevolent force that no one saw coming has now completely neutralized the evil intentions of the Trilotew.

"Here with me tonight to enlighten you are several very important guest speakers. Their significant part in this worldwide-televised event will become clear to you, while you listen to what they have to share. My first guest speaker will be Mr. Ted Carter. Many of you may know him as the most wealthy person on Earth. However, he is actually the Chairman of the classified secret hidden government. He and his associates have gone through their own liberating transformation, and he will relay what has happened that will change the direction of the destructive destiny of our planet to one of amazing liberation.

"My second guest to speak will be the newly liberated and transformed Trilotew Ambassador Grotzil himself. He will relay how he and his Trilotew associates have also gone through an entirely unexpected change brought about by a new liberating energy Ray that is beginning to manifest on Earth even while I'm speaking to you tonight. What was subconsciously driving the Trilotew race to behave in an evil covert manner for hundreds of thousands of years no longer exists. This new benevolent energy completely removed it. Rest assured, I know from personal experience that all Trilotew who were secretly operating on Earth have already left our world, other than Ambassador Grotzil who remained behind to relay his own experience about what is creating this great change.

"Then there are two other very important human beings with us tonight who wish to speak with you but they are not from Earth. You may know of Mark Santfield from his successful first conspiracy theory novel that revealed very prophetic revelations about a suspected hidden government and their involvement with a sinister extraterrestrial race. His second book just released two weeks ago has already skyrocketed far beyond the *New York Times'* bestseller list. In fact, worldwide sales are dramatically climbing through the roof, and you should know what is contained in this second book is one hundred percent accurate in every way. There is a reason for this. Mark Santfield and Chairman Ted Carter's adopted daughter, Janice Carter, are actually emissaries from an extraterrestrial organization called the Galactic Inter-dimensional Alliance of Free Worlds. This organization is comprised of over four hundred and fifty million human, humanoid, and other highly intelligent benevolent space faring races. They are coming here to help us make a great transition to becoming a planetary member of their organization. Mark is actually Galactic Alliance Ambassador Shon-ral and Janice is actually Prime Galactic Alliance Scientist Moon-teran. They come from a planet over five hundred light years from Earth called Norexilam. We finally have the answer to that great question of whether or not we are alone in the universe.

"They will directly share with every man, woman, and child living on our planet what they went through: starting with how they were trapped by the Trilotew; how they were finally freed from a torturous subconscious programming; how this reawakened their originally very evolved extraterrestrial human natures; and how the even greater expansion of their beings recently took place. Once they have finished imparting their truth to you, each one of you will remember your own much more advanced human natures that were originally available on Earth before they were purposefully genetically suppressed a very long time ago.

"Fellow citizens of planet Earth, you have all been deceived about a great many things by your governments for more than sixty years. To sum things up, the military industrial complex was being run by a secret second government that was being controlled by the extraterrestrial Trilotew before this great change began. Now our planet and our lives are about to transform into something truly beyond wonderful. Prime Creator or the Ancient One, the benevolent central source or great power that sustains all life, recently gave a great gift to the Galactic Alliance. They are now openly engaged in sharing this with us. Our planet will become a space faring member of the wondrous Galactic Alliance, and you will actually know the experience of what it is like to travel to the stars. The end of evil as an experiment, like the extinction of the dinosaurs, is finally occurring on our world."

The President paused to let his profound last statement sink in to the television audience.

"I will now introduce my first guest speaker, Ted Carter, chairman of the classified secret second government. First, know that he and his associates have all gone through a liberating change back to their natural benevolent natures." He nodded smiling at Ted, who was standing with the other guest speakers along the sidewall, and then he stepped away from the podium. Ted smiled at the cameras that focused on him as he walked behind the podium and took a relaxing breath.

Then he solemnly began, "My fellow citizens of planet Earth, I am the nominated Chairman of a Council of secretly classified men who have been collectively running the major governments of the world. However, your votes did not elect me to this position. My forebears started down that dark road of deceit and covert misdirection after World War II. Originally, they created their secret control at the beginning of the Cold War with the former Soviet Union to maintain a consistent level of government that would survive if nuclear war destroyed the duly elected government officials. They felt they were doing the right thing at the time.

"Then a wild card was thrown into the works. Many unidentified flying objects began to appear around the world after the first nuclear bomb tests, and soon direct secret contact with both benevolent and totalitarian extraterrestrials began to take place with certain world leaders. The highly evolved benevolent human Galactic Alliance representatives who first contacted them required that all Earth governments give up their nuclear weapons before they would share any of their extraterrestrial technological wonders. The Earth leaders of the time turned them down because of fear, and then the Trilotew made contact. They did not require nuclear weapons be given up, and the United States leaders who wanted to remain technically dominant over any future adversary were compelled or blackmailed into signing a treaty with them.

"To elaborate, a great traumatic fear remained in our leaders after the destructive Second World War ended that made our President and his generals at the time very paranoid of the sincere Galactic Alliance offer. However, several months later, the totalitarian Trilotew emissaries, with their own sinister designs upon our planet, met with our leaders to make them an offer they could not refuse. They claimed they were willing to provide what the U.S. military industrial complex leaders wanted without requiring they first give up their destructive nuclear bombs and radioactive toys. After that, our leaders stepped into a blackmail trap because the Trilotew Ambassador stated that if the United States refused to sign a treaty with them, they would take their offer to the Soviet Union and they would become the preeminent super power on Earth. The Trilotew compelled that past President and his generals to sign the treaty, against their better judgment. However, they did not know the Trilotew were in Moscow at the same time offering the same deal to the former leader of the Soviet Union.

"After the treaty was signed, the Trilotew began to infiltrate and dominate the leaders of our secret second government. I inherited my position from my father's position before me in what many people on Earth have labeled the Illuminati or what we actually call the Triumvirate World Council, or the TWC for short. According to Galactic Alliance scientific historians, like my foster daughter known as Janice or Moonteran off world, the unconsciously perversely driven Trilotew tyrants were driving us in a direction that would have unexpectedly ended in the destruction of our planet.

"My fellow human beings, you will come to know for yourselves that the former twisted nature of the Trilotew that orchestrated this direction, and all of our hidden secret TWC Council members have gone through a liberating transformation. The negative drives in our subconscious minds are permanently gone, and it is my privilege to announce that our hidden government no longer exists. All worldwide members have unanimously committed their lives and our collective monstrous fortunes to liberate all of you in harmony with the coming uplifting transformation of our world. I have been informed that everyone, without exception, will soon have their own experience with this liberating Ray that comes from the source behind all life, or whatever you may conceive that to be

Please hold back any anger and frustration for just a few moments longer, and each one of you will know what we now know to be true beyond any doubt whatsoever. There will be no more secrets between us. We will soon disclose everything that has previously remained hidden from you. Your freed rightfully elected President Martin McCoy is now benevolently in charge as he should be. He is now openly accepting the guidance, wisdom, and assistance of the entire Galactic Inter-dimensional Alliance of Free Worlds. Thank you for listening, and for your considerate understanding."

Ted stepped away from the podium, and the President stepped back up behind it and announced, "Now, it is my privilege to introduce to you Trilotew Ambassador Grotzil," and he nodded at the ambassador as he stepped back away from the podium.

The Trilotew Ambassador walked past him and stepped up behind the podium. In his dark blue suit, he appeared to be similar to any member of the President's staff but with oddly penetrating eyes.

"Thank you, Mr. President, for your kind introduction. First let me state we Trilotew would deserve only the worst fate after what we have secretly done here on Earth. If this new Ray from Prime Creator or the source behind all life had not been sent here to intervene, we would have all gone up in flames."

"Fellow beings living on Earth, we of the Trilotew were your bitter enemies, and your fate under our control would have caused you unimaginable suffering. However, we were set free from a terrible subconscious programming that we have been suffering under as a race for so long. Fortunately, the Galactic Alliance President McCoy mentioned received a new liberating power that removes all genetically limiting and tyrannical evil drives that operate on a subconscious level in beings who live on many planetary systems throughout the many galaxies of the universe. When they brought this liberating force to Earth we were the first Trilotew to be set free, and now the entire Trilotew race is about to become benevolent loving beings again like we once were in the ancient past. I say to all of you that my fellow Trilotew, who were secretly operating on Earth, have been set free from any desire to dominate your world. We are now your committed friends. We will do all we can from now on to help liberate everyone living on your world so that you too can play among the stars.

"Please forgive us for the harm that we caused to the relatives of some of you that disappeared without a trace over the years. Although many of them were killed when we were not in control of our behavior, know their real selves still exist. It is true that many have lost their bodies. However, as you will each soon discover they are still alive in their true spherical energy or Atma forms or what you refer to as Soul, and you will all see them again soon in a very special way. I know this to be true. It has also been my great privilege to speak the truth to all of you at last. There will be no more secrets. Now the time has come for me to introduce to you all my true Trilotew Ambassador bipedal reptilian physical form. You may be shocked at first, because I am not actually the human male you see before you. What you are seeing is a projected illusion. However, know I am now a benevolent eternal being even as you really are. Behold!"

Grotzil touched his belt buckle device and the energy screen projection of a tall lanky human male rippled around his body revealing his true reptilian nature.

Gasps of surprise came from the mouths of the camera operators and President McCoy encouraged, "Don't be frightened by his appearance. Stay at your cameras. He is not harmful."

They obeyed, and while they gazed through the cameras at his vertical, red cat-like slits, centered in his horizontal oval violet eyeballs, they began to perceive they were emanating a gentle nature. His smooth green scaly skin actually appeared to be strangely elegant to them without their understanding why, even though they could also clearly see the two receding rows of sharp fanged teeth lining the inside of his upper and lower jaws. His wide smile was unmistakably warm and friendly toward the operators, and to all human beings watching from all around the Earth. He stepped aside and bowed with the palms of his hands placed crossed over his chest upon each shoulder. Then he rose back up, smiled again, and walked away as President McCoy walked back behind the podium.

"Please do not indulge in anger or fear, my fellow citizens, for your futures are very bright, beyond even your finest dreams. Now I have the distinct privilege of introducing to you Mark Santfield, who I mentioned is actually Ambassador Shon-ral, and Janice Carter, who I also mentioned is actually referred to as Prime Scientist Moon-teran from the Galactic Inter-dimensional Alliance of Free Worlds."

The President nodded to them as he stepped away from the podium again. Then Mark and Janice stepped up together to stand side-by-side behind it smiling, and they nodded their heads toward the main camera.

"First of all," cordially began Mark, "I want to thank all of you who purchased my second book. You will discover it is now operating as a channel of this new liberating Ray. I can also assure you, and those close to you who may not have read it yet, that you are all about to receive vastly more in liberating new awareness and freedom."

Janice kindly added as she stepped a little closer to the podium, "In a few moments, you will all begin to experience the liberating Ray on a grand scale all over the planet, and finally you will remember your true advanced benevolent natures as human beings that was genetically taken from you a long time ago."

Mark boldly stated, "You should all see us as we really are, now that we have been returned to our original human extraterrestrial natures that were suppressed until recently. Your greatly unexpected destiny is to become enlightened members of the Galactic Inter-dimensional Alliance of Free Worlds, and free space faring adventurers that can confidently state you are from the completely transformed planet Earth. Behold!"

They both stood to the side of the podium and looked away to envision the coming miraculous change. The desert-like heat wave affect appeared washing down over their bodies revealing the true radiant advanced human characteristics of Ambassador Shon-ral and Prime Scientist Moon-teran. Then a pulsing series of golden expanding donut-shaped energy waves began to radiate from their bodies out through the walls of the conference room.

Shon-ral's deeper melodious voice carried upon the waves to every human being on Earth telepathically stated, *Experience now all we went through starting with how the Trilotew captured us after we arrived to help the people of Earth not destroy yourselves. Then witness how we were set free from the Trilotew subconscious brainwashing technology, and observe how the full realization of our greatly expanded awareness as highly evolved human beings resurfaced. Know that all of you will soon be experiencing this awakening for yourselves.*

From outside the White House, the concentric circles of luminous golden energy waves expanded until they encompassed the surface of the entire planet in under a minute. People everywhere were suddenly experiencing a great uplifting feeling and clarity of awareness they had never known before. They quickly discovered that all fear, hate, bigotry, prejudice, jealously, greed, and vain religious superiority attitudes had simply dissolved away within their consciousness. People about to commit murder or shoot a weapon in conflicts taking place at different locations around the globe simply could not fathom why they were about to do what they were about to do. Child molesters and rapists were free from all impulses to behave in any other way than benevolently toward all life. They all began to realize that evil as an experiment was being retired from creation because the time had finally come to replace it with something far more effective, true, necessary, and kind. This new awareness was beginning to inspire each individual to embrace the wonder of becoming a liberated co-worker with the source that supports all life and all beings living in the vast multi-dimensional universe.

Then, twenty-foot-high luminous golden pyramids began appearing in the central parks of major cities and in ideally centrally located places in the countryside all over the Earth, until ten thousand had appeared. A short time later, childlike wonder began to dominate the entire attention of everyone on Earth. An irresistible force was drawing them to approach the pyramids in a peaceful loving manner that absolutely amazed them.

Then everyone heard Shon-ral's loving vibrant telepathic voice encourage, ***Now be at peace on this world, and enjoy together this mighty gift from Prime Creator or the source behind all life.***

The pyramids began to simultaneously radiate a brighter light. Then the mysterious fountains, with the majestic Angelic being standing up inside the white granite bowls, began to become visible through the walls of the pyramids that were starting to turn transparent. The walls then faded away, leaving the fountains permanently grounded to the Earth.

There stood the strongly built bare-chested youthful but completely bald majestic angelic statue of a man in perhaps his mid-thirties with light-bronzed skin. Two golden bracelets encircled each of his upper arms, and a white cotton-like skirt extended from the waist down to just above his bare feet that were standing upon a raised square granite platform centered in the bowl. The golden-white vibrant liquid light pouring out of his open palms held facing outward in front of his hips was streaming down into the wide white granite bowl below his feet. A round granite column supported the wide granite bowl full of the luminous liquid that was flowing over the entire circumference of the outer rim like a shimmering smooth curtain of nectar to mysteriously vanish in the ground. Twelve ornate golden jewel encrusted cups hung from golden hooks were set into the circumference of the outer rim of the bowl. A flat circular, two-foot-wide white granite seat, supported two feet above the ground by a dozen intricately carved white granite legs, encircled the fountain bowl a foot away from the water.

The loving vibrant voice of Moon-teran then said for all to clearly hear, *Drink freely from these wondrous fountains and be free from all the subconscious nightmares that have driven your lives for countless generations. Your two-stranded DNA helix that has limited your full potentials as human beings from surfacing on Earth is returning to your original four-stranded DNA helix. Then they will become an eight-stranded helix in time, and your creative horizons will open up beyond your most sacred dreams. Know that Shon-ral and I, and all the vast number of your fellow beings in the Galactic Alliance, wish you all only the most uplifting enlightening good will.*

Shon-ral's telepathic benevolent soothing voice cheerfully added, *Something amazing, something wonderful is also coming to your planet. Thousands of Galactic Alliance star ships filled with scientists, scholars, medical personnel with cures for all disease, biologists, botanists, builders, engineers, and teachers of every advanced benevolent discipline will be landing all over the planet to assist you all in attaining your true potential. Useful benevolent products, transformed from the dangerous forms of energy you now use, will come into existence, and teleportation units will replace your automobiles. Anti-gravity propulsion systems in spacecraft capable of traversing the vast distances of outer space and into many parallel dimensions will replace your polluting aircraft. They will also be capable of freely traveling under the oceans.*

You will become a welcomed planetary culture that can then freely explore the wonders of other worlds. You will meet the people of many advanced cultures you have not dreamed existed through prearranged exchange programs. After their natural creative talents are encouraged to blossom to their full potential, your children will grow up in a world of wonder free from fear. It is our privilege to assist all of you to go through the coming great world transformation that has in our view, taken far too long to come to Earth. For now, farewell!

Back in the White House in Washington, D.C., the combined vision of Ambassador Shon-ral and Prime Scientist Moon-teran of the coming planetary changes underway returned to focus in the Oval Office. Childlike expressions of amazement were now on the faces of Ambassador Grotzil, Chairman Ted Carter, President Martin McCoy, Secretary of Defense Daniel Samuelson, and the three camera operators who were experiencing wondrous changes in their own awareness.

The President, standing beside them, stepped up to the podium and said, "I don't know how many of you are actually still at a television set that have not already headed out the door on your way to visit one the fountains. All of us in the White House somehow saw the same vision of what is starting to take place all over the Earth. We are all in this together. It is clear that our current forms of government will be retired and money, as we have known it, will no longer exist. Fellow citizens of planet Earth, we are no longer alone. Good night and may God bless the United States of America and every other country and people, as well as all animal and other life living on our soon to be purified world. We will remember this day as the day we were reborn into a higher life of wonder. God bless you all and good night."

The President nodded to the lead camera operator, who then indicated they were no longer on the air. Ambassador Grotzil was now radiant with kindness as he gazed with true friendship at everyone in the conference room.

"I am honored to have been a part of this change coming to Earth. Now I will return to the last of our ships waiting in orbit for me. I am very anxious to be among those of us who will witness what these mighty pyramids will do to our fellow Trilotew living on all our empire worlds, to our military forces, and then to the Emperor. Know that I will witness the last days of our worlds ruled by an Emperor. Then we too will look forward to becoming part of the entire Galactic Inter-dimensional Alliance of Free Worlds. Farewell, my new friends."

He bowed again with his arms crossed over his chest and his palms placed upon his shoulders. Then he stood back up smiling from ear to ear, touched his belt buckle three times, and a moment later he was dematerialized in a golden-white teleportation beam.

The President looked fondly at Shon-ral and Moon-teran, and

then happily stated with new found confidence, "Well, we've got a lot to do now that really counts. Ted, I believe we should coordinate our efforts together to combine funds from all over the world to help heal this stricken planet, even though in the near future it will not be necessary. If those Galactic Alliance ships show up soon, we may not need money any more. Anyway, in the meantime, we should see what the two of us and all your disbanded secret government TWC Council members can do to clean things up. What do you say?"

Chairman Ted Carter grinned like a giddy child, shook his head and replied, "You're on, Mr. President. I will contact all of them and have them come to the White House. Will that do?"

"You bet your ass it will," replied Martin, now greatly relieved and uplifted.

All is well gentlemen, telepathically interjected Shon-ral with an impish grin, and they both gazed surprised at him.

That's an understatement if ever there was one, replied Ted Carter with his own impish grin.

That's the truth of all truths, cheerfully chimed in Martin.

The three astonished camera operators gazed at them in wonder and stated aloud almost simultaneously, "We heard you... in our heads!"

You see, gentlemen, telepathically confirmed Moon-teran with a wry grin, *These fine cameramen are already starting to remember who they really are, and this is only the very beginning.* She gazed longingly at Shon-ral and asked, *Well, cousin, are you ready to return home to rejoin our families before we get into hot water with them?*

She chuckled with Shon-ral, who then nodded and curiously replied, *Well, cousin, when you're right, you're right.*

He comically gazed at President Martin McCoy and Ted, and said, *Thanks for all the hospitality. We will have to do this again sometime.*

Right, we'll do lunch, chuckled back Moon-teran, picking up on his reference to an old Hollywood cliché.

They cracked up laughing and after the levity died down, Shon-ral calmly said using his own vocal chords, "We will return when the massive fleet arrives, which is scheduled to take place in the near future. Things are going to get very interesting on this planet during the next few months, and Moon-teran and I want to bring our families here to stay for a while. Our children would receive quite an education observing the complete overhaul, and uplifting transformation of an entire world and its people. They will want to help. What do you think, cousin?"

"Well, cousin," she jovially shot back using her vocal chords, "When you're right, you're right."

He playfully grinned, and they both nodded a simple farewell. Then they looked away to visualize their families back on Norexilam and then... They just vanished.

"Wow! They really do get around, don't they?" President Martin McCoy mused.

"They sure as hell do," wholeheartedly answered Ted.

"What do ya say we get some lunch?" inquired Martin, grinning with raised eyebrows.

"I thought you would never ask, and I'm starving," answered Ted, rubbing his empty stomach.

Then Martin impishly grinned at Daniel and requested, "Daniel, my friend, would you care to join us?"

Daniel grinned wide and nodded, and they cheerfully walked side-by-side out of the television conference room with a newly transformed profound zest for life.

CHAPTER TWENTY-EIGHT

DAWN
OF
A NEW BEGINNING

There is no going back when what is behind has forever changed to a sublime new truth, and the world turns an entirely unexpected page to reveal a wonderland for all. The people of Earth will be left with only one query to ponder as the planet is changed in tremendous ways right before their amazed eyes and under their feet. All over the world, people will be asking each other in astounding joy, "How could this be happening?"

They will come to know they were not actually free to imagine a better world, for their imaginations were fixated on oblivion. Many understood they had fervently been praying for the end of the world to cease their lives of meaningless toil and fear. This was not because they had an inkling of a chance to turn around the destructive direction the planet was going. They will become aware they were not really in control of their lives because true freewill had successfully eluded them. The wonder of their newly liberated lives will be gratitude enough for they will not be able to explain how this new Ray works.

Something beyond what they know was not earned will liberate them, and they will begin to remember their true God-like characteristics as benevolent human beings. As startling as the new revelation will be, when they use their imaginations in the years to come they will only create visions that will benefit all life. They will begin to see that everything, including people, animals, plants, and stones, have a presence of Atma or Soul, an evolving nature they could never see before, not even within themselves.

A new appreciation of their pets will began to take on a far deeper light of understanding, which will reveal they are also committed, loving and evolving eternal spherical energy beings that temporarily reside in various animal physical forms. People all over the planet will find their former desires to kill and slaughter animals without regard to their feelings will fade away. At the same time, they will discover an innate ability surfacing which will enable them to consume vibrant food for pleasure or take in any necessary nourishment, vitality, and longevity by simply breathing the air or drinking the subtle form of energy derived directly from the liberating Ray. They will know this awareness is being radiated throughout the Earth's atmosphere, coming from the fountains within two giant golden pyramids sitting on the bottom of Earth's deepest oceans and from a third one located deep within the Himalayan mountains. Then, one day it will just happen.

They will began to hear each other speak inside their own beings without the need to use their vocal chords, and they will know certain genomes on their DNA double helix have been turned back on. Then the human population on Earth, including those who are suffering from various diseases, will start to recover from genetic distortions in their bodies as their double DNA helix transforms back to the advanced four-stranded human DNA.

Soon after this begins, the massive mile-long cylindrical Galactic Alliance space ships, radiating a pale blue light around their silver-blue hulls, will begin to arrive and hover in the skies all over the planet. However, no one will be afraid for fear or evil will begin to be retired from everything living on the planet above or below the surface. Nearly seven billion people will be quietly beaming joy to their fellow beings aboard those magnificent space ships as they began to hover down and land in parklands, in fields, and in the countryside near every major city on Earth. Then more ships will arrive with highly trained specialists aboard. Thousands of Scout class saucer shaped ships will emerge from their massive parent carriers during this second visiting wave. Their Galactic Alliance pilots will maneuver them in an acrobatic dance in the skies for the delight of the watchers below before they start landing them nearby every government Capital center all over the planet.

The advanced human beings aboard comprised of different skin colors, shapes, and other striking characteristics will be breathtaking to their Earth brothers and sisters as they emerge from the ships to joyfully greet their equally jubilant new Earth friends. Almost at once, special molecular engineers will begin to take surveys of all the major congested cities where people had been unnaturally stacked on top of each other in small creativity stifling spaces they return to each day, after trying to eek out a living. These technicians will be using very unusual handheld crystalline devices, similar to a crystal wand, that are programmed to analyze and record the entire internal structures of the massive city skyscrapers and surrounding facilities.

Teleportation chambers will be set up all over the planet. Dozens will appear in the big cities in vacant lots and public parks, and every small town will receive one. The serene people of Earth will be telepathically encouraged to go to the teleportation chambers to beam away in groups of a dozen and reappear in vast unpopulated fields, forests, and plains that are still numerous all over the planet. After that, their new Galactic Alliance friends will escort them to their new waiting domed and rectangular energy self-sufficient homes, which will have materialized intact about every twenty acres. The energy generators in these homes derive their power from the electromagnetic field surrounding the planet that interconnects with worlds throughout the universe. These gifts from the Galactic Alliance have no moving parts, and nothing in them can wear out or pollute the environment in any way.

Six and a half billion people will soon witness, inside their own inner vision, the seven other prepared Earth-like planets that await them in close parallel dimensions of the physical universe. Galactic Alliance specialists will ask which of them would like to volunteer to leave Earth to have wondrous adventuresome lives on other worlds as new colonists. Oddly enough, exactly six and a half-billion human beings will volunteer and the implementation of the Earth's massive relocation aspect of *The Seres Agenda* will begin.

Far away on another world, Shon-ral and Moon-teran appeared standing side-by-side in Shon-ral's garden outside his three-domed complex on planet Norexilam. They looked fondly at each other, hugged, and then nodded their understanding of each other's silent communication. Moon-teran stepped back and looked away to visualize her husband and three children, and then she just simply vanished. Shon-ral grinned and turned to greet his loving wife Lorun-eral and their two children as they appeared walking out of the dome's entrance to welcome him back. His wife jumped into his open arms, and the two happy children watched as he joyously spun her around while they passionately kissed. Then he sat her down, and the children surrounded their parents that cheerfully began to hug and kiss them.

"Well, I'm back and the Earth planet is finally being transformed. Dearest Lorun-eral, it is breathtaking to observe first-hand. I wish you and our children could be there to assist with this great change."

"We want to go, Father!" shouted their excited children.

Lorun-eral coyly smiled up at Shon-ral and stated, "We have already talked it over and the children and I agree. We want to travel back to Earth with you for an extended stay to experience the rare monumental changes taking place there, and to observe the moment when our brothers and sisters on the planet Earth are formally accepted into the Galactic Alliance."

Shon-ral grinned satisfaction, and then he kissed his wife with tender gratitude for her evolved insight.

"I sensed you were ready, dear children, to make the journey. Now run along and play in the pool. Your mother and I will join you in a few moments."

The young boy and girl ran back inside the dome laughing and giggling, while their parents listened to the patter of little feet running until one splash followed another as they leapt and jumped into their magnificent indoor swimming pool.

Shon-ral passionately continued, "Before we travel back to Earth, you and I have some catching up to do. I want us to stay home for a while, perhaps for six months, before we depart. I have said this before, but there really is no place like home. However, I am beginning to see we can have a second home on Earth. There the children can spend time helping out and thereby appreciate what the Earth parents and children are going through. Beloved wife, they will have invaluable experiences that will help them reach their full potential while growing up they could not realize in any other way. Now we should head back inside and join them. Then tonight, after the children are asleep, I want us to spend quality time alone together."

They kissed again, and then walked hand-in-hand inside the living room by the swimming pool under their spacious dome.

Moon-teran simply appeared on another continent a third of the way around the planet's equator standing before her husband Donum-tuma and their three children who were eagerly expecting her return. He grabbed her into his arms and they kissed long and tenderly, while their three children excitedly surrounded them. They soon parted to hug and kiss them, and then their young ones walked together back inside their elegant domed home.

"I'm so happy to be back home with you again," joyfully stated Moon-teran as a single tear ran down her left cheek.

"And I have missed you dearly, but at least this time you were not gone for long," replied her grateful admiring husband.

"Dearest husband, the Earth planet is being transformed. The golden luminous pyramids have appeared all over the planet's surface, and the true enlightened nature of the people is awakening from a deep unconscious slumber. It's just amazing what's happening there so quickly that has never occurred on any world in the entire history of the Galactic Alliance."

"Yes, I know, sweet wife. While you were away, we also experienced this in our inner vision," confirmed Donum-tuma.

"My cousin and his wife are going to take their children back there," continued Moon-teran. "They wish to provide them with the great opportunity of spending part of their young lives growing up on a world of constant uplifting benevolent change. Donum-tuma, it would be good if we also had a second home there amongst those who were once from our own planetary system, before those malevolent beings forced them to reincarnate there unaware so long ago. We could help them build a bridge between worlds, and some of them could spend some liberating time back here."

He cheerfully encouraged, "I've already talked it over with the children and they are eager to go."

"Oh, that's wonderful," she cheerfully replied with a relieving sigh. "Then all is well. As one of the Prime Scientists, I will have the unique opportunity to scientifically study and document the extraordinary rare historical change that is taking place on Earth and in the Galactic Alliance. I would not want to miss the reward of the new awareness this will bring to the entire Galactic Alliance. You know I love you, dear husband, even beyond time and space."

"And I'm still entranced by the expanding love I always discover is still manifesting between us, dear wife. Yes, all is well. We can venture back to Earth as a family perhaps six months from now. Will that do?"

"Yes, it will do," she delightfully replied, relieved it had been so effortlessly settled.

Moon-teran and Donum-tuma blissfully walked back inside their large domed home to join their children with their arms wrapped around each other's waists and her head trustfully resting on his shoulder.

Six months went by before the two cousins and their families were together again standing in front of one of the mysterious fountains with that youthfully strong male statue pouring the luminous liquid light from his palms down into the white granite bowl at his feet. It was located on Norexilam at a point equidistant between their two domed home complexes. They were wearing their customary clothes but they did not bring other belongings with them because they knew nothing would be required upon their return to Earth. Everything they might wish to have could be easily manifested, including artistically well designed and entirely energy self-sufficient second homes.

"Well, cousin Moon-teran," cheerfully began Shon-ral, "Is your family ready to venture to the planet Earth?"

Excited cheers from all five children went off like an Earth rocket, and they began jumping up and down.

"Well, cousin Shon-ral," cheerfully shot back Moon-teran, "We are here and we're more than ready."

Shon-ral smiled at Donum-tuma, at all the excited children, and at his lovely wife Lorun-eral, who was patiently grinning while she stood by his side.

"Then everyone hold someone's hand," continued Shon-ral, "while Moon-teran and I visualize the cottage home of our friends Boun-tama and Lean-tala in the mountains in a place they call Northern California in the United States. They are expecting us, and we must not keep them waiting. Here goes," and they both looked away in an imaginative gaze across time and space, and then they all simply vanished.

They reappeared holding hands standing in the round grass field beside their jubilant friends, Boun-tama and Lean-tala. Their cottage home was in the immediate background behind them.

After hugs and jubilant greetings were finished, and the kids were off playing together in the tall grass that surrounded the now unshielded and clearly visible Galactic Scout launch hangar, Shon-ral merrily said to Boun-tama and Lean-tala, "Dear friends, it's so good to see you two again."

Lean-tala shot back with a twinkle in her eyes, "Maybe now you two can finally have that good cup of tea and fine meal we promised you some time back that always managed to somehow get interrupted."

Moon-teran took in a peaceful breath, sighed and calmly replied, "Sounds wonderful. We were both looking forward to spending some tranquil moments with you two this time around."

Donum-tuma waved his arm around at the beautiful surrounding forests and said, "You have really beautiful country around here. Have you really found twenty acre parcels for us to establish our second homes?"

Boun-tama smiled nodding and proudly answered, "We did indeed. We were given several thousand acres to allocate to individual families by the United States President in full agreement with the Galactic Alliance Council, while the nearest cities are being disbanded and transformed."

Bubbly with joy, Lean-tala stated, "Your children are certainly going to have a good time playing in this nature wonderland. So much has changed so quickly. Boun-tama and I have missed company from our home world systems and we are very glad your two families have arrived to join us."

"If you like," Boun-tama cheerfully encouraged, "Lean-tala and I can take your families aboard our Scout ship. We could give you a real first class tour of the wonderful changes that the new Ray is emanating to the planet, as well as the transforming changes the Galactic Alliance technicians and engineers are making to repair the polluted worldwide environment."

Shon-ral and Moon-teran looked at each other, their spouses looked back at them, and then they all happily replied in telepathic unison, *That's why we came here.*

Later that afternoon, the cousins, their spouses, and their combined five children were aboard Boun-tama's and Lean-tala's sleek, disc shaped Scout class spaceship. It had been just six months since Shon-ral and Moon-teran left Earth to be reunited with their families. The projected view screen above the control console was revealing a true wonderland on the planet's surface. The relocation of six and a half billion people from Earth to seven other amazing Earth-like worlds in parallel dimensions was now complete. The senseless massively congested and polluted cities were about to be transformed back into the virgin forested lands, and natural unspoiled ecology of the planet that existed before so-called civilized man built them.

Several thousand mile-long Galactic Alliance Emerald Star Cruisers sent thick green matter reforming beams down over the cities and all the molecules that formed them dissolved back into pure energy. The radiant light then took the form of a giant transparent white-light domed energy that rematerialized back in place the natural environment that was still stored in the planet's memory. This was true, for the Earth planet is also an Atma or living Soul: a spherical energy being that waited oh-so-patiently for this event to finally arrive.

The planted food producing acres all over the planet remained in place. However, the farmers that remained on earth experienced the astonishing transformation of their barns and homes into individually uniquely designed, spacious domed homes with indoor swimming pools. They were equipped with special food processors that could materialize whatever healthy food may be required to supplement their produce, and if any emergency occurred that temporarily interrupted their shared food distribution, they could provide emergency supplies to those in need. Each home produced pure water from the air, even in the deserts, and stored all they might require for future use.

The newly enlightened farmers, with the help of Galactic Alliance Botanists and food producing engineers, had transformed their farms into growing wonderlands of healthy, nutrient-rich vegetables, fruits, and hydroponics facilities. They were now capable of growing ripened food all year round, including many new varieties with much higher nutritive properties the advanced human specialists had brought as a gift to the people of Earth.

The special extraterrestrial human visitors to Earth perceived and observed all these changes as they continued their tour in the Scout ship around the surface of the planet. They were witnessing changes to planet Earth that were exponentially increasing at a wonderful phenomenal rate. It was a thing to behold watching the masterful advanced assistance of over ten million Galactic Alliance specialists who were diligently applying themselves individually and collectively to their chosen tasks.

First, they neutralized all radioactive materials and transformed them into non-harmful sources of free energy. Then they molecularly transformed all nuclear reactor buildings, nuclear bomb casings, and nuclear storage facilities into teleportation stations and spacecraft. Recombined molecules also produced advanced extraterrestrial building materials with amazing properties Earth scientists never dreamed existed. The molecules that made up power lines and sewer systems transformed into natural soils that stimulated accelerated plant growth. The molecular transformation of all human and animal waste into odorless, pollution-free fertilizers took place inside matter recombining tanks underneath each new home. Every public art, science, and cultural facility created thereafter was for the mutual enjoyment and advancement of all the people of Earth. Galactic Alliance scientists also transformed many now antiquated structures on the planet into useful household necessities such as toilet paper and paper towels that looked and worked even better than any former tree-based products. Once used, they were recycled into other non-polluting and non-toxic products by the household matter-transforming units.

All forms of money and taxation, as well as police forces were retired for good. The people who occupied these professions naturally awakened to be happily creative contributors in ways that had been sleeping in their former suppressed selves. This was true for all other people, even those who were out of work before this whole marvelous change to Earth began.

The people of Earth no longer cared for such things as money accumulation, and tyrants were no longer tyrants. All the people on Earth had freely available all the necessities of living life abundantly, and none had to work for a living for the right to be born on the planet. Instead, they naturally loved to toil at those necessary occupations that were already naturally dear to the true dreams of their creative liberated potentials. They were also now able to use a hundred percent of their brain, discovered their photographic memory and telepathic capabilities, and their IQs rose through the roof.

Many of the five hundred million people left on the Earth were soon scheduled to go on exchange field trips with their families to other worlds, and many citizens in the vast Galactic Alliance worlds had already enthusiastically volunteered to come to Earth just to be part of the great world change that was taking place all over the planet. Such transformations to entire planets and their people were beyond rare, for no planet had ever gone through such a swift liberating transformation after being on the brink of annihilation in the entire Galactic Alliance history dating back over five hundred thousand years.

In order to bring the massively overpopulated planet down to a healthy five hundred millions inhabitants, the other six and half billion people were relocated so that the planet's maximum healthy supportable ecosystem could be brought back in balance and sustained with Galactic Alliance assistance. Everyone was already gaining tremendous new insights into creation by participating in the phenomenal event.

The people of Earth had a hidden destiny to be saved from their own subconsciously driven negative imaginations, even though they had no idea this monumental liberating change was actually coming, and now they were all well beyond grateful.

CHAPTER TWENTY-NINE

OUR EVER EXPANDING HORIZON

Now the most important story ever foretold about the wondrous new Ray that few people living on Earth today know exists is accomplished. As human beings, we have only one great talent we can apply to create beneficial change here and now on Earth that we take with us after we depart this lifetime. That wonderful gift is childlike loving imagination. This eternal nature in us neutralizes destructive childish greed that selfishly gains a temporary power over others at the expense and good will of every living thing in creation. When it comes right down to it, the only benevolent freewill choice we have is to use our creative imaginations in only benevolent ways regarding our future together on this planet for the greatest beneficial outcome to all life, not just for human beings but also for animals, plant life, and our environment as well.

What is coming to Earth that has finally been unexpectedly green-lit is not reversible by anyone or any power. This dynamically unique revelation, recently provided for our great benefit, discloses the hidden galactic history off-world origins of human beings and our planet's recently changed future destiny, as per my agreement with *The Seres Agenda*, the coming return of the mighty Seres race, and highly evolved enlightened beings most people living on Earth today have not known existed at any time. Now, we can choose to align our imagination with this new liberating gift Ray that is beginning to manifest to permanently retire evil as an experiment from creation or we can fall prey to negatively manipulated news on television, the radio, and in newspapers. For the most part, their misguided endeavors channel a negative imaginative stream that is designed to trap our celestial gift of imagination like a slave in the subconscious mind, and bind our normally unlimited constructive imaginations to the very limited destructive misuse of vision toward the world's terrorizing end.

What is here already, which will only briefly remain a mystery to almost all of humanity living on our planet, will continue to make its presence known in ever more obvious ways. This astounding new Ray will provide every man, woman, and child with the personal liberating experience of their suppressed highly evolved true self. One day soon, all the people of Earth will know without doubt that vast numbers of human, humanoid, and highly evolved benevolent beings actually thrive in the multi-dimensional universe beyond planet Earth.

Even those people who refuse to correctly use the great secret of imagination, that can lead to liberation from oppression, suppression, fear, hate, and evil as an experiment, will soon experience this liberation for the benefit of all life. This new coming Ray is about to awaken in everyone the expanding awareness of our true benevolent human natures that has been purposefully suppressed for far too long. Our world's negative destructive destiny is beginning to change forever, because a new omnipresent force or liberating Ray from the source behind all life has finally come into existence to save us from ourselves. This new dispensation of grace is emanating down into the lower dimensions to reach all the way down to good old planet Earth, and our future is wondrous beyond our wildest imaginations.

My fellow human beings, we must choose wisely for once to use our imaginations together with this coming liberating Ray. You will experience for yourself how this uplifting transforming gift is actually emanating to us from the highest dimensions of creation far beyond the lower dimensions and physical worlds of time and space. Look for it, and be ready to behold this coming liberating worldwide change. Gaze into the skies with your heart to behold that which you have never seen before, but suspected might just someday come true. Expect the unexpected, for it is most certainly coming to our world. This is certain. Let us look into the truth of what our hearts are really beginning to tell us now. Discover for yourself what we are privileged to experience. After all, as human beings we are all in this together on our beautiful blue-green water covered jewel of a world.

The revealing of this great part of *The Seres Agenda* for the first time is gratefully serving to spearhead our coming entirely new unexpected destiny - our new future. Although this book now ends, the special Ray flowing like an expanding celestial river of luminous Light and vibrant Sound through its pages remains open. Whether one knows it now or not, our future is very bright indeed.

From this moment onward, the reader will uncover more hidden truth deep within that is waiting to surface, while the far... far greater adventure continues to unfold on planet Earth.

THE END

...is only the BEGINNING...

GLOSSARY OF CHARACTERS AND TERMS

Characters:

Agent Jacobson - He is the NSA agent working with the benevolent Galactic Alliance, who helps Mark to secretly integrate back into Earth society as Mark Santfield.

Alec Johansson - He is the local Deputy Sheriff, under Sheriff Pat Donyfield, of a small northern California town near the cottage home of Dan and Mary Allison Crystal (Boun-tama and Lean-tala).

Boun-tama (Boon-tah-mah) - He is an advanced extraterrestrial human secretly stationed on Earth and Mon-tlan's associate known by the cover name Mr. Dan Crystal or Mr. Crystal.

Corel-shana (Cor-el-shah-nah) - She was Ambassador Shon-ral's mother who arrived on the Trilotew home world to accompany her husband to get an agreed treaty signed with the Trilotew Emperor, who then betrayed and killed her and her husband.

Cynthia Piermont - She is the snobbish, very wealthy Vice Chairwoman under Chairman Ted Carter of the worldwide secret second government.

Dan Crystal or Mr. Crystal - This is the Earth cover name for Boun-tama, who is married to Mary Allison Crystal – the cover name on Earth for Lean-tala.

Dan Waymeyer - He is the Chief Editor and CEO owner of Waymeyer Publishing and Mark Santfield's book publishing agent.

Daniel Samuelson - He is the United States Secretary of Defense.

Danim-tama (Dan-him-tah-mah) - He is the seven-year-old son of Moon-teran and Donum-Tuma.

Donum-tuma (Don-oom-two-mah) - This is Moon-teran's handsome middle-aged husband on her home planet, Norexilam.

Dun-tal (Doon-tall) - He is an extraterrestrial human male Lieutenant aboard the flagship of the Galactic Inter-dimensional Alliance of Free Worlds.

Elon-tal (E-lawn-tahl) - Lieutenant Elon-tal is a control board and view screen operator in the Mt. Shasta base.

Fimala-tanis (Fee-mall-ah-tan-iss) - She was Moon-teran's Prime DNA Biologist mother, before she was killed with her husband aboard their Galactic Alliance deep exploration research ship. A mysterious meteor collided with it right after the stationary ship's protective energy shield surrounding the vessel was down for repair.

Gonshockal (Gone-shock-all) - He is the Trilotew Imperial Overlord Fleet Commander located in a secret underground base deep in the jungles of Brazil.

Gorsapis (Gor-sahp-iss) - He is a nine-foot tall bi-pedal reptilian extraterrestrial from the malevolent (evil) totalitarian Trilotew race.

Grotzil (Graht-zeal) - His official title is Supreme Illumined High Lord Ambassador of the Trilotew.

Harold Van Tipton - He is a tall, middle-aged but dashingly handsome man with wavy brown hair and a handlebar mustache. He wears an expensive Italian suit. He is one of three men in the hidden second worldwide government who first approaches Ambassador Shon-ral in the secret Galactic Alliance Mt. Shasta base. He thanks them for helping them become transformed by the new Ray, along with ninety-seven other hidden government members.

Henry Throckmorton - He is Mr. Carter's general counsel attorney.

Jameson Rockefeller - He is a bald, slightly rotund man of medium height, about seventy years of age, who also wears an expensive Italian suit. He is also one of three men in the hidden second worldwide government who approach Ambassador Shon-ral (Mark Santfield) in the secret Galactic Alliance Mt. Shasta base to thank him for helping them become transformed by the new Ray, along with ninety-seven other hidden government members.

Janice Carter - She is Mark Santfield's fiancée on Earth, who is actually Ambassador Shon-ral's advanced extraterrestrial human cousin - known as a Prime Historical Trend Scientist Moon-teran from the Galactic Inter-dimensional Alliance of Free Worlds.

Jason Armontel - He is a middle-aged trim man of medium height with thick black hair neatly combed back over the top of his head, who also wears an expensive Italian suit. He is also one of three men in the hidden worldwide Government that approach Ambassador Shon-ral (Mark Santfield) in the secret Galactic Alliance Mt. Shasta base to thank him for helping them become transformed by the new Ray, along with ninety-seven other hidden government members.

Jin-trean (Jinn-tree-ann) - She is a lovely young human extraterrestrial technician aboard the Galactic Inter-dimensional Alliance of Free Worlds flagship.

Joanne - She is also a close college friend of Janice Cater.

Jon-tral (John-trahl) - He is the extraterrestrial human Commander of a mile-long cylindrical or cigar shaped flagship of the Galactic Inter-dimensional Alliance of Free Worlds.

Kantal-teran (Can-tall-tear-ann) - He was Moon-teran's Prime DNA Biologist father, before he was killed with his wife aboard their Galactic Alliance deep exploration research ship by a mysterious meteor that collided with it right after the stationary ship's protective energy shield surrounding the vessel was down for repair.

Lean-tala (Leen-ta-law) - She is Boun-tama's wife, whose cover name on Earth is Mary Allison Crystal.

Lorun-eral (Lor-oon-air-all) - She is Ambassador Shon-ral's wife back on his home planet Norexilam beyond the Pleiades star group.

Mark Santfield - He is Janice Carter's fiancé on Earth, who is actually an advanced extraterrestrial human being known as Ambassador Shon-ral from the Galactic Inter-dimensional Alliance of Free World.

Mary - She is a close college friend of Janice Cater.

Mary Allison Crystal - She is the wife of Boun-tama (alias Dan Crystal), who is actually an advanced extraterrestrial human known as Lean-tala.

Mathew McConnell - He is the head editor of Waymeyer Publishing owned by Mr. Dan Waymeyer.

Mon-tlan (Mawn-tlann) - His official title is Special Officer Mon-tlan. He is a highly evolved human extraterrestrial space ship pilot from another world beyond the Pleiades star constellation. His nickname is Monti.

Moon-teran (Moon-tear-ann) - She is the advanced extraterrestrial human historical and sociological scientist, officially known as Historical Trend Scientist Moon-teran or Prime Scientist Moon-teran, from the Galactic Inter-dimensional Alliance of Free Worlds. Known as Janice Carter on Earth, she is actually Ambassador Shon-ral's cousin from beyond the Pleiades star group from her home world Norexilam in the Starborn Cluster.

Oceanans (O-she-ann-ons) - They are the benevolent humanoid people of planet Oceana, who are relatively tall and trim, have pale blue skin and slightly pointed ears, and that evolved with the ability to breath on land or under water with tiny unobtrusive gill slits at the back of their chins by the top of their necks. They are much more highly enlightened than Earth humans, and they emit an uplifting vibration that any person on our world would find to be elegantly beautiful – like tall benevolent Elves.

Pat Donyfield - He is the local Sheriff of a small northern California mountain town near the cottage home of Dan and Mary Allison Crystal (Boun-tama and Lean-tala).

President Martin McCoy - He is the President of the United States.

Razjewl (Razz-jewel) - He is the Trilotew Second Officer revealed to be covertly operating inside the secret underground classified second worldwide government.

Seres (Say-rays) - These majestic, highly spiritually evolved eighteen to twenty feet tall extraterrestrial human beings seeded human and humanoid races throughout the many galaxies long ago before they vanished from galactic history. The very recently decided to return.

Shan-dreal (Shawn-dree-all) - He is the eight-year old son of Ambassador Shon-ral and his wife Lorun-eral back on their home planet Norexilam.

Shanal-teal (Shahn-ahl-tee-ahl) - She is Prime Biology scientist from Shon-ral and Moon-teran's home world.

Shaoulnoom (Sha-ool-newm) - He is the Trilotew controller of the Russian President disguised as a human being.

Shon-dema (Shawn-dee-mah) - He was Ambassador Shon-ral's father, the previous Galactic Inter-dimensional Alliance of Free Worlds Ambassador. He and his wife arrived on the Trilotew home world to have an agreed treaty signed by the Trilotew Emperor, who then betrayed and killed them both.

Shon-ral (Shawn-rahl) - He is the advanced extraterrestrial human Ambassador of the Galactic Inter-dimensional Alliance of Free Worlds known on Earth as Mark Santfield. He comes from beyond the Pleiades star constellation from his home world Norexilam in the Starborn Cluster.

Shul-non (Shool-none) - He is the Pilot Shul-non of the Galactic Inter-dimensional Alliance of Free Worlds flagship.

Skondrilm (Skawn-dree-alm) - He is also a Trilotew Lieutenant under Gonshockal's command in their hidden underground base deep within the jungles of Brazil.

Sun-Deema (Sun-dee-mah) - This is First Officer or Second In Command Sun-Deema, who is Jon-tral's wife aboard the Galactic Inter-dimensional Alliance of Free Worlds flagship.

Susan - She is President Martin McCoy's personal secretary.

Suzanne - She is the secretary and receptionist for Dan Waymeyer, CEO owner and Chief Editor of Waymeyer Publishing.

Taluna-tala (Tao-loona-talla) - Back on their home planet Norexilam, she is the ten-year old daughter of Ambassador Shon-ral and Lorun-eral.

Tam-lure (Tam-loor) - He is the benevolent extraterrestrial human Commander of the secret Galactic Alliance extraterrestrial base inside Mt. Shasta in northern California.

Tamal-shan (Tahm-al-shawn) - He is the physicist husband of Shanal-teal on their home world Norexilam.

Ted Carter - He is the father of Janice on Earth, the richest multi-billionaire, and Chairman of a hidden classified second worldwide government.

The Silent Mentors - They are the most evolved mysterious beings in creation who take care of keeping everything in balanced order in the many parallel and higher dimensions: the stars; planets; galaxies; and in general all the balanced mechanics of creation. They have unlimited power and freedom, can come and go to any place or anywhere in creation from the highest dimension to the lowest in the blink of an eye, and can take any form they wish without being detected if they choose. The mighty Seres have direct contact with them, for they are the ancient Mentors of the Seres.

Torellian (Tor-el-ee-un) - He is the eighteen-foot tall mighty Seres Ambassador from the most highly evolved and most ancient mysterious human extraterrestrial race that seeded all human and humanoid races long ago throughout the many galaxies.

Trel-una (Tree-al-oo-nah) - She is a young human female teleportation technician at the Mt. Shasta base.

Trilon-Kal (Tri-lawn-cal) - They are the white-winged reptilian race from a parallel dimension that invaded our dimension over five hundred thousand years ago, conquered the genetically related Trilotew, and then used them to start a galactic war. They were defeated by the Galactic Inter-dimensional Alliance of Free Worlds with secret help from friends in the Andromeda galaxy known by benevolent extraterrestrials as Medulonta – our nearest galactic neighbor.

Trilotew (Tri-low-two) - They are a race of malevolent eight to ten-feet-tall, bi-peddle totalitarian reptilian extraterrestrials, who do not respect human beings.

Trondshopa (Trond-show-pa) - He is a Trilotew Lieutenant under the command of Gonshockal in their hidden underground base deep within the jungles of Brazil.

Una-mala (Oo-nah-mahl-lah) - She is Second Commander Una-mala and Tam-lure's wife, who also oversees the secret extraterrestrial Earth base inside Mt. Shasta.

Vera-tima (Vera-tee-mah) - She is the nine-year-old sister of Yoral-telan and younger daughter of Moon-teran and husband Donum-tuma back on their home world Norexilam.

Yalgoot (Yee-owl-goot) - He is the High Divine Imperial Commander Yalgoot aboard the Trilotew flagship – one of two Destroyer Class spaceships secretly hovering above each of Earth's poles.

Yoral-telan (Yor-all-tee-lawn) - She is the eleven-year old daughter of Moon-teran and husband Donum-tuma back on their home world Norexilam.

Zin-tamal (Zin-tuh-mall) - He is the pilot officer of the three hundred-foot long Medium Transport Carrier ship of the Galactic Inter-dimensional Alliance Free Worlds.

Zorbok (Zor-bock) - He is the Trilotew First Officer revealed to be covertly operating inside the secret underground U.S. desert base of the classified second worldwide government.

Zushsmat (Zoo-shmawt) - He is a more than eight-foot tall bipedal extraterrestrial from the malevolent (evil) totalitarian Trilotew race.

Terms:

Atma - This is the Galactic Alliance of Free Worlds term for what people on Earth call Soul. They know this to be the eternal, deathless, true energy spherical form of all living beings.

DNA Transverse Molecular Reconstructor - This recently perfected extraterrestrial device developed by Galactic Inter-dimensional Alliance of Free World scientists can transform the suppressed two-stranded DNA of human beings on Earth back into the normal four-stranded advanced human DNA. Four-stranded DNA is common among millions of other human populated world systems. Also referred to as the DNA Reversion Process, the device can transform the unique human DNA characteristics of one world to that of the human DNA characteristics of another world.

Energy Field Dampening Device - This Galactic Inter-dimensional Alliance of Free Words technology can shut down, without damage, electronics or computer systems anywhere on Earth, should the need arise to prevent a nuclear war. During the cold war between the United States and the former Soviet Union, it was secrety very effectively used twelve times to prevent this catastrophe after either side, for one reason or another, actually pushed the button to destroy the world.

Frequency Harmonizing Mind-link Activator - This off-world device is very effective in removing subconsciously implanted three dimensional mental image pictures containing sight, sound, smells, motion, tactile sensations, and every possible negative imagery that can compel an individual to forget who they are and behave in an abnormal manner for suppressive control purposes.

Frequency Modulators - The device connected to the back closet inside the cottage home of Boun-tama and Lean-tala shields the doorway entrance to the hidden teleportation pad located in a slightly higher molecular frequency, or parallel dimension. It also lowers or raises the molecular frequency or time rate of human physical bodies from one parallel frequency to another.

Galactic Alliance Deep Penetration Observation Magnifyer - This advanced technology allows the observer to peer through any material barrier and underground as well to undetectably observe what is there.

Galactic Alliance Courier Scout Class Ship - They are much larger one hundred-foot in diameter and thirty-foot high long range transport ships. They are capable of carrying over a hundred people and much more cargo than the smaller thirty-foot in diameter Scout Class transport and defensive interceptors, and they are capable of traversing greater distances between star systems than the smaller Scout Class ships, without needing to be recharged.

Galactic Alliance Emerald Star Galaxy Class Space Ship - These massive mighty ships of the Galactic Inter-dimensional Alliance of Free Worlds are from one mile-long to over ten miles in length. They are cigar or cylindrically shaped mother ships or parent vessels with smooth flattened top and bottom hulls. The Interstellar Emerald Star Class spaceships have special anti-gravity propulsion drives that give them the ability operate in planetary atmospheres, under oceans, travel between planets, into parallel dimensions, to stars systems anywhere in our galaxy in a very short period of time, as well as to and from other galaxies.

Galactic Alliance Inter-stellar Medium Transports - These are 300 to 900 feet long, slightly flattened cigar or cylindrical shaped interstellar capable spaceships of the Galactic Inter-dimensional Alliance of Free Worlds. They have anti-gravity propulsion drive systems that give them the capability to travel between the stars and vast distance of outer space in our Milky Way galaxy in a very short period of time. They can also travel between parallel dimensions within our galaxy, within planetary atmospheres, and under oceans.

Galactic Alliance Scout Class Spaceships - These Galactic Inter-dimensional Alliance of Free Worlds' reconnaissance, transportation, and defensive interceptor disc shaped spacecraft are thirty feet in diameter, with three convex semi-spherical pods facing downward in triangular position on the bottom of their hulls. A characteristic pale blue antigravity light enshrouds their hulls when they travel between lower and upper parallel dimensions in the physical universe, in planetary atmospheres, under oceans, between worlds, and under certain conditions between star systems.

Galactic Inter-dimensional Alliance of Free Worlds - This is the largest and most prominent benevolent organization of independent worlds systems and space travel capable races in our Milky Way galaxy. It is comprised of more than 450,000,000 inhabited planets in just ¼ of the galaxy, and it has a harmonious relationship with the more advanced benevolent races that inhabit the Andromeda Galaxy known by extraterrestrials as Medulonta – our nearest galactic neighbor.

Maldec or Maldek (Mall-deck) - A very long time ago, a special bomb blew apart this inhabited planet, and it became the asteroid belt circling in the orbit of a planet around the sun of our solar system between the planets Mars and Jupiter.

Matter Annihilator Bombs - They are Trilotew energy ray spherical bombs that bury themselves deep underground and then implode, creating a disintegrating effect of the molecular bond of all matter within a mile wide radius of the intended target. It turns matter back into energy that quickly dissipates, leaving nothing but a semi-spherical hole in the ground.

Matter Disruptor Implosion Bomb - If set off, this extremely powerful oil barrel sized Trilotew implosion bomb will blow apart an entire planet.

Matter To Energy Conversion Beam - This Galactic Inter-dimensional Alliance of Free Worlds device can neutralize any explosion or exploding device, even nuclear bombs, and transform the energy back into the natural terrain, landscape, plant and animal life that existed in the area.

Mayan Calendar (My-yann) - This pertains to the ancient Maya (My-yah) culture or people: a member of a major pre-Columbian civilization of the Yucatan Peninsula that reached it speak in the 9th century A.D. They produced magnificent ceremonial cities with pyramids, a sophisticated accurate prophetic mathematical calendar system, hieroglyphic writing, sculpture, painting, ceramics, and gold icons and jewelry.

Medulonta (Med-you-lawn-ta) - This is the Galactic Inter-dimensional Alliance of Free Worlds extraterrestrial's name for the Andromeda galaxy – our nearest galactic neighbor.

Morphing Device - This Trilotew device, built into their belt buckle symbols, tightly bend light around their reptilian bodies to make them appear, in shorter stature than they actually are, as human beings with normal appearing human eyes and appropriate clothing. However, it does not alter their molecular structure or DNA, and it is not capable of hiding their covert attitude to look at human beings like cattle they want to kill or eat alive on the spot, if they did not restrain themselves.

Novissam System (No-vis-sam) - The star and solar system nearer to the galactic center of our Milky Way galaxy that has the central governing world of the Galactic Inter-dimensional Alliance of Free worlds circling around a bright white-blue star in the fifth planetary orbital position. It is often referred to as the central Novissam system.

Oceana (O-she-anna) - This mostly water covered planet, with an atmosphere very similar to Earth, has several large island masses near or centered over the equator. It exists in our Milky Way galaxy in a slightly higher parallel dimension of the physical universe.

The New Expansion Ray - This is the new consciousness uplifting and transforming Ray that was very recently brought into existence, emanating from the omnipresent, omniscient, and omnipresent source behind and supporting all life. It emanates from the highest realm many dimensions far beyond the lower worlds of time and space. It has been brought into existence to permanently remove (retire) evil as an experiment on Earth, in our galaxy, and eventually throughout the many parallel and higher dimensions of creation. It functions only one way and it cannot be compromised, controlled, or altered in any way by any power or being.

Transverse Carrier Waves - These special frequency carrier waves contain the imprinted patterns of original advanced four-stranded DNA human genome codes.

Trilotew Demon Scout Interceptors - The slightly elongated triangular and slightly bat-wing shaped hulls of these space ships are thirty feet long, measured from the two rounded pointed ends at the base of its triangular shape to the third rounded pointed apex. They are antigravity powered reconnaissance, transportation, and offensive attack interceptors. Similar to Galactic Alliance Scout ships, they have three convex semi-spherical pods pointing downward from the bottom hulls. Their hull surface glows pale-red when they fly in outer space or travel in planetary atmospheres. They can travel under oceans, between worlds, between lower parallel dimensions of the physical universe, and under certain conditions between star systems.

Trilotew Fast-Attack Destroyer Class Spaceships - These Trilotew heavily armored hundred-foot-long oval shaped fast-attack spacecraft are designed for very destructive hit-and-run missions.

Trilotew Medium Galactic Destroyer Class Spaceships - They are massive oval-shaped, charcoal-black Trilotew mother ships, nearly half a mile long, with a characteristic luminous red ionized antigravity light enshrouding their hulls. They are about half the size of the mile-long Emerald Galaxy Class mother ships of the Galactic Inter-dimensional Alliance of Free Worlds.

Waveform Transmitters - This once benevolent device, perverted by Trilotew scientists long ago, transmits controlling terrorizing implants into a victim's subconscious mind. The Trilotew then gain initial influential control over their intended victims.

Zetranami (Zee-traw-nom-ee) - This is the central world of the Galactic Inter-dimensional Alliance of Free Worlds located nearer to the galactic center of our Milky Way galaxy in the Novissam star system.

About the Author

Photo by: Jungle Jim (Behrens)

After over forty years of extensive experiential research, R. Scott Lemriel has finally put forth this first published hidden-truth revealing novel, *The Seres Agenda*, from among four completed book manuscripts. This published book, created for the purpose to share this uniquely transforming and uplifting adventure channel with his current and future readers, is now here on Earth.

Lemriel was originally inspired to write *The Seres Agenda,* for the benefit of his readers, based upon many awareness-expanding events that occurred during his childhood, while growing up, and throughout his adult lifetime. They involved a series of experiences with the UFO and extraterrestrial phenomena, journeys via out-of-body travel into parallel and higher dimensional realities, as well as numerous excursions along the past time track. These adventures eventually revealed a hidden history of Earth and our solar system that subsequently helped to confirm the depth of suppressed truth he was uncovering. In addition, the music compositions and productions he developed throughout his life from his early twenties continue to kindle the fire which drives his ongoing explorations into knowing ever deeper hidden truth by direct experience - in contrast to believing or theorizing.

Today, his continuing journeys into our vast multidimensional universe and his unique uplifting music continue to serve as an inner channel of inspiration to further explore and awaken ever-so-much-more about our true nature as knowing eternal beings."

Lemriel is genuinely passionate about sharing the eye-opening adventure story, based upon many enlightening experiences and unusual personal encounters with revealed hidden truth, he is grateful to have discovered. For the first time, he discloses how our planet is about to be unexpectedly benevolently transformed in the near future instead of destroyed because of a recent off-world decision that was finally made concerning changing Earth's current destructive destiny. He takes the reader on a personal journey to discover the reality of UFOs or advanced alien spacecraft, extraterrestrials both benevolent and malevolent, the true nature of the everlasting Soul; its non-destructible energy form that people from other worlds call Atma, and the reality of the existence of parallel and higher dimensions.

He further reveals to his audience what he discovered about our Earth's most important missing ancient history, and discloses how he experienced much about the depth of purposefully hidden truth from the guidance of masterful teachers the majority of the human beings dwelling on earth today do not know existed at any time.

Lemriel gratefully acknowledges his mother for being the first person to read and experience the revealing depth of the transforming truth-revealing channel the pages of this book represent. She discovered, greatly surprised, much about her son she never knew or even imagined, because he kept silent about his uplifting, extraordinary life-changing experiences - until now.

Originally, from Salt Lake City, Utah, where Lemriel spent the first six years of his life, he spends a lot of his time writing about his continuing explorations into hidden truth through his ongoing out-of-body journeys and direct experiential explorations into the UFO and extraterrestrial phenomena. The culmination of his passion for writing numerous books and screenplays, musical compositions, and his current endeavors with feature film and episodic TV story development, coupled with a series of uniquely distinguishing awakening lifetime events, places him as a conduit on the coming horizon for grand new transforming adventures to be opened up to the worldwide book reading public.

The new promotional video about the *The Seres Agenda,* and *The Parallel Time* trilogy books, as well as various overviews of his feature film projects and feature film related music productions are easily accessible at his very unique website, www.paralleltime.com. The video and website are also accessible on Facebook, Linkedin, Twitter, and under the author's official copyright pseudonym R. Scott Lemriel, or his legal name R. S. Rochek.

CPSIA information can be obtained at www.ICGtesting.com
Printed in the USA
LVOW08s0152180414

382202LV00001B/35/P